T0037507

Dead and Gondola

Dead and Gondola

A Christie Bookshop Mystery

ANN CLAIRE

Bantam
New York

Dead and Gondola is a work of fiction. Names, characters, places, and incidents are either the products of the author's imagination or are used fictitiously. Any resemblance to actual persons, living or dead, events, or locales is entirely coincidental.

A Bantam Trade Paperback Original

Copyright © 2022 Ann Perramond

All rights reserved.

Published in the United States by Bantam Books, an imprint of Random House, a division of Penguin Random House LLC, New York.

BANTAM BOOKS is a registered trademark and the B colophon is a trademark of Penguin Random House LLC.

ISBN 978-0-593-49634-3
Ebook ISBN 978-0-593-49633-6

Printed in the United States of America on acid-free paper

randomhousebooks.com

2 4 6 8 9 7 5 3 1

Book design by Virginia Norey
Title page art created from original art by
redchocolatte/stock.adobe.com

For my mother, my first reader

Dead and Gondola

CHAPTER 1

A Perfect Day for Murder

I swung open the heavy oak door and blinked at the figure taking shape in the blizzard.

"What a perfect day for murder!" The woman strode into the Book Chalet, glowing like a summer sunbeam and a vision from the past. Feathers trembled atop her flapper-style beret. Pretty pin curls framed her face. Snowflakes swarmed at her sides.

I gaped, not at the greeting—that was perfectly appropriate—but at its giver.

Morgan Marin. *The* Morgan Marin, Hollywood legend known even to book-dwellers like me. Movies were nice, but they hadn't rendered me tongue-tied. Morgan had reportedly retired (once again) from acting. In its place, she'd turned her superstar dazzle to my beloved medium: books. Her online reading club, Shelf Indulgence, attracted tens of thousands of devoted bibliophiles, myself among them.

I'd been dying to meet her.

And here she stood, in the lobby of my family's bookshop in little Last Word, Colorado.

Morgan stomped faux-fur boots so plush they should have been hibernating. "You must be Ellie." She beamed at me. "The missing Christie, returned to the roost."

I basked in her glow, then remembered my manners and the door, still gaping as wide as my mouth. I switched to a giddy grin and shoved the door shut against suicidal snowflakes. Cowbells dangling from the door latch clonked, buying me time to formulate a sparkling reply.

"Yes," I said.

Hardly scintillating.

"That's me!" I added. "It's an honor to meet you, Ms. Marin."

I cringed. I'd gone too gushy. According to my grandmother, Morgan Marin wished to be treated like any other small-town neighbor. Essentially, she was. Unlike many of the vacation-mansion set who jetted in for weekend getaways in our remote mountain valley, Morgan had settled in Last Word permanently.

Morgan brushed snow from a long emerald coat cut like a cloak. "Please, call me Morgan, and the honor is mine. Your darling grandmother told me *all* about you. Traveling the world from Torquay to Tokyo on literary jobs? A Christie giving tours of Agatha Christie's hometown?"

I bit back my usual disclaimer. If Morgan had chatted with Gram, then she truly would know *all* about me. My resume, my favorite books, those wince-worthy cute grandkid tales grandmothers love to overshare. Morgan would also know that, sadly, we Last Word Christies had yet to uncover a genealogical link to our favorite mystery author. That didn't stop us from loving Dame Agatha like family.

"You've returned to run the Chalet with your brilliant sister?" Morgan patted her miraculously immaculate curls and hat feathers. "The era of the Christie sisters, how grand!"

My cheeks flared.

"It's my dream job," I said. Trite but oh so true. I'd had some great gigs since leaving home straight after high school. Like managing a beachside bookshop on a South Pacific resort island and leading tours of Agatha Christie's stomping grounds, Torquay. Most recently (and far less fun), I'd served as a private librarian for a persnickety antiquarian book collector in London.

It was there, feather duster aimed at a leatherbound Sherlock Holmes, that I'd gotten *the call*. Mom, informing me that she and Dad wanted to retire early and set off on their own book-inspired travels. They hoped to hand over the Book Chalet to a fifth generation of family caretakers: my older sister, Meg, and me.

"Only if you really, truly want," Mom had stressed.

If I really, truly wanted?

After the world's tumultuous years, I was more than ready to come home. I yearned to savor time with Gram and my niece, who'd somehow metamorphosized into a teenager in my absence. Most of all, I *really, truly* wanted to work with my big sis in my favorite bookshop in the world.

I'd been home for about three weeks now and was still pinching myself silly.

Morgan unbuttoned her voluminous coat. Layers of flapper silk glistened under lasso-length strings of dusky pearls.

"Amazing outfit," I said. Here I'd been feeling pretty put-together in my nice jeans, cable-knit sweater, and on-time arrival via the best commute in town, down the steep stairs from the loft above the shop.

Morgan shimmied, silk and feathers jitterbugging. "Can you guess who I am?"

I could. I'd bet my freshly minted library card that Morgan was the star of the day's book, *The Sittaford Mystery* by Agatha Christie. "Emily Trefusis."

"Yes! Emily, amateur sleuth, at your service! Now, where is Ms. Ridge? Has she started yet? I brought props."

Ms. Ridge, our indispensable shop assistant, organized Mountains of Mystery. I hadn't been home for a meeting in years, but I knew Ms. Ridge operated with the precision of a punctilious typesetter. At exactly eight o'clock, she'd sent me to the lobby to watch for stragglers. In deference to the storm, she was allowing five extra minutes for arrival.

"She's in the Reading Lounge," I said. "She'll be starting soon."

She'd be counting down the seconds until launch.

Morgan frowned at the door, a furry boot tapping like an agitated yeti.

On cue, the door whipped open. A young woman stomped inside. Her shoulder dipped under a bag the size of carry-on luggage. She wore a scarf so elaborately knotted it could rig a schooner, along with a look of harassed ennui I recognized from her rare appearances on Shelf Indulgence.

"There you are, Renée-Claude, finally!" Morgan fussed at her assistant. "Hurry now. We can't miss the murder."

I checked that the door was unlocked for any members still trekking through the wintry wonderland. Then I trotted after Morgan and Renée-Claude, heedlessly thinking that I didn't want to miss the murder either.

* * *

At the entrance to the Reading Lounge, I paused the way I might for a sublime work of art or stunning vista. Bookshops in general had that effect on me. The lounge was particularly special. It was a sanctuary, a refuge for readers.

A bookshelf arched around the opening, filled with covers the colors of a muted rainbow. Light beckoned from the far wall of windows. Pine logs crackled in a river-rock fireplace, its chimney flanked by bookshelves rising to meet soaring beams and trusses.

I stepped inside. Ten hardy readers sat in a wobbly oval of armchairs. Earlier, two members told me they'd snowshoed in. Now, that was book-club commitment. Morgan and Renée-

Claude would have braved the slick hairpin road down. Most members, however, likely took the serene route, the gondola line that glided between our mountainside hamlet and the larger base village down below. The best commute around, after mine.

Ms. Ridge held up a book. She sat upright, her spine as straight as her blunt-cut salt-and-pepper bob.

"*The Sittaford Mystery*," she said.

Good. I hadn't missed anything. I tiptoed toward my seat between Gram and Meg but found it taken.

The fluffy occupier, Agatha C. (as in "Cat") Christie, slit open a blue eye, assessed me, and slid the eyelid shut.

Pretending to sleep?

My new roommate was too adorable to begrudge, even if last night she'd purred into my eardrum and kneaded my scalp with the aim of overtaking my pillow. She'd succeeded, but I could get my cuddling revenge.

I scooped up the long-haired Siamese and sat, easing Agatha onto my lap.

The queen of the Book Chalet did all things on her own terms. Agatha rose, treated me to her signature ornery frown, and hopped over onto a dozing Gram. Gram startled, wrapped her hands around Agatha, and they both closed their eyes again.

I shared a grin with Meg. We'd been doing that a lot lately, delighted to be reunited.

Ms. Ridge held up another edition. "The story was first published in the United States under the title *The Murder at Hazelmoor*."

This dust jacket featured a manor alone on a snowy moor. I glanced outside. Snowflakes pirouetted over the meadow and cloaked the distant mountains. With the crackling fire and snowy landscape, I could easily imagine us transported to Hazelmoor.

At Ms. Ridge's prompt, the book clubbers debated title preferences. Sittaford or Hazelmoor?

Piper Tuttle, a local society reporter and gossip maven, had a firm opinion. "The murder title. Readers *love* murder. It makes them happy to be alive."

I could see that. Kind of . . .

Emmet Jackson pensively stroked his handlebar mustache. If pressed, modest Emmet described himself as one of Last Word's top-100 cowboy poets. Counting Emmet, I knew of two, yet I preferred his image. Droves of lyrical cowpokes reciting sonnets to their herds.

Emmet also favored the Hazelmoor title, but for a different reason. "Sounds lonesome. A good place to wander and ponder."

Ms. Ridge nudged the discussion onward. "Let's talk about our sleuth, Emily Trefusis. How do you think she compares to Agatha Christie's more well-known sleuths, Poirot and Miss Mar—"

"Ohh, ohh!" Morgan waggled her arm like a schoolkid with the A+ answer.

"Yes?" Ms. Ridge said.

Morgan bestowed her glow on Ms. Ridge. "My dear Ms. Ridge, first let me compliment you. You've arranged an absolutely *perfect* day for murder. How *do* you do it?"

Emmet Jackson belly-laughed.

Piper's eyes glittered, and I wondered if she was here for the book or the bookish celebrity.

"Thank you, Ms. Marin," said Ms. Ridge with her usual polite formality.

Ms. Ridge had a first name. Katherine. I'd never felt right addressing her by it. Even when we'd first met—way back when I was in college—I'd had to practically beg her to call me Ellie.

Meg and I agreed: Ms. Ridge could time-travel to St. Mary Mead in Miss Marple's era. She'd fit right in as the competent village woman known for her punctuality, efficiency, and tea cakes. Not that Meg or I wanted Ms. Ridge to go anywhere in time or place. We needed her. With Mom and Dad off globe-trotting, Ms. Ridge was our encyclopedia of all things Book Chalet.

Ms. Ridge smiled thinly. "You're also, ah, very well attired for our discussion of Emily Trefusis, Ms. Marin. Now, to return to . . ."

But Morgan wasn't done.

She stood, shimmied, and beamed at each book clubber before returning to Ms. Ridge. "As you so wisely noticed, Ms. Ridge, Emily has inspired me. She gave me the best idea! Renée-Claude, show them."

With a sigh, Renée-Claude rose and held the massive bag aloft.

"We can re-create the séance!" Morgan declared. "I didn't have a tippy table like they used in the book, but I did rustle up an Ouija board."

"Rustling," Emmet chuckled. "Nice . . ."

Morgan dubbed him a "doll."

Emmet reddened to the tips of his prominent ears.

Was Emmet a fellow Shelf Indulgence fan? Or was he smitten? Cowboy poets were romantics. Hopeless romantics, I thought, if as bashful and blushing as Emmet.

Morgan bubbled on. "This way, we can all inhabit the characters, examine their fears, their motivations . . ."

Heads bobbed. Emmet was already merging side tables for the Ouija board. Even Gram and Agatha fluttered awake.

I looked to Meg, raising my eyebrows in a silent question. *Was this how book club worked?*

"Let's see how it goes," she whispered.

Meg had told me about Morgan too. More like warned me. Morgan was a star, Meg had said. A mega-influencer.

I knew that.

Morgan could bestow bountiful publicity on the Book Chalet with a social-media post. Or devastate us with a single negative word.

Meaning we sure shouldn't squelch Morgan's séance.

"It'll be fun!" Morgan clapped her hands.

"Fun?" Ms. Ridge repeated weakly.

"Great fun," Morgan insisted. "I promise, Ms. Ridge, we won't re-create the *actual* murder. Although, you *did* order up the perfect setting." She added in ominous delight, "Who knows what will happen . . ."

Book clubbers laughed along with her.

I didn't join in. I ached for Ms. Ridge. Her chin dipped to her notes as her careful schedule veered off course.

I felt something else too. In the warm, snow-bright lounge, a chill tiptoed up my spine.

Absurd, I assured myself. Yes, the wintry scene resembled our book, but little Last Word was no setting for cold-hearted crime.

✳

CHAPTER 2

The Stranger Visits

"Eyes shut, everyone." Morgan's voice bounced to the rafters and back. "Minds honed. Focus. Concentrate."

She made spirit summoning sound like a spin class.

I squeezed my eyes shut. As in spin class (the few I'd grudgingly attended), I sure didn't want to be singled out for lack of effort.

"Silence," Morgan commanded. "Strong silence. Shhh . . ."

Silence only made sounds louder. Agatha and Gram softly snored. Meg was restless, I guessed. Her corduroys swished as she crossed and recrossed her legs. The fire wheezed. Paper rustled. Wind moaned in the eaves.

I forced myself to sit still despite tickles at my temples. Before I left London, my stylist had chopped my wavy hair to shoulder-length layers and a "face-framing fringe." In dry mountain air, fringe tended to turn into face-tormenting static. I momentarily obsessed—again—about whether to grow out my bangs, then chided myself. *Focus, Ellie. Summon!*

But . . . summon whom? In all her instructions, Morgan had failed to specify.

I defaulted to the obvious, the spirit I'd most like to meet: Agatha Christie. I imagined her in sturdy middle-age, tweed-clad and strolling our aisles. Perhaps she already had visited in spirit. Once, in a Poirot mystery, she'd written the perfect description of the Book Chalet.

I attempted to summon her words. *The books owned the shop rather than the other way around? Books, left to multiply and run wild?*

Later, I'd track down the exact quote. Emmet would enjoy the image of great milling herds of books.

Appropriately, cowbells roused me from my musings.

Morgan huffed. Eyes popped open.

"I'll check," I offered, scooting my seat back.

Morgan abandoned silence. Her voice, deep with melodrama, wavered after me.

"Spirit, speak. Speak! We feel your presence . . . Become manifest!"

Morgan really was a great actor, I thought, hurrying through the shop. I did feel a presence, an unsettled air. Yet when I reached the lobby, I saw no one, ghostly or otherwise.

"Hello?" I called. "Is anyone here?"

Someone had come inside. Zigzags of tread-packed snow speckled the mat. I turned in a slow circle, scanning the lobby. Books looked back from neat stacks on the display tables. No one sat in the club chairs tucked in the corner or browsed the wall of new-release mysteries.

The lobby, however, was just the tip of the Book Chalet. Previous family caretakers hadn't simply allowed our books to multiply. They'd actively encouraged their spread, squeezing in aisles wherever they could. Some stopped in dead ends, others in unexpected nooks. All were perfect for discovering new reads and getting lost in a book.

As well as actually lost. The visitor might have taken a wrong turn.

A floorboard creaked back in the shelves.

Whoops rose from the lounge.

Morgan's voice rang above the others. "D! Spirit, tell us the next letter."

They fell silent, waiting for a sign. I listened too.

Creak. A pause. *Creak, creak.*

Slow footsteps.

I tiptoed toward the dark aisles, then stopped short. I read mysteries. I would *not* be one of those ill-fated characters who skips off to dark spaces to check on bumps and thumps.

I returned to the entry and flicked on every overhead light.

Books lit up before me, but there were still those blind corners. Now that I'd conjured the thought of someone—something—lurking, the image stuck. An active imagination was an occupational hazard of a life with books.

"E! The spirit talks," Morgan exclaimed. "D. E . . ."

I could guess where she and the spirit were heading.

I started with history and regional nonfiction. Enticing titles tempted me to browse. I resisted, peeking around corners and into dead ends. No one appeared, but someone had come before me. I didn't have to be Miss Marple to spot more rectangles of boot-packed snow.

Annoyance overtook trepidation. Why not simply answer?

Unless they hadn't heard. Most likely it was an innocent misunderstanding and an entirely innocent visitor.

However, when I turned a corner and bumped into a figure, I nearly jumped out of my slip-on sneakers.

"Ms. Ridge!" I slapped a hand to my heart. "Sorry! I . . ." How to explain I'd talked myself into a fright?

Ms. Ridge hadn't flinched, and she balanced a coffeepot on a silver tray. "Is something wrong, Ellie?"

"No, no. I thought someone was in the shop. It's nothing."

Blunt bangs covered Ms. Ridge's forehead to her eyebrows. I could still detect fretful furrows.

"I loved your introduction and the different covers," I said, hoping to cheer her up. "The title discussion was great too. So much fun!"

She shot a grim glance back toward the lounge.

A cheer rose.

"A!" Emmet bellowed. "D. E. A!"

"Not as fun as that, I'm afraid," Ms. Ridge said.

"Even more so, truly." I meant it. A parlor game was nothing compared to the tricks, twists, and turns of Agatha Christie. "I hope we get to your other discussion points. What's next on your list?"

"Red herrings?"

"Love them!" I over-enthused.

"I do too," Ms. Ridge murmured. Chin dipped, she turned on her sensible soles and headed toward the storeroom and its fickle old twenty-cup coffeemaker.

I hurried on with my search until a strange sound stopped me. Rather, a lack of sound.

Morgan had just announced another letter, *D*. The final piece in the word I'd been totally expecting: *D. E. A. D.*

No cheer rose. No excited clapping, crowing, or chanting.

The lounge had gone deadly silent.

* * *

I noticed Gram first. She and Agatha still snoozed, models of doing what they wanted. The other book clubbers sat tight as teeth around the Ouija board. They stared at a man turned to the wall of windows.

His hands disappeared into the pockets of a wool overcoat, oversized and out of place in its businessman cut and shoulder pads straight from the '80s. Snow-white hair tufted. A thin satchel in faded black dangled from his right side.

He wasn't doing anything, just standing. Yet somehow his stillness set me on edge.

Meg scooted back from the armchair circle and approached the visitor. "Hello, sir?"

Her move snapped me from spectator mode. I hurried to join my sister.

To my relief, the man turned and smiled. At least I thought it was a smile. Thin lips stretched across a pale face.

"That view," he said.

I relaxed even more. Just another visitor mesmerized by our wall of glass.

"Even better when we can see the mountains," Meg said. "I'm sorry, sir. We're not open yet."

His face reminded me of a prematurely aged child. Round cherub cheeks, etched with lines too deep and numerous for an age I guessed to be fifties or sixties.

Caught staring, most members pretended to study their books. Morgan didn't bother. She leaned back with the air of a disdainful queen. Legs crossed. Fingernails tapping on red velvet armrests.

She was ticked, I guessed. He'd disrupted her grand finale.

"Apologies," he said, neither sounding sorry nor making a move to leave.

"Are you looking for something?" I asked tentatively. "A book?"

The smile stretched thinner. "I *am* looking. I lost something important."

He turned back to the windows.

Morgan removed her hat and rearranged its feathers as if that task was ever more fascinating than our visitor. Efficiently, she turned one tuft into two, like an iridescent horned owl.

The other members—except for snoozing Gram—dropped their reading ruses and stared once again. We were all mystery fans. We wanted to know. What was he seeking? What had he lost?

I broke first and asked.

"Sadly, a treasure that appears to be absent." He kept his stare fixed out the windows.

No one spoke for uncomfortable minutes.

Emmet broke the silent standoff with a cowboy drawl. "Well, now, partner. If that's the case, I'd say it's time for you to saddle up and mosey on out."

He didn't move.

"Mosey along, then," Emmet repeated and made to get up. Chair legs scraped against floorboards. A book fell with a slap, and flustered apologies ensued.

My chest tightened.

I glanced at Meg. My big sister pushed back her glasses, new frames she'd chosen for their descriptor: bookish. The frame designers had envisioned "bookish" as the mahogany of vintage leather covers, flecked with golds evocative of gilt fore-edges and aged pages. The colors highlighted Meg's hazel eyes and chestnut hair, traits we'd both inherited from Mom. The overall feel—serious mixed with fun, artsy, and all-around fabulous—perfectly captured both "bookish" and my big sister.

At the moment, Meg was leaning into serious.

"Sir," she said, squaring her shoulders. "This is a private gathering."

I drew a breath and willed him to leave.

To my surprise, he did. The stranger turned and actually moseyed, pausing to peer down each aisle he passed.

Meg and I followed.

My sister remained seriously silent.

I succumbed to a bad habit when nervous. Chirpy chatter. "We open at ten. We offer hot cocoa at our Coffee Cantina. Coffee too, of course, and books. Lots of books. Obviously. Mysteries especially. We're known for mysteries."

No response until he reached the door.

"I'll be back then. I'm looking forward to it."

I wasn't.

The door shut behind him as laughter sailed in from the lounge.

"M," Morgan sang out.

Meg and I leaned over the window display, watching as the man slowly ambled down Upper Main.

Behind us, the spelling spirit picked up speed.

"A," Morgan cried and then a moment later, a chorus of voices, "N! Man!"

Dead man.

Good, I thought. The spirit had spelled. Maybe now Ms. Ridge could serve up her red herrings. Which made me realize— Ms. Ridge hadn't been in the circle of readers.

"Where's Ms. Ridge?" I scanned the lobby again.

Meg did the same. "Didn't she go to make coffee?"

We headed for the storeroom. The carafe sat by the sink, empty.

No fresh coffee.

No Ms. Ridge.

"Something feels wrong . . ." I waited for Meg to do that comforting big-sister thing and convince me otherwise.

She didn't. Behind her bookish frames, Meg's serious expression took on a worried frown.

*

CHAPTER 3

Absent in the Autumn

"Eleven forty-five," I announced as Meg joined me at the register counter. "No sign of Ms. Ridge."

We'd opened at ten on the dot. Meg had confirmed that she'd never known Ms. Ridge to be a minute late. Just the opposite. Ms. Ridge was usually a good fifteen minutes early.

"There's probably a perfectly reasonable explanation," Meg said. "We just haven't thought of it yet."

We had come up with several *unreasonable* explanations.

Ms. Ridge might have flubbed her schedule. She may have ditched work and gone out shopping or to brunch or a matinee in a bigger town down the valley.

I looked to the bay windows. Snow fell as if the clouds were tossing it out in handfuls. Ms. Ridge wouldn't go for a drive on a day like this. She wouldn't miss work or flub her schedule either.

Meg sighed and tucked back her hair, which fell just below her shoulders in a sensibly elegant single length.

I lowered my voice. "It's that man, the stranger. He's making me nervous doing nothing."

Out loud the words sounded absurd. I waited for Meg to scoff. When she didn't, I hardly felt reassured.

"He's still sitting in the lounge? Not reading?" Meg asked.

"Not reading. Not even wasting precious bookshop time on his phone."

The stranger had returned promptly at ten. He'd then paced all the aisles before settling into the lounge in a chair positioned to stare toward the entry.

We'd asked if we could help him. He remained mysterious. He was waiting for someone special, he said. He wouldn't say whom.

Meg said, "We can't kick him out. Lots of our guests spend all day here relaxing, waiting for folks on the slopes, watching blizzards by the fireplace. . . . We're a reading refuge."

"Keyword being 'reading.' " But Meg was right. We had no reason to evict the man.

Meg returned to the storeroom to process new inventory.

I updated our social media accounts, including Agatha's Instagram. Her adorable ornery face had more followers than the shop. I was ringing up a customer, when movement caught in the corner of my vision.

The stranger! He moved fast, beelining for a blond woman in a cherry-red ski suit. She stood at the regional-reads display, engrossed in a back cover.

Distracted, I rang up a vastly wrong amount.

"Twenty-seven thousand and eighty-one dollars?" my customer laughed. "Books are as pricey as the real estate here."

"Oh goodness, sorry!" I glanced again at the woman in red. She was smiling, seemingly okay. I focused on the customer and her delighted horror at the local real estate market.

"Where do people live?" she asked. "Everyday people, I mean."

"The loft in their family's bookshop?" I nodded upward, knowing I was lucky. The other day, I'd stopped to peruse glossy flyers in a realtor's window and realized I couldn't even afford a yurt. A yurt needing work.

The woman left with a smile and books—always a bargain.

More customers stepped up to keep me busy. I tallied purchases, gave sightseeing recommendations, and helped a customer decide among three mysteries (she bought all three). When I looked around again, the stranger was gone.

The woman in red approached the register with an armload of novels. In a Texan twang, she praised the Chalet. "What a sweet place. Y'all are just bursting with history!"

"Thanks, we sure love it." In other circumstances, I would have chatted about our history. I'd have told her how my great-great-granddad, a gold prospector, built his refuge for reading from a single lucky strike. If she'd still seemed interested, I might have mentioned that my ancestor fashioned the chalet from images in his favorite travelogues, inspiring the alpine style of the entire upper hamlet.

My mind, however, dwelled on more recent history. "That man who approached you earlier . . . Did he bother you?"

She clicked her tongue. "He mistook me for someone else."

At my prompting, she said, "Someone called Cece. Like the letter C twice? 'Someone special,' he said." She fluttered heavily made-up lashes. "I get that a lot."

"Cece?"

She laughed. "No, hon, I mean *men* and hokey pickup lines. You know, 'I thought I was seeing an angel come down to earth.'" She snorted. "Hogwash."

Her resolute use of "hogwash" suggested she might enjoy Emmet Jackson's latest chapbook, *Odes on the Range*. I added his bookmark to a complimentary Book Chalet tote. When she'd hefted away her purchases, I slipped back to the lounge.

To my happy surprise, Agatha lay in the stranger's former chair. Gram sat beside her, dressed in her "work uniform." Gram's retirement work involved modeling how cozy reading was done. Today's uniform included peach slippers and a matching cardigan.

"I was frolicking," Gram reported, patting fluffy white curls damp from snow. "I simply had to make a snow angel. I felt like a kid again, until I couldn't get up."

"That happens to kids all the time," I said supportively.

Gram smiled. "A nice young man helped me. Very pleasant. He had a firm grip and good manners."

Uh-oh. Gram was drifting into dangerous matchmaking territory.

I switched subjects. "Did you see a man with a wrinkled baby face? He was sitting right there most of the morning." I nodded to Agatha's seat and silently praised her for stealing it.

Gram would not be so easily sidetracked. "That nice young man was closer to your age, Ellie. He knew you too. I told him that you were back home and single."

"Gram . . ." I'd broken off a long-term relationship several months back. I wasn't eager for another.

Gram straightened her cardigan in a prim just-doing-my-grandmotherly-duty move. "Yes," she said. "I did see a white-haired man. Was he the man I missed in book club? You girls should have woken me. I hate to miss fun!"

I apologized again and assured her that it hadn't been fun. "What was he wearing?"

Gram described a long coat with big shoulders.

That sounded like him. "Where did you see him?"

My grandmother huffed. "Well! He caught me changing."

I gasped and not because he'd caught Gram in her knickers. She'd been swapping boots for slippers. No, it was *where* they'd met.

"In the storeroom," Gram said. "He'd gotten lost."

Lost in a room marked PRIVATE/STAFF ONLY? However, only that sign barred entry. We left the door cracked so Agatha could access her kibble buffet. The door had a custom cat flap, but the bookshop queen objected to mussing her whiskers.

He wouldn't have wanted cat treats or my meager pantry supplies. Coffee? We sold delicious hot drinks at our Coffee

Cantina. Otherwise, the storeroom contained books to mail, miscellaneous inventory, staff lockers, and the might-come-in-handy-someday clutter saved by generations of frugal mountain folk.

Nothing particularly valuable or important except . . .

The stairs leading to my loft!

Our storeroom used to be part of a family residence attached to the shop. Over the decades, hungry books and their shelves had nibbled away much of the family space. So had the coffee nook that Mom and Dad installed. What remained was a spacious room with tall windows, a 1950s-vintage kitchenette, and steep wooden stairs leading up to a cozy loft space.

I'd loved that loft since childhood. It featured dormered ceilings, a private bath, and a bed with fabulous views. Constellations twinkled through a skylight, and I could turn on my pillow (when Agatha hadn't stolen it) and look out over the postcard-pretty hamlet.

Every place has its drawbacks, though. Right now, one far outpaced the lack of closets. The stairs opened straight into my loft. No door. No way to add one either, unless I wanted to come and go through a hatch.

I pictured the stranger emerging into my space. Was he there now? Touching my books? Rearranging my to-be-read stack? Lounging in the loft's most luxurious feature, the cast-iron clawfoot tub, hoisted upstairs by a legendarily determined great-aunt? Why, I'd—

"He left," Gram said before I could dash upstairs, armed with indignation. "He got a call and seemed agitated. Or maybe excited? He wanted to rush right out the nearest door. I let him out the back and warned him to watch out for snow angels."

"When was this, Gram?"

She pondered. "An hour ago?"

Wow, I really had been caught up in work.

"Fifteen minutes?" Gram frowned behind her bifocals. "I may have napped on and off. You know how naps are. A moment can feel like hours or years back in time." Gram smiled, recalling past joys or perhaps just happy naps.

I was pleased too. The man was gone.

"He was sitting in Agatha's seat?" Gram asked. "Agatha is guarding his property, then. He'll be back."

I examined the adjacent seat more closely. Floral upholstery. Cinnamon and cream kitty fluff, curled in a bun. A tarnished metal buckle and faded black canvas. Agatha lay on the stranger's satchel.

I feared that Gram was right. The stranger would be back.

* * *

Meg strolled into the lounge a little while later. "Ah, El? What are you doing?"

I knelt in front of the floral chair, attempting to peek inside a bag with a wild-eyed Siamese on top. I could have moved Agatha. However, if the man returned, Agatha C. Christie was my cover.

No, no, I could say. *I'm not snooping. I'm entertaining our cat.*

Agatha played along beautifully, batting at my fingers.

"Just playing with Agatha," I said, giving the line a go.

Meg made a sound of rightful skepticism.

My big sister has always been able to see through my ruses. I used to attribute her fib-detecting superpower to our age difference.

When I was kindergarten five, Meg was a savvy fifth-grade ten. When I reached ten, my big sis was a worldly teenager. I'd assumed that somewhere along the line (say, our current thirty-three and thirty-eight), I'd catch up.

Turns out, I'd always be the little sister, and now I was totally fine with that.

Agatha snagged my sweater sleeve.

"We're snooping," Gram said. Gram couldn't keep a secret and rarely wanted to. "Ellie's peeking in that stranger man's handbag. Agatha's a foil. I'm keeping watch. It's a team effort."

"The stranger's bag?" Meg asked.

"He left it behind." I gave up on the ruse and lifted Agatha, untwining my sleeve from her claw as I did.

Gram told Meg about meeting the man in the storeroom. We all stared down at the bag, now mottled in creamy cat fur.

A few readers glanced at us over their covers. Among them was Piper Tuttle. The gossip columnist had returned earlier to purchase and "power skim the good parts" of Morgan's Shelf Indulgence book of the month. The online meeting was this evening. I wanted to tune in too, though I hadn't had a chance to even skim chapter one.

Piper looked up, pages still flipping fast. She gave a little wave of ring-heavy fingers before ducking back behind the cover. Her spiky copper hair clashed boldly and beautifully with sparkly pink reading glasses.

"Who wants to look inside first?" Gram asked.

Meg frowned down. "We can't pry inside customers' private property the moment they step away."

"The airport would," Gram countered. "They'd have dogs sniff that bag and robots blow it up."

"Exactly," I said. "We're not going that far. Plus, he hasn't just been gone a moment. He might have been gone an hour."

"Or fifteen minutes," admitted Gram. She was way too honest.

I added a more helpful reason. "What if he forgets where he left his bag? We can check for contact information. A hotel card, a wallet . . ."

"And if there's anything suspicious, we'll toss it out in a snowdrift," Gram said cheerfully. "The avalanche-mitigation team keeps dynamite. They could blow it up."

Meg smiled at us. An indulgent, patient smile. "You know,

it's hard being the responsible big sister and elder grand-daughter sometimes."

"You make it look easy, dear," Gram said.

Meg rolled her eyes.

I placed Agatha on Gram's seat and reached for the bag, all eagerness until my mystery-reader imagination kicked in. What would Agatha Christie leave inside? A viper? A poison pen? A poisonous letter dripped from a toxic tongue? A bomb?

Ridiculous, I told myself, yet I held my breath until my fingers touched a hardback.

"Oh my," Gram said when I held up the book. "I'm certainly glad we didn't blow that up. *Absent in the Spring* by Mary Westmacott."

"Who?" Piper Tuttle had slipped into our little circle. I'd been so focused on the bag and its contents that I hadn't noticed her approach.

"Agatha Christie's pseudonym," Gram said and explained. Agatha Christie had penned six novels under the name. "Sometimes they're called romances, but they're more like psychological studies. They explore relationships, possibly even Agatha herself."

Piper peered closer. "Are there murders?"

"No . . ." Gram said.

Piper tutted. "There you go. That's why that man left it behind."

So, she'd overheard us talking about the stranger. I couldn't fault her for eavesdropping from behind a book. I'd have done the same.

"Find any contact info?" Piper asked, winking conspiratorially. "You better keep looking."

I planned to. I gently flipped pages, having learned from working in used books that people leave all sorts of things tucked between pages. Cash. Bank cards. Locks of hair. Love letters. Once, working in a bookshop in former East Berlin, I'd discovered one spy's note to another, a warning read decades too late.

However, it was Meg, searching the satchel, who discovered the only other items. A gum wrapper and a plain white envelope, unsealed.

"We're only checking for ID," Meg said in what sounded like reassurance to herself.

She opened the envelope. Its contents reminded me of the spy's correspondence, deceptively common yet obtuse. A slender stack of sticky notes, pale pastel with cursive script in smudged pencil.

Meg read the upper note aloud. "Love is, *indeed,* a terrifying thing."

"Indeed!" exclaimed Piper. "That's why people love it. The *terror.* That's why everyone loves murder mysteries and horror flicks too."

I wasn't sure I agreed, but then everyone had their own reasons for reading.

Meg flipped through the little squares before tucking them back in the envelope.

"Hey," Piper protested.

Now we were on the same page. I wanted to read the rest too.

Meg, however, kept us to her word. "We were only looking for contact info, which these are not."

What they were, we couldn't decide.

"Maybe he's a writer," suggested Gram. "They're always scribbling down random thoughts and then forgetting where they put them."

Piper had little interest in absentminded writers. She returned to skimming her book.

Meg inspected the Westmacott, which wasn't entirely empty. "Look . . . Agatha Christie's signature as Mary Westmacott. That's a treasure, even with this minor water stain at the corner. He'll be back for sure. We don't have to worry about that."

His return was what worried me.

However, by the end of the day, the stranger hadn't reappeared. Neither had Ms. Ridge, which concerned me more.

"Let's swing by her house on the way home," Meg proposed.

Gram had already gone home, taking the gondola down to the comfortable Victorian she'd shared with Meg and Rosie since our beloved Gramps passed away. She and Rosie were fixing their specialty tonight: lasagna.

"You'll join us, Ellie?" Gram had asked.

My favorite meal and most favorite people? How could I resist?

Meg tucked the Westmacott into the lost-and-found shelf under the register.

I served Agatha her favorite fishy dinner and promised I'd return by bedtime.

"Unless Ellie misses the last gondola," Meg joked to the frowny feline.

Agatha couldn't fool us. We knew she liked her alone time.

"My ulterior motive is to keep my little sis for a sleepover," Meg said as we set out on the short stroll to the gondola station.

Snow fell softly, icing the chalets like gingerbread houses. The streetlamps cast golden halos, and the air smelled of woodsmoke and pines.

Meg was saying, "We could do a puzzle, watch a movie, make s'mores in the fireplace . . ."

"Sounds perfect." I went to loop my arm through Meg's. Her arm shot out.

"Ellie, look! Is that him?"

The station lights glowed before us. The metal pavilion had a chalet roofline with scrolled trim and a minty-green patina.

Two wide openings allowed entrance on either side. Inside, an overhead track chugged and churned, circulating the gondolas in a long oval up and down the mountain. Passengers hopped on the slow-moving cars unless they requested a pause from the gondoliers manning the upper and lower stations. The cost was the best deal around: free.

A man had entered from the side opposite ours. I took in mussed white hair and a long, loose coat. He ran with a bobbing lurch and lunged into the nearest gondola.

Meg grabbed my sleeve. "Let's go! We'll flag him down at the base and see if he wants to come back up for his bag."

I balked, thinking of things I'd rather do. Like find Ms. Ridge. Invite her to lasagna. Joke with my favorite niece in Gram's warm kitchen.

"If we return his book tonight, we don't have to worry about him tomorrow," Meg said.

We took off, boots slipping in snow. As we entered, the upper-station gondolier, Rusty Zeller, ambled in the opposite entry. Around our parents' age, Rusty was a proud member of the Wolfe Pack, devotees of fictional detective Nero Wolfe. He was also a reigning champ of the Book Chalet's literary trivia nights. Usually, we'd stop and talk mysteries.

Meg called out, "We're chasing that gondola, Rusty. Its rider lost his Mary Westmacott!"

Rusty hesitated only a moment before displaying his literary knowledge. "A Westmacott, eh? You Christie gals'll set that straight!"

The stranger's gondola inched out of the station. Meg and I dashed, just managing to catch the gondola behind his. Our doors slid shut. The glass capsule eased out, wobbled, and plunged downhill. My stomach pitched. I'm no fan of heights, but the magic of floating over treetops always assuaged my fears. Snowflakes wafted by like millions of butterflies. Lights from the ski slopes to the west cast a peachy glow.

Dim solar lanterns lit each cabin. I could barely make out the man ahead, leaning against his window.

"Right," Meg said, as the base station neared. "What's our strategy? Jump out and yell 'Westmacott'?"

"Sounds good to me," I laughed, then noticed a problem with the plan. The stranger's gondola was inching past the disembarking point. Was he riding back up?

The base-station gondolier, a young man with lanky shoulder-length locks, noticed too and stopped the line. Our gondola wobbled to a swinging stop, leaving us a few meters from the station entrance and several more above the ground.

"Ah, sir? Hello?" The gondolier's voice floated up to us.

Meg and I leaned forward.

The stranger didn't move, not until the attendant stepped inside and prodded his shoulder. That caused a reaction. In horrifying slow motion, the stranger slumped, sank from his seat, and disappeared from our view.

Meg and I stood, our mittened hands pressed to the glass.

"He's sleeping," I said. "Or passed out or fainted or . . ." *Drunk, please let him be drunk . . .*

The attendant turned to us, face stretched in shock, before fumbling into a baggy jacket. He produced a phone and jabbed at the screen.

Meg and I froze as his frantic words reached us.

"Dude! I've got a problem. A dead guy on the gondola!"

✳

CHAPTER 4

A Murder Is Announced

"What are they waiting for?" I asked, looking down from our safety-latched bubble. Two EMTs stood outside the stranger's gondola, stoic and still as palace guards.

The young gondolier had attempted CPR, urged on by Meg's miming and my bellowed, off-key rendition of "Stayin' Alive," the song with the perfect chest-compressing beat.

Except the bouncy rhythm hadn't brought the stranger back. Nor had the EMTs, who'd dashed in and then almost as quickly stepped back out.

I stared down at the EMTs. They'd arrived in an ambulance, lights flashing. Surely they had a stretcher, a blanket . . .

Meg puffed frosty breath. "Maybe they're waiting for the coroner? A hearse?"

I shivered and scootched closer to my sister. Down in the station, a crowd gathered as steadily as the snow, drawn by the spectacle. Unfortunately, that included Meg and me, suspended above a tragedy.

Eyes stared our way, along with the camera ends of cellphones and a massive zoom lens. The guy wielding the zoom had arrived moments before the EMTs. They'd pushed by and waved him away, but he hadn't gone far. His lens turned to us again.

I can see you! I wanted to yell. *It's rude to photograph people trapped in glass bubbles!*

I scrunched into my scarf and scowled. He noticed and waved. Friendly. Grinning. Vaguely familiar. Here was a distraction from the awful scene below. I could sleuth out the identity of camera guy. I tucked clues into a mental list.

Around my age. A former classmate?

Strawberry-blond hair jutting from a green beanie. Outdoorsy-ruddy complexion. Snow pants and jacket, fashionably baggy and bright. A lanyard thick with IDs. A snowboarder?

Summation: a snowboarder I might know.

Hardly a Sherlockian feat. Then again, Sherlock Holmes had never faced the case of former classmates who had—shockingly—aged.

Since returning home, I'd embarrassed myself by failing to recognize some former classmates and teachers. I'd readily admit that I wasn't great with faces. I would have known close friends, but most of them had moved away, off to cities or suburbs with more jobs and homes affordable for families.

Now that I was back to stay, I wanted to reconnect. I'd reach out, I vowed. I'd overcome my natural impulse to stay home, curled up with a book. I'd say yes to—

Screeeeech!

Meg and I slapped mittened palms to our ears as the acoustic equivalent of braking train mixed with caterwauling tomcat ricocheted through our gondola.

Meg glared up at a quarter-sized intercom in the ceiling.

I spotted the original source. Down in his glass cabin, the young gondolier hunched over a microphone.

"Ah, hello?" He leaned closer to the mic. Our cabin filled with heavy breathing.

"This is the Last Word Base Village Gondola Station and your gondolier for the evening, ah, Trevor?"

Poor Trevor. I empathized with his uncertainty.

Trevor picked up a binder and read in a rote monotone. "Welcome. I mean, *attention,* valued riders. The Last Word Gondola—your premier gondola service—will be pausing service momentarily for routine . . . ah . . . um . . ." He flipped pages.

Meg shuddered. "Oh dear, let's hope death doesn't become routine."

"We're stopped for a delay?" Trevor suggested and then added, "There's no cause for concern." With that, he dropped the binder in a deafening clatter.

Meg winced and said, "If we were upslope, swinging above the cliffs in the dark, would 'no cause for concern' comfort you?"

"Just the opposite."

We Christies weren't catastrophists. We were practical. We were also avid mystery readers and thus knew what could go wrong. Anything and everything, often with a twist.

I wished Rusty Zeller would chime in from the upper station. He'd be gruffly calm. He wouldn't pose questions either, unless they were literary trivia to pass the grim time.

Meg's phone buzzed. I looked away to give her privacy. Her screen soon slid into my vision.

"Does this sound like your favorite niece?" Meg asked.

Solid text filled the screen. Like any self-respecting teen, Rosie texted in minimal letters and ample emojis. Interpretation was akin to deciphering code.

"Gram?" I said, incredulous. "Since when does Gram text?"

Gram had an emergency cellphone she routinely forgot to charge and carry. We'd called her rotary landline earlier to let her know about the death and delay.

"Ever since I got Rosie her new phone last week. She and Gram discovered the voice-to-text function," Meg said.

"Oh no . . ." Voice to text was a minefield for blush-worthy mistranscriptions.

"Yep," Meg agreed. "Let's see . . . Gram hopes we're not frostbitten and says 'huzzah is hot in loving.'"

My rumbling stomach readily translated "huzzah" to "lasa-gna" and "loving" to "oven."

"Thank goodness," I said.

Meg continued, "They're at book club and it's stuck too? Do you understand that?"

I didn't understand the stuck part, but I got the rest. "Shoot, we're missing Morgan's Shelf Indulgence chat!"

"Gram says you'll be kidnapped." Meg scrolled on.

"If it's by you, Gram, and Rosie, I'm in." No way was I getting on another gondola tonight.

My sister had gone silent.

"What?" I asked.

Meg sighed. "Gram wonders about the cause of death. She's listed possibilities: heart, lung, *deep veiled trombones*? Deep vein thrombosis, I bet." Meg hesitated before reading Gram's next suggestion. "'*Unnatural* causes'? Do you think she means . . ."

I did. I'd already thought it. *Murder?*

Meg answered her own question. "No, that's impossible. We saw him get on the gondola, alive and alone. The most likely explanation is something medical, right?"

When I didn't respond right away, Meg raised expectant eyebrows.

"Right," I said. "Much more likely."

Meg turned her attention—and an index finger—to her phone screen. Unlike Rosie, and apparently Gram, Meg texted by single-finger jabbing. She also wrote in full sentences with proper punctuation. Her texts took a while.

"I'll tell Gram that he slipped away peacefully while sailing in the sky," Meg said.

She tapped.

My eyes caught movement below. I stood for a better view. "Ah . . . Meg."

"Just a sec. Oh, this autocorrect! *Not 'naturalist dentist,' 'natural demise.'*"

"Meg," I said urgently. "Hold that thought."

The crowd had parted. A woman, tree-trunk stout in thick layers of winter wear, strode through. Pale curls poked from her plaid earflapped hat.

Her, I recognized immediately. I'd seen her in the newspaper last week, front page, smile as bright as her name: "Sunnie" Sundstrom, Last Word's new chief of police. A coup for our tiny town, the paper declared. Sunnie Sundstrom was a former big-city detective. A real hotshot.

The article quoted her saying those things urbanites do when they move to Last Word. She sought fresh air, small-town charms, a healthy lifestyle, and hopefully the joy of sighting a moose. She dearly wanted to see a moose.

Our new chief had then added another anticipated perk, not commonly cited but a definite plus: "fewer incidents of major crime."

My stomach clenched. Meg stiffened beside me.

Sunnie Sundstrom wasn't smiling now. She stopped near the dead man's gondola. In a voice louder than the intercom, she boomed, "Folks, I'm sorry—truly sorry—but this is a potential crime scene. I'm gonna need everyone out."

A rumble rose. The crowd closed in.

"Out," the chief commanded. "Now."

The crowd siphoned toward the exit.

"Everyone but witnesses," declared Last Word's new police chief and pointed up to us.

CHAPTER 5

✳

Tripping Down Memory Lane

One by one, gondolas inched along like reluctant pill bugs. Meg and I stood back on solid ground, unsteadily waiting to give statements.

"First priority is getting the rest of the riders out," Chief "call me Sunnie" had said as we disembarked. "Can't have a bunch of frozen bodies floating up there, can we?"

I'd initially taken that as grim humor. Chief Sunnie seemed to mean it.

She'd moved here from somewhere far less snowy, I recalled. San Francisco? San Diego? Santa something? Was that all it was? Fear of the unfamiliar chill? Or did she have reason to suspect further trouble?

She was elusive about the crime itself.

"Let's not label anything yet," Chief Sunnie said, smiling in a way that was probably meant to reassure. It didn't.

Murder, that's what it had to be. A man had died in front of Meg and me, and we hadn't noticed a thing.

The chief had viewed our witness potential differently, especially after learning that we'd met the man earlier. "You're key witnesses," she said. "I want to talk in-depth. Will you wait?"

Of course we would. Meg and I had taken shelter on the

downwind side of Trevor's small hut, warmed by the thought that we might help.

I bundled my coat tighter and allowed myself a heroic fantasy. The Christie sisters serve up a clue that catches a killer. I lowered my eyelids and replayed the scene at the upper station. I saw snow lit by streetlamps. Happy skiers. Kids bundled in snowsuits. A pug in a puffer coat.

What had we missed?

Had the killer walked right past? A shadow slinking by—

Pssst . . .

The sound brushed my ear. I jolted into Meg. We spun to face the sheepish grin of zoom-lens guy.

"Hey, Christies," he said. "Sorry! Didn't mean to scare you."

After the chief ordered everyone to leave, he'd approached her, holding up his lanyard, fanning through cards, and pointing to his camera.

Reporter, I'd deduced, which still failed to place him.

Now I added another clue. A big one. He definitely knew us, meaning I should probably recognize him.

His grin widened to Cheshire-cat frisky. "El, great to see you. Your grandma said you were back in town. And on your own, eh?"

Oh dear. Was this the firm-gripped, well-mannered hero who'd extracted Gram from her snow angel? If so, I bet Gram had practically asked him out for me.

He was good-looking. And oh-so-frustratingly familiar. I had to say something.

"Yep, I'm back," I said, perky and smiley as a cheerleader after a gallon of espresso.

"We should get together sometime, catch up." He grimaced and glanced toward the gondolas, where the chief was interviewing disembarking riders. "Someplace nicer than this."

"That'd be great!" I said, digging myself in deeper. Now I really couldn't ask his name.

I nudged Meg, hoping she'd toss me a clue. She knew about my memory mishaps. Last week, I'd lamented that old classmates didn't come with nametags. She'd supportively championed my memory wins.

"You have an amazing memory for books, El. And characters—like when you recalled the name of the vicar's cat in *A Murder Is Announced*? What was it again? Tilly Pilsner?"

Meg was the best big sister. I'd assumed she was feigning forgetfulness to make me feel better. Because *of course* the cat's name was Tiglath Pileser, named after an Assyrian king. Who could forget that?

Thankfully, Meg provided more than a hint.

"Sydney Zeller!" she exclaimed in mock chastisement. "You nearly gave us heart attacks, sneaking up on us like that. Do you want more deaths in this gondola station?"

His grin fell.

Mine rose for real.

Meg gasped. "Oh, sorry! That was awful and tactless of me. This whole terrible thing has me off balance."

Me too, and now a whoosh of memories added to my wobbliness. Sydney Zeller! How could I forget Syd?

I offered myself excuses. Syd *had* changed. A tall, broad-shouldered adult had replaced the loose-limbed teen. However, the easy smile was the same, confident and disarming. And now that I knew, his identity seemed blatantly obvious. I updated my mental list.

Syd, a year ahead of me at school, a cool-crowd guy, far out of my realm except when he'd dated a friend.

Syd, a top student but so prone to ditching school for the slopes, his name became a code. *Pulling a Zeller!*

Syd, son of upper-station gondolier and mystery-buff Rusty Zeller. How embarrassing for my detection skills! I assured myself that they looked little alike. Rusty was rounded, red-cheeked, and gravelly gruff. He also hadn't mentioned

Syd. We'd spoken about the weather and my travels. Mostly we'd talked of books, especially Nero Wolfe mysteries, whose characters Rusty spoke of like family.

Fritz is sure cooking up some feasts. That Dol Bonner, now she's a clever one . . .

Syd who—for heaven's sake—one-twelfth stood me up for senior prom. Only one-twelfth and probably twice removed because he'd been dating a friend of a friend and a bunch of us went as a group. And then . . . yep, a massive springtime snowstorm hit and he'd pulled a Zeller.

Clearly, he was still a skier. Good for him. He'd always known his passion and hadn't gone off searching elsewhere.

Eyes I hadn't remembered being so blue twinkled at me. One winked. Sagely.

"You didn't recognize me, did you, El? Don't deny it. I could tell when I snapped your photo. Guess I'm getting so old I'm unrecognizable." Syd pointed to the barest crinkles that spoke of smiles and hours outdoors.

"No, no! We were far away and the glass was foggy and . . ." I was fooling no one. "It's me—my memory!"

Meg said, "Ellie focuses her memory on books, you know that, Syd."

He laughed. "I remember El reading at football games." He made this sound unfathomable.

Really? Helmeted boys in stretchy pants, tossing balls and forever huddling? Who *didn't* bring a book to football games?

Not that I didn't think fondly of sporting events. I'd always recall the satisfaction of turning page six-hundred-something of the nineteenth-century classic *The Woman in White* during a college basketball game, attended to support a roommate. Also memorable, that great first line: "This is the story of what a Woman's patience can endure." A lot, if she has a good book!

Then there was my brief romance with an English cricket fan. We weren't meant to be, but during those incomprehensible matches, I developed an enduring devotion to the logic of Dorothy Sayers.

However, I've learned that unintentionally favoring fiction can offend. Thus, I protested that *of course* I remembered Syd.

"You're a photographer? A reporter?" I remembered Syd as a guy of action rather than words, but people changed.

Syd gave a modest shrug. "Freelance photog. Mostly I do outdoor-recreational guiding and videography. Stuff like this when I come across it. Just until I can land funding for my business. Heli-skiing, that's where it's at. Did you know that Last Word doesn't have a dedicated helicopter service for backcountry skiing?"

He launched into a business pitch about the desperate need for helicopters to carry extreme skiers to cliff-tops.

Airy vertigo spun in my head and not because I'd ever ski off a peak. I was thinking of his other gig. Had my hometown changed so much that freelance crime-scene photography could be a side hustle? I must have murmured the words aloud.

"There's always a market for crime," Syd said. "I can sell to the local papers. Regionals and nationals if I have something really good." He flipped over his lanyard to show an ID for *Last Word Weekly*.

"Our new chief wasn't impressed," Syd said. "She basically told me to shove off. Then I ran into Piper Tuttle outside the station. She said it's murder? Something about terrifying love and a séance at your book club predicting his death?" Incomprehension tinged his words.

Meg said firmly, "Coincidence, that's all it is. That poor man visited the Chalet when our book club was reenacting an Agatha Christie scene."

"A scene predicting a death," I said and then wished I hadn't. I quickly added, "Like Meg said, coincidence."

"*Weird* coincidence," Syd said. "So, who is—was—the guy? Anyone important?"

"Everyone's important," Meg said crisply.

I felt the need for honesty after my fib about recognizing Syd. "No idea. He said he was looking for someone. He came by again and left a satchel and book behind. When we saw him getting on the gondola tonight, we hoped to catch him at the base station."

Meg said, "By the time we got down here, well . . ."

Syd grimaced. "That's awful. But, wait. You saw him get murdered?" His blue eyes widened. "In the gondola?"

Meg and I shared helpless shrugs.

Meg answered. "We only saw him get on. Alive. Obviously. Sometime on the way down, he passed away."

"Whoa." Syd shook his head in disbelief. "All alone, but they still think it's murder? Man, this'll get Dad going. He'll think it's one of those mysteries he reads. Something convoluted. Poison in the dead guy's beer. No, a poison orchid! You know that Nero Wolfe character Dad loves? He's into orchids. Obsessed. So now Dad is too. Has a whole room filled with them. Crazy for orchids and those mystery books."

Crazy for mysteries? Ah, who did Sydney Zeller think he was talking to? His comment, however, had sent my mind churning.

How had the man died?

Syd had joked about a poisoned drink. What about poison in a pill bottle? Say the soon-to-be deceased got a headache, a common affliction at high altitudes. He'd pop an aspirin, but one of the tablets would be deadly.

Or death came from within the gondola? Poison in the air? All the air sucked out?

I didn't like that scenario. Too dark and terrifying. Anyone might have been the victim. Kids. Vacationers. Bookseller sisters.

I returned to the more comforting notion of targeted murder.

"Probably wasn't poison . . ." I murmured.

"Why not?" Syd asked. "Do you know what it was?"

His interest was flattering. I wished I had more than speculation. "The EMTs called the police right away. Determina-
tion of poisoning would require lab tests and—"

"Oooh!" Syd snapped his fingers. "What if it was a poison
dart? It's easy enough to get wildlife tranquilizer 'round here.
Yeah . . ." He looked as pleased as if he'd solved the case.

Meg said, "The scent of bitter almonds?"

"Cyanide," I explained, reading Syd's perplexed frown.
"Fictional detectives can always tell the almond scent of cyanide from, say, almond extract in a scone."

But could Last Word paramedics? Doubtful. And surely
poisoners prowled mystery novels more than real life.

My mind wandered from poison frogs (not a lot of those
hopping around Colorado in November) to a limber killer
shimmying down the gondola cables (we would have noticed
that).

When I tuned back in, Syd was saying that his dad would be
disappointed. "All that time reading mysteries, and he missed
one a few feet away in real life?"

I felt oddly sad for Rusty. Then another thought flickered.

"Syd, how did *you* happen to be here?" He photographed
crime scenes. Maybe he had a secret crime obsession and was
dissing his father as a cover? *The gentleman snowboarder doth
protest too much?*

"Elementary, my dear Watson," Syd said, chuckling at his
own wit. "I was on my way up to see the old man before hitting the slopes for some night boarding. This snow, man . . ."

Dear Meg, in a massive mistake in small talk, asked Syd
about the skiing conditions. He launched, rapturously, into
words the bookish rarely see as positive.

Scorching. Shredding. Ripping. Tearing. Dropping. Totally
sick.

"Sorry," he said, the endearing sheepish look returning. "I get carried away. First big snow, you know?"

I understood. I'd peeked out the window this morning with the giddy glee of a kid on a snow day. Except I'd seen the wintry wonderland as a perfect day for reading.

Until it had turned into a perfect day for murder.

Syd's enthusiasm bubbled up again. "Did you hear the best part? I mean, not good but great for us local skiers. A rockslide came down this afternoon and blocked the road out of town."

Last Word was nestled in a box canyon. In canyon terms that meant a dead end. One main road led in and out. In addition, a treacherous gravel track wound into the mountains, but no one except wildlife, hikers, and snowmobilers would venture that way until the snow melted.

"The slide took out part of the bridge over Camp Creek too," Syd said. "No city skiers are getting in anytime soon."

Which also meant that the killer wasn't getting out.

Syd hadn't clued in to this downside. He clasped his hands like a cartoon villain in greedy glee. *This snow is mine, mine, all mine . . .*

As if realizing he'd veered off track, Syd said, "Yeah, so, I heard the ambulance coming this way, hustled, and beat 'em by a full minute."

Syd, I recalled, liked to be first.

"First thing I saw was you up in the gondola singing, El. I figured the line got stuck and you were passing the time." He grinned and patted his camera. "Thought I'd snap a good human-interest shot."

The grin slumped. "I wish I'd noticed the guy. I might've helped. I do mountain rescue and ski patrol. I know first aid."

Meg soothed that there was nothing anyone could have done. "Trevor, the gondolier, tried CPR. It was too late."

I zoomed in on a much more minor and personal problem. "You photographed me singing?"

The grin returned. "Nah."

Thank goodness!

"Singing's the stuff of video."

I gasped and reached for his camera.

He backed up, holding it just out of my reach. "Okay, I get it. It was an emergency songfest. I'll delete the video on one condition."

"No conditions," Meg said.

I was prepared to listen.

"Come out to the slopes with me sometime," Syd said, addressing us both but singling me out. "El, bet you need to get your snow legs back . . ."

Was he blushing? Was he asking me out?

Syd shrugged. "Or we can get the old gang together. Lifties still makes awesome nachos."

Meg bumped my boot with hers.

"I'll think about it." I was thinking of the fun we used to have, sitting by the firepits at Lifties, a rickety A-frame shack with a million-dollar view. We'd sprawl on deck chairs, treating the snow like our beach. Lifties's owners didn't believe in shovels. You waded out, carved spaces to sit, and cooled drinks in drifts.

"They have these gourmet s'mores kits now," Syd was saying. "They're awesome. Homemade marshmallows . . ."

I had a huge weakness for s'mores. Plus, I had just vowed to get out and reconnect with friends.

"If that video disappears," I said, aiming to sound firm.

Syd made a dramatic show of punching delete. "Shoot," he said, frowning over my shoulder. I turned to see the chief, her finger pointing from Syd to the exit.

"Fine," Syd said with a dramatic heave. "If you hear anything about the victim, will you let me know? Might help me sell my shots." He jogged off but swiveled after a few steps. "Hey, El, if we make a ski date, I promise I won't ditch you. Not like prom."

I grinned, but chilly reality soon swept my smile away. The chief had turned her pointing finger to us, beckoning. Time to reveal that we were witnesses with more questions than clues.

✳

CHAPTER 6

The Unwitting Witnesses

"A book?" Chief Sunnie held a pencil over a pocket-sized notepad, as if waiting for Meg and me to reveal a real clue. A gust lifted her earflaps.

I shivered. We'd stepped a few yards from the protective shield of Trevor's hut. The young gondolier sat inside, hunched over his phone, ears muffled in headphones the size of hamburger buns.

The chief repeated, "You were *chasing* a man about a book?"

I didn't like her emphasis on "chasing." I could guess where she'd heard the word. Rusty Zeller, although he would have considered returning a book a noble mission.

Patient Meg explained. "Like we said, the man left his satchel in our shop. We were trying to catch him and give it back."

Chief Sunnie tugged down the wayward earflap. The other lifted. "Okay, let's make sure I have this straight. He returned to your shop after interrupting your book club. He wandered around, presumably looking for someone named Cece . . ."

Meg and I nodded.

"Then he left, leaving behind a satchel, which you then examined. Why? You go peeking into all your customers' things?"

To her credit, Meg didn't shoot me a that's-what-I-said look. She did let me field the question.

I hesitated, feeling a twinge of guilt. The deceased lay mere yards away, having just returned from his final ride. To allow other riders off the gondola line while preserving the crime scene, a grim-faced deputy had ridden up the mountain and back with the dead man. The deputy had burst out as soon as the doors parted, declaring a need for coffee.

"He was, well . . . acting odd . . ." I glanced his way. *Sorry!*

"Odd how?" The chief perked up like a bloodhound catching a scent.

Not reading in a bookshop? I doubted the chief would consider that suspicious.

Thankfully, Meg stepped in with our practical reason for snooping. "We thought we might find some ID in his bag. From his attire, he didn't seem like a local. We didn't want him to leave town without his property."

The chief took an entire page of notes.

I approved of her pencil-on-paper approach and the notebook too. I'd recently ordered the same brand to sell at the shop. Orange cover. Creamy pages with light-blue gridlines. Perfect for plein-air sketching, poetic musings, geologic illustrations, and, it seemed, murder investigations.

"Right," the chief said, finally. "So where are these items now? I'll take them and log them in as evidence." She scanned us up and down as if we might be making off with stolen goods.

Meg had a slender cross-body purse. I carried only my wallet, phone, and keys, tucked in various pockets of my parka.

"The book is safe back at the Chalet," Meg said.

"Under lock and guard cat," I added.

The chief glanced up into the dark. "Right, I suppose a book is safe in a bookshop. I'll come by and pick it up tomorrow morning. The gondola's not moving tonight, and no one should be driving on the road." She muttered, "Not that that's stopping some folks."

She returned to her questions, asking again if we could recall anyone mentioning the man's name.

We couldn't.

"And you found nothing else in that satchel, other than the book and those sticky notes? Luggage tags? Store cards? Library card?"

We *definitely* would have noted a library card.

"The only name he said was Cece," I said. "If you could find her, she'll probably know him, but didn't he have a wallet? A phone?"

"Not that we've recovered yet," Chief Sunnie said.

I felt absurdly pleased by this crumb of information.

The glum-faced deputy returned, carrying steaming paper cups. "No cream," he reported with an air of tragedy. "Internet's still out at the station, so prints'll have to wait."

Chief Sunnie accepted a cup with a sigh and jerked her head to the side. They stepped away to speak in low voices.

I leaned close to Meg. "They're searching fingerprint records. The chief wanted to know about names and anything that would identify him . . ."

Meg filled in the conclusion. "They don't know his name yet. How sad."

"How suspicious!" I countered. "Who goes around with no ID?"

"Maybe it was stolen? A robbery?"

My first impulse was to scoff. Robbery in Last Word? Yet a murder had occurred on this seemingly peaceful snowy evening.

The chief was returning. Before she could resume her questions, I blurted my own.

"Can you tell us what happened? How he died?"

She issued a blanket "no," stating procedure. "You read mysteries, you get that, right?"

We did. She was speaking our language.

"But," I countered, hardly a convincing argument. I barreled on anyway. "But how could we miss a murder right in front of us? What killed him? Poison? A dart?"

Okay, I'd stolen the dart idea from Syd. If that was the murder weapon, I'd give him full credit.

The chief replied in a rote monotone. "Cause of death will need to be examined by autopsy."

A sensation of little feet trotted up my spine. Someone was behind me. My mind screamed, *Killer!* I spun so fast my neck twinged.

Trevor shuffled his boots, hand raking shaggy locks.

Last I'd checked, the young gondolier had been absorbed in his headphones, rocking to a beat we couldn't hear. Or maybe he'd been listening to everything we said. Headphones were useful that way, like books.

"Dude," he said with more anxious hair tugging.

I interpreted this "dude" as his version of "hey" or "excuse me."

"I'll be with you shortly, Trevor," the chief said kindly.

"Dude," Trevor said, more urgently. "I mean, Chief Sunstrummerston? Ma'am?"

Chief Sunnie smiled patiently. "Yes?"

Trevor stammered on. "That cause of death. Was it, ya know, that knife wound or whatnot in the dead dude's back? I swear, I didn't know anything about that until those ambulance guys turned him over."

He held out his palms and stared at them accusingly.

"You two encouraged me to thump on his chest," he said, casting watery eyes to Meg and me. "What if I killed him?"

My heart thudded. Meg gasped.

"CPR didn't kill him," the chief said. Her voice turned steely. "Someone did, though, and I'll find them."

The killer should be worried, I thought. But then, so was I.

* * *

"We should still go check on Ms. Ridge." I wiped snowflakes from my eyelashes. More landed to take their place.

"We promised the chief we'd go straight home," Meg said.

My sister was big on promises. I was too. Usually.

We stopped at a crosswalk. Meg turned to me. "We'll call Ms. Ridge again when we get to Gram's, but I've been thinking, El. What if she was upset by that séance overtaking her Mountains of Mystery discussion?"

"She *was* upset," I said.

Meg nodded. "Right. Well then, what if she left in a huff? I know it's totally unlike her. She's so reserved, which means she'd be mortified now. If we hound her, we'll only embarrass her more."

Meg made good points.

My sister continued, her tone upbeat, as if trying to convince us both. "I bet she'll be at the Chalet extra-early tomorrow. She might not even mention missing work today if we don't."

Pretend it never happened . . . If only that could alter reality. I wished the murder hadn't happened. That didn't make it or our unwitting involvement go away.

Before Meg could step from the curb, I blurted, "Do you think we should have told the chief about the séance and 'dead man'? I almost did, but then it seemed kind of . . ." I debated between "silly" and "suspicious."

Meg offered other suggestions. "Unnecessary? Unhelpful? Distracting? I thought about it too, but I don't think we held anything important back. The chief wanted to get to the good parts, didn't she?"

Like Piper, skimming to the juicy parts of Morgan's book selection. Piper would view the séance as a must-tell item. Syd had already gotten a confusing earful from the gossip columnist. I imagined embellishments morphing into tall tales all over town.

Meg proceeded into the empty street. I hustled to keep up. My sister crossed streets with brisk purpose. She faced problems that way too. I guessed that her mind was spinning at high speed, propelling her legs along with it.

At the other side, Meg said, "If the Ouija had spelled out a name, then of course we would have told her."

We fell into silence, watching our step on slick patches. I slowed at a house I used to know as well as my own. Lights glowed in all the windows. Filmy curtains blocked the view. I wished I could part them or, better yet, step inside again. Growing up, one of my best friends had lived in the old Victorian. No longer. A few years back, her parents had sold and retired to Arizona.

"Their lottery ticket," my friend had told me sadly. "They made a bundle, but I can only come back to Last Word as a tourist."

She could bunk with me in the loft like when we were kids. I knew it wouldn't be the same.

Meg and I turned onto Lower Main Street. Last Word was a single village in two distinct parts. The upper hamlet had its chalets, vast views, ski center, and webs of trails leading to the bald-capped peaks. And, of course, the premier (and only) bookshop.

The base village was larger, if you could call a place with no red lights big. The downtown hosted several blocks of vibrant brick-and-mortar businesses, ringed in residences and the steep slopes of the box canyon. I usually saw the canyon as protective, snuggling us in, sheltering us from storms and the bustling world. Now I thought of the killer, trapped here by the blocked road.

Would he—she?—be plotting an escape? The unmaintained track over the mountains wound through public lands. There'd be thick snow, dangerous drop-offs, and no settlements other than a ghost town for at least forty miles. If the killer scrambled across the rockfall, the main road reached the next town in about fifteen miles.

Either way would be risky. A more cunning killer might stay put and blend in. I mulled that scary prospect as we walked. Other pedestrians passed. Most offered pleasant greetings that we returned.

"Are you suspecting everyone of murder like I am?" I asked Meg after a woman trekked by, hiking poles stabbing with each step.

"Not *everyone*," Meg said, nodding down the street.

I smiled at a familiar figure. Emmet Jackson came our way, bundled from the top of his Stetson to the tips of his handlebar mustache. He saw us and stopped to wait under the awning of a squat brick building capped with a towering false façade. The Flying W Lounge billed itself as a western speakeasy and hosted open-mic nights for readings, stand-up comics, and local bands.

Brave performers, I thought, which sparked a memory of the first time I met Emmet. A summer's day long ago. My fifth birthday party. Emmet had freshly retired from the army and was testing out other careers requiring courage and mettle, such as rodeo clown, cowpoke poet, and party entertainer.

I'd been the kid who hadn't wanted a birthday party. I had a better plan. Cake for breakfast, followed by long, lovely hours lording over my haul of new books, like Smaug on his mountain of gold.

I was big into Smaug. Dad had been reading *The Hobbit* to me before bed.

Mom had other plans. The people person among a family of bookish introverts, Mom decided I needed a party, whether I knew it or not. Friends, relatives, a piñata, and a cake arrived. So did Emmet Jackson, striding out from a dramatic puff of dry ice. At his side was a young rescue pony named Calamity Janet, who'd trotted in with an I-own-this-party attitude and some thrilling restrictions.

Don't, under any circumstances, step behind her, we children were warned. Duh! That was basic. Every five-year-old knew that.

Don't let her see or eat your fingers. Also Pony 101.

Don't kiss her on the lips. Disappointing. Pony lips are velvety soft, but we'd reluctantly agreed.

Don't call her Janet. Apparently, Calamity didn't favor her given name and its utterance could provoke violent outbursts. My family has chuckled about that ever since, our in-joke anytime we met a dappled pony or a Janet.

At the time, I'd taken Calamity Janet's name issues with solemn seriousness. My full name is Eleanor. At age five and for many years thereafter, I'd failed to appreciate it.

Now my favorite cowboy poet greeted us with a symbolic tip of his hat. A real tip would have required loosening the scarf bundled up to his nose and over his hood.

"Christie sisters," he said solemnly. "I suppose you've heard of the sad and sorrowful business."

We'd more than heard. We told him about our unfortunate gondola ride.

"Unheard of." Emmet's voice was muffled by the tightly wrapped scarf. "Unprecedented. And you're certain it was the same man who interrupted our book club?"

"Yes," I said. "Did you recognize him this morning?"

Emmet frowned. "I recognize trouble."

The door to the Flying W flew open. A man poked his head out. His beard—chest skimming and curled at the tips—could rival Emmet's mustache for extravagant facial hair.

"Emmet, you made it," he said with obvious relief. "We're up next. Five minutes tops."

"Be right with ya," Emmet promised. The man ducked back

in. On the back of his jacket, elaborately embroidered, I read *The Sideburners, cowpoke poets with altitude.*

So, there were more cowboy poets roving town than I'd known.

"Did you get stuck on the gondola too?" I asked. I hadn't seen him disembark while we waited. Maybe he'd tried to get on at the upper station and found the line stopped.

Emmet said he'd driven down. "I have a bunch of props to haul back later. I got delayed. There's an accident on the road down. A bad night to be out." He nodded toward the club. "I best get ready."

The movement caused his scarf to flip. He quickly raised it, but not before I saw an angry scratch on his chin.

I drew a breath. "You didn't wreck too, did you? Are you hurt?"

Emmet wound the scarf tighter. "Nothing but a scuff. Nothing to do with anything that should concern you." He abruptly turned and yanked open the door. Laughter filtered out.

Before the door closed, he paused. "You gals be careful. There's bad business about and you're best to stay far clear of it."

I looked at Meg. "That was more than a scuff. He didn't have it this morning."

My sister was frowning. "I take it back. Maybe I do suspect everyone."

But Emmet? He'd told the stranger to leave. But then the man had. No fight. No scuffle. I replayed his answer to my question. Did he recognize the man? He hadn't actually said. He'd called the man trouble. He'd also seemed awfully intent on covering that "scuff" and warning us away.

No, I assured myself, the kind poet of my childhood memories wouldn't hurt anyone. Yet I matched Meg's stride as we ducked our heads against the storm, hurrying on to the warmth and safety of Gram's.

✳

CHAPTER 7

Muffins and Murder

"Quick, she's coming! Hide the knife!"

I froze at the bottom step. The voice was Meg's. The words came from the kitchen, the source of tempting scents that lured me from warm, cozy quilts.

Fresh coffee. Baked goods. Possibly even chocolate, unless I was dreaming.

I hadn't slept much last night. When I did, my dreams had morphed into nightmares. In one, I'd been in the gondola, inching up, up, up in a classic setup for a plunge. In other fever-dream adventures, I'd found myself on skis, desperate to flee a shadowy figure raising a knife. Being a totally trite nightmare, my legs had refused to move.

Shushing hissed from the kitchen. A clatter, a gasp, and a grandmotherly titter.

My legs moved, meaning it couldn't be a dream. I stepped into the kitchen. Meg and Gram stood shoulder to shoulder. Their hands were hidden behind their backs and they both wore slippers, glasses, ruffled aprons, and caught-in-the-act expressions.

Something was going on.

"Ellie!" Gram exclaimed. "Oh, good, we were afraid you were Rosie. She has to be up early."

Gram unclasped her hands. One held a cleaver.

"Give me a hug, dear," Gram said. Thankfully, she left the cleaver on the counter. Her hug smelled of lavender soap, sugar, and love. I almost didn't want to ask.

I decided I'd wait.

Meg offered me a steaming mug of coffee. I gratefully took it and slid into the spot at the breakfast nook that had always been "mine."

Outside Gram's lemony gingham curtains, a snow-frosted world sparkled under a bluebird sky.

Meg checked on the oven and the source of the divine scent. Chocolate chip muffins.

"Three and a half more minutes," Meg declared. Rosie would get seven more minutes before Meg went upstairs to rouse her.

Everything was warm, comforting, and precisely timed. Except, what was up with the cleaver?

After downing half the mug, I felt sufficiently caffeinated to ask.

Meg and Gram shared a look I read as conspiratorial.

Meg deferred to Gram.

"Reenacting," Gram said.

I groaned, guessing the topic of said reenactment.

Gram confirmed before I asked. "The murder." Gram smoothed her apron and specified, "The murder on the gondola last night."

I sure hoped there hadn't been *more* murders overnight. I pictured Syd and his zoom lens, snowboarding from one crime scene to the next.

Gram was saying, "I called Lottie Nez over at the jail this morning. I knew she'd be in, and she's always so nice and chatty in the morning. I learned bunches, just not what I wanted most."

Lottie, jail receptionist and passionate reader of police procedurals, was clearly more of a morning person than me. I couldn't fathom being chatty in the morning. However, I liked listening any time of day, especially to Gram. Gram busied herself wiping already immaculate countertops and sharing the information she had gleaned.

"That accident you heard about?" Gram said. "A man was speeding down from the hamlet in a Porsche. A convertible!"

"Rental plates?" I asked. In Colorado, license-plate color gave rentals away.

The convertible had, indeed, sported telltale red-and-white plates.

We tsked about car choices in blizzards.

Gram reported damage to the soft top—the car, thankfully not the driver.

Meg pulled muffins from the oven. A lot of muffins. Three trays.

"The driver made it to the first hairpin curve and crashed," Gram said. "The police and ambulance were on their way to help him when they got the call about the deceased man. That's why they were delayed getting to you."

I shivered, thoughts of melty chocolate and warm muffins replaced by the memory of our frosty gondola, swinging above a man growing cold.

"No one else was injured?" I asked, recalling the bruise on Emmet's chin.

"Only the convertible," Gram said.

I sipped more coffee and reasoned that there were many ways to acquire a bruise. A slip on the snow? A brush with Calamity Janet? Age, according to Emmet, hadn't made the opinionated pony any less feisty.

I returned to the bigger question. "Gram, what about the deceased? Did you learn anything about him? His name? Whether he's a local?"

Gram clicked her tongue again. "That's where I failed."

"No!" Meg and I said as one.

Gram remained hard on herself. "Lottie knows his name, but I couldn't get her to tell me." She brightened, demonstrating that Christie information-gathering spirit. "Which suggests to me that he's someone big. Probably a visitor too. Otherwise, a name would have gotten around. *Someone* would have recognized him."

"See?" Meg said. "You learned a lot."

Gram smiled. "I'll get more. I'm going to take Lottie some muffins after we finish breakfast. A little treat."

"A little bribe?" I asked, grinning.

Gram patted her curls, her tell that I was right.

I amended, considering the quantity of baked goods. "A big bribe? That's a lot of muffins." Gram could bribe Lottie's entire extended family.

"Triple recipe," Gram said. "I'd like to send some over to Ms. Ridge too."

"You've heard from her?" I asked, hope sparking.

Then I registered Meg's grim expression. "No messages from her. Maybe she's having trouble with her phone. I'm sure she's fine . . ."

I didn't feel sure. It didn't help that Gram had returned to the knife "reenactment."

Gram picked up the cleaver again. "We had time while all the muffins baked, so your sister and I tried to work out how a murdered man outran you girls at the station last night."

Okay, put that way, I really needed to up my exercise regime. "Regime" sounded so unpleasant, though. Maybe I'd take Syd up on his skiing offer, with s'mores as a perfect après-ski reward.

Meg said, "We speculate that the victim didn't know he was hurt, or that he didn't realize the severity. I've read that adrenaline masks pain. The knife—or whatever stabbed him—must have been slender. Which could also explain why we didn't notice blood. Rusty didn't seem to, either, and he entered the station from the same direction. If he's on duty this morning, we can ask him."

She and Gram then proceeded to go full CSI with talk of blood splatter, puddling, and droplets.

I didn't consider myself delicate, certainly not about murders in books. But talk of real blood at breakfast? No wonder they hadn't wanted Rosie to overhear. On the other hand, I'd read some of my niece's young adult mysteries. The body counts could rival Agatha Christie's.

Gram waggled the cleaver. "We ruled out something like this. It would surely cause too much splatter—or is it spatter? Who carries around a cleaver, anyway? You'd need big pockets, too, or a very spacious purse."

"Yeah," I said, ever the supportive granddaughter. "That makes sense."

None of it made sense, including splatter and spatter.

"It doesn't help narrow the suspect pool, though, does it?" Gram said. "Anyone could thrust a little knife and by luck, skill, or accident hit just the right—deadly—place."

Meg turned a paring knife in her hand, then slid it in a muffin.

I bundled my robe tighter.

Pop music filtered down from upstairs. The bouncy music morphed to a frantic buzzer, a thump, silence, and then the thud of teenager feet.

Meg smiled. "Good, Rosie's up."

"Isn't it a little early for teenagers?" I asked.

Meg explained that Rosie was teaching ski lessons. "For absolute beginners, including our new chief of police. I suppose Chief Sunnie will be too busy with murder today. Rosie's also teaching a toddler class. They call them the Little Rippers. Isn't that cute?"

Cute. A tiny bit terrifying too. I bet that if the chief knew, she'd be suspicious.

Rosie shuffled into the kitchen. She wore puffy pink slippers. Her dark hair was knotted in a messy bun, the ends recently dyed cotton-candy pink. Her oversized hoodie featured an angry-face emoji. If she was trying to look surly and unadorable, it wasn't working.

Rosie kissed Gram on the cheek, mumbled a general greeting, and slumped into a seat next to me. She brightened when Meg slid the muffin platter in front of her.

"Chocolate chip muffins? What's going on? Is it someone's birthday?"

"Oh, nothing special," Gram said. "Just a pretty snowy day and your auntie Ellie staying over."

I knew whom I'd inherited my poor fibbing qualities from. If I was as obvious as Gram, no wonder Syd saw right through my of-course-I-remember-you fib.

Rosie wasn't fooled either. "Uh-huh. Okay, so, these aren't feel-better chocolate chip muffins because Mom and Aunt El saw a murder?"

"Maybe," said Gram, reinforcing her bad-liar status. "Or maybe these muffins actually are for your aunt Ellie, and your mother and I were using the baking time to act out knife crimes."

Maybe I'd underestimated Gram.

"Cool," said Rosie. Grinning, my niece tucked into her muffin. After a glug of juice, she said, "Mom, did you and Aunt El see your picture online? You're kinda famous." She pulled a sparkly-cased phone from her hoodie pouch, tapped, and turned the screen to us.

Meg closed her eyes as if pained.

I felt a sting of betrayal. Syd! I looked closer. The photo was blurry. Syd was a professional. He wouldn't sell a poor-quality image like that. Someone else had taken this terrible shot.

"You both look beautiful," Gram said, in a sweet grand-motherly tone I didn't believe.

Rosie enlarged the image with her fingers, which had even Gram grasping for something nice to say. "You look, ah . . . limber," Gram said. "Always good to stretch."

I saved Gram from further fibs. "Oh my gosh, that's the worst photo ever!"

Rosie covered a giggle. "Sorry," she said through her hand.

I knew Rosie wasn't laughing at the situation but at the exceptionally horrible photo.

The photographer had caught me with both hands cupped to my mouth, head tipped up like a county-fair hog-calling contestant. Meg, meanwhile, might have been doing yoga squats at the gym. Knees bent, linked palms pressing down. Both of us squished in a gondola with fogged windows.

"Your aunt was singing 'Stayin' Alive,'" Meg crisply told her daughter. "I was demonstrating CPR. Important life-saving efforts." Then she relented. "It's an *awful* photo."

An awful photo now floating around online. "Where did you get this?" I asked Rosie.

"First Word Last Word." Rosie took another bite of muffin.

Meg removed her glasses and rubbed her eyes, as if that might improve the image. "First Word Last Word is a community discussion forum, El. Kind of like Facebook, but for Last Word residents. I don't use it much."

Meg actively avoided gossip.

Gram sought it out.

"I like it," Gram said. "Rosie made the font extra large on my computer, so I can check it every day." Gram spread butter on a muffin, sounding pleased with her technological savvy and helpful great-granddaughter. "People discuss all sorts of interesting mysteries. Like last week, Margaret O'Neal saw a space-ship. It turned out to be a kite, but it was quite exciting while it lasted. You can learn about lost pets too and grocery sales."

I got the forum's appeal to Gram.

But Rosie? Did kids today hang out on forums discussing extraterrestrial kites and grocery sales?

I asked Rosie as neutrally as I could. "Do *you* check this site often?"

Rosie's snort was answer enough.

At her mother's prompting, she said with a shrug, "Pash told me."

Pasha Witten was Rosie's BFF since toddlerhood, a competitive skateboarder, and all-around cool teen. Pash seemed another unlikely fan of community discussion forums.

Rosie said, "Pash's mom saw the photo and read about that séance and said you guys could be in big trouble." She bit her lower lip. "Stupid, isn't it?"

Seeing her mother draw a breath—likely to issue thoughts on the rudeness of "stupid"—Rosie amended. "Silly, that's what I mean. False. Right? You're okay?"

Rosie, who'd recently grown into teenage bravado, actually sounded worried for us.

"Your aunt and I are absolutely fine," Meg said. "No one blames us for the murder, and 'silly' is the right word. That's all the séance at book club was—a silly game. Not real, just like you said."

Gram passed the muffin plate around supportively.

Everyone took another except Rosie, who squirmed with exasperation. "Of course, I know Ouija's a game. Pash has one. We played it when we were, like, ten."

Ouch.

Gram didn't feel that burn. "Games go through phases, dear. All my friends are hooked on coloring books, puzzles, and Candy Crush these days."

Rosie, grinning, challenged Gram to Candy Crush before turning serious. "No, I mean . . . Not that kind of trouble. Mom, you and Aunt El are in that photo. Everyone's talking about you. Your names, the bookshop. How you chased after the dead guy and have clues and are going to go all 'Christie' and catch the killer."

Before I could interject, Rosie threw up her palms in exasperation. "I know, I know, you're clueless. You didn't see anything, but what if the killer *thinks* you did?"

✳

CHAPTER 8

Lace Curtains

M eg and I crossed a stone bridge over a tumbling mountain stream. A basket of goodies swung at my side. The world sparkled. Like a fairy tale, I thought, just as a fairy tale–appropriate tingle scampered up my neck.

"We're being watched," I whispered. "I feel it."

Emmet had warned us to stay clear of bad business. Rosie worried we'd attract a killer's interest. Hopefully, we'd reassured her. Meg and I would go about our business with vigilance, we'd told her. At the same time, we'd keep our eyes and ears open for clues that might help the police.

"Like Miss Marples," Gram had said, which cheered Rosie a little too much.

"I can be extra careful and watch out too," Rosie insisted, putting Meg in a maternal pickle. What mother could say no to extra caution?

But had we already let down our guard? I scoured the pretty scene for places a murderer might lurk. There were way too many. Chubby frosted pines. Looming landscaping boulders. An autumn scarecrow cloaked as a snowman.

Meanwhile, my cheery sister waved and called out a friendly hello. "Hi, Glynis! Lovely morning, isn't it?"

Down the lane, a woman in a calf-skimming purple parka leaned on a snow shovel and stared at us.

I took it as a lesson. Don't overlook the obvious suspect. That and be friendly to watchful neighbors.

The now-named Glynis gave us a sharp, upward chin jab before returning to shoveling. Snow flew, cascading onto the cleared street. A thick silver braid danced down her back.

Meg pointed beyond Glynis. "Ms. Ridge lives in the cute red cottage."

All the cottages were cute, shaped like a kid might draw. Little rectangles with peaked roofs and tippy tall chimneys, fringed in red-berried hollies and plump pines, and brightly painted in the colors of a crayon box.

"Pretty street," I said.

"Nice and quiet," Meg agreed.

Nothing jinxes quiet like complimenting it. A puffed-up man in an equally puffy snowsuit marched out to start up a snowblower approximately the size of his cottage. It belched and roared. He gazed upon it as I might lovingly admire a kitten or a book.

Meg, raising her volume, informed me that the block had recently earned historic-district status. "I hope it protects the houses. These are the original miners' homes. Historic treasures."

Our great-great relatives would have strolled this lane. I wondered if they'd ever come by on a snowy day to check on a friend. My boot slipped on an icy patch. I caught myself but not a slippery thought.

Would Ms. Ridge consider *us* friends? I wanted to think so. But then why had she left work without saying? Why hadn't she returned our calls?

In our few blocks' walk, I'd built up a rosy fantasy. We'd find Ms. Ridge stepping out her door, efficient, polite, and flustered to learn of the mix-up. We'd apologize for safety-stalking her. She'd apologize for the misunderstanding. We'd all ride up on the gondola, with no delays or fatalities.

Since this was my happy daydream, I went all in: The police would nab the killer, Agatha wouldn't kitty guilt-trip me about her delayed breakfast, and we'd sell avalanches of mysteries.

Meg and I had reached the cute red house. Snow slumped down the tin roof like waves of meringue. A brick chimney rose from the center.

I frowned at the chimney. No smoke.

No matter, I told myself. Practical Ms. Ridge wouldn't waste wood when we'd have a fire at the Chalet later.

No lights in the windows, nagged the gloom-and-doom voice in my head. Lace curtains, I countered. They'd let in lots of sun.

"The sidewalk is shoveled," Meg observed. "That's good, right?"

"Yeah, sure . . ." My sunniness was clouding over.

Down the street, snow-machine Glynis moved on to shovel out another house. Was she doing the whole block? Had she done Ms. Ridge's sidewalk?

Meg followed my gaze and frowned.

"The walkway to the front door isn't shoveled," I said. "Maybe she's just not up yet? It is Sunday."

"It's well after nine. Ms. Ridge is an early-bird. Who do you think set book club for eight o'clock in the morning on a Saturday? Not me."

We studied the silent cottage, giving it time to live up to our hopes.

"Have you ever been inside?" I asked Meg.

Meg had, but only a few times. "I dropped off a paycheck, maybe last spring? Something had gone wrong at the bank, and Mom insisted we couldn't put Ms. Ridge out. It's a gem inside. Sweet old-fashioned kitchen, bookshelves everywhere. But she's a private person, isn't she? I think Mom goes over sometimes, but you know Mom."

I certainly did. Our mother's bubbly social nature wouldn't be squelched by the lack of an invitation.

"I wouldn't just drop by," Meg was saying. "That's why this seems wrong."

"None of it seems right."

We slogged over a snowdrift to the sidewalk. The latch on the picket gate was frozen shut.

I wiggled it. The whole gate wobbled.

"We can climb over," I said. "This snow mound is so high we're halfway there." Climbing would have been fine if we were, say, the nimble Little Rippers in snowsuits.

I dropped the basket of muffins over first. Then I clambered up the drift, hefted a leg over picket teeth, and landed in a crouch approximating a superhero stance. That is, if super-heroes got snow up their sleeves and ankles, down their necks, and landed by baskets of muffins. Meg fared better, staying upright.

I was about to press the doorbell when a voice rang out. Agatha Christie would have called it "stentorian," a word I loved but rarely got to use.

"She's not home." Glynis stood at the gate, shovel resting jauntily on one shoulder.

Meg answered brightly. "Do you know where she went?"

"Nope."

"Do you know when she left?"

"No."

I pressed the bell. Inside, chimes echoed into silence.

Meg persisted. "Did you see her today?"

"Sure didn't. Why do you think I'm out here?"

I gave up, turned, and flashed Glynis my great-to-see-you

smile. I was pretty sure I'd never met Glynis, but I wouldn't swear to it. "How do you know she's gone?"

This earned me a crooked smile. "Well, now, I'm glad you asked. I know because I beat her to the sidewalk shoveling. Usually, that one's up by six, out here as silent as a library mouse."

Meg introduced me, confirming my guess that Glynis Goodman and I had not met previously. She added, "Ms. Ridge left book club early yesterday and didn't return for work. We're hoping she's not ill."

Or hurt. Or worse. A wave of worry and guilt swept over me. We should have checked last night.

Glynis frowned. "She left book club? She loves that club, always after me to join. I tried to explain that I read solo." She turned her scowl to the closed door. "If she's in there, she's gotta be seriously ill or immobile. There's mail in that box. See?"

A supermarket flyer stuck from the brass mailbox like a mocking tongue.

Glynis said, "Mail lady comes by around noon on Saturdays. I got the sidewalks last night, 'round six and then later 'round ten. Let me tell you, it felt good to get to 'em first, aside from my aching back."

My kind sister inquired about Glynis's back.

Glynis predicted she'd suffer for days. She sounded delighted.

"You could rest up with some reading," Meg suggested with bookseller savviness. She asked if Glynis was looking forward to the new release in a bestselling Scandinavian noir series.

I hadn't read the series. Even the back-cover blurbs gave me goosebumps.

Glynis, however, cheered at the prospect of a fresh Nordic death spree. Momentarily. She lowered her shovel and leaned on it. "Since you bring it up . . . What if it's that?"

"Ah, sorry," Meg said. "What if it's what?"

Oh, I knew. I was about to whisper "psycho spree killer," but Glynis was coming our way. She gave the gate a firm whack, hefted the latch, and stomped up.

"I mean, what if something's *really* wrong?" She lowered her voice to an ominous whisper. "Like, *dead* wrong." She glanced suspiciously over both broad shoulders.

I couldn't help it. I looked too, the prickly feeling dancing up my spine again.

Glynis caught me. "Yep, I'd be wary, too, if I were you. I read all about what happened last night. You two, predicting and then witnessing a murder, and now the killer's trapped here with us."

That about summed it up, but Glynis wasn't done.

"Mark my words," she said. "Once there's one murder, there's apt to be bunches. Like termites and rabbits and such."

In a strained voice, Meg said, "The murder is likely nothing to do with Ms. Ridge. We're just getting a bit worried."

"A *bit*?" Glynis sputtered. "A murder and her missing? You should be big-time worried. But, you know, there are only two broad options. She's either dead or alive. Let's look around and see if we can narrow that down. I'll go first. Not to brag, but I have a certain talent for this kind of thing."

Meg murmured assent.

Did I want to know?

Glynis tromped down the steps and around to the south side of the cottage, shovel at rest on her shoulder. Leaving the muffin basket on the steps, Meg and I followed, lunging to step in Glynis's wide footsteps.

At the first window, Glynis stopped and peered in. "These curtains are what give me the creeps. Lace. Not even fully closed. Anyone could peer right in. Stalkers, peepers . . ."

Bookshop keepers . . .

"Who puts up curtains like this?" Glynis demanded.

An honest person? Someone who likes natural light?

We continued on, peering in empty rooms. A small sitting room lined with books. Even Glynis approved.

A bedroom with a twin bed, tidily made with a white quilt and four pillows, symmetrically arranged.

"What's that tell you?" Glynis demanded.

"That she makes her bed?" Meg said.

Glynis had an alternate interpretation. "That she's gone for good. Let's say, best case scenario, she's not dead. Where is she? Not here. I think the conclusion is obvious."

When neither Meg nor I responded, Glynis said, "She's done a runner. What if *she* killed that gondola guy? I don't mean to butt in on your detection work, but it seems kind of obvious to anyone who *reads*."

It seemed absurd! Glynis, I thought, read too many mysteries. I immediately chastised myself. Reading too many mysteries was impossible. Glynis simply had an active imagination. I could relate.

"Ms. Ridge isn't a killer," Meg protested. "Would a killer shovel her neighbor's sidewalk?"

Glynis thought that's exactly what she'd do. "They hide among us. Shoveling walks. Sharing cookies. Anyway, you aren't a killer until the first time you kill."

We pondered this undeniable truth as we slogged up snowy back steps. Meg called Ms. Ridge's number, and we pressed ears to cold window glass, listening for ringing or footsteps. Nothing. I didn't know whether to be relieved or more concerned.

"What about her car?" I asked.

"That's snappy thinking," Glynis said.

A small shed sat at the end of the back garden, bare-shingled and weathered. Glynis yanked open creaking hinges. An older-model sedan filled the space.

Glynis was disappointed. "That shoots my theory. Unless

she stole a car, which makes sense, doesn't it? You don't take your own vehicle on the lam. Too easy to spot."

The sedan was trustingly unlocked and thankfully empty of bodies. It did have a safety kit, a road atlas, and an Agatha Christie paperback tucked in the glove compartment.

Glynis read much into the title: *Murder Is Easy*. "Getting some tips, was she?"

I recalled the story with a different dread. "It's about a woman who thinks her village harbors a serial killer."

"That sounds great," Glynis said. She was downright chipper by the time we returned to the front walkway. "I'm glad—real glad—we didn't find her body. If she was there, I'd have felt it."

This time I had to ask.

Meg answered. "Glynis is part of Search and Rescue. She's very good. Renowned, in fact."

Glynis shrugged, suddenly modest. "Eh, well, I'm not someone you necessarily want finding you." She grinned. "I tend to find the goners. Someone has to. I like to think, knowing I'm coming gives the living extra incentive to rescue themselves."

I was relieved when the belching snowblower drowned out further discussion of Glynis's talents.

Glynis cursed. "Gotta go. Hank can't beat me to my own sidewalk. I've been doing everyone else's. If he gets mine . . ."

She left the thought dangling, a horror she couldn't bear saying.

Meg moved faster than Glynis and Hank. "Let me text you, Glynis. That way you'll have my number. If you see Ms. Ridge, you can let us know."

Glynis glanced nervously toward the roaring machine.

"I can text you when we get that new book in too," Meg said. "We ordered some signed copies. I'll reserve one for you."

They exchanged contact info. I offered Glynis the basket of muffins, which she happily accepted.

"Sustenance for when I'm laid up from all this shoveling," she chuckled.

Snow flew from her shovel as Meg and I walked by on our way to the gondola station. Gram had called ahead earlier to make sure the line was back up and running.

"Ms. Ridge's car is there, but she's not," I said as we crossed the stone bridge. "Where could she be?"

"Before last night, I'd have said we were being overly concerned," Meg said. "Now . . ."

"We'll tell the chief," I said. "She'll be coming up for the book."

✳

CHAPTER 9

Lost and Gone

As we neared the gondola station, my mystery-reader's imagination galloped ahead. I pictured the crime-scene gondola waiting for us, doors clacking like teeth. A malevolent fog, crouching in crevices, hovering in the eaves. At the very least, police tape, eerily cheery.

Reality proved both better and worse. In both cases because the gondola station looked completely normal. If I'd stayed in last night, reading and avoiding all gossip and news, would I have known anything awful happened? Unlikely. I certainly wouldn't have guessed that a man lost his life.

Gondolas glided smoothly. A family boarded, hefting in a giggling toddler and colorful plastic sleds. Meg and I held back, waiting until a friendly female gondolier waved us to the next gondola. Our very own private coach. I planned to use the ride to pepper my sister with questions neither of us could answer. The doors were easing shut when the clack of running footsteps approached.

"Hold the doors!"

Meg reached out automatically, but Piper Tuttle already had both hands inserted. The gossip columnist forcibly parted the doors and slid onto the opposite bench seat with a *whoosh* of winterwear, an oversized purse, ample perfume, and exclamations.

"Christie sisters! Just the women I wanted to find. I call first dibs on your tell-all."

The doors slid shut. Our glass bubble bobbled, dipped, and surged upslope.

I looked to Meg. We shrugged first at each other and then apologetically to Piper.

Piper enunciated. "Your tell-all. You lovely ladies tell me all you saw. The murder. The wild chase. The singing!" She lowered her voice, although there was no one to overhear. "The killer . . . Don't hold back. My readers love the juicy, gory details. Let's give the people what they want!"

"Sorry," I said, wondering why I was apologizing. If anyone deserved an apology, it was the dead man. We'd missed his murder.

Meg stressed that we hadn't seen anything, juicy or gory. She added, a touch pointedly, "We hope people don't get the wrong idea about what we witnessed from First Word Last Word."

Piper waved a hand sparkly with rings. Her frilly canary-yellow scarf, combined with her avid eyes and fluttery movements, reminded me of an intent bird. I guessed her age as around fifty, give or take a decade either way. Taut skin made it hard to tell.

"You might not remember right now," Piper said, "but you're sure to recall *something* eventually. Think back . . . put together the pieces."

Simple, her tone implied. Like a jigsaw puzzle, if the pieces had been hidden, destroyed, and/or scattered all over town and possibly beyond. That's all.

Wise Meg turned the questioning back on Piper, with compliments. "What do *you* know, Piper? More than we do, surely. You know *everything* that goes on in Last Word."

"I try," said Piper with unconvincing modesty.

"Did you recognize the man or learn his name?" Meg asked. "We heard that the police have identified him but haven't released a name yet."

"Is that so? No one told *me*." Piper's scarf feathers ruffled. Then she came to the same conclusion Gram had. "That means something in itself. Do you think he was famous? That could explain why the police are so tight-lipped. But then if he's famous, why didn't *I* recognize him?"

Meg and I had no answer. Silence filled the gondola. I was fine with that.

Piper wasn't. "Speaking of famous," she said, "did you attend Morgan Marin's book club last night? Oh, that poor woman! It's like they say, isn't it? Stars are just like us."

Just like us? During Morgan's Shelf Indulgence chat, Meg and I had been trapped in a frigid gondola swaying above a crime scene.

Piper thumped at her puffy-coated heart. "Her Internet was acting up. She couldn't upload live video. Of all the times!"

Yep, even book celebrities had Internet troubles. Piper chattered on about Renée-Claude's valiant but failed efforts to salvage the video feed.

My eyes drifted to the pretty scene outside. A grove of aspens passed by, bone-white trunks and a few shivering leaves. We were nearing the midpoint of the ride, where a rocky cliff divided the aspens from pines above.

The cliff sparked a memory I wished I could forget. When I was about twelve, my friend Reva and I had set out to hike down the gondola line. Only two and a half miles and the cliff stood in our way. I didn't particularly want to. At twelve, like now, I preferred thrills from books. Reva had twisted my arm. If I didn't go, she said, I was a bad friend. She also claimed to know a secret path.

Her path took us as far as a rocky ledge, where we got stuck, too scared to go up or down for hours. Eventually, we'd inched our way sideways, scrabbling on our knees, clinging to slippery saplings. We'd arrived back home after dark, sore and scuffed but alive.

Reva made me promise never to tell. She didn't want anyone laughing at our failure and fears. As it turned out, she didn't like me knowing either. Reva pretty much ditched me after that. She hadn't been the friend I thought she was.

I caught a glimpse of "our" ledge before it disappeared underneath the gondola. What was Reva doing these days? She'd once tried to "friend" me on Facebook. I'd quietly declined.

Piper chatted on about Morgan. "She managed to post some still photos. Oh, she shared the most gorgeous photo of herself in her library, reading this month's book. Simply divine."

This snapped me back to full attention. "That library is amazing!" I'd ogled it during other Shelf Indulgence chats. "I could live there."

Then I remembered that I could one-up a celebrity book influencer. I lived above an entire chalet of books. My loft just needed a few more cozy touches. Throw pillows, fluffy blankets, stained-glass reading lamps. Little touches to distract from the current décor theme of unpacked suitcases and stacks of books.

"Wouldn't we all love to live there?" laughed Piper.

Meg spent as little time as possible online. She hadn't seen the library.

"Oh, you must!" Piper produced her phone and hunted down the photo. We all sighed in shared library lust.

I read the caption. *Well, such is life in the wilderness! Heroic, darling Renée-Claude is working to fix it all. Until then, we shall discuss the book the old-fashioned way.*

"Call me old-fashioned," Meg said with a laugh.

The upper station came into view. Piper sped up her praise

of Morgan, as if trying to squeeze it all in. "Such a champion of books and female authors and, oh, wasn't she amazing at our séance? To think, *we* predicted the murder."

"No," Meg stammered. "I'm sure we didn't."

"We most certainly did," Piper countered. "Dead man? And then a man dies?"

She leaned across the few inches of space separating our knees. "Ladies, this is exactly why I wanted to talk to you. I already left a message for Morgan through Renée-Claude. We *must* hold another séance."

Meg and I opened our mouths to protest.

Piper waggled an index finger. "Believe what you like, but what if . . ." She paused for effect. "What if we summoned that man too soon? What if he was already destined to die?"

I let my big sister handle this one.

"Surely no one's destined to be murdered," Meg said, as our gondola swung into the station.

Piper shrugged. "Who can say? The mysteries of the great unknown are not for us to understand. We do know he's dead, though, so now we know exactly who to summon. Besides, in the right atmosphere, one of us might remember something important. Like you ladies. I wonder if Morgan knows hypnosis too? Maybe she could put you into a trance and tug out details buried in your subconscious."

Piper gathered her purse and inched toward the doors, in preparation to launch out. "Will you ask Ms. Ridge to set up the séance space again? She did such a wonderful job last time. A perfect day for murder, indeed!"

The doors opened. Piper burst out with a trilled, "*Ta-ta*, ladies. Remember, I've called first dibs on *everything* you know."

She was already trotting out of the station as we stepped off.

"Ms. Ridge won't be thrilled about another séance," Meg said.

No, she wouldn't. But if that was our biggest worry regarding Ms. Ridge, I'd take it.

* * *

In mutual and unspoken agreement, Meg and I took the exit leading away from the Book Chalet.

The stranger had come from this direction last night. At the time, I'd thought nothing of his wobbly jog.

Now I saw his movements differently. He'd been wounded. Had he been fleeing his assailant? If so, why hadn't the attacker followed? Maybe because he'd spotted witnesses—us—and fled back into the darkness?

Rosie might have been right to worry.

We stepped outside to light so bright my eyes watered. This side of the station opened to a park, overstuffed with park-ish stuff. Two picnic tables. A cute stone cottage housing restrooms. A platform large enough for solo musicians or poets. Antique mining equipment with wordy plaques. Lots of statues: a donkey hauling ore, a weary miner, a wearier Ute chief, a ski jumper, and—my favorite—an approximation of the hamlet's founder, our great-great-grandfather, reading.

"What was he doing back here?" I asked.

"Restroom?" Meg guessed. "Either that or he cut through the park from anywhere along this side of Upper Main."

I mentally strolled the stretch of street. What would attract a soon-to-be-murdered man? There were inns and private chalets, many now rentals. Had he been staying in one? The police would be looking into that if they didn't already know.

I continued my tally. Outdoor gear boutiques. Fancy gifts, a chocolate shop, the pizzeria, and an oxygen bar. Beyond was the ski center, a launching point for the downhill slopes and miles of cross-country trails. The man hadn't been dressed for skiing. He hadn't been dressed for Last Word either.

At the far end of the park, a cross-country skier glided

along the Rim Trail, which ringed the hamlet and its meadow. Kids launched toboggans and flying saucers, disappearing downslope with squeals and laughter. Syd would be equally giddy. I wondered if he'd remember our ski "date."

Throat clearing interrupted my mental meanderings. Another Zeller, Syd's dad, greeted us somberly. I scanned his face and now detected a few likenesses between father and son. Keen blue eyes and a few rust-red strands among scraggly silver locks.

"You're working?" I asked. "You deserve time off after last night."

"I don't deserve anything," he said, his voice extra gravelly. "You two do. Syd told me you faced down all the bad stuff."

We tried to shrug it off. If only shedding the memory was that easy.

I asked, "Did you talk to the police last night?"

He had. "That deputy, Garza. He rode up with the dead guy. I'm sorry if I got you gals into any trouble. After I said you were 'chasing' that man, Garza radioed down to his boss, and I worried."

We assured him that we were okay.

Rusty spluttered. "I told Garza, I don't miss much. I could list everyone coming and going, all day. Darn it, I stepped out for a rest break at the wrong moment." He hung his head.

I nixed the restroom as the scene of the crime. Rusty would have heard a scuffle and stepped in to help.

Meg said soothingly, "Your memory is legendary, Rusty. We're hoping you remember something for us. You know Ms. Ridge? Did you happen to see her yesterday? She would have come up early in the morning, before eight. We're wondering when she went back down."

If she went back down. I thought of her car and mail. Those open lace curtains and the snowy sidewalk leading to her door. But if she didn't go home, where did she go?

Rusty looked alarmed. "Why? Is something wrong?"

We explained that she'd left book club early yet might not have gone home.

"We're worried," I admitted. "What with the murder . . . It's unlike her."

Rusty ran a hand through already mussed hair. "She's a fine lady. I wish I could help, but I missed it all, didn't I?" He told us he hadn't come on duty until noon. "Came up around eleven for a bite to eat before my shift. I didn't see her go down. I was reading off and on, but paying attention, I can assure you." He reeled off a long list of locals and tourists he'd greeted in the afternoon.

I wished I had even half his recognition abilities.

Meg asked if Rusty had recognized the murdered man.

He frowned. "I only saw the back of his head and you gals chasing after him."

I felt bad, like we were rubbing salt in the wound of all he'd missed. I still needed to ask. "Did Chief Sunnie show you a photo?"

A laughing group tumbled out of a gondola. Rusty raised a pained smile and waved. The smile quickly fell to a grimace. "Yeah, she showed me a photo, but I can tell you honestly, I did not recognize that man." He pressed up a sad smile. "Nero Wolfe would be very disappointed in me. I missed everything important."

"Miss Marple would be disappointed in us," Meg said.

"Poirot too," I added. "And Emily Trefusis."

This cheered Rusty. He winked. "Not if you gals solve the case, they won't be."

As Meg and I strolled toward the Chalet later, I said, "How would Miss Marple go about solving this case?"

"Gossip and knitting," Meg replied promptly. "If those are the keys, then Gram will have it wrapped up before anyone."

We were listing Gram's other Marple superpowers—fluffy

sweaters, gardening, a passion for justice, and keenness for spotting the peculiar—as I unlocked the front door of the Chalet. We stepped inside, and I called out for Agatha.

The feline bookshop queen wasn't in the bay window, snoozing or engaging in exhibitionist grooming. Nor was she in the entry to the lounge, complaining about her delayed breakfast. I listened for the thump of ten pounds of Siamese hopping from a high shelf.

Silence.

Meg shivered. "Does it feel chilly in here?"

I set the thermostat for good-sleeping brisk at night. This air was frosty. Oddly fresh too, unlike the usual Book Chalet perfume of paper, ink, campfire, and coffee.

I zipped back up my coat. "Has the furnace been acting up?"

Meg groaned. "Last fall it kept blowing out its pilot light. Mom thought we'd upset it by waiting until September to turn it on. It was a hot autumn!"

Mom ascribed feelings to most inanimate objects. The cash register had "spicy" days. The antique safe was "standoffish." The furnace, it seemed, was sensitive and easily offended.

Meg and I headed to the storeroom, where a hatch door opened to the furnace's basement domain. As a kid, the furnace had scared me, looming in the gloom with octopus arms and a red glowing eye. To be honest, it still scared me. So did the cost of furnace repair.

"Do you know how to relight it?" I asked Meg. "If we can't, could we light a fire and hold off on an emergency Sunday repair call?"

Brave Meg was saying she'd try when a sound stopped us cold.

Click, click, click. Then a wheeze, followed by a whooshing roar. Sounds you'd never wish to hear from a basement, except when they indicated a working, breathing furnace.

Warm air puffed from a nearby vent.

Cold air rushed from the storeroom door. It stood ajar and wasn't alone. When we stepped inside, I saw that the back door hung wide, wedged open by a snowdrift.

Meg gasped.

My insides clenched. *Agatha! Where was Agatha?*

*

CHAPTER 10

A Thief in the Night

I ran to the back door and searched the snowdrifts for paw-prints. Two Christmases ago, I'd been home for a visit and opened this same door to discover a shivery fluffball. Kitten Agatha had clawed her way up my jeans and into our hearts.

Only a few months earlier, Mom's beloved bookshop cat, Macavity the Mystery Cat (named after the T. S. Eliot poem rather than *Cats* the musical, Mom always stressed), had passed away at the impressive age of twenty-two.

Mom was bereft. She was also adamant that she wouldn't seek out a replacement. Macavity, she believed, would send her a sign.

If that was so, Macavity had skipped signs and sent a feline queen in search of a castle. Even as a kitten, Agatha resisted any attempts to remove her from her realm. Mom, Gram, Meg, and Rosie had all tried to take Agatha home after hours, offering cuddling, pampering, and treats. Agatha spent her time away plotting her escapes. Once, she did break out from Gram's. After a frantic, two-day search, Meg discovered Agatha sitting on the Chalet's front stoop, sour-faced and dusty-furred.

Agatha would never willingly walk away from the Chalet. But what if she'd been scared? Awful images swirled. Whirling

snow. Nocturnal creatures. A kitty kidnapper? Agatha was undeniably adorable, not to mention a semi-celebrity.

I called her name, toeing at the low snowdrift slumped over
the threshold. Sharp shards glittered. The back door had an
upper window divided into nine panes. Only one was broken,
the pane above the knob and locks. My stomach sank as I took
in what else was missing.

The doorknob had a simple twist lock on the inside. Above
was a sturdy deadbolt that could only be turned with a key. A
key I'd been leaving in the inside lock for convenience and—I'd
thought—for safety too. In an emergency, no one would get
trapped inside, searching for the key. The burglar hadn't had
to search. The key was gone. Stolen.

I wanted to stomp and kick myself. That wouldn't fix the
door or turn back time. I could do something, though. I was
hustling to get a broom to remove paw-threatening broken
glass when I glanced up.

Agatha sat at the top of the steps, looking extra rumpled,
fluffed, and grumpy. Showering her with kitten talk, I scooped
her up. She purred as I carried her to her throne by the fireplace.

"I found her! She's okay!" I called to Meg.

My sister appeared at the arched entry to the lounge.
"Thank goodness," Meg said, although a frown clung to her
forehead.

Not good news, I guessed. I arranged logs and crumpled
newspaper in the fireplace and touched a match to the tinder.
My frustrated sigh fueled the flames. We couldn't afford to
lose days of profits.

"We'll have to start using the safe," I said, watching fire nib-
ble at newsprint. "Do you think we could keep this from Mom
and Dad when they check in next week?"

Our parents were house-sitting a moody stone home on a
remote Scottish moor. Amenities included a library and no

Internet or phone reception, much to our father's delight. No one could interrupt their reading.

"They'll just worry," I said, justifying my childish urge to hide a flub. Worse, they might be disappointed in us. To my knowledge, the Book Chalet had never suffered a break-in. Some pilfering, yes. Some overzealous book "borrowing," surely. But never a robbery. We'd know. Gram would have woven that into her loop of lore.

Gram. My desire to fib by omission fizzled. Gram couldn't keep secrets. Meg and I would have to embrace our illustrious family first.

Meg's frown deepened. "No, El, that's what's so weird. The register is fine, all the cash is there. It's not even scratched."

"What did they take, then?" We kept our higher-priced editions in glass cases behind the register. Then there were the books we'd never sell. Family treasures with our ancestors' signatures in lovely looping calligraphy. My favorite was a novel from the late 1880s, a gift to my great-great-grandmother from her teacher. My ancestor had gone on to teach too, down in the base village in a one-room school.

Meg adjusted her glasses, tipped askew by her scowl. "I'm not certain, but I think something important is missing. Come tell me I'm wrong."

Agatha and I followed Meg out front. The glass case seemed intact. So did the high shelves holding our family collection.

Meg moved behind the register. "I'm losing my mind, right? I thought we left the Westmacott and satchel on the lost-and-found shelf. Did you move it, by any chance? Please tell me you did."

I couldn't because I hadn't.

Agatha hopped onto the cash register and swished her tail.

"What happened, Agatha?" I asked. "Where's the bag?"

Agatha purred but declined to say.

I crouched to shelf level. Our lost and found included a

cardigan in residence for as long as I could remember. Base-
ball hats piled in a stack. We could sponsor a read-during-
sports team. Winter hats and mittens in a fluffy clump. A
single adult-sized clog filled with various international coins.

"It's not here," I said, lifting and patting the cardigan as if
the book and bag might appear.

Meg got out her phone. "I'll call the police," she said.

Just then, thumps struck the door. Agatha puffed to double-
fluffy and bolted in a skittering of claws. Meg reached the entrance first. We peered through the wiggly antique glass,
breath fogging the diamond panes.

Chief Sunnie squinted back, the morose deputy at her side.
They made a pair of opposites. Her, short and stout. Him, tall
and gangly. Both a very welcome sight.

Meg swung open the door. "Come in, come in!" she urged,
as if they were belated guests of honor.

The chief removed her earflap hat. "This is Deputy Garza,"
she said. "Don't know that we got around to introductions
last night."

The deputy surveyed the shop with a melancholy rarely displayed in our chalet full of books. He removed a brown knit
hat, then promptly tugged it back on.

"Chilly in here," he said. "You having trouble with the
heat?"

"Let's not worry about that," the chief said.

Garza looked unconvinced.

"We are having trouble," Meg said. "We were just about to
call you."

"We've come about the book and notes," the chief said patiently. "Regarding the murder."

As if we could have forgotten.

"It's about that book," I said.

The chief drew a plastic bag from an inner pocket. With it
came disposable gloves, snapping over stubby fingers. "I'll col-

lect the property and get it logged into evidence, and then we can—"

"It's gone," I interrupted, adding a truly heartfelt, "Sorry!"

"Gone?" the chief repeated, eyebrows rising.

"Stolen," Meg said. She hurried on, explaining.

The chief's expression had gone blank. She stared from Meg to me. Sizing us up, I thought. Deciding whether she believed us. I had the uneasy feeling she didn't.

* * *

The Westerns aisle ended in a right-hand turn to an abrupt dead end.

"Good place for an ambush," the chief observed.

I held back a stress-induced giggle. An ambush in the Old West section? *Ha! Good one!*

Except the chief was deadly serious, and I knew I should be too. As far as we could tell, the burglar had taken only the satchel and its contents.

"And who would care about those?" the chief had asked and promptly answered: someone connected to the victim.

Someone like the killer?

"If you could tell us the victim's name . . ." I said, desperate for something tangible to explain how our bookshop might be involved.

The chief couldn't. "We have to try to track down any next of kin first."

Sadness swept over me. Someone was about to receive the most awful news. And if there was no one? That was tragic too.

In the Romance section, we bumped into Deputy Garza, scowling at cover art. A lusty duchess and bare-chested duke, swooning dangerously on horseback.

"Nothing happening upstairs in the bedroom," he reported glumly.

Nope, I thought, anxious giggles threatening to bubble up. Nothing going on there!

"Thank you for checking," I said, gulping back the laugh. "Did it seem like anyone's been up in the loft?"

"Bed's partially unmade," he said. "Cat fur on the pillow. Books everywhere."

"All's right and as I left it, then," I said, with such brittle brightness that the deputy took a step back. He departed for the crime scene to collect evidence. "If anything's still there."

Yes, yes, I felt properly chastised for sweeping away a crime scene. I read mysteries. I should have known better.

"I was worried about broken glass and our cat," I told the chief, once again rationalizing my shoddy crime-scene behavior. "I wasn't thinking straight."

Chief Sunnie was more understanding. "Happens all the time. Garza's taken a bunch of crime-scene courses. He thinks that only physical evidence will crack a case. Prints. DNA. Lost buttons, snagged threads, blood, and whatnot. Me? I say, it's mind games. We need to understand the criminal's psychology. Their motivation."

Human nature. That's what Miss Marple would say. So would Poirot.

The chief stopped to ponder an aisle Mom had labeled Supernaturalist. Resident books covered everything from New Age philosophy to wilderness nudism.

Chief Sunnie frowned and moved on to Mystery. "Hypothetically, say the burglary was about the Westmacott book. Who'd want it?"

"Anything Agatha Christie is desirable to her collectors and fans," I said. "But—"

"Something you'd like for yourselves?"

Was she accusing us of staging a robbery?

"You sure have a lot of books here . . ." Chief Sunnie said, running a finger along a line of spines.

I reminded myself that just last night, Meg and I had declared ourselves suspicious of everyone. Everyone but us Christies. The chief wouldn't make that distinction. Thus, with a strained polite smile, I led her to our Westmacott display among the Christies.

The chief inspected our copy of *Absent in the Spring*. "Based on your description, this has a prettier cover than the stolen one's. Guess I'm not supposed to judge books by their covers, though, am I?"

"I like this cover better too," I said. Our edition featured a pensive woman set against a desert backdrop of yellows and blues. This cover revealed the author too: "Agatha Christie writing as Mary Westmacott."

I also admitted that we'd love a first edition. "Any bookseller would, but we didn't swipe it. It's not *that* valuable."

The chief turned to the sticky notes we'd found in the satchel too. "You remember anything more about them?"

I wished that we'd peeped more. "They didn't *seem* that important."

The chief was still inspecting *Absent in the Spring*. She flipped to the back cover, then the first page. "Do you recommend it?"

One of my absolute favorite things about my job was giving book recommendations, finding that perfect book for a reader's mood and desires. However, the chief hadn't dropped by for my book-taste interrogation, so I gave her my abbreviated impression. "I do, although it's quite a depressing story. A woman realizes uncomfortable things about herself and her relationships. As a psychological study, it's amazing, especially when you consider that Christie wrote it in three days. Three! This was the book she felt compelled to write."

"Like I said, psychology," said the chief, sliding the book back onto the shelf.

Meg joined us. She'd been trying to track down a handyman to repair the door. From her vexed expression, I guessed she hadn't found one.

"So, who knew you had this book?" the chief asked.

We listed the obvious. Us, Gram.

Meg said, "We yelled out 'Mary Westmacott' to Rusty Zeller at the gondola station last night. He's a big literary trivia fan and knew what we meant, but we didn't say the title or mention the satchel and notes."

The chief had out her notebook, pencil poised. "Good. Not so many folks, then."

Oh, I hated to disappoint her again.

"Well . . ." I got out my phone. "Do you know the community forum, First Word Last Word? I didn't until this morning." I'd signed up at Rosie's urging.

To see what murderers might find out about you, Aunt El!

I decided to let the chief see—and read—for herself. I handed over the phone and listened as she read Piper's post aloud with rising incredulity.

"Bagged and booked. Strange and stranger. Did the dead man leave the Christie sisters a bookish clue? A Christie that's not a Christie? Will the sisters' little gray cells decipher the meaning or must the spirits again be summoned?"

She handed the phone back. "Piper Tuttle? She's on the list of book club attendees you gave me last night. How's she know so much?"

Meg described Piper's status as "society" reporter for the weekly local newspaper and full-time stirrer of gossip on the online town forum. "She was here when we found the Westmacott."

The chief allowed herself a sigh. "She doesn't give the book's title or the author's pseudonym. I'll talk to her. Ask her to keep it back."

Meg looked rightfully doubtful. I didn't know Piper well,

but I guessed a professional gossip would also be a poor keeper of secrets.

The chief asked us to keep the name quiet too, before stomping her way through a quick search of the remaining aisles. We all ended up in the sunny lounge, where the chief sank into a wingback and got out her notebook.

With Agatha watching from a high shelf, Meg and I went over our evening. I probably waxed on too long about Gram and Rosie's excellent lasagna. The chief indulged me. When she did interject, she asked who knew that I wouldn't be returning to my loft.

"I did," Meg volunteered. "My teenage daughter, Rosie. You know her from ski lessons, Chief. Our grandmother, but she said that she didn't tell anyone."

I was thinking about the question. Two scenarios came to mind, neither of which I liked.

One, the burglar—who could very well be the killer—knew I'd gone down to Gram's. Which meant they knew who and where I was.

Two: The burglar didn't care if I was upstairs in my loft or not. What if I had been?

The chief tapped her pencil to her notebook. "Do a lot of folks *know* you're living here?"

I relaxed slightly. "That's a good point. No one's lived here for years. A local magazine interviewed us as new owners, but I don't think they mentioned me living here."

Meg confirmed that they hadn't.

"Wise to keep things private," the chief said. "I was featured in the local news recently too. Blabbed way more than I intended. Like I said I was learning to ski. What was I thinking? Now I've said it out loud and on paper, I'll have to keep going to lessons."

Once words got onto paper, they tended to stick around.

For years, decades, forever. I felt for the chief, especially since the residents of Last Word held people to their word.

"You can always hide out from the slopes here," I said. "We're a bookshop, but we're also a refuge. In the winter, we get a lot of guests who want a break from the snow, work, their ski-obsessed friends and relatives . . ."

"It's usually peaceful," Meg added. "And crime-free."

I pictured those signs in factories: no accidents in X number of days. We could get one. NO BOOKSHOP BREAK-INS: 0 DAYS. NO WITNESSING OF MURDERS: 1 DAY.

The chief gazed around as if finally seeing the bookshop as something other than a crime scene and/or criminal hideout. "I like the sound of ski refuge and crime-free. I'll drop by for a book when this investigation is over. I'll admit, I wasn't expecting murder and burglary my first month on the job, but at least a spree hasn't come in threes. That's what my grandmother used to go on about. Bad luck in threes."

She stood, saying she'd better go check on Deputy Garza.

"There's something else," I blurted, overlapping with Meg's "one more thing."

"What? Did you remember something?" The chief's eyes flashed with eagerness.

"No," Meg and I said as one.

"Yes," I corrected, "but nothing to do with the break-in."

"Or the murder," Meg said.

When Meg hesitated, I said it. "It's our co-worker, our friend. She's gone missing."

*

CHAPTER 11

Ghosting

We sat in the lounge, four of us in three seats by the fire. Our fourth was Agatha, curled up on my lap.

The chief had out her notebook again. I'd worried that she'd dismiss Ms. Ridge's absence. Ms. Ridge hadn't been gone all *that* long, and the chief did have a murder on her plate.

Now I worried that we'd dunked Ms. Ridge into trouble. The chief was all too serious and suspicious.

"So." Chief Sunnie tapped her pencil eraser to the page. "Your co-worker left without explanation. Her departure coincided with the arrival of a man—who would subsequently be murdered. Have you ever known Katherine Ridge to be violent?"

"No!" Meg and I exclaimed.

The chief made a note a lot lengthier than "no."

Agatha raised her head and frowned all around. She'd been napping in fits, paws and whiskers twitching. I hoped she dreamed of chasing grasshoppers in the meadow, not hiding from scary burglars. Which made me wonder what I'd dream of tonight.

If I slept at all . . .

What if the door and lock remained unfixed? I couldn't leave the Chalet and Agatha unattended, open to any criminal with the key. But if I stayed here, I'd jump at every creak and bump in the night. The old building had a lot of those, even without illegal entry.

On the other hand, if I gathered up Agatha and went down to Gram's, I wouldn't get a wink either. I'd worry about our building and books. Agatha would prowl the halls, yowling to return to her castle.

The chief said my name and I blinked back to attention. "Ellie, you said you saw no interactions between Katherine Ridge and the deceased?"

I had said that. I replayed the scene once again. Me, jumpy. Ms. Ridge, calm and efficient but clearly feeling down about the raucous séance. She'd headed to the storeroom and the coffeepot. Surely, I'd have noticed if she returned to the lounge. I definitely would have detected fresh coffee.

"Coffee," I said out loud.

Meg nodded encouragingly, and I continued, "When we couldn't find Ms. Ridge, Meg and I looked for her in the storeroom. The coffeepot was empty. The machine's reservoir hadn't been refilled."

I told the chief way more details than she likely wanted about a coffee machine that hadn't made coffee. She had assured us that no detail was too small. I added, "Ms. Ridge probably left out the back door. I don't remember hearing the cowbells at the front."

"That's good," the chief said. "Very good. When you went by her house this morning, you didn't see any evidence of a struggle? No blood? No broken glass? Furniture tossed around? Empty closets? Open drawers? Nothing that caught your eye as odd?"

Lace curtains. Highly suspicious according to Glynis. A tidily made bed. Her unlocked car right where it should be, stocked with an emergency kit and a book about murder being easy.

Murder might be easy, but deciphering mysteries sure wasn't.

Meg said, "Ms. Ridge didn't pick up her Saturday mail or shovel her walk. That suggests to us that she didn't go home yesterday. Or make it home."

I put an arm around Agatha and scootched her warm, purring fluff closer.

"It's completely unlike Ms. Ridge," Meg stressed.

In the fireplace, red embers winked. Outside, a cloud had sneaked over the range, casting a long shadow over our meadow.

The chief made a noncommittal *hmm*. "I hear what you're saying. Let's say that your friend wasn't involved in a crime, either as instigator, perpetrator, or victim. You say her book club discussion was taken over by . . ." Chief Sunnie consulted her notes. "Morgan Marin, a celebrity book influencer and former movie star?"

I marveled that the chief hadn't heard of Shelf Indulgence, not to mention Morgan's many movies, some of which even I could name.

Meg tried to explain. "Ms. Ridge was disappointed, I'm sure. She had an outline for the discussion. She always runs a wonderful book club. That's why we know she wouldn't abandon us or Mountains of Mystery. That club is very important to her."

"So important she might run off in a huff when someone else takes charge?" the chief suggested.

Meg winced. She'd had the same thought last night. "She wouldn't abandon *everything*," Meg said quietly.

"Right," I said, jumping in to support her. "If I were upset or embarrassed, I'd run home and hide out in bed with a book. I think Ms. Ridge would do that too."

The chief made another noncommittal sound.

"Ms. Ridge is beyond reliable," Meg said. "She's always on

time. She shovels her neighbors' walks. She came in early and fed our bookshop cat until Ellie moved in. Because she wanted to, not because we asked. She's generous and kind and . . ."

When Meg paused for air, the chief said, definitively, "Ghosting."

"Ghosting?" Meg repeated.

"You know, like in dating?"

Oh, *I* knew. That was something I never wanted to deal with again. What were the odds that my one true love would stroll into the bookshop like Prince Charming? Prince Charming with great taste in books and no glass-slipper fetish. Did Syd like reading? I shoved that silliness from my mind. Syd and I had chatted once, at a crime scene.

The chief, meanwhile, was recounting missing persons who'd walked away from their lives. "One time or another, don't we all think we'd like a fresh start? We don't act on it. Too many entanglements. Work, family, cats to feed. Some people, though, they pick up and go. They don't tell anyone, because they've already written them off as their old life. That or they're too embarrassed or scared of the hurt they've caused. Either way, they dig into being gone."

The idea hurt, most of all because I could imagine it. To my knowledge, Ms. Ridge had no relatives in Last Word, no commitments other than the Book Chalet, now under new management. Us.

Had Meg and I bugged her with our many questions? Annoyed her without realizing? Had she simply wanted to move on and couldn't find a way to tell us? Morgan and the book clubbers, whooping it up with the séance, might have pushed her to make the leap.

The chief said kindly, "We'll make up a missing person's report. But unless I find evidence that Katherine Ridge is in danger or a danger to herself or others, I can't do much. It's no crime for a lucid adult to go off without saying."

She turned to a fresh notebook page. "So, tell me her particulars. Birthday. Age. Photo if you have it."

I had no idea. I looked to Meg.

My sister bit her lip. "I don't think I know her birthday. That's awful, isn't it?" She added, somewhat defensively, "Mom once said that Ms. Ridge would kill us if we tried to throw her a surprise party."

I flinched at the wording.

Meg realized it too. "Not literally, of course! You have to understand, our mother is *really* into surprise parties. They can be too much. Way too much. Flash mobs dancing. Surprise singing. One birthday, I was grocery shopping and a choral group jumped out and sang 'Happy Birthday.'" Meg hurried to say, "Sweet, of course, but kind of terrifying."

"That time in Japan," I said, commiserating. To Chief Sunnie, I said, "I was teaching English there. By mistake— a mistranslation—Mom sent a team of exotic dancers to my classroom."

The dancers had brought cake, which was always welcome, but Mom had intended a poignant haiku recital evoking snowy mountains and nostalgia for home.

Meg swerved into guilt. "Oh dear, what if Ms. Ridge secretly wanted a party? We've never celebrated for her!"

"I've seen folks run off over less," the chief said, too agreeably. "On the flip side, I'd run off if I got wind of flash mobbing and dancing. Do you have an employee file on her? That'll settle the dates and such."

I dislodged Agatha and her don't-move-me claws. We all trooped to the chilly storeroom.

"Find anything good, Garza?" the chief asked brightly.

He stood by the broken door, scowling at his phone. "I did, actually." He jerked his head for his boss to join him. They huddled over the phone.

Meg and I searched. We pawed through the overstuffed

boxes that were Mom and Dad's nonorganizational system. No file under "R." No luck under "Katherine" or a misspelled "Catherine." We even checked "Ms." As we did, an absurd thought kept running through my mind. We needed Ms. Ridge. She'd know where to find the file.

Meg was checking twice, when I looked up. The chief had on her assessing, suspicious look. Garza was actually smiling. Both expressions made me uneasy.

"D. E. A. D., 'dead man'?" the chief said in a light tone I read as dangerously intent. "Your so-called parlor game spelled out death, and I'm hearing of it first from a gossip site?"

✴

CHAPTER 12

Bad Business

"Murder and robbery are good for business," Meg noted grimly, joining me behind the register counter.

"Definitely not worth it." I lowered my voice. I didn't want to be overheard complaining. Any business was good business. And yet . . . "A whole bunch of locals suddenly need single pencils, postcards, and books from the dollar trunk. Is that usual behavior on a snow day?"

Meg sighed. "Gossipers."

"Yep. You wouldn't believe what people are saying," I said, tidying the overstuffed one-dollar-bill compartment.

Meg said she probably would.

I gave her a sampling anyway. "The nice baker down the way? She'd heard that we'd been serenading the dead man. She tried to get me to sign up for the town choir. At least three people thought we were chasing him, as in running him out of town. Others wanted to join Mountains of Mystery because they think we'll predict death every month."

Meg blew out a breath, fogging her glasses. "I just hope we tempered the chief's suspicions about Morgan Marin and that silly séance. I don't want Morgan associating us or the shop with any trouble."

"She can't blame us," I said. "We pointed out her alibi. The best in town."

The chief had questioned us about the séance. *Who thought up the so-called game? Who spelled out 'dead man'? Whose hand was predominantly guiding the whatchamacallit?*

Morgan, that's who. Our star customer, our biblio-celebrity had guided the planchette, directed the séance, and brought the Ouija board. Morgan had called out the letters too. D . . . E . . .

And that's when it had struck me.

"Dead!" I'd exclaimed. "Dead was already half spelled when the stranger arrived." I rushed on, laying out my case. None of us could have known he'd appear, and none of us could have summoned him. We'd all been seated in a tight circle of silence, summoning no one in particular. The séance was just what we'd said it was—a game, reenacting a scene in a book.

Better yet, during the actual murder, Morgan had an alibi of thousands and her beleaguered assistant too. They'd been live, hosting her Shelf Indulgence club, Morgan bravely overcoming that stars-are-just-like-us challenge of shaky Internet.

"Thank goodness for her alibi," Meg said again. "Morgan's always been lovely to us, but I've seen her get, oh . . . What's a nice word? Imperious? She can be touchy too. We all get irritated sometimes, but most of us don't have thousands of followers and fans to vent to." My sister gave a wry smile. "It's not just Morgan—I don't want *any* Last Word local involved, but it looks increasingly unlikely, doesn't it? Would an outsider know to target our shop?"

"A stalker?" I said, more hopefully than I'd ever imagined speaking that word. "Maybe someone followed the man to town."

I snapped my fingers. "Cece! He thought they were meeting here. She knew where he'd be."

Cece the stalker . . . It had a nice ring to it.

Meg's phone buzzed. She stepped away to take the call, likely from another handyman. So far, the few that had called back had been overbooked, stuck on the other side of the rockslide, or busy skiing.

I continued to mull my Cece theory, so much better than suspecting anyone I knew and liked. Like Emmet, with his poetry, party performances, and opinionated pony. Did he have an alibi? Perhaps the hassle of getting stuck behind that accident would save him from suspicion. On the other hand, from where he lived, he'd have to drive through the hamlet to get to the road down.

The cowbells clanged. I flexed my cash-register fingers and set myself a small deduction challenge: gossiper or bona fide book browser?

The man looked like a well-to-do tourist. Middle-aged but denying it with platinum hair and a tangerine tan. He wore a snowsuit of baby-blue crinkly fabric and strode in with an air of impatience.

I could guess his type. A man puffed up with his own sense of importance, too busy to wipe his snowy boots or hold the door for two women entering behind him. He made for the nearest display table and grabbed a book.

Kudos. I was never so decisive in bookshops. Even if I knew the book I wanted, I still circled the displays, tempted by more.

Book in hand, he paused and raised a nose pitched like a ski jump. He gave the air a disdainful sniff.

I patted Agatha, who lounged beside the register. "Some people . . ." I whispered. Agatha purred her agreement.

Most visitors find the Book Chalet charming, as evidenced by clasped hands and exhalations of glee. But you can't please everyone, even in a bookshop. Some people only delight in picking out faults. Others—like snowsuit guy—feign boredom, as if they're so worldly they've seen it all.

That's absurd. No one can see every book, and no two bookshops are alike.

He approached with pursed lips.

I smiled and reached for his book. He jerked it away.

Odd. Perhaps he wasn't so certain about his choice. Book doubt happened, and when it did, I was ready to step in as biblio-therapist and matchmaker.

I guessed this guy craved admiration. "Great choice," I enthused. "This one is getting wonderful reviews."

The book was the latest spy thriller by a mega-name author. The spy was known for going undercover as a dashing yachtsman. He blended in with designer deck shoes and noticed details like sailing knots, martini garnishes, and silencers. Just like characters in cozier realms of the genre, except watchful women in knitting circles, bake-offs, and bookshops rarely received super-spy recognition.

Snowsuit guy glanced at the back cover as if only now noticing. He still didn't hand over the book.

I stood, smile frozen, doubting my earlier judgment. He hadn't come here for a book . . .

"You had a visitor here yesterday," he said.

A gossiper! I'd judged too quickly. There was a lesson. Perhaps he was a local, a new-mansion resident. I feigned cheery obliviousness.

"Yes," I said, still smiling. "We had lots of visitors yesterday. Snowstorms are perfect for sitting by the fire and reading."

"A *certain* visitor? A visitor who later *died*?" My teenage niece employed the same tone for sentences prefaced with a silent *duh*.

He looked around in a rude show of bafflement. "What would he want *here*?"

Ah, a book? I bit back my snark and realized something extraordinary about him. He appeared to know the dead man. He didn't seem broken up by the dead part either.

"Oh, yes, that poor gentleman," I said.

He snorted.

Okay, he had to know him. No one's *that* rude about a murdered stranger. I guessed snowsuit guy wouldn't give up information for nothing. Maybe if I offered a little something . . .

"He was looking for someone," I said. "But she didn't show up."

The ski-slope nose twitched. "She? Who?"

"Who was the murdered man?" I countered.

Another scoffing snort. "If you don't know, it's none of your business. Who was he looking for?"

"Who are *you*?" Seriously, who was this rude man? Agatha flicked her tail.

"Simon Trent," he said, tone implying I should know, smug smile suggesting I owed him for this gleaming nugget of knowledge.

He waggled the book. "How about this? I buy your over-priced book. You tell me what 'she' our dead friend was looking for."

He seemed like a lot more trouble than the totally reasonable price of $28.95 for a fresh-off-the-presses hardback. On the other hand, he knew something, and the chief had only told us to keep the Westmacott title a secret, not Cece. If I found something out, I'd tell the chief. She'd encouraged any and all tidbits of information.

I patted Agatha, soothing us both. I sure hadn't gotten into books and bookshops because I liked bargaining and confrontation. "You might enjoy that book more if you read the first three in the series."

This earned me a slimy grin. "I see what you're doing. A savvy businesswoman. Nice. I *like* you . . ."

I didn't like him. A line of one had formed behind him, a patient woman browsing covers and shooting me sympathetic eye rolls.

"Hold my place," he demanded to either or both of us. He strode to the display table and picked up two more of the yachtsman spy series. "Three books," he said, slapping them on the counter.

Agatha threw her ears back. Yeah, I'd meant the first three in the series *plus* the book he'd originally grabbed. However, three books were better than one or none. I punched in the amounts with extra force. He handed over a credit card, gold and weighty, which I supposed made him feel important. The embossed name read Simon G. Trent, just like he'd said. I still didn't recognize him. I put the books in a bag, which I held back, watching him closely.

Pursed lips. A smarmy expression that suggested he was enjoying this. "Well?" he said, flashing too-white teeth.

"Cece." I stared at him hard, searching for any clues of recognition.

His eyes narrowed. The puckered lips opened, forming—I guessed—a "who." Then, suddenly, they stretched into an alligator's smile. "Cece . . . ? Here?"

Before I could react, he snagged the bag of books and turned to leave.

"Hey," I said, feeling cheated, although I now realized that I hadn't bargained a name in return. "Who's the murdered man?"

I thought he was going to ignore me, but at the door, he waved without turning. "You'll know soon enough."

The woman waiting in line issued an "Ugh." "He's staying at my hotel, and let me tell you, he's the type that always wants more than he's owed."

I asked which hotel. I wanted to keep track of Simon G. Trent.

"That lovely big chalet inn across the street, L'Auberge." She chatted on about how she'd won a stay in a raffle.

"It's absolutely lovely, but he's awful," she said. "He can

clearly afford to stay there, but he's been badgering the owner for room upgrades and free spa treatments. You know the type."

I put her book in a complimentary tote bag—organic cotton with an image of the Chalet, designed and printed by a local printmaker. "I do know his type, but am I supposed to know *him*?"

The woman looked delighted, both by the tote and my nonrecognition.

"No one would know him," she said with a happy smile. "Not without his famous half sister. Morgan Marin?"

My mouth fell open as if unhinged. When I got it to move again, I said, "He's related to Morgan Marin? She's so . . ."

"Nice? Kind, intelligent, generous, into books, a true class act?"

Morgan was all those, and related to rude Simon Trent? I couldn't hide my confusion.

"I know! They're *half* siblings, but I still can't believe they're in any way related." She introduced herself as Daphne and issued a disclaimer regarding her Simon Trent knowledge. "I follow Morgan for her wonderful book recommendations, not for the gossip about her personal life. I wouldn't ever have recognized him, but I overheard the innkeeper talking with a local woman—very excited about him and incredibly nosy. I mean, she wanted to know what kind of rental car he had and when he went to dinner. A news reporter, I suppose, but surely there's more to report on than rental-car choices. I mean, there's been a murder!"

And a robbery. Then my mind clicked, first on an easy deduction. Enthusiastic, nosy, and possibly a reporter? That had to be Piper Tuttle.

But that car . . .

"A Porsche?" I asked. "Is that what kind of car he has?"

Daphne's raised eyebrows suggested that I—and possibly all of Last Word—was crazy about car choice.

I hurried to halfway explain. "My grandmother said a Porsche had been in an accident. She wondered who was driving." I wondered what Simon Trent had been doing, speeding out of town when a murdered man was taking his last breath on the gondola. Could Trent have been chasing him? Fleeing?

Daphne moved on to a happier topic. Morgan Marin.

"I can't believe she lives *here* in this tiny town! I thought I saw her walking when I was out for dinner last night. If my husband hadn't been with me, I would have run out and made a fool of myself. She's changed my life with her book picks!"

That warmed my heart. Book recommendations were important work.

Meg joined us as Daphne was asking whether Morgan visited the shop.

"She does," Meg said with a smile. "We love seeing Morgan—but then, we love all our customers."

Except for Simon Trent, I silently qualified.

Daphne left, promising to be back soon. The road closure had extended her vacation. "Forced relaxation and reading," she laughed. The laugh turned into a nervous titter. "And hoping the police nab that murderer. My husband tells me not to worry, that it must have been someone local. Nothing to do with us."

That's what I hoped, except for I wanted an out-of-town culprit. When Daphne had gone, I told Meg about Simon Trent. To my surprise, my sister had heard of him.

"From Gram," Meg said. "He was the talk of First Word Last Word over the summer. He flew in looking for mountain-view properties to buy up, being a real bully to some locals. I haven't seen him come in here before. I guess he ran out of books."

Hardly. I told her about our book-for-info swap. Meg bristled. "Then he didn't tell you anything? No name? Not even a hint?"

He'd told me a lot, actually. "He knew the dead man. It took him a bit, but he recognized the name Cece too."

"That's good to know," Meg said, but then she frowned. "But also bad."

I guessed her meaning before she explained. If Morgan's half sibling knew the dead man, maybe Morgan did too.

✳

CHAPTER 13

The Goods

In a shop where books climb the walls, crowd the ceilings, and conspire to roam free, disarray can be hard to distinguish. This afternoon, I had no trouble. The shop looked like a book-swirling tornado had swept in with the gossipers.

Volumes lay abandoned on reading chairs. They huddled on side tables and sprawled across shelves that were not their own. The display tables in the lobby—so orderly when we'd first opened—were decimated (a good thing) and a study in disarray (not so good).

As I worked to straighten and re-home our stock, I yearned for Ms. Ridge. She'd have this mess tidied in minutes. No, correction. She wouldn't have let things get so out of hand in the first place.

Eventually, I'd corralled most of the wild books back in the aisles. One volume, however, continued to baffle me. It was the heaviest of the lost books, of course, and written in a language I couldn't read. Greek, I thought. The vintage cover was a rich red leather, and the fore-edges shimmered in gilt. Inside its parchment-yellow pages, elaborate etchings suggested a guide to herbal remedies, witchcraft, maybe both, or perhaps something else entirely.

Ms. Ridge would know where the book lived. She thrived on order. Which, once again, made me think that she wouldn't just walk out on us. If she wanted to leave, she'd tidy up first. She'd arrange for someone to take over her work hours and continue the book club. She'd let Glynis know and drop off apologetic baked goods.

I stared at the book and made up my mind. Here was a problem I could solve immediately. The fine old book deserved a day to shine.

I was carrying it to the lobby when Meg intercepted me.

"Rosie just called. She said, and I quote, 'Gram has the goods.'"

"Good!" I leaped to a conclusion. "The murdered man's name?"

Meg said, "I'm guessing so. Rosie wouldn't say more. She insisted that great detectives make dramatic reveals."

A name and a grand reveal sounded great to me.

We continued on to the lobby, where I perused the display tables. Which would be best for the old book? Colorado guides and histories seemed out, given the Greek. Nonfiction—a possibility. Cookbooks, also possible. Mysteries? Always a good choice and the book was a mystery to me.

Meg wasn't as thrilled about the incoming "goods." "My fourteen-year-old daughter and our grandmother think they're amateur sleuths investigating a murder."

"Gram was offering up muffins for gossip," I soothed. "Nothing dangerous in that except to waistlines. Besides, information is always good, and the name is bound to get around. Simon Trent knows it, and he's not even from here. Piper Tuttle is on the hunt too. And the police know. They'll hold a press conference eventually."

"True," said Meg, drawing out the word skeptically.

I smiled reassuringly at my sister. "Gram and Rosie won't

do anything risky. You know those two. They look out for each other."

Gram felt particularly protective of her youngest relation. Rosie had similar feelings about her "ancient" great-gram. Each also saw it as their duty to teach the other the tricks and trends of their respective generation. Thus, Gram knew way more about TikTok than I ever would. Rosie could bake cakes without a recipe and mend both frayed socks and failing book bindings.

I stepped to the mystery display table. Books lay scattered like autumn leaves. I tidied, straightened, and stacked. When I was done, a book easel stood empty and waiting. I set the vintage book on it, moved the easel front and center, and stepped back to admire. Lovely. I had a feeling the mysterious book would find its perfect match. Someone would understand it, treasure it.

Meg cocked her head. "What's that?"

"I don't know, but *someone* will."

Just like someone had to know something, anything, about Ms. Ridge. People might want to become ghosts, but they couldn't disappear entirely.

* * *

Gram and Rosie arrived as Agatha and I were busy arranging the window displays. I propped up books in overlapping angles. Agatha toppled them with affectionate headbutts. Her approach had already lured in a few customers, eager to meet her.

Gram stomped her boots. The pom-pom atop her knit hat quivered. "A robbery! Never in my eighty-two years. How rude!"

"How *creepy*," Rosie said, frowning all around. She went to kiss and cuddle Agatha, cooing about the little cat's bravery.

"Exactly," I said, to all those sentiments. Except I couldn't help smiling at the messengers. Gram and Rosie wore ski jackets and snow pants in the splotchy colors of tropical flowers. Gram's outfit, I was pretty sure, was a hand-me-down from Rosie.

"You two hitting the slopes after this?" I said, half-joking. Rosie might be, but Gram would be here for work, as in to relax by the fire with a book.

"Nope, we're here to make snow angels," Gram said resolutely. "They will not defeat me again. We're also here to dish the goods."

Rosie and I shared a grin and helped Gram remove her boots and slip into comfier slippers.

"Do you want to see the door damage?" I asked.

"I want to give that burglar a talking-to," Gram said. "But first I want to give you a hug."

I gladly accepted, sinking into Gram's crinkly coat and comforting scents of muffins, lavender soap, and face powder. Meg joined us and hugged both snow-angel sleuths. She proposed that we all get hot drinks and sit out on the porch.

Mom and Dad had added the glassed-in porch and coffee stall back when coffee among books was considered a risky novelty.

"I'll keep my coat on, then," Gram said.

Wise. Dad grandly called the porch all-season, which it was. The space could swing to every seasonal extreme in a day, sometimes within an hour. Intense heat. Bitter chill. Helicopter-force drafts. Meg and I had window replacement and insulation on our repair list, but far down the expensive line.

"I'll just find Teesha and ask if she can watch the register," Meg said.

Teesha, our occasional part-timer, had a full-time plus overtime job of mothering her twin toddler sons. Lucky for us, she'd been free to come in this afternoon and help out. Lucky for her, she'd said when I'd called, issuing apologies for the late request. The twins were having boy time with their dad. Teesha craved book time. Books that didn't require her to read aloud with farm-animal noises.

Before Meg left, she said, "Gram, will I know his name?"

"Oh, you'll know," Gram said. "Even dead, that man's still causing trouble."

CHAPTER 14

✳

Criminal Characters

"Oh, my goodness!" Meg drew a sharp breath.

"Right?" Gram said, word and tone picked up from Rosie.

My niece had stayed long enough to order fancy cocoa and issue an ominous *"dun, dun, dun."* She'd then left to "investigate" our new inventory of graphic novels.

Gram elaborated on her information source. "I had a hunch who'd know, so I dropped by the German bakery. One of the baker's daughters is married to the brother of the coroner's assistant, who recognized the dead man. He's been on the news. The dead man, I mean. So, you see, I got it straight from the horse's mouth."

My head spun. That sounded like a whole herd of chatty horses.

"It's shocking." Gram paused to deal with her drink.

She and Rosie had ordered the same thing, Italian hot cocoa. Think melty chocolate pudding under a mountain of whipped cream. The trick was getting to the chocolate without a face full of cream. I usually resorted to a spoon. Gram was going the old-fashioned route and slurping.

I tapped my nose, a polite hint to Gram that a dollop of

cream perched on hers. Helping my grandmother seemed better than giving in to a silly, selfish emotion.

You are being childish, I informed myself, which didn't help. The emotion only dug in deeper. Namely, I felt left out.

Meg tutted, "Last Word is the *last* place on earth I'd expect him."

"How did he get out of prison already?" Gram said.

Prison! Shocking. Last place on earth!

I was definitely missing something.

I raised my cup, tipped, and tipped some more. A tepid drop of peppermint tea fell to my lips. I regretted my order. I'd convinced myself I needed something soothing and healthy. Crazy! Like whatever Meg and Gram were on about.

"But who *was* he?" I blurted.

They opened their mouths, likely prepared to repeat the name they'd whispered across the table earlier. Prescott St. James. Greater enunciation and volume wouldn't help. I had no idea what he was. Gram must have read my exasperation.

"Oh, Ellie, that's right." Gram put down her mug. "You were probably gone then. Now, when was it? I suppose you were in college?"

"Junior year," Meg said, often quicker with my chronology than I was. "When you interned at the British Library?" She dimpled at me. "Lucky thing."

Yes, incredibly lucky. I blushed, knowing I had no right to feel left out when I was the one who'd left.

"How to describe Prescott St. James?" Gram mused, dabbing at her nose. "Without foul words, since we're among books and readers?"

Foul? Gram? My grandmother's strongest word was "sugar," which she inserted for all other known epithets.

Meg shook her head and gazed outside. Clouds hid the peaks, making the landscape look strangely flat and unfamiliar.

"How about this?" Gram said after a long minute of pondering. "Prescott St. James was a cad. A swindler. He orchestrated a massive financial scheme. The national news covered it, but only because he'd stolen from some of our newer residents—wealthy, famous folks."

"Oh." My new feeling? To be honest? Let down.

A cad and financial crimes didn't have the spine-tingling chills of Glynis's Nordic noirs. I tried to imagine a fictional scenario: *Devilish financier traps couple in a backwoods mansion, forces them to invest in questionable mortgages.*

No . . .

What about a more Christie-ish version?

Cunning cad returns to the scene of his crimes, only to be trapped by an avalanche and hunted by his well-to-do enemies.

That was better, in fiction. What about reality? Would someone still be murderously mad?

Gram read my thoughts. "It wasn't just bank accounts that Prescott destroyed, Ellie. I know of at least two marriages that fell apart. A couple of family businesses lost, a ranch, and even . . ." She shook her head, reluctant to go on.

"A suicide," Meg whispered. She named a man and my memory twitched. A high school teacher? Librarian?

"A principal at the grammar school," Gram supplied. "Very nice man but terribly unworldly. He handed over his retirement income. Lost every bit and then some." Gram thought the man's family had moved away from Last Word, mostly removing them as suspects.

Meg searched on her phone and brought up an article about Prescott's arrest. "An anonymous local informant provided evidence against Prescott St. James. I wonder who that was?" She held up her screen. "Look, here's Prescott, right before his arrest."

The man in the photo had thick dark hair, broad shoulders filling a well-tailored suit, and a sly smile. The smile, I recognized immediately. Like he was in on an inside joke, just like the ghostly man who'd visited our shop.

"I can see why you didn't recognize him," I said.

Meg and Gram didn't recall meeting him in person before his deadly return. Meg had been busy raising a daughter. Gram allowed herself no excuses.

"I'm disappointed in myself," Gram tutted. "I knew *of* him before his arrest. He was one of our most famous criminals, especially in recent times."

I made a note to ask Gram about famous criminals of Last Word. Later. After the murder and burglary were cleared up and Ms. Ridge was found, safe and sound. I didn't need to worry about who else might be lurking around.

"He did have a distinctive voice," Gram was saying. "A touch of a Midwestern accent, I think. Didn't he go to prison there?"

I typed this query into my phone. "A federal prison outside Chicago. They were overcrowded and let him out early under a special parole condition of house arrest."

"Surely not a house here in Last Word," Meg said. "I thought he had to forfeit everything."

Google had the answer. I read the highlights. "House arrest in an eight-thousand-square-foot mansion in Chicago. What hardship! Jacuzzi, library, marble staircases . . ." The article temptingly offered links to photos of the library and chef's kitchen. I resisted and kept skimming.

"Twice divorced. Single at the time of his arrest."

"What a catch," Meg muttered.

I grinned and kept on. "Two kids from a first marriage, one's in Hong Kong, the other California . . . Ah, he was supposed to have an ankle monitor."

"A lot of good that did," Gram said. "He must have hacked it off."

Probably so. That could also explain why he wasn't carrying ID. He'd come here covertly.

"Up to no good," Gram said decisively. "What, though? Why come to the Book Chalet? We never fell for his fraud, and I still can't recall any Cece or employees with C names."

I succumbed to the link showing photos of his library. A massive space, gorgeous, if a bit chilly and spartan with the books. I showed Gram the photo.

"Oh!" she exclaimed. "I should have remembered. That library sparked my mind. He used to own the house that Morgan Marin lives in now."

My stomach sank. Another connection to Morgan. Had she recognized Prescott? Did that explain her disdainful gaze when he'd interrupted her séance? Her brother, Simon, had sure recognized him, and not in a happy way.

I told Gram about Simon's visit and how he'd held back Prescott's name.

"*He* knew? Before I did?" When Gram was done sputtering, she realized a positive. Actually two. One, she'd obtained her favorite pretzel buns along with the name. Two, she agreed with me. Simon Trent had provided us with a clue.

"Not many other people recognized Prescott, did they?" Gram said. "The baker's daughter's husband's brother only knew because he's a true-crime fan."

My mind boggled at Gram's outstanding memory for personal relationships.

Meg cut to a sensible question. "But would Simon Trent admit to knowing Prescott if he killed him?"

Gram—in the wise ways of Miss Marple—thought he might. "A small crumb of honesty can throw off suspicion. Like a touch of truth can hide a lie."

Meg had told me that Gram knew of Simon Trent, but I was still surprised at how much she knew. While Gram loved to gather information, she kept her foraging local. Gram, for instance, probably couldn't name all the Kardashians, if any at all. On the other hand, she considered Morgan pretty much a local now, which I supposed made Morgan's relatives fair game.

Gram was talking about Simon's earlier visit, citing her sources as First Word Last Word and "everyone." "He and Morgan are estranged. I gather that she wouldn't even acknowledge him during his visit. Sad, but perhaps wise of her."

Yeah, more than perhaps. Earlier, in between customers, I'd done what anyone with a cellphone in her back pocket would do. I'd googled Simon Trent. I'd mostly found his name in tabloid mentions, always associated with Morgan. He'd been Morgan's manager for years, bullying his way into her life, relationships, and especially her finances. He'd seemed most keen on leveraging her name and fortune for his benefit.

I tuned in to Gram's version.

Gram said, "He was all around town over the summer, looking for properties to buy up. Such a rude man. He'd insult people's homes, calling them shacks and tear-downs, demanding too low a price. Sadly, such behavior wouldn't be notable these days, except for his relationship to Morgan. He claimed he wanted to move here to mend fences with her. That would have been nice, if he truly meant it." Gram sounded doubtful.

Having met Simon Trent, I agreed with the doubt.

I glanced at Meg, feeling fortunate that we'd always gotten along so well. My big sis was smiling. I smiled back.

As it turned out, her reaction hadn't sparked from tender sibling emotion. Nope. Meg's mind was on the killer.

"Simon Trent is the perfect suspect," she said. "He had a motive—Prescott St. James cheated him, and Simon sounds like the sort of man who won't let go of an insult. He knew that Prescott came to the Chalet. He's not a local, and definitely not someone we know and like. The gossip and publicity would be awful for Morgan, but if she's had nothing to do with him, she'll be safe from suspicion. Plus, she has that wonderful alibi."

Rosie came in as we were toasting this wisdom. My niece held an armload of graphic novels. "What's going on? You guys closed the case without me? You were supposed to wait for me if you had something big."

I said, "You're just in time for a grand reveal. We have a more important case to investigate." I raised my eyebrows to Meg and Gram and saw that they agreed.

Rosie frowned. "More important than the murder and the creep who broke into our bookshop?"

I could feel Meg's glow next to me. *Our bookshop*. She'd never pressure Rosie into working at the shop or taking over one day, but we all secretly hoped that another generation would love this place as much as we did.

"Much more important to us," her mom said. "The chief will be busy with the murder and our robbery. That means someone needs to look for Ms. Ridge."

"Cool," Rosie said. "I like her." A frown creased her young forehead. "We need to find her fast. Her birthday's coming up. She said I could make her cake."

"You know her birthday?" I said, with Meg exclaiming pretty much the same simultaneously. We really were in sync as sisters, and mutually clueless about Ms. Ridge.

"Dun, dun, dun . . ." Rosie sang dramatically, realizing a belated grand reveal. She quickly returned to teenage nonchalance. "Whatever. She said it was a secret, but all I had to do was ask when to make her a cake."

✳

CHAPTER 15

An Open Door

When we finally turned our door sign from OPEN to CLOSED, Meg exhaled in relief. "Whew, I'm ready for a day off."

I was too. Chief Sunnie had officially announced the victim's name late in the afternoon, sparking a fresh wave of gossip seekers. But although the bookshop was closed on Mondays, I couldn't rouse that Friday-on-Sunday feeling.

I groaned. "What are we going to do about the back door?"

"Come see my repair," Meg said, fringing "repair" with air quotes. She waved like a game-show hostess as we entered the storeroom.

Burglary repair had me in knots, but I couldn't help laughing. Cardboard covered the broken pane, held in place by enough duct tape to wrap a moose. "We have to take a photo for Dad. He'd be so proud." Dad specialized in tape-based fixes.

Meg pushed back her glasses and summarized her futile handyman quest, ending on the barest of positives. "The hardware store will be open tomorrow. We can buy a lock and install it ourselves. A glass guy can maybe, possibly come by on Thursday. Oh, and a lock guy told me not to worry. He says, if someone wants to get in, nothing will stop them."

Yeah, that didn't help.

"We'll rig a lock fix for tonight," I said. "We're Christies—we have Dad's tape supply and a whole lot of how-to books."

A little while later, I stood on the breaking-and-entering side of the door. On cue, snow began falling, fat flakes that perched on my eyelashes.

"Give it a shove." Meg's voice easily cut through the cardboard patch.

I wanted to cheat and call it done. *Let me believe,* I begged the door. Let me go up to my loft and join Agatha in a nap. From which I'd awake in terror if the door was unsecured.

Meg and I had pushed a heavy table in front of the door. No book had suggested this fix. Reading, as always, provided understanding, enlightenment, and sparkling rays of ideas. Sadly, it also pointed out what we lacked. Saws, glue, chisels, glass, locks, and most of all handy skills.

We did, however, have a heavy soapstone-topped work-table where we packed mail orders and Gram and Gramps used to conduct book surgeries, repairing broken spines, torn pages, and sagging covers. Now that I was back, I hoped that Gram and her apprentice, Rosie, would teach me.

"Okay," I called back. Summoning a powerful burst of frustration, I pressed a shoulder to the door. It didn't move. *Yay!* I turned my face upward and let snowflakes plop onto my cheeks. Magical.

Hot chagrin soon melted them.

"Great! I'm unlocking the deadbolt now."

Right, the deadbolt, which Meg could unlock because she had a key to that lock, just like the burglar did.

I gave the door a heave. It opened a centimeter, two, three . . . an inch. Shoving and entering would be a cinch.

"We could stack some books on the table," Meg proposed. "Chairs? Rocks?"

We'd need boulders. I leaned my forehead against the frame and focused on refraining from thumping it.

"We could trust," kindhearted Meg suggested from the other side. "Remember when Gram fell asleep and woke to find customers ringing up their own charges? Hang on, sorry, I'm getting texts from Rosie."

Gram's deep-nap story was legendary in the family. Sweet too. A heartwarming tale about the goodness of humanity and solid sleep.

But no. I was no longer feeling trusting when a criminal was still in town. I allowed my forehead a single thump against the doorframe.

"El?"

I spun. A figure approached, masked in goggles, anonymous in snow gear, and gliding silently on skis. The goggles came up. Syd Zeller grinned at me.

Something struck me. "*You're* cross-country skiing?" I'd thought Syd's version of fun involved flinging himself down cliffs.

He did that endearing sheepish grin again. "Yeah, shhh . . . don't tell anyone. I was guiding a bunch of 'influencers' earlier. They wanted to experience the 'silence of the forest.'" Irony and air quotes drenched the keywords.

"Not so serene?" I guessed.

"Not when we had to stop every five minutes so they could photograph themselves looking meditative. Staring at trees. Yoga posing at vistas . . ."

He sounded exasperated. I supposed staged serenity could do that.

"However," he said, smiling and waving grandly toward his feet. "These are no ordinary cross-country skinny skis. They're ATs."

"Oh," I said, unsure.

"Alpine touring skis." He elaborated on how they could go downhill, uphill, and glide along a path.

Climb tall buildings, I thought, smiling encouragingly. I liked to hear about other people's passions. I always learned something and loved to see eyes light up. Plus, I figured it was conversational good karma. I'd undoubtedly overloaded many a listener in book talk.

Syd said, "I already had these on, so I thought I'd take the Rim Trail over and check on you. Are you okay after last night? Did I see you, ah . . . headbanging?"

Before I could explain a single forehead thump, he looked beyond me.

"What happened? Was it the storm?" His scowl scoured the landscape, landing on a blameless nearby spruce.

I appreciated his suspicion and something else too. Syd, unlike most of the town, hadn't come by for gossip. He'd skied out of his way to check on me.

"You didn't hear about our break-in?" I asked.

"Break-in! No, sorry. I was . . ." His eyes drifted out toward the hillslopes and forests.

He'd been skiing all day. Correction, working and enduring staged serenity.

I gave him the highlights. "The crook didn't take much, but the deadbolt key is gone. I feel like a fool—I left it in the lock and the thief stole it, which means they could come back and get in and we can't find a handyman and our friend is missing and our cat won't stay overnight anywhere else and . . ."

And I was rambling, the stress of the day spilling out as if from a broken faucet.

"I could help," Syd said. "With the door. I'm not sure about all the rest."

"You could?" I regretted the two words immediately. More precisely, the emphasis I'd landed on "you." I stammered to cover. "I mean, I'm sure you're really busy with work and . . ."

And extreme sports and fun. Did Syd know something as practical and dull as door repair?

Thankfully, he chuckled. "I'm actually pretty handy, if I do say so myself. I've made my own snowboards. Fixed up Granddad's old cabin too so I could live there. Made it so desirable, I'm fending off offers, not that it'll ever be for sale." He grinned at the tape. "I'm also good at improvising on the spot, as I see you are too."

He stepped to the door.

I opened my mouth to warn him about our table barricade.

No need. We might as well have blocked the way with a stack of paperbacks.

Syd easily pushed inside. I stepped in just as Meg returned.

"Hey, Syd," she said, sounding distracted. "I guess our fix didn't work."

"Syd saw me out fighting with the door," I told her. "He's going to give it a look."

"Is that how to get a handyman on a fresh-snow Sunday?" Meg smiled. "Send my little sister out to break in?"

I almost felt bad. Here she'd spent all day calling around.

Syd was saying that it wouldn't be a professional job. "Just something to keep you and the shop safe until you get a pro."

Meg's phone buzzed. She shot me an apologetic look. "I am the world's worst mother. I forgot that I'm supposed to drive Rosie to a science club meeting. Seven on a Sunday in a snowstorm, why?"

I knew the answer to this. "Because it's for science and Rosie and you're the world's best mom. Go, go! You weren't even supposed to be here today."

Meg hurried off. Syd already had a plan.

"You have a screwdriver?" he asked.

"Not that we could find. I have a butter knife. I could rummage in the old book-repair bins . . ."

"No problem." He'd put his backpack on the soapstone

table. Now he opened it and pawed around in a jumble of gear.

"You're prepared," I said.

"Matches, snacks, extra layers, warming blanket, gloves, camera, headlamp, flare, cleats," he reeled off. "The basics, plus rock-climbing gear so those influencers could pretend to climb. You would have laughed. They got like two feet up, tops, posing a pick at a rock. Their photographer had to lie on the ground, aiming up so it looked like they were scaling a mountain. Fake muscle-flexing. Fake serenity. Ridiculous."

We shared a laugh, and I enjoyed my own tranquility, a little burst of feeling like a local again. Sure, I might not scale mountains, but I knew how to truly enjoy a serene walk in the woods. Quietly. No posing or selfies involved.

Syd eventually fished out a multitool with everything from a tiny saw to a corkscrew.

He pointed to a drawer latch on our soapstone table. "Can I borrow this padlock latch?"

"Sure," I said. "One problem, though. We don't have a padlock."

"I do." Syd again dove into the backpack and brought out a chunky padlock. "I always carry an extra in case I have to stash my gear in a locker."

"Meg and I always carry a book." Before ebooks, I carried a paperback, preferably an Agatha Christie that I could read over and over and still pick out new clues. Now my phone held a dozen electronic books, all ready to spring forth like life preservers in case of a reading opportunity and/or emergency.

"Also practical." Syd chuckled. A few minutes later, he stood back to admire a rigging that would also make Dad proud. Syd downplayed it, saying—like the lock guy—that a determined burglar could still get in.

"But you don't have to worry anymore," he added. "You

were already robbed. It's the other businesses that should be bolting their doors."

"Right . . ." I appreciated the no-worry sentiment. Always welcome. However, unless Prescott St. James had left books, satchels, and odd sticky notes at other businesses around town, everyone else should be safe.

Agatha trotted in. She frowned at me, Syd, and me again before issuing a feed-me-now meow.

"You want your dinner, Agatha C?" I asked, pitching my voice to kitty talk. "You deserve it. You had a busy day, didn't you?"

She did. The gossipers had included a subset similar to Syd's perfect-pose influencers. Those who wanted a social-media-worthy photo to prove they'd visited the "little Book Chalet of murder prediction." Getting a selfie with frowny-faced Agatha was the ultimate photographic prize. I hadn't told Agatha, but she was trending under the hashtag "mur-derkitty." She might be offended. Or a little too pleased.

I opened a fresh can of her favorite fishy dinner. Agatha meowed her approval.

"I'd like dinner," Syd said. "Let me take you out, El. Sounds like you had a hard day too, and I know the cure. Pizza. There's a great new place. Wood-fired. Amazing crust."

My stomach rumbled. I adored pizza. The door was se-cured, and I had vowed to say yes to friend opportunities. Plus, Syd was giving me that charming smile.

"Nope," I said, grinning. Before his smile could flicker, I said, "I'm taking *you* out. You protected the Chalet. It's the least I can do."

Syd eventually relented. "Okay, I'll get the next one." He winked. "But I should warn you. I may have an ulterior mo-tive."

✳

CHAPTER 16

Motives

My first thought upon entering Fratelli's: I'm not dressed for a date.

Second thought: This is not a date.

Thought three: I'm not dressed for this place, which would be a fine spot for a date.

Syd had assured me that we could go as we were. Me in jeans and a sweater. Syd pared down to techie layers and ski boots boasting an extraordinary technology called "walk mode."

I'd believed him about the casual. It was pizza, after all. Plus, I knew the place. I recalled it as a woodsy vintage chalet selling tourist trinkets and treats. Stuffed moose. Postcards. Silly T-shirts. Yummy taffy, caramels, and fudge.

Some time since, the building had undergone the real-estate version of extreme plastic surgery. Gone were the folksy finishes. Moose remained, but not the cuddly variety. Great paddles of antlers hung in a chandelier I could imagine doing mortal damage in a mystery novel. Servers in long white aprons whisked about in the brisk ballet of a five-star restaurant. Candles flickered on linen-topped tables and bottles in amber, green, and crystal clear sparkled behind an antique saloon bar dressed up in modern metal touches.

As we settled in at a cozy corner table, I gawked—politely, I hoped. What a transformation! Syd had been right about the dress code. I did, indeed, spot many combos of jeans, leggings, knitwear, snow boots, and ski jackets draped over chairbacks. The distinctions came with the price point. I spotted designer duds trying to look casual at eye-watering prices.

It wasn't that I was into fashion. Far from it. Give me sweats and sweaters any day. However, I could spot wealthy clientele, thanks to some of my previous gigs. The beach-shack bookshop, for instance, had been a rustic prop at a resort so exclusive it owned an entire island. Then there was the persnickety antiquarian collector and his swanky library soirees. I suspected he wanted the ambiance of a library more than the actual books.

Syd said, "Sure has changed, hasn't it? Remember getting milkshakes here as a kid?"

I did. "Meg would bring me here to spend my 'salary.'" I smiled at the memory and told Syd how, even in elementary school, I'd insisted on "working" at the shop. My working consisted of tagging behind Mom, pulling out books, and putting them back, mostly where I'd found them. In return, Mom gave me a weekly paycheck of a dollar or two and more to Meg to chaperone me on a candy expedition.

"I'd get saltwater taffy," I said.

"Taffy?" Syd snorted. "It's a wonder you have any teeth left. Nah, chocolate malt shake, hands down."

We bantered about favorite sweets, a far happier topic than my day of murder gossip and worries about Ms. Ridge.

"Who'da thunk?" Syd said, laying down a menu framed in metal and wood. "Last Word, middle of nowhere-ville, now the hot new place to be. I suppose I shouldn't complain. The fly-in crowd and all these second- and third-mansion owners, they pay my bills. No local needs to hire a ski guide."

"They help with our bottom line too," I said. Little Last Word had a big community of devoted readers. However, visitors on vacation mode were eager to snap up the mountain version of "beach reads." We sold a lot of fun fast-paced reads, as well as gifts and mementos. Regional cookbooks. Gorgeous coffee-table collections by local photographers and artists. Guidebooks, works by local authors, and merchandise like our tote bags and prints by Last Word artists.

Our waiter glided back. We ordered two small pizzas and a bottle of wine, all to share.

Syd bemoaned the sky-high cost of everything. Lift passes, groceries, and especially homes and land. "You and me, we're lucky to have some family places here. Otherwise . . ."

Yeah, otherwise, forget it. I thought of my childhood friend who no longer had a landing pad in Last Word. If—horrors—my family no longer lived here, I couldn't afford to live in Last Word. I told Syd about the fixer-upper yurt I'd seen listed by the local Sotheby's realty office. A yurt—listed by Sotheby's!

Syd unexpectedly brightened. "You saw my work!"

Not the yurt, it turned out. Syd had yet another side gig, doing "glamour shots" for realtors. "It might look promising— if you're in the market for a yurt—but it's a dump in real life. Reeks of mice and moldy felt."

I wrinkled my nose and focused on much more pleasing scents of wood-fired dough.

Syd dubbed this branch of his photography work as painfully dull.

I could see how ski videography and crime-scene photography might be more thrilling, yet I'd pick the real-estate gig. It sounded fascinating. "You get to see all the rooms, how people live." I knew where I'd zoom in. "You can check out their bookshelves. That's where you'll get clues to who they are."

Syd chuckled. "I better check my bookshelves, then, in case you come over and profile me."

I already had a clue and I approved. Syd owned bookshelves, presumably containing books.

Our pizzas arrived with backstories. Solemnly, the waiter described the origins of the cheeses, the grower of the single-estate arugula, and the pastures the sausages once roamed. Fresh parmesan was offered and grated with aplomb. Wine was poured as if it were the highest end and not the second-least-expensive bottle.

Before the waiter left, he glanced toward the bar. A besuited man with a name tag was making obsequious little bows at a sour-faced customer. I guessed besuited was the manager. I knew sour-faced: Simon Trent. He perched on a too-tall bar-stool, holding a wineglass, which he swirled, sipped, and assessed with a cat-smelling-lemons look. He thrust the glass under the manager's nose.

With his boss distracted, the waiter broke character. "Enjoy," he said to Syd. "That pistachio pesto is awesome."

He and Syd bumped fists. Syd introduced us. Demetrious, he grandly described as a "champion snowboarder and all-around excellent person." Me? Well, I was "El Christie, beautiful new proprietor of the best bookshop in Giltridge County."

Still the *only* bookshop, I might have qualified, if I hadn't been busy blushing.

"Demetrious's a great guy," Syd said, as his friend glided to the next table. "He's partnering with me on the heli-ski business concept. All we need is funding."

That's all. I knew next to nothing about heli-skiing, but I guessed a helicopter couldn't be cheap.

Syd explained that he and Demetrious had met at college in Boulder. "Every break, we'd come here and ski, competing for 'radness' points." He rolled his eyes at himself. "Silly stuff, but I still think of it as the good old days, you know? We were all about going extreme, challenging ourselves. The highest points were for having fun."

He gave examples of point-worthy fun feats. Calling his dad in the middle of a run. Making first tracks in new snow.

Thumping ski poles and yelling bluster. "'Cause if no one sees you do it, does it happen?"

It sounded silly, absurd, and, yes, fun.

We came up with parallels for my world: a numerical assessment of reading radness.

First to (very carefully and tenderly) crack a new hardback. An all-night read. Slippers closest to the cozy fireplace. More than two cats sitting on a lap. Syd came up with the cats on laps. I approved. Agatha would not. She enjoyed her reign as sole queen of the Book Chalet.

As Syd poured us more wine, I realized I was having fun. Maybe that's what broke the spell.

Syd suddenly turned serious. "You know how I said I had an ulterior motive?"

I had indeed noted that. I'd deemed it as clumsy flirtation, not something that had him unable to meet my eyes.

"I need your help, El. It's my dad."

"Rusty? What's wrong?" Rusty had been disappointed to miss his moment of crime-stopping, key-witness glory. Otherwise, he'd seemed okay.

"He's . . ." A din of voices swelled around us, punctuated with loud hoots. Syd looked around. I followed his gaze, which had stalled at Simon Trent. Simon jerked his chin in a greeting and raised a glass in our direction. Or, rather, Syd's direction. I suspected that Simon wouldn't remember a bookshop clerk, even one he'd recently bribed for information.

"Client," Syd said. He lowered his glass and the smile he'd raised with it as soon as Simon looked away. "Guy's a first-class jerk but filthy rich and connected. Considers himself an extreme skier too. He's my dream investment candidate. When I find the right moment, I'm gonna pitch him on the heli business."

Earlier, I would have pressed Syd for details about Simon

Trent, our prime murder suspect. Now Rusty was more important.

"Your dad . . ." I prompted.

Syd leaned across our table. In a voice so low I almost couldn't hear, he said, "El, he's in big trouble. The police think he killed that guy."

Our candle flickered at the words.

My mind did the same. What Syd had said didn't compute. "Rusty? You know who the murdered man was, don't you?"

"I sure do," Syd said ruefully. "For a while, Prescott St. James was kind of like a favorite uncle to me."

As a proud favorite (albeit only) aunt of the world's best niece, I was taken aback.

"Dad was Prescott's silent business partner." Syd stared at the candle flame. "Except nothing's too secret around here, is it? Probably everyone knows. You know that Dad didn't always sit around reading mysteries in a gondola station, right? Remember? My family used to have money?"

"Oh," I said, attempting to cover another massive memory lapse. Or maybe I'd never known. Syd and I hadn't hung out in school. He'd been the friend of a friend, a year above, a coolness level above too. I actually didn't know much about him, let alone his family.

Syd was saying that Rusty had helped Prescott set himself up in Last Word. He'd been the local guy who made other locals feel comfortable investing.

"Dad wasn't the same laid-back guy back then. He was driven. Addicted to the money game." Syd studied his wineglass. I thought I saw a blush. "Prescott getting caught, that's what snapped Dad out of it."

Prescott had gone to jail. How could I ask if Rusty had too? Thankfully, I didn't have to.

"Dad gave evidence against Prescott," Syd said. "He felt

rotten, but it was finally the right thing to do. This is gonna sound sappy . . ." He hesitated, looking embarrassed.

I murmured encouraging words and waited.

Syd sighed. "Okay, I wouldn't admit this to most people . . . My family lost everything when that business went south, but I got my dad back. And now . . . Now he might actually go to jail and I'd lose him forever."

"No, that won't happen," I said automatically, but I wasn't sure. Rusty was a logical suspect. He'd been at the scene. He and the victim probably weren't on good terms. Prescott was the one with the gripe, though. More than a gripe. He'd gone to jail. Had he returned to confront Rusty? If they'd fought, Rusty might have a case for self-defense.

I didn't want to bring that up. Syd was already upset. Instead, I poured us each more wine and said, "Meg and I talked to your dad this morning. He said he didn't recognize the victim when the police showed him a photo. But Prescott had changed a lot—white hair, thinner, a whole lot older looking. Gram didn't recognize him."

But Gram hadn't met Prescott in person before he "caught her changing." Rusty, on the other hand, had seen Prescott so often that his son considered the man a favorite uncle.

Syd's sigh nearly extinguished our candle. "Yeah, that's what he told me and the police too. Makes it worse, doesn't it? Don't repeat this to the police, *please,* but how could Dad *not* recognize him? Every time Prescott visited Last Word, he'd come over to our place. He had Dad out to his place in L.A. a couple times. Had me out once too." He hurried to add, "I'm not saying Dad did anything. He couldn't have. *Wouldn't* have."

I felt bad for Syd, and Rusty too.

Syd was saying, "That's my ulterior motive. To beg for help. Do you know *anything* that can help Dad? Did you and Meg see anything?" He reeled off a list of what we might have helpfully seen. Rusty, asleep in his hut? A masked man with a knife running off? Anyone strange? Anything at all?

"I'm sorry." I was. What Meg and I had seen—and what we'd told the chief—only looked bad for Rusty in retrospect. We'd seen Rusty hustling into the station moments after Prescott lunged onto his last ride. We hadn't seen a man with a knife, but that also included Rusty. He'd seemed like he always did. Jolly, friendly, and quick with literary trivia.

Syd slumped back into his seat. "The police took Dad in for questioning this morning. I was about to go out guiding. There was nothing I could do to help him."

I debated whether to tell Syd about our "perfect" suspect, his perfect investment candidate. I didn't want to give him false hope. Or come off as a fool. Earlier, at Meg's urging, I'd called Chief Sunnie and told her about Simon Trent and how he'd known the dead man. The chief clearly hadn't rushed out to arrest him.

That didn't mean he was innocent, though.

Syd said, "Could you keep an eye out for, I don't know, anything that might help? You're into mysteries and observant, and I'm out of my depth."

I couldn't see friendly, book-loving Rusty as a killer. I assured Syd that of course I'd try to help. Keeping my promise, I glanced toward the bar.

My stomach flipped. Simon Trent raised a slimy smile along with his wineglass. He'd been keeping an eye out too, and I'd been wrong. He hadn't forgotten me, but now I wished he had.

✳

CHAPTER 17

Should Haves

As a rule, I tried not to dwell on "should haves." The opportunities that slipped by, unrealized until too late. All those tricky red herrings, in books as well as life.

The next morning, however, I woke to a should have I couldn't ignore.

Namely, I should have appreciated the gentle version of Agatha's kitty wake-up calls. Purring, head-bumps, even a drop of affectionate drool . . . All were preferable to her springboard lunge at dawn.

Claws skittered on floorboards, skidded around a corner, and tore downstairs.

I bolted upright, heart thudding.

I'd actually slept soundly above the scene of a burglary. Good food and exhaustion had helped, as well as Syd's chivalry. He'd walked me home last night, coming inside briefly to check dark corners. After confirming the absence of burglars and broken windows, he'd bid Agatha and me a gentlemanly goodnight. I'd called Gram and Meg as a check-in, then conked out as soon as my head hit the pillow, unperturbed by the night creaks of the old chalet and Agatha snoring in my ear.

All traces of sleep bounded away as fast as Agatha. I gripped the covers and held my breath, listening. The scrabbling of claws had ceased, allowing another noise to surface.

A squeak and rattle, distinctive and recognizable: the back doorknob turning.

Fear tingled to my fingertips. As I saw it, I had two choices.

One, stay frozen under the covers, hoping the terror fizzled away. But what then? Stick my head under a pillow and pretend I'd heard nothing?

Option two would have to do. My bare feet hit cold floorboards. I didn't stop to find socks. I tugged on my robe and grabbed a hefty compendium of Golden Age mysteries.

I pictured the book as my shield, blocking blows from knives and fists, possibly even inflicting its own damage if I aimed a good, solid whack. In either case, I'd be conflicted. The book was innocent, and I had five more stories to read.

Halfway down the steps, I found Agatha hunched in a scaredy-cat loaf.

Not helpful, I thought, but of course Agatha was as blameless as the book. Heroic too. I stopped on the step above my guard cat and crouched low enough to see the doorknob. Syd's lock still held. Thank goodness!

Gripping book and banister and watching my step, I maneuvered over Agatha. When I looked up, a blur passed by the window over the sink. Muffled words slithered in. I tiptoed down the rest of the steps, nearly getting knocked over by Agatha, bolting to secure her food bowl. So much for her guard-cat priorities.

"Hello?" I called out, immediately wishing I'd gone for something more forceful.

The voices quelled, replaced by woodpecker-strident knocking.

"Yoo-hoo!" Piper Tuttle's face appeared at the glass, peering through in cupped hands. Her breath fogged the glass. She wiped it down and waved energetically.

Dread fled, replaced by the minor terror of hosting a gossip-hungry guest before coffee. I put down my defensive book, stuffed my bare feet into a pair of Gram's fluffy-lined snow boots, and fumbled to twist Syd's combination lock correctly. After two tries, it opened.

Piper burst in like an enthusiastic flurry. "Ellie Christie, my goodness, haven't you been busy! Crime, more crime, and a hot date too? Or were you grilling our prime suspect's son? Romancing clues out of him? Don't try to deny it. I was in a booth at the back of Fratelli's and saw you two cozying up."

To my fresh horror, Piper raised a sparkly cellphone and snapped a picture. "Cute! I'm guessing Mr. Hunky Ski Guide didn't stay over?" She raised eyebrows at my plaid bathrobe and puffy snow boots, as if they provided evidence enough.

"No-o . . ." I stammered, which covered pretty much everything. No to romancing, grilling, cozying up, staying over, and especially to book-loving Rusty Zeller as prime suspect. Also, no, no, no to another embarrassing photo!

Before I could elaborate on any of these, another visitor stepped in. Lena Bruner owned and managed L'Auberge, the grand three-story chalet inn a few buildings up the street. Lena had been out sweeping her entry the other day, and I'd stopped to introduce myself. She'd been polite but reserved, like an elegant model gazing just beyond her audience.

She assessed the storeroom and old-fashioned kitchen with an eye that likely read clutter. Books were stacked everywhere, to inventory, ship, shelve, repair, donate, and simply linger. Then, of course, there was me. I fought back the urge to apologize for the mess and my appearance. They were the ones showing up before eight A.M. on our day off.

Lena held two large canvas bags. She laid them on the soapstone table and elegantly removed calfskin gloves, tip by tip.

Agatha hopped up to inspect the bags. Her feline inspection, I suspected, would include curling up for a nap. The fabric was nubby black canvas, ideal for showing off cinnamon and cream kitty fur. I plucked her up and distracted her with breakfast. Then I overloaded the coffeemaker with grounds and willed it to hurry. I offered some to my guests.

Piper lamented that her doctor had banned coffee. "Makes me too jittery," she said, hands fluttering.

Lena declined too. "Thank you, but I mustn't stay. I left Paolo with the breakfast service."

Gram had given me the scoop on Lena and her husband, Paolo. Both were originally from Switzerland. She'd managed fancy inns all over Europe. He was a retired Olympic ski jumper.

"Paolo's like a retired greyhound," Gram said. "Happiest to lie down. You know that summer has arrived when you see him in a hammock with a book or two on his chest." Those sounded like great summer goals to me.

Piper waved off Lena's concern. "Paolo's fine. He's a grown man, and you have staff. Delegate." Before her frowning companion could answer, Piper said to me, "I *forced* Lena to come over here. She didn't want to *bother* you so early."

Not bothering me sounded lovely. I shot Lena a grateful smile. She missed it, being engrossed in plucking cat hairs from her bags. Agatha must have willed some fluff that way.

"Lena needs *books*," Piper said, as if revealing a scandal.

"We sure have those. We're closed today but—"

"She needed them *yesterday*," Piper interrupted. "You need to stand up to those guests of yours, Lena. So demanding. Just because they're snowed in during a crime spree? Boo-hoo!"

Lena looked pained.

I felt for her. Plus, I wouldn't—couldn't—keep people from books. "We're neighbors. Of course you can get books. I can recommend some . . ."

But Lena knew exactly what she wanted. She had a typed list.

"I'll help you find them," I said, reluctantly glancing at the dawdling coffeemaker. Mom would call it coy, dripping slowest when needed the most.

I bolstered myself with positives. The pot would be full by the time I returned. I'd have an unexpected day-off sale, and maybe I could get some information too.

Simon Trent was staying at L'Auberge. Syd wanted him as an investor, but he'd surely welcome another prime suspect if that would clear his dad. Rusty would need all the help he could get, too, if Piper was talking up his suspect status all over town.

I could also check another item off my investigative to-do list. Gram, Meg, and I had a busy day ahead. We'd formulated a plan last night. We would spend our day off looking for Ms. Ridge.

Gram was going to call around to hospitals. My grandmother loved chatting on the phone, especially about medical conditions.

Meg would check hotels, motels, inns, and vacation rentals down in the base village. I would do the same up in the hamlet. We planned to be discreet, still hoping that Ms. Ridge had gone off on her own accord. Discreet meant I should be careful what I said around Piper.

I decided I'd look for Lena's books first. If I helped her, maybe the innkeeper would reciprocate. We stepped into the main shop, Agatha and Piper tagging at our heels. I flicked on lights and smiled. I always loved waking up the books and all the worlds, knowledge, adventures, and mysteries they contained.

Lena tore her list neatly in half and handed me the top part. "Thank you. These, you will know, I think."

Mysteries. I sure did know them. I peeked at her half. Books from Morgan's club and several local fishing and hiking guides. Conveniently, all were likely in the front. I directed her to our

Morgan Marin Shelf-Indulgence display and the Colorado table.

Agatha followed Lena.

Piper nipped at my heels with rapid-fire questions. "So . . . what did you learn about Rusty Zeller last night? Anything juicy?"

"I was just catching up with Syd, he's an old school friend." That had been true when dinner started.

"Ohhh . . ." Piper said suggestively. "So, Sydney didn't tell you about his father? Do you realize, you might have shared a pizza with the son of a killer?" Piper conversationally swerved, extolling both the pistachio pesto and waitstaff as yummy.

I needed caffeine. The last thing I wanted to do was verbally stumble and get Rusty in more trouble. I considered sprinting back to the kitchen and gulping straight from the pot. That wouldn't look good for Rusty, Syd, or me.

I said carefully, "Syd told me about his father's prior business dealings with Prescott St. James. He's confident that his father is innocent. Rusty has no motive to hurt anyone."

I sure hoped he didn't. Rusty was a man who loved to read, a caring man who'd taken our worries about Ms. Ridge seriously. "*I* think he's innocent," I added for the record. I assured myself that I did. I *wanted* to.

"Perhaps," Piper said ambiguously.

We'd arrived in the Agatha Christie section. I paused to admire the beautiful spines. Agatha Christie had written sixty-six mysteries and over a dozen short-story collections. We had them all, in multiple editions and collections. The two on Lena's list were chilling selections—*Crooked House* and *Endless Night*—and good reminders for me to trust no one.

No one, I repeated to myself. No one but us Christies.

Which meant I shouldn't be so sure about Rusty. And Ms. Ridge too? All we'd discovered about Ms. Ridge so far was how little we knew about her.

Before Piper could pepper me with more questions, I turned one on her. "Did *you* know Prescott St. James?"

"Did I?" Piper laughed in roller-coaster ripples. "Oh, honey, he's how I got my money."

While I searched for more books, Piper happily dished on her "fool" second husband, Frankie, who'd gotten in early on Prescott's scheme. "Before the pyramid crumbled. That's how it works. Someone has to get rich to lure in the rest." She tapped her taut temple. "Bait. That was Frankie. You know, I think I might actually be psychic . . . I timed that divorce just right."

I complimented her. Good timing was everything. "You have no hard feelings toward Prescott, then?"

Piper laughed. "Are you suspecting me?"

I couldn't hide anything.

"Good for you, Ellie Christie!" Piper exclaimed. "I'm sorry to disappoint you, though. If I'd recognized him at book club, I would have made a scene and hugged him."

Patting her coppery spiky locks, Piper went on about how *old* Prescott had looked. "I'd only seen him in the news, but he used to be very handsome. Nice thick dark hair . . ." She went on, listing good teeth, fine clothes, and a commanding presence.

I considered this. So, Rusty wasn't alone in failing to recognize Prescott. Syd wasn't the only one with kind words. But someone sure hadn't liked him. I murmured the last aloud.

"I'll say," Piper said. She lowered her voice. "Did you hear? He was in a fight before his death. I heard from someone who heard it straight from the coroner's office."

I vowed never to reveal anything to that loose-lipped guy at that coroner's. Piper laid out what she knew. It wasn't much.

"Prescott had a bruise on his knuckles, probably acquired several hours before he died. I heard that the police were ask-ing business owners up here in the hamlet if they saw any sort of disturbance. Early afternoon, I was told. Around one or half past? I'm just sorry I missed it! I got lured into reading at your place."

She looked slightly put out, as if reading was ever a bad thing.

I repeated the bigger question. "Disturbance?" The police hadn't asked us if we'd seen anything. They must have had a general idea where it happened.

"Fight. Brawl. Scuffle. I don't know, but I'm trying to find out. If you hear anything . . ."

"Scuffle" pinballed around my brain, along with an image of Emmet Jackson with the bruise on his chin. Just a scuff, he'd said. Stay clear of bad business, he'd warned.

I only half listened as Piper returned to her ex and her foresight in picking the perfect divorce date. "I was going to put it off until after Christmas. Who wants to ruin the holidays? It's so hard to find movers in December too . . ."

I pulled the remaining book on my half of the list, an illustrated version of Edgar Allan Poe stories that my niece would like. In the lobby, Lena already waited by the register.

"Your guests will love these," I said, ringing up the stack. Nine books. A good sale for our day off.

Lena shrugged. "L'Auberge has no televisions. I must provide entertainments."

Piper's phone rang. She pounced on it. "Hello? Hang on, the reception's awful . . . Who?" She unlocked the front door and stuck her head and phone outside.

With Piper distracted, I saw an opportunity. I asked about Ms. Ridge first.

"The older woman who works here? With the hair?" Lena made a gesture by her chin to indicate pageboy hair.

My hopes soared. I imagined success—victory before coffee, still in my bathrobe and snow boots. "Yes," I said eagerly.

"Katherine Ridge. We're checking around at local inns and hotels."

"No," said Lena. "There is no Katherine Ridge checked in at my inn."

Given the high prices of L'Auberge, I wasn't surprised. So much for that fantasy, but even my first strikeout was somewhat satisfying. If we could determine where Ms. Ridge wasn't, we'd be closer to finding her.

I checked that Piper still had her head out the door.

"One of your guests stopped in yesterday," I said.

"Mmm," said Lena and stopped at that.

I'd have to get specific. "Simon Trent? I heard he was in an accident Saturday evening. How scary. Do you know where he was going?"

Lena's narrowed eyes suggested she knew where I was going with my questions.

"My guests enjoy complete privacy at L'Auberge," she said tersely.

Piper popped her head back inside. "See, Lena? *Everyone* knows. You might as well tell us what your infamous moocher was up to when he raced off in that ridiculous convertible."

Lena's stony face said everything. She wouldn't be saying a thing.

Piper trotted back to us. "Ellie, you're looking into Simon too, are you? I thought I saw you staring his way last night. You should be more subtle, dear."

Lena cracked a smile at that. "Says the kettle to the . . . what is the saying? The frying pan?"

"Pot," said Piper, undeterred. "Did you know, Ellie, that Simon Trent sped out of town right around the time the murdered man stepped onto his final gondola ride? Mmm? Poor Morgan must be horrified. Such a man as her half sibling. Of course, I'm sure she'd be thankful to have him out of her life. Jail would accomplish that."

Lena hefted her bags and headed briskly for the door. "Thank you for the books."

Piper followed, pausing to waggle a finger. "Remember, we're all looking for the same man—or woman. The killer! Call me first if you find out anything juicy. And have Ms. Ridge get back to me about that séance. Where is she?"

The cowbells jangled. I locked the door behind them, feeling unsettled.

Had Piper overheard me asking about Ms. Ridge? I was back in the storeroom, seeking clarity from a second mug of coffee, when pounding sounded at the front door. When I rushed back, I found Lena standing outside, looking impatient.

What had I done? Rung up the wrong charge? Missed a book? Well, it was early and we weren't even open and . . .

My mental excuses fled when I saw what Lena held.

"Agatha!"

"Your cat," Lena declared unnecessarily, struggling to hold a squirming Agatha. "She followed me and refused to leave. L'Auberge has a strict no-dander policy."

I gushed thanks and apologies and reached for Agatha, who scrambled from my embrace and huffily sashayed back to the Reading Lounge.

Lena, in a moment bordering on camaraderie, shrugged. "It has been an oddly disturbed morning."

With that, I heartily agreed.

✳

CHAPTER 18

Poetry in the Park

B y noon, I'd walked the length of the upper hamlet, up to the ski center and back down through the chalets and shops. I'd popped into local businesses, chatted, and acquired goodies. Fancy chocolate truffles, decadent brownies, sunglasses that promised to prevent snow blindness and disorientation, postcards to send faraway friends, and coupons for bottled oxygen. I'd also acquired sore feet, a smaller bank account, very little about Prescott's scuffle, and zip-all about Ms. Ridge.

The scuffle, I learned, had possibly taken place in the narrow sidewalk-width passageway between the oxygen bar and the chocolatier. The chocolatier's assistant told me that her boss had stepped out to admire the snow and seen a man in a long overcoat stomp by, rubbing his knuckles.

"He was muttering," the assistant said, reporting this secondhand witnessing with titillated thrill. "Something about people minding their own business." The chocolatier had then seen a shadowy figure (of course!) heading down the passageway, away from Upper Main Street.

"A large shadow," said the assistant, handing me sample truffles as she talked. "Keiko—that's my boss—she thought the shadow person was kind of big? Or wearing a bunch of coats? Anyone can look big in puffer jackets. It's something, though."

It was something, and more than I learned about Ms. Ridge. The baker claimed she'd never seen Ms. Ridge. This, even though Ms. Ridge would have passed her shop twice daily between the gondola station and work.

A man at a ski rental place raised my hopes. He'd recently rented cross-country skis to an "older lady," he said. Further prompting revealed that the woman had had a few strands of silver among otherwise ebony hair, as well as two young children.

At residential chalets, I met friendly but unhelpful visitors. From them, I received an invitation to an après-ski bonfire and an offer of morning hot toddies.

Locals, once reminded of who I was, wanted to talk only of the murder and robbery.

"Never had a burglary at the Book Chalet before," observed the elderly man who ran the hardware store, where they were fresh out of deadbolts. "Never a killing on the gondola either."

I could have quibbled with the latter statement. The fatal stabbing surely occurred *before* the deceased lurched onto his last ride.

Maybe right around here, I thought, finding myself in front of Gondola Park. Prescott St. James would have had to come through the park to get to the station. There would have been lights, but still loads of places for an assailant to hide. Behind the restrooms, beside a statue, or tucked into a puddle of darkness.

Bright sunshine lit the park today. A small crowd gathered around the central pedestal, on which my favorite cowboy poet stood holding a microphone. I went in to listen. Emmet appeared to be dabbling in more modern poetic forms. He dramatically pronounced words and let them linger.

"Cowpoke," he boomed.

"Cowful," he pronounced and let the crowd ponder. "Goodness in droves."

I skirted the statue of the weary miner for a better view and was rewarded with a joyful sight. My favorite pony, Calamity Janet, stood beside the pedestal, enthusiastically demolishing a green apple. Munching, tossing, and spitting out shards to stomp on.

I forgot my sore feet and treated myself to another truffle and a listen.

Emmet launched into what he called a love sonnet, full of sorrow and grief. I noted quite a few kids in attendance. Some sat cross-legged in their snowsuits, rapt to Emmet's words. Others launched sleds and plastic saucers down the slope at the end of the park.

Desperate to deduce something, I made the easy guess that the schools had called another snow day. Rosie would be pleased. I wondered if she'd ski or read. Probably both, maybe with a dash of sleuthing with Gram.

When I was a kid, Mom always sent me outside on snow days for that motherly treasure "fresh air" (and getting out of her hair). I'd dutifully sled or made snow sculptures, always anticipating the best part of the day: returning inside for an afternoon reading binge.

Floating on Emmet's words and happy memories, I gazed out to the edge of the park. A group of kids had launched a snowball fight. Projectiles and giggles flew. A familiar figure stoically skied through the fray. As if sensing my gaze, Glynis Goodman changed course and glided over.

She shook her head in the negative before I could ask if she'd seen her missing neighbor.

"Nope," she said. "I've been shoveling her walk, and I bet her mail will be there when I get back."

I told Glynis that Meg, Gram, and I were looking for Ms. Ridge. "I'm just taking a break," I said, offering Glynis a truffle.

"A crack Christie detection team," she said seriously. She accepted a chocolate and turned her attention to the poetry, declaring it "nice" after Emmet produced a few near rhymes.

"Poignant," I said. "The unrequited romantic cowboy."

"Hardly unrequited," Glynis declared.

Emmet was telling of a lonesome cowboy, wandering the plains. His herd was lost. His horse was old and swaybacked.

It sure sounded sad to me. I said so to Glynis.

She shrugged. "Eh, poetry. You can't take it literally. Poets exaggerate and get all soppy. Same with that pony—such a little drama diva."

Calamity Janet was hoofing a baguette, tossed to her by a misguided fan.

Emmet announced a brief intermission. "For my tired pony to rest her weary hooves," he said.

Calamity gave the baguette a vigorous thrash and stomp.

Emmet descended the podium and took up her lead. I raised my clapping hands high. Glynis lifted her ski poles and yelled, "Bravo!"

Emmet smiled and came our way, Calamity Janet sauntering behind like the drama diva she was.

"Ladies," Emmet said, with a little bow. "Thank you for stoppin' by."

The bruise on his chin had turned to a garish purplish gray, the scratch a dark line. I noted that Emmet had let his chin stubble grow fluffy. His handlebar mustache was also unusually untamed and bushy.

Calamity too had grown a fluffy winter coat of gray dapples over white. "You look beautiful," I told her. "It's so good to see you."

She raised velvety lips to show off hay-yellow teeth, either grinning or reminding me to respect her boundaries.

"Yep, she's looking fine. Can't keep a good woman down," Emmet said.

Glynis heartily concurred.

"You doin' okay?" he asked, directing the question to me. "Heard you were robbed."

"Everyone's heard about that," Glynis said.

I assured Emmet that we were fine. "We got a temporary lock fix from Syd Zeller," I added, thinking he deserved praise for coming to our rescue.

"Has to be hard for him," Emmet said. "Especially for Rusty. He's turned into a good man, Rusty."

"You know about—?" I cut myself off. I didn't want to be the one to spread Rusty's so-called secret.

Emmet and Glynis guffawed. Janet joined in with a lip-ruffling raspberry.

Glynis said, "We know all about Rusty Zeller's past business endeavors. You can't keep a secret in Last Word. The last to know are the ones who *think* they're keeping the secret." She winked at Emmet, who looked away.

"So, you both knew Prescott too?" I asked.

Glynis promptly denied having any personal contact. "I don't ski in those circles."

Emmet said he knew *of* him. "A poor poet doesn't get mixed up with such sorts."

That wasn't an answer. "But you *knew* him?" I pressed, thinking of the vague description of the shadowy figure leaving the scuffle. Large. Emmet was tall. Imposingly tall, now that he was looking down at me within reaching distance.

"Who knows anyone?" Emmet said ambiguously.

Why was he being so evasive? I tried another approach. "There's a rumor going around that Prescott St. James got into a fight on Saturday afternoon. Right up here by the choc-olate shop."

"Darned shame," said Emmet. "Sweet shop."

"That man had a bad day," Glynis opined.

I held out my truffle box. Maybe chocolate would help. Emmet declined. Glynis took another. I did too. I needed for-tification for my next question.

"Did you see anything, Emmet? The fight, I mean? Maybe, ah . . . try to break it up?" I touched my own chin, on the spot where his bruise glared back at me.

He gazed down at me, saying nothing.

Glynis took another chocolate and interpreted. "Ellie here's trying to ask if you fought and/or killed the man, Emmet."

A scowl flickered. His drawl dipped low and slow. "Nope, can't say that I did."

Glynis helpfully provided a follow-up. "She's looking for my missing neighbor too. Know anything about that?"

This was safer territory. I described how Ms. Ridge had gone missing during book club and we hadn't seen her since.

Emmet's face softened. "That is concerning. Katherine is a kind soul and a true sage of book recommendations."

"Sure is concerning," agreed Glynis. "Woman disappears. Leaves her car in the garage and her curtains wide open. That's why I'm out, you'll be happy to know."

I guessed I wouldn't be happy.

Glynis gazed at the kids battering one another with snow-balls. "Weather like we had the other day, heck, she might've gotten lost walking to the gondola station. Disoriented. Frost-bitten. Could be anywhere, five feet from us."

Yep, not happy.

Emmet checked his watch and announced he should be moseying back to his stage.

Moseying. The term hadn't seemed so friendly the other

day. For someone who said he didn't know Prescott St. James, he'd been pretty firm about kicking him out of our bookshop. He'd been downright evasive about my questions too.

I concentrated my goodbyes on Janet. She raised her soft muzzle, as if for a kiss. I recalled my birthday party so long ago and its warnings: *Don't kiss the pony!*

An air kiss would be safe, right? Janet was lingering, looking wanting and almost affectionate. I leaned in . . .

"Stop right there." A male voice, authoritative.

I jerked upright, guilt zinging. I'd been caught, doing what I knew was forbidden.

Janet reared.

Glynis calmly pivoted.

Emmet touched the brim of his hat. "Howdy, Officer. What can we do you for?"

Deputy Garza approached, the stern statement giving way to glum. "Sorry, Emmet. I know you're in the midst of poetry, but I need to talk to you. Alone, please?"

Chief Sunnie stomped up, boots slipping in the snow, looking grouchy under flopping earflaps. "I'm going to need a moment of your time too, Miss Christie."

"What about me?" Glynis demanded.

Emmet handed her the braided pony lead. "Will you kindly manage my herd?"

The crowd was gawking and making no bones about it. I whispered to the chief, "Everyone's looking."

She looked around and then bellowed, "Good afternoon, folks. Nothing going on. Nothing to see here."

Kids put down their sleds. I felt like even the statues were staring. The morose miner. The not-so-alike likeness of my great-great-granddad. The very disappointed Ute leader.

"Does that ever work?" I asked. " 'Nothing to see here'?"

"Nah. Not that I've found, but it doesn't mean it won't someday. What works is boring a crowd. I'm going to show you something on my phone. Nothing more boring than watching people stare at phones."

Garza and Emmet had moved under the wide eaves of the gondola station. Emmet had a regal stance, gazing out at the distant vista, head high, hat tipped back.

A phone screen jutted into my vision. I leaned back and tried to focus my vision. The video remained blurry and dark no matter which way I looked at it.

"You're right," I said. "This is boring." More like terrifying, but I didn't want to admit that. What—who—was I about to see?

I made out a snowdrift under the dim glow of a streetlamp. Snow sheeted across the screen in a diagonal blur. I squinted. Was that the wrought-iron fence in front of L'Auberge? If so, the Book Chalet would be a few buildings down the way.

"Wait for it," Chief Sunnie said.

A shadow appeared, dark and pixelated. I caught my breath.

Chief Sunnie stopped the video and rotated her phone so it showed a wider horizontal frame with a date and time stamp in the upper-right corner. Sunday at 4:34 A.M.

Meg and I had left the Chalet on Saturday evening. Soon after, a man was killed. Sometime later, the Book Chalet was robbed.

If I were a robber, I'd choose the darkest hours just before dawn, when most folks were asleep.

"Strange time to be out for honest business," the chief said. "Recognize him?"

Him. "I can't tell if it's a man or woman or . . ."

The chief rewound a few seconds, paused again, and pointed to the shadow's head with a stubby finger. "Recognize that?"

A hat, broad-brimmed, tucked under a hood. Like Emmet had been wearing on the night of the murder.

The chief said, "He has a pretty fresh bruise on his chin too. Did he have that injury at your book club Saturday morning?"

The chief was assuming I'd identified Emmet. I felt my head shaking no.

No, Emmet hadn't had the bruise in the morning. No, I didn't want to acknowledge that it was him.

Emmet sauntered up with Deputy Garza a step behind. He seemed unconcerned. He tipped his hat to the chief.

"Ellie, darlin'," he said. "Will you do an old cowpoke a favor?"

My head automatically bobbed in a yes.

"I'm going to chat with these folks. Would you or Glynis or both of you fine ladies escort my Calamity home?"

I was too busy being stunned to respond. Emmet? Emmet wouldn't rob a bookshop. But then, as Glynis had so astutely translated, I'd wanted to know if Emmet killed a man.

"We gotcha covered," Glynis said, breaking my spell with a teeth-shaking shoulder thump. "Come on, Janet, giddyap, we're going home."

We were a half mile down the snowy road when I realized something astounding. The grouchy pony had let Glynis call her "Janet."

CHAPTER 19

✳

Probable Improbables

Rosie supplied the corkboard. I spread out a map, the tourist kind with streets, attractions, and ad-paying businesses in exaggerated cartoonish perspective.

We, the crack nondetection team plus teenage niece, had gathered at Gram's for a debriefing. Also, for Gram's mac and cheese, the ultimate comfort food. We needed comfort, having already established that we'd failed to find Ms. Ridge.

The casserole bubbled in the oven. The fireplace glowed with red embers. Meg sat in Gramps's favorite recliner at full recline, which meant head tipping downward as if awaiting a root canal. On the sofa, tucked under a blanket of her own creation, Gram knitted. She was making a fluffy hooded sweater in pale pink. Earlier, I'd told her that the sweater reminded me of Miss Marple in one of my favorite scenes.

"Nemesis," Gram had said, guessing the scene. "I am nemesis."

Chills had danced up my arms, just like they had when I read those words. Gram would be a formidable nemesis.

"Where's the first one go?" My niece waved a thumbtack over the tourist map.

Rosie and I sat on the floor by the coffee table, a rag rug as cushioning, the fireplace crackling warmth. Rosie circled the tack ominously over the map.

No one answered except for the softly whispering fire.

Finally, Gram said, "We know a lot of places where Ms. Ridge *isn't*. That's important. Detection is a process of elimination."

I felt affirmed. Exactly what I'd thought.

From her extreme recline, Meg quoted, " 'When you have eliminated all which is impossible, then whatever remains, however improbable, must be the truth.' "

"Spock!" exclaimed Rosie.

"Sherlock Holmes and Spock," I said.

Rosie approved. "Then you guys found out a lot. Maybe she's not even missing, because you can't find her."

We pondered that teenage Spockian logic.

"Could be," Gram said supportively. "Ms. Ridge doesn't appear to be at any local hospitals. I called all the way to Durango and talked with the nicest people."

Gram regaled us with the many blizzard-related emergencies she'd learned of in her calls. Blocked roads. Cars trapped in tunnels. Drivers trapped in cars trapped in tunnels, one including an ill-tempered marmot.

"Clinics," Rosie murmured. She found a dermatology clinic and stabbed it. "Where else?"

"The Book Chalet," I said.

Rosie launched another pin. "Oh my gosh, what if she's been there the whole time? Now, that would be weird."

"Improbable," Meg said.

"And therefore probable," Rosie countered. "Aunt El, have you checked your closets?"

I laughed, not revealing that last night I'd had Syd check the coat closet. It was huge, practically a room. A whole brigade of burglars and murderers could have hidden there. After he'd left, I'd also pulled a heavy trunk over the trapdoor to the creepy cellar.

Meg said, "Improbably, Ms. Ridge is also not at her house. The walk's shoveled but none of her neighbors has seen her."

I could confirm that from Glynis. "It's safe to say that she's nowhere near her home block or she'd feel compelled to shovel everyone else out." I pointed to Ms. Ridge's street so Rosie could pin it.

"Glynis has been watching," I said. "No one but the mailman has approached, she reported."

Walking the high-spirited Calamity Janet back home, Glynis had been downright loquacious, pointing out landmarks. To Glynis, these meant trails, cliffs, and innocent-looking meadows where people had gotten themselves lost, sometimes fatally. I figured that Glynis was kindly trying to distract Calamity and me, knowing we were rattled. Or maybe she'd been rattled. She and Emmet seemed to be friends.

I'd say more about the video and Emmet when Rosie was out of the room. Gram and Meg already knew, and we didn't want to upset Rosie, who liked Emmet. He'd performed at some of her birthdays and school events too. He could be entirely innocent. I hoped he was.

"How is Glynis's back?" Gram asked.

"Aching," I said. "Yet she managed to ski the entire Rim Trail. Ms. Ridge is not there either." Not within ski-pole stabbing distance, at least, which was how Glynis had conducted her search of the fallen snow.

Rosie jabbed a rainbow line of pins along the upper contour of the hamlet. The map looked quite festive, aside from marking our failure.

"My turn," Meg said before we could think too much about Glynis's under-snow search. She cranked the chair to a more upright position. "Ms. Ridge is not at motels, hotels, or bed-

and-breakfasts down here that I can tell. Most people said that they couldn't give out information, but I got some hypotheticals and winks from front-desk workers and cleaners who wanted to help."

With effort, Meg extracted herself from Gramps's recliner. She slid down to the floor and pointed out bunches of places for Rosie to pin. Then she moved a finger to the far edge of the map.

"I did find something out," Meg said. "I discovered where Prescott St. James was staying. Trail's End Motor Lodge. You know, that place with the giant moose statue that's all shot up?"

Even Rosie knew it. "It has that creepy vacancy sign that flashes a smiley face. Why stay there? Wasn't he, like, rich?"

No one would expect him to be there, we theorized. He'd be harder to recognize, so out of place. That and he'd supposedly relinquished his ill-gained fortune. Except for that marble mansion he'd been house-arresting at in Chicago. My mind drifted to trunks of cash, buried in the mountains. Is that why he'd returned? Money? Another sketchy business venture?

"How'd you figure it out, Mom?" Rosie asked. "Did you trick it out of the motor lodge people? Threats?"

Meg downplayed her detecting. "There was police tape sealing a door. I offered the front-desk clerk a coupon for a free book if she'd answer my questions. I asked about Ms. Ridge first, of course. Then about Prescott."

"Bribery!" Rosie crowed. "Cool, Mom."

"Sounds like promotion of reading to me," I said.

"Book philanthropy," Gram said. "In the pursuit of justice."

"Mom the briber. Awesome . . ." Rosie whispered to me, and we grinned. Meg *was* awesome.

Rosie planted more pins on Upper Main, Lower Main, the library, the community center, several churches, and the grocery store. The oven timer dinged. Gram went to uncover the casserole dish for the last half hour, the key to her crispy golden crust.

Rosie's sweatshirt pouch beeped with an incoming text. "Pash wants to talk about our science project," she declared. She clumped upstairs.

When we heard Rosie's bedroom door shut, I told them what I'd learned. First, about the reported scuffle, then about the poetry reading. "The poetry started off great. Calamity Janet was there. She looks fabulous! There were a lot of poetry fans, kids having snow-day fun."

"I loved snow days," Meg said fondly. "I'd go up to the Chalet and read for hours."

Exactly what I would have done today if we hadn't been out detecting. Reluctantly, I returned to the events at the park. "Chief Sunnie showed me a security-cam video from Upper Main. Probably the fondue place. I stopped in there earlier and they gave me a two-for-one dinner coupon and . . ."

And, okay, I was delaying. I needed to channel Glynis and come out and say it.

"The video was blurry and dark, but someone was out walking at four-thirty in the morning. I think it was Emmet. It looked like his hat. He was coming down the street—toward the Book Chalet. Chief Sunnie knew about the bruise on his chin too."

Meg filled Gram in on the bruise Emmet had been evasive about on the night of the murder.

"He was evasive this afternoon too," I said, recounting how he'd answered without answering.

"Maybe he was being poetic?" Gram suggested. "You know poets, how they make those glancing blows at the truth." But she looked concerned. "Emmet . . ." she said, shaking her head. "He loves books. Surely he wouldn't break into the Chalet."

"None of *our* books or money were taken," Meg pointed out.

I was glad to see that I wasn't the only one resisting the idea. Gram said, "But why? It's entirely improbable. Emmet's a *poet*. A *cowboy* poet. Besides being a sensitive soul, I can't see him investing in Prescott St. James's shady scheme. Why, the dear man can't even afford those cattle he's always rhyming about."

Gram then fondly recalled a cow Emmet had rescued from an animal shelter, a golden Guernsey he'd take hiking.

"Now, what was that cow's name?" Gram could never let a name be forgotten. She pondered the cow. I worried about Emmet. Meg studied the map as if it might show us a direction.

Suddenly, Gram declared, "I know what to do."

Good! She sounded decisive, and I yearned for a solid plan.

Gram went to the hallway and returned with her cellphone. "I'll text Lottie Nez over at the jail. She said she's working late this week because of the murder. She'll know if Emmet's still there. I bet she'll remember that charming cow too."

The oven timer went off. Meg and I bolted to get it and avoid what was sure to be a lengthy and confusing voice-texting exchange.

"We're awful," Meg said. "One of us should go back there and stop Gram from interrupting Lottie at work."

"As if we could," I said. I didn't want to either. I wanted to know if Emmet was cleared. And, yes, I wanted to know the cow's name. Evasive names bugged me too.

I hauled out the hefty casserole dish. Crispy breadcrumbs atop gooey cheesy goodness.

"Are *you* doing okay?" Meg asked. "I know you're fond of Emmet. We all are. The police are talking to everyone, you know. It could mean nothing."

"Sure," I said, because Meg was trying to cheer me up. But how could I forget the figure in the video? My gut impression was that it was Emmet, but would I have thought so if he didn't have that bruise?

"I'm just tired," I told Meg, which was true. "I walked miles in the snow."

"All uphill?"

It felt like it. I described my route around the hamlet and then down to Emmet's small farmstead to return Calamity.

"We passed the Zeller cabin on the way," I said. "What a view, and Syd's fixed it up beautifully. It looks so good he's stuck a NOT FOR SALE sign out front." The little log cabin had a wide roof swooped so low it nearly touched the ground.

Meg reported that properties out that way were getting snapped up for luxury mansions. "The views are priceless, but so's a family property. I can see why the Zellers wouldn't want to sell." She asked about Emmet's place. "I haven't been out there in ages."

I described Emmet's little homestead. A sweet log cabin and a shingled barn ringed by a grove of aspens. Clucking chickens, a donkey bray, and a big-horse whinny had greeted us. Carved wooden bears waved at the entry, and antique blacksmithing equipment hung under the covered porch.

I said what I hadn't dared utter to contrarian Glynis. "Emmet's place didn't look like somewhere a killer would live. We tucked Calamity into her barn and got everyone fresh hay and grain. Glynis said she'd check in on them again tonight unless she heard otherwise from Emmet. She's good with horses. Better than me . . ."

"Oh?" Meg raised an eyebrow. "You didn't call Calamity by her angry name, by any chance?"

I dodged her gaze by gathering salad ingredients. When I sensed she wasn't going to give up, I justified my reckless action. "Glynis did it first! She called her Janet, and there was no reaction other than a happy pony."

I decided to come clean. I went to the nearby mudroom and returned with my coat, displaying the sleeve with its fresh rip, ringed by toothmarks.

Meg—my sister, my protector and confidant—laughed. "That's quite a bite mark. That was just from calling her Janet? Did you try to kiss her too? Come on, El, I *know* you did that as a kid. You can't hide anything from me."

I couldn't hide anything from anyone. I shrugged, mumbled, and pumped the salad spinner.

"What'd you say?" Meg persisted.

I sighed. "In the park, I tried. I was about to give her a kiss—an air kiss! Deputy Garza appeared and barked something like 'stop right there.' He meant Emmet. I thought it was for me."

Meg was pink-cheeked with laughter when Gram popped in, beaming.

"Bessie Moo. That was the name of Emmet's cow," Gram announced triumphantly. "How could I forget such a glorious Guernsey? I have other good news too. Emmet's back home. He's a suspect, all right, but not under arrest. I simply cannot see that nice man as a murderer. Ellie, remember when he came to your birthday party? To think, you didn't want a party. Oh, but remember your seventh birthday, when we got that clown? You were right about him . . ."

Gram launched into reminiscing. Rosie thumped downstairs to help set the table. Meg was still smiling. No one wanted to ruin the comforting feast with talk of murder.

It wasn't until the dishes were cleared and Rosie had retreated to her room that we returned to our plan, or lack of one.

"What if asking around discreetly about Ms. Ridge doesn't work?" I asked after we'd carried mugs of peppermint tea back to the den. The fire was down to winking embers.

Meg suggested, "We go back to the police?"

We could, but they were busy with murder and burglary, and we had nothing new to tell them.

Gram picked up her knitting. "We could be indiscreet?"

I knew just who to ask for that. "Piper Tuttle," I said. "She'll get word around."

Meg winced. "Gossip is like a wildfire. You don't know which way it's going to flare."

"A controlled burn?" I suggested. Firefighters sometimes lit little fires to contain raging infernos.

We agreed and clinked mugs again, less enthusiastically than before, hoping that both gossip and the crime spree wouldn't spread out of control.

✳

CHAPTER 20

Making Waves

The next morning, Meg and I rode up the mountain in a gondola filled with so much sunlight, I could almost believe that everything was all right. Almost.

Meg used our commute to catch up on bookshop business. She did the majority of book buying for the Chalet. Book buying was part mathematics. Meg considered price, sales data, shelf space, and "window titles" that would draw customers inside. She read up on bookish buzz and followed influential reading clubs like Morgan's. Another part of the decision— a big part—involved art, instinct, and a passion for books.

While Meg worked her magic, I watched the aspens glide by and stewed on problems.

I warmed up with the smallest. I owed Agatha an apology. Once again, I'd lied when I told her I'd return home last night. Gram's cozy guest room had snared me. Agatha had thus missed out on her bedtime snack and the joy of stealing my pillow. Correction: She'd missed out on strong-pawing my head off said pillow. She'd likely still slept there.

This problem was easily solved. I'd serve up gushy praise of Agatha's beauty, and her favorite tuna treats.

Much trickier—although, I supposed, still minor in the realm of troubles—was crafting a reply to Syd.

Reluctantly, I slid my phone from a pocket and brought up his texts. Last night, he'd sent a single word in exuberant all-caps.

THANKS!!!

Thanks didn't usually provoke dilemmas. This one did. I'd considered feigning misinterpretation.

Thank you *for accompanying me to dinner! Thanks for suggesting pizza! Thank you for walking me home!*

Syd wasn't thanking me for dinner, I was sure of that. He thought I'd had a hand in pinning prime-suspect blame on someone other than his dad.

I'd chickened out last night and said nothing. I didn't want fibbing to become a habit in this new relationship. I also didn't want Syd to spell out his meaning.

This morning, Syd had texted again.

I owe you dinner! 2 dinners!

He'd punctuated this with a smiley face and a heart that I didn't know how to interpret.

I wanted no thanks for Emmet Jackson becoming the new prime suspect.

I could say so . . .

We glided over the cliffs. My finger wobbled over the small screen. After a ridiculous amount of dithering, I replied with a text version of my anxious too-chipper smile.

Dinner would be great!

And, yes, I added a smiley face.

I immediately wished I could rephrase and delete that grinning yellow circle. Not because I didn't want to go to dinner with Syd—I did—but because I hadn't stood up for Emmet.

And there was the biggest problem.

I sank into my seat as we flew over the frosted tips of tall pines. I wasn't sure I believed in Emmet's innocence anymore. That was crushing. Could a man who'd brought poetry and ponies to our family celebrations be a killer?

"El, we're here." Meg nudged me.

I registered the dim light of the station. Our gondola doors had already slid open, and we were inching toward the tight curve in the oval that would take us back down the mountain.

I hustled out after my sister. We were turning toward the exit closest to the Chalet when Rusty stepped out of his station hut, as bright and sunny as the day.

"Christies! Hey, gals, did you know, Agatha Christie was one of the first European women to surf?"

Literary trivia was his lure, and Meg and I happily let ourselves be reeled over. It was nice to see Rusty smiling.

"I just added the surfing tidbit to my wall of knowledge and inspiration." He pointed inside his hut to a whiteboard covered in a rainbow of writing, ringed in rays of neon sticky notes. "My favorite quotes from books and interesting trivia I've learned. Habit I picked up long ago, so I can remember to share with folks with bookish inclinations."

"That's us!" Meg laughed. "No wonder you're the champ of trivia night, Rusty. Agatha Christie surfing . . . That's a great one."

I had no doubt that Meg already knew all about the surfing.

Rusty beamed. "Do you know where it was?" He answered his own question. "South Africa, on a surfboard with the name Fred on it. She chose that board because her dad was named Fred. Bet no one gets all those right."

I would. As a tween, I'd had a poster of Agatha and her "Fred" longboard on my bedroom door, a gift from Dad. Other kids hung heartthrobs or bands that shocked their parents. I thought Dad was the coolest for having my favorite mystery writer specially printed to nearly life-sized.

Where was that poster? There was the kind of mystery I

wished we faced. *The Christie sisters locate missing childhood treasures.*

I chimed in with our own "did you know." "Rusty, did you know our Gram was one of the first women in Last Word to snowboard? December 1971. The meadow by the Book Chalet."

Gram loved to tell the story. Snowboarding was still in its infancy and considered disruptive, rebellious, and low-class by the elitist world of skiing. Some resorts had banned boarders.

If there was anything Gram couldn't stand, it was a ban on harmless enjoyment, especially if that enjoyment involved reading or the great outdoors. She went all out on Banned Books Week, insisting that we keep up our displays for the whole month.

There were more fun items to find: Gram's recommendation lists of banned books. She tracked her reading the old-fashioned way: writing out lists on lined paper, with notes and one-liner reviews. I'd also love to find a photo I remembered fondly. Gram, young and happy, surrounded by a group of grinning rogue boarders. We could have it enlarged and hang it in the Book Chalet, right by Agatha Christie and her surfboard.

Rusty chuckled happily. "Your grandmother is a notable woman. Wise. Generous. Ripping up the slopes. I hear she's been . . . how should I put it? Marpling?"

Marpling! I wanted that to catch on as a verb and activity.

"She's been knitting and chatting," Meg concurred.

And suspecting everyone. Gram was definitely Marpling. So were Meg and I and Rosie too. The Marpling Christies . . .

"Where did you hear about the Marpling?" Meg asked. "Have you been Wolfing?"

The Nero Wolfe fan liked that. He listed an elaborate web of informants, all spinning out from the gondola and Piper Tuttle.

Running a hand through already mussed hair, he said, "Piper's been by. She said that you gals and your grandma have been all over town asking questions. That killer has to be quivering in his boots."

A tremor rippled up my middle. I hoped the killer had no thoughts at all about us.

Rusty was saying that he approached detecting in the manner of his favorite armchair detective. "Sitting in my station, waiting for the information to come to me." He patted an ample belly and added, "In between fine dining. I aim to up my cooking game, that's my almost-new-year's resolution."

It occurred to me that Rusty had noticed Ms. Ridge more than most people we'd spoken with. As he'd just said, he also heard and saw a lot here in the station.

I asked him if he'd heard anything about Ms. Ridge. "We're worried," I said. "We're going to enlist Piper and have her spread the word on First Word Last Word."

Rusty frowned. "First Word Last Word's nothing but a gossip parlor. It's nice of you to be concerned about Katherine Ridge. Well intentioned and all . . ."

I sensed a "but" coming. I was right.

"But . . . well . . ." Rusty hedged. "I get the impression she's a private woman. Have you gals considered that she might not want to be found? That she's lying low for a reason?"

"What sort of reason?" I said, realizing too late that I'd sounded demanding and skeptical. Which I was.

Rusty frowned. "Her own business, I'd say. I'm sure she's fine."

But what if she wasn't? A murderer was on the loose. Rusty couldn't know she was okay.

Unless he knew more than he was letting on. I resisted the urge to step back, dragging my sister with me. Suspecting everyone was making me jumpy, a definite drawback of Marpling.

"We have considered that," Meg said. "That's why we were trying to be discreet, but—"

"Discreet is good," Rusty interrupted. "As someone who's suffered through cruel, hurtful gossip, I can tell you, it's not something you'd wish on an enemy. If I were you, I'd leave it be. Not that it's my business to tell anyone else their business." He added, with a chuckle that sounded forced, "Especially not Christies going Marpling."

Meg assured him that we wouldn't pry or bully Ms. Ridge into returning to work. We wouldn't even ask for an explanation.

Rusty waved to a group of tourists in neon snowsuits. The next gondola carried the baker who'd sold me the brownies yesterday. We waved, and she called out that she'd have a chocolate chip cookie special today.

"I'll be there," Rusty hollered, back to friendly and sunny. "I'll be by the Book Chalet too," he said to us. "I'm treating myself to a new book."

"That's great," I said, which seemed to be my go-to response today. It was great if he'd been cleared of suspicion. Chief Sunnie also suspected everyone. If she'd deemed him innocent, I could too, couldn't I? I wanted to ask Rusty, yet the rules of manners rarely touched on how to bring up murder-suspect status.

I skirted around the question and asked if he'd heard about Emmet. I added, "I was here at the park when the police came by. Glynis Goodman and I walked his pony home." I held up my pony-bitten sleeve as evidence.

Rusty bristled. "I heard. And there was some surveillance video too? Outrageous! A man has every right to go snow-shoeing whenever he wants. Then to be hauled off in front of his audience *and* his horse?" He huffed and offered up explanations he was sure the "big shot" chief hadn't considered.

"Has she never had insomnia and taken herself out for a walk? I know she hasn't a clue about the lure of fresh snow. It's like a siren to us true mountain folks."

Meg murmured about the lovely snow.

I thought of the sirens of mythology, luring the entranced to their doom. I couldn't imagine what would lure Emmet to violence and burglary. Money? Love? Fear? Those seemed like the top hits in many a crime.

Rusty rumbled on. "I saw Emmet on Saturday. I stepped out for my coffee break around one o'clock or so, and we chatted for a spell. In no way did that man look or sound murderous. In fact, he planned to spend the afternoon wandering the forest, composing poems. If that chief comes by, I'll tell her. I don't care if it puts me back in a bad spot. I'll say, no man who's making poetry in the snowy woods goes out and kills someone later."

I had no plans to become a criminal, but if I ever did, I'd be sure to take up poetry beforehand as a cover. Everyone seemed to think that poets were too sensitive, sentimental, and tenderhearted to kill. What if it was the opposite? To me, putting feelings into words seemed incredibly brave. Maybe poets could just as easily be deemed tenacious, tough, and sly.

Rusty was blatant in his agitation. Red flared across his cheeks. I'd wanted to find a way to ask him about Prescott St. James, but this did not seem like the right time.

Meg agreed. My sister shot me a look, a silent *let's go* yell.

"Yes, yes, I agree," I exclaimed, in answer to both Rusty and Meg.

Meg said, "Rusty, you should tell the chief about seeing Emmet on Saturday. She puts a lot of stock in human nature, but she doesn't know folks personally yet. She's trying to pin down . . . ah . . ."

She'd been trying to pin down who Prescott scuffled with

on Saturday. Perhaps the chief already knew. A man with a bruise?

Rusty had inadvertently confirmed that Emmet was in the hamlet around the time of the alleged fight. Not wanting to further upset Rusty, I switched back to the happy subject of books.

"Do come by the Chalet this afternoon, Rusty. You've earned a free book as a frequent reader." Maybe a free book would make him more willing to chat about his old business partner.

"I have? Well, it's truly my lucky day. I'll try to make it by." He waved us off with refreshed good cheer and "Have fun Marpling, gals."

Meg waited until we were well clear of the gondola station to give a long exhale. "Whew, Rusty seemed kind of . . ." My word-loving sister struggled for a word.

"Mercurial?" I suggested. "Worked up about Ms. Ridge, a gondola passenger who he says is private?"

As we passed by L'Auberge, I glanced up. The flower boxes on the balconies burst with autumn décor. A lace curtain twitched in a second-floor window. Someone else Marpling?

I was about to turn away when the lace parted. Simon Trent looked out. Not a just-checking-the-weather look either. His stare lasered down, straight at us.

I jerked my gaze away and slipped my arm through Meg's.

"Mercurial," my sister repeated. "That's the perfect word. Of course, I can see why. Imagine being accused of murder. How horrifying if he's innocent. He must be hugely relieved that there's another suspect but still terrified."

Relieved, terrified, gathering news, watching from windows . . . watching us. A murderer might feel and act the very same way.

✳

CHAPTER 21

A Famous Disappearance

Piper Tuttle burst into the Book Chalet as muted cuckoos sprang from their clocks to celebrate noon. Wooden woodsmen chopped logs in faint hollow clonks. Couples in lederhosen and swirly skirts twirled in softly squeaking dances. Miniature woodland creatures leaped as gargantuan cuckoos clacked their beaks.

Mom had silenced the clocks as one of her first executive actions at the Book Chalet. As a kid, I'd sided with Gramps and lobbied against the cuckoo-muting. *But I love them,* I remembered crying. I surely *thought* I did, even if giant menacing birds figured prominently in my recurring childhood nightmares.

Mom acknowledged that the clocks were handmade wonders, treasured heirlooms, and that her younger daughter *said* she loved them. They were also poor business practice.

Of course, Mom was wise. I saw that now. Peaceful readers should not be reminded of passing time in frenetic outbursts. They also shouldn't be scared out of their seats by hourly reenactments of *The Birds.*

Piper stopped under an elaborately carved chalet-style clock. Her hands fluttered. Round birdlike eyes glittered.

I felt slightly guilty. I'd texted Piper, saying we had important news. Of course, she'd assumed we had info about the murder. However, she had called dibs on our "tell-all." Right now, this was all we had to tell.

"You found the killer?" Piper said hopefully. "You found a clue?"

"No," I said. "At least, we hope it's nothing to do with the murder."

Piper had been unwrapping her canary-yellow scarf. She stopped, hand and scarf extended, poised to wrap back up and move on to other gossip wells. "Not about the murder? You said it was *important*."

I wished Gram and Meg were here. Meg was in the storeroom, tucking books into mailing envelopes. Gram was "working" in the lounge, reading or snoozing.

We'd already agreed on what to tell Piper, though. The basics. The facts, as much as we knew them.

"Ms. Ridge is missing," I said. "She left book club on Saturday morning and we haven't heard from her since."

Piper gave an elaborate sigh, somewhere between exasperated and gratified. "It's about time you asked for my help."

"You knew?"

Piper unwound her scarf. The fluffy fabric writhed as if alive. "Of course I knew. You and Meg and your grandmother were hardly being discreet. Your niece has been slightly better."

Meg came in holding a stack of mailers. She stopped when she saw Piper.

Piper waggled her fingers in greeting.

"She already knows." I attempted a covert mutter from the corner of my mouth.

"I most certainly do," Piper affirmed.

"And you haven't said anything?" Meg said, not even trying to hide her incredulity.

It hardly mattered, I supposed. We were all too obvious.

Piper's eyes took on the gleam of a raptor. Hungry. Intent.

"I hoped you might find the killer along the way. Or maybe—just maybe—our Ms. Ridge and the killer are the same person?" She issued an admonishing index finger at our protests. "I *know* you've considered it. You're mystery readers. You must know that the quiet ones are the most dangerous."

Had she been talking to Glynis?

Meg put down her armload of envelopes. They sprawled over the counter. I felt like joining them.

Meg said, "We're worried that Ms. Ridge could be in danger. What if she saw something related to the murder? She could be a witness, scared and in hiding. If we find her, she might point us to the killer."

"That would be juicy. A real feather in the cap of our mystery book club too." Piper steepled her fingertips like a well-manicured cartoon villain. "Here's what I'll do. I'll talk up Ms. Ridge's disappearance on First Word Last Word. That's why you enticed me over here, am I right? You could offer a little incentive too. A reward for tips? Free books?"

Meg and I nodded enthusiastically. This wasn't flaring into the gossip inferno we'd feared.

"Yes, free books," Meg agreed. "A gift basket full of new releases? A book a month for a year?"

"Lovely," Piper said. "I have an even better idea too. Keep open minds . . ."

Oh no. That phrase made my mind twitch, ready to clamp shut like a trap.

"The séance," Piper said. "If we're already gathered to summon the murdered spirit, we can reach Ms. Ridge's too. Oh, don't look so skeptical. Free books are nice and all, but what'll whip up major interest is us—Mountains of Mystery—detecting clues from beyond. I feel we can do it. Ever since Morgan's séance, I've felt a psychic tingling."

"Ah, okay . . ." Meg said.

Because what else could one say to psychic tingling?

"But let's hope we aren't summoning her 'spirit,'" Meg continued. "We want Ms. Ridge alive. Safe, happy, and well."

Piper said we could "work with that." "Famous psychics locate pets, missing husbands, true callings, pretty much anything. I just have to get a hold of—"

The door swung open. Cowbells clonked and Morgan Marin sailed in like a beam of sunlight.

Piper gasped. "Morgan! I was just about to say your name. I *do* have the gift!"

* * *

Morgan gripped my shoulders and issued air-kisses that left me dizzy.

Pfff... Bored disgust rode in on a frosty gust. Renée-Claude followed, muttering a few French words I recognized. Some regarded the weather, spoken in the same tone as the curses.

Morgan reported that she'd been on her way down to the base village for a facial. "Then, halfway there, I felt the overpowering need to read! 'Turn around,' I said. 'I must get to the Book Chalet!'"

Two sighs overlapped, Morgan's dreamy, Renée-Claude's weary.

"You're so brave." Piper addressed Morgan. "To be out in these dangerous conditions. The storm. The crime spree!"

Renée-Claude flicked an eye roll and drifted toward a sci-fi display.

"It's Ellie and Meg who are brave," Morgan declared. "You ladies witnessed a murder and suffered a robbery, and through it all you keep selling books! My heroes."

My cheeks flared. A riff on the post office motto danced on my tongue. *Neither snow nor sleet nor gloom of murder . . .* I bit it back.

"Meg and Ellie are investigating," Piper said. "Thrusting themselves front and center in the killer's sights."

Meg attempted a clarification. "We're not investigating the murder, we're looking for—"

Piper shushed her. "I'll reveal the juicy developments." She did, with enthusiasm and embellishment.

Morgan thumped her heart. "Ms. Ridge? Dear Ms. Ridge is missing? And you think she might be kidnapped or hiding and that it involves that awful Prescott St. James and his murder?"

Meg paled.

I noted that Morgan had declared Prescott awful instead of his murder.

I said, "She *might* have witnessed something, but we don't think Ms. Ridge knew Prescott St. James. She moved here after he was arrested. We can't see them moving in the same circles."

"Nor can I," Morgan said rather haughtily.

Morgan's brother had run in Prescott's circles. Had she? She'd just given me an opportunity to ask. My heartbeat sped to a jittery trot.

"Your brother knew him?" I asked, nice and gentle. Or so I'd thought.

Morgan went as frosty as the icicles spiking from our eaves.

"My brother?" she said, so sharply that Renée-Claude frowned up from a fantasy novel.

Piper clasped her hands in thinly veiled delight. At least she no longer regretted stopping by.

Morgan said, "My *half* brother knows all manner of unsavory people. Yet another trait we fail to share." With that, she clamped her ruby-red lips shut.

I got the message. Make that, several messages. Morgan Marin was no fan of her half brother, his company, Prescott St. James, or me asking such questions.

Agatha, thank goodness, stepped in to rescue me. The little

cat wove around our shins, demanding affection and attention.

No one could resist Agatha's pouty pet-me face.

"Agatha, darling," Morgan said, her warmth returning so swiftly, I blinked.

Morgan was an actor—an award-winning actor, I reminded myself. She could put on false emotions as easily as a mask. However, by all accounts, she and Simon had been estranged for some time. And Prescott? Dislike didn't lead to murder . . .

Morgan cooed down at Agatha. "You must be worried too, sweet kitty."

"She adores Ms. Ridge," Meg said. "We're all worried. Hopefully, her absence has nothing to do with the murder."

Piper gave a skeptical snort.

Morgan clicked her tongue. "It's a true mystery, isn't it? Just like Agatha Christie going missing. Did you know, Agatha Christie disappeared for eleven days? Oh, you Christies surely know."

We did, but in a day of "did you knows," this was one of my favorites.

"I didn't know," said Piper, much to Morgan's delight.

Morgan said, "Piper, you'll *love* this story. Mrs. Christie said goodnight to her little daughter, drove away, and poof!" She waggled her fingers like a magician.

I jumped in, unable to resist. I used to tell the story in my Torquay tour gig. "Her car was in a ditch, but she was nowhere to be found. All of England looked for her." I smiled and nodded to Morgan. She could tell the best part. The discovery.

"She was at a spa. A spa! She checked in under the surname of her husband's mistress. Can you imagine?"

"Interesting . . ." Piper said. "Is Ms. Ridge married?"

"She's single," I said. Actually, I didn't know. I looked to Meg, whose nod and shrug said the same.

I returned to slightly firmer ground. "Agatha Christie always said she remembered nothing. There's a theory she experienced a dissociative fugue and amnesia."

Morgan clasped her hands. "It gets even better. Arthur Conan Doyle—Sherlock Holmes's creator? He took a pair of Mrs. Christie's gloves to a medium and . . ."

Piper practically vibrated. "Oh my goodness! This is fate! I was just telling Ellie and Meg, we need to do another séance."

Morgan gasped in apparent glee. This time, I was pretty sure she was acting.

I wished she'd continue the story of Arthur Conan Doyle's psychic intervention. It hadn't helped one bit. A spa worker finally recognized the famous writer.

"So, Conan Doyle used gloves for his séance?" Piper said. "Do you have Ms. Ridge's gloves around here? Anything? A shoe?"

"I'll go check," I said. Agatha bounded ahead, hoping for kitty treats. I gave her some as penance for deserting her last night. "You were nice to Morgan too," I whispered.

Agatha meowed for more treats. I caved, then went to the lockers Dad had salvaged from an elementary-school renovation. They were metal, dented, and painted in happy crayon colors. Red, blue, leaf green, singing-dinosaur purple, and the yellow a kid would pick for the sun. I made my way down the line to a dented yellow door marked with a piece of practical masking tape and the name K. RIDGE.

The door stuck. I pulled up, down, and yanked before it burst open. Agatha and I stared in.

A single mitten lay on the floor next to a fallen coat hanger. Other hangers hung empty.

Agatha stepped inside to bat at the mitten.

"Where's the rest?" I asked Agatha.

Ms. Ridge usually kept her indoor shoes here. An extra cardigan. A change of clothes, a toothbrush, and a first-aid kit. She was always prepared.

Maybe I had the wrong locker.

I checked all the lockers. Gram, Mom and Dad, Meg, me, Teesha, Sadie the barista, Liz the sometimes part-timer, a locker filled with extra boxes of cat food and—oddly—potato chips. Good to know about the snacks. All the labeled lockers had items inside. All except Ms. Ridge's.

I scooped up Agatha. She purred in my ear.

"What does it mean?" I asked her.

Ms. Ridge had cleared out her locker. She'd left her car behind and her curtains open. She'd kept her birthday a secret, except from my cake-baking niece.

Agatha had no answer. I had a bad feeling. The chief would see this as evidence of a ghosting, but even as a ghost, Ms. Ridge would be tidy. It looked to me like she'd run. The worrying question was, why?

✳

CHAPTER 22

Little Lies

When I returned to the lobby, Meg had stepped away to help a customer. Renée-Claude held an armload of books, which Morgan stacked higher. Piper perched on the window seat, frowning at her phone. My carefully arranged window displays lay shoved aside in disarray.

Only Renée-Claude noticed my "discovery" of the long-abandoned sweater in our lost and found.

"Aha, here it is!" The words came out as rigid as a hardback. I wanted a redo. Maybe I should have gone with the truth? That would have been easier. Or unleashed a can of proverbial worms. I needed to talk with Meg and Gram first.

I held up the sweater. Yikes! I'd forgotten it occupied the realm of knitwear between gloriously awful and glaringly atrocious. Zigzag stripes of mauve, neon green, and dusty cream. Molting velvet elbow pads. Wood-toggle buttons. No wonder its owner hadn't returned.

I lowered the garment. Renée-Claude raised an eyebrow.

"Her, ah, around-the-house cardigan," I improvised, poorly. "How about I keep it under the desk since we'll be holding the séance here?"

Renée-Claude managed to look even more bored.

"Lovely idea!" Morgan exclaimed, adding a hefty psychological thriller to Renée-Claude's armload.

"Yes, good, preserve the energy here," Piper said. She sounded hassled. "My reception is terrible. Too much wood and paper in here."

Too much paper? As in, too many books? Impossible!

Piper stood, scarf fluttering. "I must go. So much to post. We'll see results soon. There'll be *buzz* about our séance."

Morgan bestowed air kisses and lingered at the threshold, calling out compliments. "You're a wonder, Piper. A woman of the people!"

Morgan's smile dimmed as the door shut. She flashed it back, making me again wonder about her true feelings. "Piper is a dear, but those community forum members are whipping up hurtful rumors. Ellie, have you seen what they've been saying about our darling Emmet?"

I'd been avoiding the forum, afraid of more awful photos of Meg and me. Now that we were offering books for tips, I'd have to force myself to check.

Morgan added another weighty selection to Renée-Claude's stack. "This séance is a wonderful idea. Looking for Ms. Ridge will give everyone something productive to do. It's a true puzzler too. Ms. Ridge wasn't upset on Saturday, was she? Everyone was having such a good time."

Everyone except Ms. Ridge. Was the chief right? Had Morgan's séance driven Ms. Ridge away?

This time, I went with the truth. "I don't understand any of it."

Morgan's expression turned beneficent. "Don't worry, dear. Talk of the séance will get the whole town looking." She smiled at me. "I've found it useful to nudge the message in a desirable direction. Do you have any clue where Ms. Ridge went? Something to get the Ouija started?"

A nudge . . .

The last time Morgan nudged the Ouija, it predicted a dead man.

"Are you okay, Ellie?" Morgan eyed me suspiciously.

"Yes! I was just thinking . . ." I couldn't say what I'd been thinking. I regrouped. "So, you don't believe that we predicted the murder?"

She laughed. "Goodness, no! You don't either, do you?"

Could she read my thoughts? I was relieved when she addressed Renée-Claude.

"Renée, I'll wear my Emily Trefusis super-sleuth dress for the séance. It will need steaming. Maybe I can find enough 1920s hats for all of us, even Emmet if we can pry him from his Stetson."

She turned back to me. "Speaking of dear Emmet and hats. I heard the police showed you a video that they claimed was Emmet. Could you say for certain it was him?"

I was glad the blurry image let me tell the truth: "Not really. The video was dark and pixelated. It looked like his hat but . . ." I forced myself beyond the bruise on his chin and the chief's certainty. "Even if he was out snowshoeing, I can't see Emmet breaking into our shop."

"Never! You're right, Ellie, he'd never, ever do that." Morgan stepped close enough to rest a hand on my shoulder.

Nudging. Directing . . .

Gripping. Morgan squeezed my shoulder blade. "It's inconceivable that Emmet would harm a bookshop, let alone a person. And the chief is basing identification on a *hat*? A hat is the easiest way to create an illusion, to transform oneself. Why, if that person had been wearing a feathered beret, would the chief say it was me? Cowboy hats certainly aren't rare around these here parts." She put the last in a western twang.

True. Yesterday, I'd visited the new-to-me Due West Haberdashery. The owner, a twenty-something woman from Atlanta, crafted the hats by hand. Stunning hats. Also stunningly expensive. I'd picked up one that promised to highlight my "mountain spirit" and "real reality." Then the real me on a bookshop salary noted the nearly four-hundred-dollar price tag. I'd put it back, thinking of Syd. We locals were even getting priced out of our hats.

Morgan released my shoulder. "I'm trying to help *you,* Ellie. You and this glorious shop. I hope you'll let me feature you someday on my social sites? My favorite book source?"

I spun between suspicion and delight. I grasped on to the latter. "We'd love that."

"You and your sister and beautiful Gram and Agatha, of course. Where is my favorite blue-eyed kitten? We'll schedule it, so my hair is up to par and we can all look like literary goddesses."

She patted glossy locks, more up-to-par than my hair could ever dream of being. Abruptly, she turned serious again.

"Don't let the chief bully you into saying you saw something you didn't. You'll do that for me? We'll help each other, won't we?"

This seemed like more than a nudge. A bribe? But why? Her insistence on Emmet's innocence made me worry that he'd done something wrong. Or that Morgan knew who had and wasn't saying.

Still, I felt my head nodding yes. Of course I'd never say I'd witnessed something I hadn't. That went without saying. Plus, I hadn't actually seen Emmet's face, and Morgan made a good point about hats.

Morgan glanced out the window and clicked her tongue. "Renée-Claude, did you forget to put coins in the meter?"

Renée-Claude had returned to browsing. Picking up books, glancing at the covers, replacing them with a wide range of disinterest.

She came to the window. "*Ça alors!* I added too many coins. Why are the police looking?"

They weren't looking at the Range Rover now. Deputy Garza pointed our way with the giddy enthusiasm of a groupie. Chief Sunnie raised a smile too, pleased as a cat who's cornered a mouse.

Inside, Deputy Garza bubbled at Morgan. "I've seen all your movies and read every one of your book selections. You've turned me into a reader, ma'am. It's an honor and a pleasure."

"A pleasure, indeed," the chief said. "Ms. Marin, I spoke to your assistant and understood you had a full schedule today. Like yesterday and tomorrow. Yet here we were, driving by, and what did I see? Your vehicle in front of the bookshop."

She took out her notebook, murmuring, "Little inconsistencies, Garza. Always look out for those small untruths . . ."

Garza blushed like a kid whose mom had just wiped his nose in front of the cool crowd.

"I am busy. *Buying* books," Morgan clarified brightly. "You officers caught me at my addiction. But I do apologize, Chief Sundstrom. My schedule gets filled up until I don't know where I'm going. I'm sure you understand."

Deputy Garza agreed vigorously.

Morgan turned to Renée-Claude. "Can we fit the officers in? Tomorrow, perhaps? After lunch? Oh, but I have that *thing . . .*"

"How about now?" Chief Sunnie said. "A quick question or two and I'll be on my way. Could we use that back room of yours, Miss Christie?" She turned back to Morgan. "There was a robbery here as well. We have something in common. I have all sorts of *things* on my calendar too."

✳

CHAPTER 23

Coffee with a Cop

An impromptu interrogation party called for coffee.

"I can make a pot," I offered. "Or get some specialty drinks from the Cantina? We have hot cocoa . . ."

The chief requested a pot. "Nothing fancy. A gallon or two would do me."

The pokey old pot in the storeroom would happily provide nothing fancy in bucket quantities. I was happy too. Fixing coffee gave me an excuse to stay and listen.

The chief jumped right in. "So, Ms. Marin, did you know Prescott St. James?"

"That man? Not my type." Morgan waved a dismissive hand. She did, however, have loads to say about purchasing his house. "All through my brilliant lawyers and broker. I got a *fabulous* price! They say a death brings down a home's value? Chief Sundstrom, let me tell you, so does dreary financial crime."

"I'll remember that," the chief said, dry as a drought.

"Do!" Morgan added, in coy tones. "I didn't kill him, Officers. I know you want to ask." She batted sultry eyelids at Deputy Garza. "I believe in cutting to the chase."

Garza stammered, "Very good, very wise."

The chief sighed. "Know anyone who did want him dead?"

Like your half brother? My pulse quickened, and I thought about my call to Chief Sunnie, basically telling on Simon. If the chief brought him up, I prayed she wouldn't mention my name.

Morgan stroked her chin pensively. She smoothed her hair and gazed at the wood-beamed ceiling.

I waited in tense suspense.

Suddenly, she snapped her fingers. "I do!"

Garza sucked in a breath.

Morgan's laughter sailed to the rafters. "My decorator, Leandro. Oh, if you'd heard his words about Prescott St. James. Foul. Simply foul."

Deputy Garza recovered and joined Morgan in merry laughter.

The chief slow-blinked as if gathering patience.

Morgan clarified the source of Leandro's rage. "Twenty-one shades of baby-food beige paint in that house and not a paint swatch to be found. Of course, I'd never touch up such dispiriting colors, but it's diabolical not to leave a swatch. Don't you think, Officers?"

Garza appeared aghast.

Morgan reassured him. Leandro overcame and repainted the interior in cool whites and pine-complementing airy grays. "The bones of the house were fine, and the library, oh my goodness. Like a book-loving fairy godmother waved her wand and brought my fantasy to life. It even came with books. Can you believe, the lawyer liquidating the property was going to have them disposed of. Books! To a landfill! Now, *that's* criminal."

I gasped. "All those books were going to be dumped?"

I admitted I'd ogled her library during her book clubs. Garza eagerly said he had too.

Morgan bestowed us both with her glow. "You're Shelf Indulgers? How sweet! Did you witness my recent livestream disaster? Thank goodness Renée-Claude managed to upload photos."

Garza, abashed, muttered that he'd had to miss the latest chat. "Work," he said.

"My grandmother and niece joined," I offered. "Meg and I were, ah . . . stuck on the gondola."

Murder investigation and hanging above a crime scene were totally reasonable excuses for missing a book club, yet somehow I still felt guilty. Garza blushed madly.

"Of course," Morgan said. "These things happen."

The chief confirmed the timing of Morgan's book club. "So, you were in your library talking books, Ms. Marin. Where was Leandro?"

In the Caribbean, decorating a villa. Morgan had referred him to a friend, but couldn't recall the name of the island. "Saint Something? Kitts? Lucia? Honoré?"

I covered a smile. If Leandro was on Saint Honoré, the lucky man had entered Agatha Christie's imagination. Miss Marple had visited the island on vacation. A vacation she'd found a touch dull until enlivened by murder.

"Nice when we can eliminate folks with airtight alibis," Chief Sunnie said, dust-storm dry.

In the silence that ensued, I might have confessed, if I'd had anything to spill.

Morgan placidly examined her nails until the chief resumed her questions.

"So, Ms. Marin, you said you bought your home here through brokers. But you knew of Mr. St. James's legal difficulties. You must have seen him on the news? You didn't recognize him when he interrupted the book club here?"

Morgan lowered subtly shadowed eyelids. "I had a *feeling*. I couldn't place it. You know how vexing it is when recognition is just out of reach?"

I knew all about that.

Chief Sunnie abruptly changed tack. "What about your brother, Simon Trent? I understand he knew Prescott St. James?"

My cheeks flared. I raised my coffee mug as cover.

Morgan brushed a speck of dust from the table, then smoothed her sleeve. I wondered if tidying was her tell, a signal that she was upset. When Prescott interrupted Mountains of Mystery, she'd busied herself with hat feathers.

"My *half* brother through the paternal line," she specified crisply. "I'm not surprised that Simon would recognize Mr. St. James. As I was telling Ellie earlier, Simon was attracted to the unsavory. He also can't stand to lose. He lost money to St. James's scheme. *My* money. Simon hardly has a right to care."

She smiled coldly. "Although I did cut Simon off after that— from me and my bank account—so I suppose he did care very much."

She sure wasn't buffering Simon from suspicion.

"What's he doing in Last Word, then?" Chief Sunnie asked.

A frown wrinkled Morgan's smooth complexion. "Simon has been looking at properties here. I've *heard* he hopes to reunite with my money."

Morgan went on to state that she had no knowledge of Simon's movements, on Saturday or any other day. "I am not my brother's keeper."

Morgan's frosty feelings *seemed* genuine. Perhaps Simon thought he could melt them by recouping her money. Or maybe he wanted the money all for himself. Either way, he had a motive to tangle with Prescott St. James.

The chief wrote in her notebook, underlining with emphasis.

"Emmet Jackson," the chief said abruptly. "Did he appear to recognize Mr. St. James?"

Questions about Emmet cascaded from there. How had

Emmet seemed before St. James arrived? During? After? Had he helped move the planchette to spell out "DEAD MAN"?

Morgan deflected with the elegance of a fencer. "We all participated in summoning the spirit, Chief. Such fun! Have you read the book? Oh, you should! The amateur sleuth is a delight. Emily Trefusis. Isn't that a wonderful name?"

Regarding the cowboy poet's feelings, she offered a philosophical question. "Can we know anyone's feelings? Even our own?"

True. I didn't actually *know* Emmet. I'd fossilized him in childhood memories as a fun, mustachioed man who appeared at parties with a temptingly treacherous pony.

He and Morgan had met at a party too, a cocktail soiree raising money for childhood literacy.

"Over canapes, we discovered our shared love of the poetry of Simon Ortiz." Morgan added, airily, "As one does."

Deputy Garza had a notebook too, I discovered. He got it out and noted the poet. The deputy was clearly smitten with Morgan. I'd thought the same about Emmet at the book club. I'd also assumed that Emmet was way out of his league. Maybe I'd been wrong. Morgan was defending Emmet way more strenuously than her own half sibling.

She described Emmet as a kind and gentle man. "A gem of a human being. So well read."

"Well read describes that whole book club, doesn't it?" the chief said wearily. "Well read in crime too."

Renée-Claude popped her head in. "Your appointment is anxiously waiting," she announced in a monotone. She gathered slightly more enthusiasm to confirm Morgan's alibi. "Yes, of course, Morgan took charge of the book club. Who else could? I was consumed with the video disasters."

The chief stood to leave soon after, much to Garza's disappointment.

"Lovely to meet you," he said again.

The chief departed with less cheery thoughts. "Remember, anyone can be a murderer. Don't base your judgments on what they read."

The door had barely shut behind them when Morgan huffed, "That silly, stubborn man!"

"Emmet?" I guessed.

She waved an agitated hand. "I will not allow this awful business to sully my new books. I have half a mind to cancel my appointments, rush home, and read."

That sounded like a fabulous idea to me. We returned to the lobby, where I rang up the hefty stack.

"Now, don't you dare give me a discount," Morgan said, sensing my finger about to subtract a frequent-buyer amount. "I heard that you had to deal with my difficult half sibling the other day. I apologize."

I focused on the unspooling register receipt and said, "He bought some books."

"Did he? Then he must have wanted something. Simon is no reader, and he always wants something."

"He did." I saw a chance to learn more. "He wanted to know why Prescott visited the Chalet. I don't know how Mr. Trent— Simon—knew that Prescott was here. Do you think they were in contact?"

I held my breath, hoping that Morgan wouldn't go cold again.

She handed over a stack of large bills and resisted my attempt to give her change. "Put it toward Agatha's kitty treats."

Agatha would have no qualms, but I might.

I was wondering how to rephrase my question, when Morgan sighed. "I have no idea other than Simon is *always* angling, looking for ways to benefit himself."

I thought of him watching me from the bar at the pizzeria. His gaze from the second story of the inn.

Morgan was saying, "By sheer accident, Simon occasionally hits on the right point. Why *did* Prescott visit the Book Chalet?"

As I had with Simon, I watched Morgan carefully. "He was waiting for a woman called Cece. Does the name mean anything to you?"

Morgan thudded a hand to her heart. She seemed truly shocked.

"Cece? I *do* know her! Ellie, darling, she's in my library!"

CHAPTER 24

✳

Agatha Makes a Move

Meg wandered in from the lounge. Engrossed in a back cover, my sister dodged patrons and displays with a honed reader's radar.

I intercepted her with exclamations. "Meg! Morgan and I found Cece! She's in Morgan's library!"

"What?" Rightful confusion clouded my sister's face, followed by worry. "She's at Morgan's? Is Morgan safe?"

"No! Yes!" I took a breath and lowered my volume. "Morgan's fine. It's good news. A clue."

I ushered Meg to the nearest empty aisle, a narrow space where nonfiction towered from floor to ceiling. Cocooned in written facts, I started over.

"When Morgan bought Prescott's house, the library came furnished with books. Morgan saved the books from being tossed out in the trash."

Meg folded her arms protectively around her book.

I returned to our discovery. "I mentioned Cece, and Morgan remembered that some of those books are inscribed. *Merry Christmas, to Cece. To Cece, with love. This book belongs to Cece. Ex libris Cece.* She thinks some also contained bits of paper. Maybe notes like Prescott was carrying?"

"But who's Cece?" Meg asked.

Oh, right. I'd gotten carried away with book details. "Prescott's ex-wife, we guess. Second ex. Cecelia Carling-Thorne. They bought the vacation home here together. She divorced him about a year before he went to prison. Morgan and I hashed out a theory."

I silently apologized to the nonfiction as I launched into pure speculation. "Say Cece lured Prescott to Last Word. She couldn't return to her library because Morgan's there, so she arranged to meet Prescott here at the Chalet and then . . ."

I let the sentence dangle, implying dark deeds. Also, because Morgan and I hadn't worked out the "and then." We hadn't wrangled the all-important why either. One thing I was pretty confident about: Morgan's surprise and excitement had seemed genuine.

I returned to known facts. "I've been trying to research Cece, but there isn't much about her online."

An understatement. All-knowing Google knew more about Agatha—as in Agatha Cat Christie—than a woman of fifty-seven. I got out my phone and showed Meg a blurry photo of Cecelia's profile, the best image I'd found. Long, pale blond hair. Slender with an upright posture.

"One story called her a 'reclusive heiress,'" I said. "The only address I could find for her was in Connecticut, but I don't know if it's current."

Meg—no fan of Internet share-alls—murmured admiration for Cece's online nonpersona. "Intriguing about the books in Morgan's library and especially the notes," she said. "You're right, this could be a big development *if* she's here in town. Gram's yet to find anyone who knows a Cece, and you know how hard it is to keep a secret here."

She handed my phone back. "If Cece doesn't live here, then why come to Last Word? We're not exactly on the beaten path.

They could have met wherever she is—Connecticut—or at his house-arrest mansion in Chicago. Plenty of space there."

Morgan and I had already pondered these questions.

"Old time's sake?" I started with our most basic speculations. "They liked the Book Chalet?"

Who can resist the Book Chalet, Morgan had said with heart-thumping emotion. I'd agreed. Of course, I hoped we wouldn't become a destination for get-out-of-prison meet-ups.

I moved on to darker speculations. "Cece's an heiress, right? He's a financial schemer. Say he got out of jail and wanted to start a fresh scam. Maybe he lured her here under false pretenses, something romantic. When she got here, she realized he was trying to swindle her again."

Which still didn't explain why she didn't simply throw snow in his face and report him for a parole violation.

When Meg didn't respond, I offered up the most powerful motive. "Love," I said. "They loved each other and vowed to meet here, in our beautiful bookshop, as soon as he was freed?"

"Touching, except for them being divorced and him being a criminal."

Love wasn't always logical. It didn't always end well either.

My sister looked deep in thought.

I waited.

"You said there were notes? Inscriptions?" Meg said. "I'd like to see those. I skimmed through all the sticky notes in Prescott's satchel. Maybe I'll remember something. Maybe something will click together."

I grinned. I'd been leading up to that.

"I already asked. Morgan's calling the police first, but when they're done, we're invited to her library!"

I basked in Meg's praise. It wasn't until she'd returned to the storeroom that I realized I'd forgotten to relay the bad news. Namely, Ms. Ridge's empty locker.

I was about to burst her joy, when a customer stepped up.

Better yet, a happy return customer. Daphne, the visitor who'd filled me in on Simon Trent.

"Is *she* here?" Daphne whispered.

I correctly guessed Morgan Marin. "She was but left a bit ago."

"Shoot! I have poor timing today. Is your precious kitty back? I was hoping for a selfie with her too."

"Back?"

Daphne pointed vaguely in the direction of the entrance. "I saw her trotting up the sidewalk a while back. I *think* it was her. Fluffy little Siamese? I called her name, but she ignored me."

Fluffy and aloof sounded like Agatha, but deserting the Chalet?

I thanked Daphne profusely, handed her a coupon for a free hot drink, then raced around the Chalet, checking all of Agatha's favorite snoozing spots. High shelves, low nooks, boxes, the best seats in the Reading Lounge, my pillow.

"Agatha ran away!" I said, thumping down the stairs from the loft.

Meg had been humming and stuffing padded mailers. She drew in a sharp breath. "What is up with her?"

I told her about Daphne's sighting while grabbing my coat and tugging on boots. "I'm going to go look."

Outside, I dodged slow-moving clumps of pedestrians, while calling in a strained sing-song. "Agatha, sweetie, here kitty, kitty . . ."

No Agatha.

I was a few buildings up the street, stooped and calling under parked vehicles when I heard my name.

Syd strode down the sidewalk, waving and flashing a smile that would have delighted me under other circumstances.

I attempted a friendly greeting, which quickly dissolved into an anxious ramble. "Agatha, our cat, she's gotten out. She never leaves the shop. Usually. Mostly. She might have slipped out when Piper or Morgan was holding the door open or when a customer came in or . . ."

"Hey, hey." Syd reached out and touched my arm. "El, it's okay. We'll find her. Let's think like a cat. Where would she go? Sushi shop for some tuna?"

This made me smile. "She'd want it grilled. She's fussy. The other day she followed the innkeeper back to L'Auberge and got herself kicked out."

"Right! To the fancy inn, Sherlock."

I appreciated that I got to be Sherlock, but it was Syd who spotted the first clue. Pawprints in windblown snow dusting the sidewalk.

"You're a tracker!" I exclaimed.

He tipped an imaginary hat. "Photographer, ski guide, and cat tracker, at your service."

I bent to get a better view. All I needed was a magnifying glass and I could have been on a Nancy Drew book cover. *The clue in the pawprints. The mystery of the disappearing kitty.*

The prints continued beyond the inn's scrolled iron fence. I pushed the gate open, anticipating a creak. The smooth silence shouldn't have surprised me. Under Lena's care, the inn was immaculate, three stories of half-timbered glory with Juliet balconies and flower boxes overflowing with ivy, colorful kale, and autumn gourds.

Syd and I followed the prints up the walkway. I finally remembered my manners. "Syd, do you have time for this? I'm sorry! I didn't even ask."

"I have time for you. In fact, I was heading for a coffee at my favorite bookshop. I've got about half an hour until I meet a client."

I flushed and covered by pointing to Agatha's path. She'd been more tactical this time, forgoing the inn's front door in favor of a winding, woodsy path along the side.

Syd sniffed the air. "I don't smell fish. An illegal catnip grow? Mouse convention?"

I could laugh now that we seemed close. Silly Agatha! I couldn't wait to scoop her up and scold her, with kisses, of course.

Poking around Lena's property seemed wrong. I knew I should ask permission, yet I also knew that Lena wouldn't be happy with Agatha's return visit. First, I'd find Agatha. Then I'd apologize. If Lena caught us . . .

We followed the path, me whisper-calling Agatha's name and taking in the garden. I wished Gram were here. Like Miss Marple, Gram enjoyed gardening and, even more, assessing the gardening efforts of others. She'd approve of Lena's landscaping, natural but carefully planned. The curves revealed new scenes at every step, like a scroll of living paintings.

We stopped at a sharp bend. A boulder, steely gray and splotched in neon-green lichen, blocked the view.

I had the tingly feeling that we were close. Or maybe the tingle was a warning that we weren't alone.

"Look." I pointed to a triangle of rooftop peeking above the boulder. "The old cabin. I'd forgotten about it."

A memory whooshed back. I'd been here before. Long ago, running among the boulders, playing hide-and-seek with a pack of bigger kids. The inn had been more of a hostel when I was little, hosting backpackers and wanderers. Mom had been friends with the free-spirited owner. They'd sit out on the back patio, tipsy with laughter and homemade chokecherry wine.

I peeked around the boulder. Smoke curled from the cabin's chimney, mingling with filmy steam.

Syd stood so close I could feel his warmth. "Must be nice. Is that a hot tub?"

I'd recently seen an ad for the inn. "Hot-spring pool. The water's regular spring water, which they heat with wood . . ." But, yeah, must be nice.

Agatha couldn't afford a spa day on her bookshop cat salary. I felt a renewed urgency to pluck her up and hustle us all away.

"We don't belong here," I whispered to Syd.

His response was way too loud. "We *do* belong here, Ellie. This is *our* hometown. Locals are getting priced out, bought out, forced out, all because of places like this catering to outsiders."

He looked around at the pretty garden in disgust. "Fake hot springs. Rich dudes buying up everything, just because they can."

"Shhh . . ." I urged, not because he was necessarily wrong, but because he was going to get us kicked out for real. That and I heard something.

Syd spluttered.

I cocked my head in the direction of a soft female voice.

Syd heard it too. He held a finger to his lips as if silence was his idea all along.

The voice floated up with the steam. *"My pretty girl. I missed you, sweet Agatha Christie."*

Agatha! And that voice . . . So familiar. But impossible. Improbable.

And therefore probable.

I rounded a boulder and stopped short.

Syd bumped into me, grabbing on to both shoulders. I was glad for the support. I blinked, attempting to take in the scene.

Ms. Ridge.

Ms. Ridge with bare feet dangling in a steaming rock-lined pool. She wore a plush white bathrobe and held a soppy-happy Agatha on her lap.

"We found your cat!" Syd exclaimed.

We'd found them both.

✳

CHAPTER 25

Ripples

M s. Ridge stared at the rippling pool. Questions rolled through my mind.

Why are you here? How can you afford this? Why have you ignored our texts and calls? Why, why, why?

Accusations crashed in next.

We worried you were hurt! Dead! Lying under the snow! You cleaned your locker and left your curtains open. Glynis has an aching back from shoveling your sidewalk!

I gulped them back and settled on the incontestable. "Tiglath Pileser."

"Pilsner?" Syd said. "You want a beer? I'd be in if I didn't have to go babysit my rich guy."

Ms. Ridge looked up, her smile tight. She rubbed Agatha's chin and said, "Tiglath Pileser. That would have been a good name for you, Agatha."

"Who?" Syd asked.

I made introductions first. "Syd, this is Ms. Ridge."

"Wait, you're the missing bookshop woman? This is awesome! So who's this Tig person?"

Clinging to this bit of solid ground, I explained. "Tiglath was a vicarage cat in a Miss Marple story. He provided an essential clue. The name is a little inside joke by Agatha Christie."

Syd nodded encouragingly.

I carried on. "Agatha Christie's second husband was an archaeologist. She traveled with him on digs and they discovered artifacts belonging to Tiglath Pileser, a real Assyrian king. I love to think of her having that bit of fun, throwing in a regal name for a cat, a nod to her own life and experiences."

Ms. Ridge said quietly, "Ellie, you'll be the perfect person to take over Trivia Night."

"No! We have you!" But did we? Ghosting, Chief Sunnie had said. Some people aren't dead, but they might as well be. Was Ms. Ridge already gone?

She didn't respond. A gray jay chattered high in the trees.

Syd said, "Sounds like a book Dad would like. Think he's read it, El? I could buy him a copy. Cheer him up. He's been down since getting accused of murder."

"That would be nice," I said, thinking he was also trying to make me feel better.

I'd imagined various scenarios of finding Ms. Ridge safe and happy. Admittedly, these had included a dash of heroic fantasy. Meg and me, humbly brushing off accolades. Most of all, though, I'd imagined the thrill, the joy.

I was happy, I assured myself. Ms. Ridge wasn't frozen under a drift or kidnapped by a killer.

However, I was confused and more than a little hurt.

Ms. Ridge said, "Suspected of murder? Oh no. No, no . . ."

Syd said, "Yeah, well, Dad was there at the scene and on bad terms with the victim. The police had their reasons. I can't hold it against them. It's just that Dad didn't do it. I know he didn't!"

Ms. Ridge sped up her petting of a pleased Agatha. "Your name is Syd? Your father is Rusty Zeller, the gondolier? You have his eyes, I think."

Syd nodded.

"He'll be okay," Ms. Ridge said firmly. "Your father is a good man. He probably would find comfort in a good book. Syd, you might like the book we're talking about too. It's called *A Murder Is Announced*. It's a delightfully devilish mystery. All sorts of characters aren't who they seem to be. I should add that book to my rereading list. I always find new clues and nuances and—"

Words flew out before I could stop myself. "Your *re*reading list? Lena came over with a book list. Was that for you?"

I stifled another flurry of why, why, why.

Ms. Ridge dropped her head.

"That *entire* list was yours?" I asked.

She looked away.

That list had more than mysteries. There had been guides to long-distance hikes and fly-fishing. Had she included those just to throw us off?

Then there was Lena, who'd known we were looking for Ms. Ridge. I couldn't fault the innkeeper. She'd told the truth about her strict privacy policy.

"Why didn't you say?" I asked. "If you wanted a vacation or to quit or . . ."

"I don't!" Ms. Ridge exclaimed. "I . . . I just needed some time away." She stared into the ripples, which ruffled in agitated waves.

Syd nudged me. "El? Bad timing, sorry, but I have to bolt. Can't keep the client waiting."

He grinned. "Want to get together later? Grab that beer? S'mores? Finding your friend here deserves a celebration."

My "yes" burst out like a demand.

Syd grinned at me, shot a perplexed scowl at Ms. Ridge, and sauntered off down the garden path.

I wished he hadn't left. I wanted backup. If I could just get Ms. Ridge over to the Chalet, then we could sit down with Meg and talk.

"Meg will be worried about Agatha," I said. "I should take her back. Would you come with us?"

Ms. Ridge studied the water. I anxiously shifted from foot to foot.

When Ms. Ridge looked up, she said, "Would it be all right if I bring Agatha over in a little bit? We're having such a nice time." She cooed down to Agatha. "Silly girl, you could have gotten yourself hurt."

She added, "I'm afraid I won't be able to put in my hours today. I need to settle some things and then . . . You and Meg have every right to be mad at me. I will explain, I promise."

I wasn't mad. Hurt, yes. Unsure, uneasy, and unsettled? Definitely. Ms. Ridge had slipped away before. What if she did it again, taking Agatha with her?

Ms. Ridge read my doubts. "I promise I'll be right over. I swear on my love of books."

What would Mom do, I asked myself. My mother would trust in the best natures of people. Miss Marple wouldn't. But I didn't have to rely entirely on trust. The road out was still closed. Ms. Ridge couldn't run far, and if she tried, Syd and Glynis would help me track her down.

"Okay," I said and added firmly, "See you both soon."

I caught up with Syd at the sidewalk and got the sense he was waiting for me.

He frowned. "Am I right about a weird vibe going on back there? I didn't want to bring it up . . ."

Definitely weird. Before I could try to explain, he pointed. "Hey, is that your sister?"

Meg half slid, half jogged across the icy street. She reached our side, breathless. "Teesha's watching the shop. Any sign of Agatha?"

"Loads of signs," Syd said. "El and I tracked her and then . . ."

I wished for Rosie and her *dun, dun, dun* . . . Here was a big reveal. I didn't feel up to it.

"That's not all we found." Syd paused, showcasing his own flair for the dramatic.

Meg looked around. "What? Where's Agatha?"

I hurried to add assurances. "Agatha's fine. She's safe at the inn. She's with . . . she's with Ms. Ridge."

"What? Ms. Ridge is at the inn? That inn?" Meg gawked at the grand chalet.

Syd's pocket beeped. He checked his phone and sighed. "Great, client wants to change plans and rock climb. I gotta go find equipment I didn't know we'd need." He paused and said, "El, you'll be okay? Will I see you tonight? I want to know what's going on."

I promised that I was both okay and very much up for meeting.

He jogged off. I watched until he'd blended into the colorful collage of jackets down by the station. Then I attempted to explain the unexplainable.

Meg enunciated each word in disbelief. "Ms. Ridge is at L'Auberge?"

In a desperate fantasy, I imagined Meg offering a happy explanation. Like, *Oh, how silly of me. Ms. Ridge won a spa raffle. We all forgot!*

"Why?" Meg said, crushing the fantasy. "How?"

I had no idea and no chance to say so.

Our names sailed in on a breeze. "Christie sisters!"

Piper Tuttle trotted toward us, amazingly stable in high-heeled boots on ice. "Oh my goodness, did you hear? Morgan uncovered a clue! She's a marvel." She registered that we were out standing in the snow. "Are you out sleuthing too?"

"We were looking for our cat," I said.

Something told me I shouldn't say anything about Ms. Ridge yet, not until she'd explained.

Piper flicked her heavily ringed hand. Gems sparkled. "I wouldn't worry too much. That kitty has a posh life and more social-media fans than I do. She'll come sashaying home. You better get back there too. I've been busy. I posted about Ms. Ridge and your gift incentives and how Mountains of Mystery will be psychically sleuthing. You're about to be overrun in interest."

I attempted to send psychic signals to Meg. *Don't mention Ms. Ridge.* I needn't have worried. My sister rubbed her temple as if pained and returned the topic to Morgan Marin, master sleuth.

Piper was delighted to repeat—and embellish—crime-solving theories she ascribed solely to Morgan. "Morgan suspects that gorgeous library of hers was the den of a killer! A murderess! A rich, vengeful, reclusive woman who lured Prescott here to his death."

Meg made polite, encouraging sounds.

Piper told us that the police were on their way to Morgan's. "As Morgan says, this should keep them from hounding poor Emmet. So what if he snowshoes at strange hours? The dead man was already long dead by then."

Had Piper forgotten about our robbery? I wasn't going to remind her. She was distracted, anyway. Lena, wrapped in a stylish wool coat, emerged from the inn and joined us. She bestowed subdued air kisses on Piper and a chilly look on us.

"The gardens of L'Auberge are for guests and their *invited* guests only," she informed me. "No pets allowed."

I opened my mouth to fib, then thought better of it.

"You knew," I said instead.

"Yes, I know your cat is pesky and persistent."

I had to admire Lena's commitment to privacy.

Piper perked up. "Ooo . . . This sounds more serious than a lost kitty. Is a 'missing cat' your excuse for snooping? What'd you find?" She waved off Lena's scowl. "Lena, be nice. There's a missing woman. Soon the whole town will be out searching gardens and sheds, snowdrifts . . ."

"I am aware of a missing woman," Lena said with frosty crispness.

"Good, but listen to this. It's truly juicy," Piper said. "Have you heard about the murderess in Morgan Marin's library?"

I nudged Meg. "We should go." I wanted to break up this little party and allow Ms. Ridge and Agatha to get by unnoticed.

Meg, however, dug in her heels. Literally. She'd stepped off the walkway and was solidly rooted in a drift. My big sis was a problem resolver. If Ms. Ridge and Agatha were at the inn, she wouldn't leave until they'd returned.

"They're coming to the Chalet," I whispered. "Let's go."

Piper was regaling Lena with tales of Morgan Marin, crime-solving wonder woman. Words sifted by me like floating snow. Library. Recluse. Biblio-crazed. Murderous! Sweetie pie.

Sweetie pie?

Piper waved in front of my nose. "Ellie, yoo-hoo, you're drifting. I said, is that your sweetie pie?"

I scanned the street for Syd, then felt ridiculous. My gaze swept toward the inn. A figure in a baby-blue snowsuit had stepped out. Simon Trent looked as sweet as a pickled lemon.

Lena inhaled, exhaled, and raised an arm in a wave. "Hello? Mr. Trent? I contacted your guide. He is collecting climbing equipment and delighted to wait for you."

If that guide was Syd, he wasn't at all delighted.

"I should hope so. I'm paying him too much as it is." Proving that he was busy, busy, Simon stalled on the second step to stare at his phone.

Piper clicked her tongue. "Come here, sweetie, come to your mamas . . ."

Lena shot her an appalled look. Her eyes quickly diverted down the garden path.

Agatha sashayed around the corner like she owned the place, cinnamon tail and frowny face held high.

"That cat," Lena said. "I forbade her to visit."

I caught my breath. Ms. Ridge followed, dressed in a beige parka, a bulging Book Chalet tote bag in one hand, her work apron draped over her elbow. She bent to scoop up Agatha, who nestled into her arms.

Piper gasped. "It's her! We found Ms. Ridge!"

Agatha and Ms. Ridge came silently down the path; Ms. Ridge kept her eyes to the ground. Agatha had on her best regal pout. They'd reached the main walkway when Simon Trent looked up.

He gawped, blinked, and boomed. "Cecelia? *Cece?*"

Ms. Ridge raised her head, bestowed a chilly look, and strode deliberately to the gate.

My head spun. *Cece?* I was about to grip Meg, but she reached for me first.

"Cece?" Meg whispered. "No!"

"Cece!" Piper exclaimed. "Oh. My. Gracious! Ms. Ridge, you're Cece? No wonder you're hiding." She drew back, eyes wide. "Oh, oh, I need to call Morgan! I need an exclusive, Ms. Ridge. I put out the word to find you—you owe me a tell-all!"

Ms. Ridge kept on walking, eyes straight ahead, back as upright as a lodgepole pine.

"I'm sorry," she whispered as she passed Meg and me. "I'm so very sorry."

CHAPTER 26

✳

In Plain Sight

We were being followed. I could tell by the heavy breathing, the *crinkle crinkle* of winter wear, and, most of all, the incessant heckling of Simon Trent.

"Cecelia! Cecelia St. James, I know it's you. Don't you try to run away again. You owe me. You owe my sister!"

Meg and I trailed a few yards after Ms. Ridge.

Except she wasn't Ms. Ridge.

The Ms. Ridge I knew would never have outright ignored someone, even such a rude jerk. She wouldn't have worried us silly or missed work or sent an innkeeper over on the sly to buy books. She wouldn't jaywalk!

I thought of Syd's game of collecting points for extreme actions. Ms. Ridge would never win such a challenge. Cece, however, was scoring big in extreme jaywalking. I tallied up her technique.

No looking before crossing.

No apologies to inconvenienced drivers.

No slowing for icy streets.

Taking the longest angle.

Double bonus points: carrying a smug, fluffy cat.

Agatha scowled over Ms. Ridge's shoulder. The furry frown

didn't fool me. Agatha loved being the center of attention. She and Ms. Ridge were certainly that.

They'd literally stopped traffic. A pumpkin-orange Jeep idled as they passed. Six well-bundled passengers sat snugly in its open-air back. As if on safari, they craned to see the local wildlife. A woman snapped photos. I imagined her thoughts. *Just in case it's someone I should know . . .*

Another woman stood and pointed. "Is that the famous bookshop cat? Ornery Agatha? Look at that adorable frown!"

Soon Ms. Ridge—aka Cece, aka Cecelia, the reclusive heiress—would be more famous than our bookshop cat. The whole village would know, thanks to my bright idea to have Piper spread the word.

News would spread beyond Last Word too. National media had gotten wind of Prescott St. James. His "great escape" from his marble mansion. His "final gondola ride to death." The small-town book club that predicted his death.

Meg waved apologetically. The ponytailed driver leaned out and returned a thumbs-up. "You found her! Way to go Christie sisters! Whoo-hoo!"

His tour group clapped and cheered.

Meg and I had just resumed our slippery pursuit when the whoop of a siren stopped us.

An SUV rolled up. Chief Sunnie leaned out the passenger window. "Ellie, Meg, imagine finding you at the center of something. Garza and I were on our way up to see Morgan Marin."

"Clever woman," Deputy Garza said. "Could be a protagonist in a book of the month."

The chief slow-blinked, then said, "So, we're on our way, when her assistant calls to 'redirect' us to a killer who's also your missing woman?"

Piper trotted up, triumphant. "She's making for the Book Chalet!"

She pointed. All of us looked, including the Jeep tour. Ms. Ridge and Agatha approached the bookshop at a firm stride. Ms. Ridge paused at the entry to stomp her boots.

Piper's eager face popped into my field of vision. "Who gets the gift basket of books? I *did* point out your missing kitty . . ."

Meg was too stunned to respond.

"Uh, I guess you could get the basket?" I said. We didn't even have a basket yet, but that was the least of my concerns.

Piper requested mysteries and do-it-yourself spirit-summoning guides. "I *predicted* we'd have good luck!" she said.

I wasn't sure about the "good" part, but I'd fulfill her book wish.

The chief sighed. "Come on, Garza. We're going to the Book Chalet."

Deputy Garza shot Meg and me a sour look, as if this was all our fault. The worst part was, he was partially right.

* * *

Back in the Book Chalet, customers browsed the display tables. Scents of coffee, woodsmoke, and ink on paper perfumed the air. Teesha greeted us from the register counter.

"They're back!" she exclaimed with joy as bouncy as her curls. Her brow wrinkled and her smile dipped as she took in the two officers accompanying us. "Is everything okay? Ms. Ridge seemed . . ."

She struggled for a word I couldn't provide.

"We need to speak to her," Meg said briskly. "Where did she go?"

Teesha pointed toward the storeroom. "I hope she's okay!"

I sure hoped so too. We found Ms. Ridge hanging up her apron in the yellow locker with the sticking door latch. Agatha purred over a heaping bowl of fishy delights.

The chief cleared her throat.

Ms. Ridge froze.

"Ma'am?" the chief said gently and introduced herself. "Can you come with us for a friendly chat? I'd like to clarify some things."

I guessed this friendly request wasn't exactly optional.

Ms. Ridge shut the locker, resting a palm on the metal. "I want to understand some things too."

She turned to us with watery eyes. "Meg, Ellie, I'm so sorry. I saw Prescott in the aisles during Mountains of Mystery. I panicked and ran off and hid. I didn't want him to see me and ruin everything. All I wanted was a quiet life with books."

Stopping an ex from ruining *everything*? That would sound like a pretty good motive for murder to the chief. I hated to admit it, but it sounded like a motive to me too.

"I get that," Chief Sunnie said pleasantly. Her words were light, friendly, and put me on edge. "But then, why invite him to come visit if you didn't want to see him?"

"Invite him?" Ms. Ridge mixed incredulity with outrage.

The chief drew out her phone. "My tech people finally accessed the deceased's email. He'd been invited to a meeting at this bookshop, the Saturday he was killed. The sender's email was registered to a CeceSJ. Is that you?" She turned the screen to Ms. Ridge.

Ms. Ridge recoiled. "Yes, but no! That was once my name, but not now and that's not my email. I never sent Prescott letters."

The chief returned the phone to her pocket. She held out her hand and gently touched Ms. Ridge's arm. "Let's go down to the station and talk about it, shall we?"

Meg and I again trailed behind Ms. Ridge. She walked with the officers, past customers and Teesha, who stared with mouth agape, fingers frozen over the cash register.

When they'd left, Meg and I kept on watching through the bay window.

"What's happening?" Our vacationing customer Daphne joined us. "Why were the police here?" She gasped. "Did you find your kitty? There hasn't been another murder, has there?"

I smiled at Daphne. She'd offered a reminder to look on the bright side. "Yes, we found Agatha. No, thank goodness, no more murders."

Remembering Chief Sunnie's earlier tactic of boring away interest, I said. "Our co-worker is assisting the police with their investigation."

The chief was on to something. Daphne's interest veered toward a book in the window display. She was reaching for it when a local man—a voracious reader of private-eye series— stepped up.

"That lady the cops just hauled away, she's likely the killer." He looped thumbs around an oversized belt buckle and rocked on his heels. "It's a breaking news alert on our community forum. She's been hiding out right here in this bookshop under an alias. That woman with the big-time book club, Morgan Marin, she figured it out."

Daphne's eyes widened. "Morgan? She's brilliant."

The man agreed. "She owns the killer's library."

"No!"

"Yes!"

"Hot drinks!" exclaimed Meg. "Go tell our barista, Sadie, that I sent you over for free drinks, anything you'd like."

They walked away, still exchanging exclamations and incredulity.

Meg uttered her own incomprehension. "Ms. Ridge? An heiress? Emails luring that man to our shop? Who would do that? I mean, if it wasn't Ms. Ridge . . . Cece."

"Someone who knew she worked here?"

Meg groaned. "Do you think Mom knew when she hired Ms. Ridge?"

I tallied up the evidence. Hiring a stranger out of the blue. The missing employee file. Mom actually respecting a desire for no surprise birthday parties.

"Yeah," Meg said, answering her own question. "She knew."

Our mother was an extreme helper. In situations where many people might look away, Mom dove in. She'd spontaneously mediate arguments on the street. She used to brake for hitchhikers before Dad—a reader of too many serial-killer thrillers—begged her to stop. She'd still pull over for any stray or needy animal. Once, infamously, she'd bundled a "lost dog" into our backseat. The pup turned out to be a hybrid wolf. Dad still cringes at the photo of toddler me, strapped in my car seat beside the toothily smiling canine.

Meg was right. Mom would be totally into "saving" a wronged woman yearning for a quiet, bookish life. We could interrogate Mom next time she checked in. Or we could wait until everything was cleared up. All Mom and Dad could do now would be to worry from afar about us, Ms. Ridge, and the shop.

Meg went to help Teesha at the register.

I lingered at the window, letting eyes and mind glaze over. Ms. Ridge was certainly good at secrets. She was Cece. Cece, whom Morgan and I had theorized was a killer. That had been easy when Cece was a stranger.

But Ms. Ridge as a killer? No . . . I couldn't imagine that, but then I also couldn't wrap my mind around Ms. Ridge as a covert heiress.

I was mentally muddling when Glynis stomped in, her thick braid swinging.

"I knew it," she declared. "Rusty Zeller just told me. Morose as all get out. Said he wanted me to ignore all scandalous rumors about my nice, quiet neighbor. Know what I said to that?"

Probably.

"I said, it's always the nice, quiet types. All how-do-you-dos and shoveling your sidewalks and foisting banana bread on you, and then, bam! They're a killer and your back's screaming murder."

Glynis pressed a palm to her lumbar. She added, with pleasure, "I told you she wasn't dead too."

I complimented Glynis's intuition. We both ignored that she had gone out probing the trail for a frozen alternative.

"Speaking of murders . . ." Glynis had received a text from Meg. The latest in her favorite icy-serial-killer series had arrived. "Signed. Make sure it's a signed copy."

"I have it right here," Meg called out, reaching under the register. She held up *The Ice Carver*. On the cover, a pale hand pressed up against an icy lake. A chainsaw and drips of red filled out the foreground.

I frowned, not at the image, but at an incongruity.

"It doesn't make sense," I murmured.

"Nothing does," Glynis agreed cheerfully. She studied the back cover. "Like this: The Dutch blindfold kids and dump 'em out in the forest at night to find their way out. They get 'em purposefully lost." She clicked her tongue. "That's something to last a lifetime if you don't die doing it. Getting lost is hard. I tried once and kept finding myself."

Meg asked me what made no sense.

"The break-in," I said, thinking of the shelf where we'd stashed Glynis's book and Prescott's stolen satchel too.

"The one they're blaming on Emmet?" Glynis asked. "All because he was out snowshoeing? Snowboarders act like they own the mountains, but it's the snowshoer who's truly free to go anywhere."

"Right," I said, because that did make some sense. "But the thief broke our door pane and stole a key. Ms. Ridge has a key. She wouldn't break in."

"You're right!" Meg's shoulders melted with relief.

Glynis countered, "Ah, but she's not Ms. Ridge, is she? What if she's a double personality, like the killer in this book? Once he has a chainsaw in his hands . . ." Glynis mimed chain-saw maiming. "Or she's throwing you off the track. Why would someone with a key steal a key? Simple. So you'd say it wasn't them. Who else has keys? That's your suspect pool."

Because Glynis looked so insistent, I gave a list. "Family and long-term staff. Sadie the barista, Teesha our part-time assistant. Mom and Dad. Meg, Gram, and me." I laughed to stress the absurdity.

"Always look close to home." Glynis raised her book in a farewell salute. "If Katherine Ridge uses her phone call from prison on one of you, will you assure her that I'll shovel her walk? She's seen to it that I owe her." She narrowed her eyes. "Premeditation? Softening up the neighbors and potential witnesses?"

"Premeditation," I murmured after Glynis had gone. Prescott hadn't just come here by chance. Someone had in-vited him, lured him.

Meg went out to mail books. Distracted, I tidied a rack of notebooks. One had a bent back cover, making it destined for the discount bin. A shame, since the front was fine and pretty with watercolor mountains. I discounted the price, fed the cash register, and opened to the first page.

Taking a cue from Poirot, I labeled my list Important Ques-tions.

Why did Cece change her name? Hiding? Running? Ghosting?
Where was Ms. Ridge when Prescott was killed? Alibi?
Who wrote the letters? Ms. Ridge? Other?
Who knew Cece?
Who recognized Ms. Ridge as Cece?
Who disliked Prescott St. James enough to kill him?
Why steal the satchel and book?

Too many questions. Agatha hopped up to attack my pencil eraser.

"Very helpful," I said, then realized that Agatha had just provided a clue.

"You were scared the morning after the robbery," I said. "Ms. Ridge wouldn't have frightened you."

Agatha scowled.

"You *were* scared. I could tell."

Agatha yawned.

"You tracked her down. You like her," I said. I did too. Ms. Ridge had always been kind to me. She loved books, the Book Chalet, and Agatha. She might have some secrets—some big ones—but that didn't mean she was a killer.

My phone dinged.

Syd's name popped up in a text. *Shoot!* I'd forgotten our "date," and now I didn't want to go. I needed to huddle with Gram and Meg and discuss all we did and didn't know.

Syd's message consisted of a shocked-faced emoji and a bunch of symbols I took as expletives.

I realized that he'd only been with me for finding Ms. Ridge, not the big reveal—*dun, dun, dun*—that she was Cece St. James. Someone must have told him.

His next text: **Can't believe she's Prescott's ex!**

He followed up with another shocked emoji face and two-and-a-half lines of exclamation points and question marks.

Yep, that pretty much summed up my thoughts too.

I hovered my finger above the screen, wondering what to say. I considered calling, using the phone as an actual talking device. But I still wouldn't have the words . . . or handy shocked emojis. I ended up texting back exclamations of shock, shock, and more shock, and an apology that I couldn't meet up. I needed to be with my family.

Gratifyingly, he replied that he totally understood. He needed to check in with his father too.

My phone buzzed again: **Dad won't believe this!!**

I stared at that line for a long time. Would Rusty believe it? Had he known who Ms. Ridge was?

Rusty had been blustery with Meg and me, warning us that Ms. Ridge might not want to be found. Plus, what had he called her? A "private" person? Ms. Ridge was private. We'd said the same, but was that another word for "reclusive?" Glynis had noted that Rusty was morose, too, and sticking up for Ms. Ridge.

Rusty had been Prescott's partner. If anyone in Last Word had met the "reclusive heiress," it would have been him.

I couldn't ask Syd over clumsy, easily misinterpreted text.

I pecked out, **Thanks for understanding. Raincheck?**

Ding: **Snowcheck!!**

I put down the phone and thought. Prescott's former wife and his former business partner. Ms. Ridge had worried about Rusty being a suspect. He'd worried about her.

A dark thought formed. *What if Cece and Rusty were in it together?*

I refused to write that down. I wanted a prime suspect I didn't like, and I still had one. Our first "perfect" suspect.

I wrote in an answer. Who recognized Ms. Ridge as Cece? Simon Trent.

I underlined his name. "Was that who broke in and scared you?" I asked Agatha.

Our bookshop queen hopped off the counter. Agatha C. Christie was done providing clues.

*

CHAPTER 27

Puzzling Pieces

Before Meg could turn her key, Gram swung open the front door.

"We have a dinner guest," Gram announced with sharp brightness.

Gram wore her best apron, resplendent in turquoise ruffles. Her cheeks flushed pink. I guessed the guest was someone important. Visions flashed of Morgan Marin and intimate book talk over dinner. I quickly rejected them. Someone else was much more important today.

"Ms. Ridge," Gram whispered. "She and Rosie are doing a puzzle in the den."

My stomach gave a little flip. I chided myself. I really, truly, almost totally did not believe that a murderer was in the den puzzling with my favorite niece.

Meg and I removed outerwear, put on slippers, and padded to the den with its squishy furniture, plank-paneled walls, and family photos. Ms. Ridge and Rosie sat on floor cushions by the coffee table. A fire crackled, and a puzzle took shape from the skeleton edges.

Rosie looked up. "Hi, Mom. Hey, Aunt El. We're making a library."

She held up a puzzle box showing a magnificent library. Floor-to-ceiling books and wooden ladders on rollers, cut into a thousand pieces.

Ms. Ridge gave a tight smile.

On the way down the mountain, Meg and I had filled our gondola with questions we couldn't answer. At the top of the list: Had Ms. Ridge been arrested?

Seemingly not, unless a bail judge was also trapped here in Last Word. I told myself that this was good news, affirmation of her innocence.

In the kitchen, the oven timer dinged.

Meg said, "Rosie, could you help Gram?"

Rosie shot her mother an I-know-what-you're-doing look, but then shrugged. "Sure. That means I get first dibs on the leftover mac and cheese."

I sniffed the air. Gram wasn't just reheating leftovers. My nose registered roasted chicken, probably with vegetables tucked all around and Gram's amazing gravy. My stomach rumbled.

Meg folded down to a cross-legged seat across from Ms. Ridge. I did the same, taking Rosie's former spot.

I was grateful for the dizzying look-alike puzzle pieces that kept our hands busy and eyes from uncomfortable staring.

Ms. Ridge efficiently clicked together a corner.

Of course she'd have a rational plan. No picking up a random piece and floating it around in search of a chance match, like I was doing.

Meg worked on a long edge.

I put down my puzzle piece and decided to broach the subject. "How did your talk with the police go?"

Ms. Ridge—Cece—looked up. Her eyes were tired but clear. "I tried to explain, but I know my actions are indefensible. Ellie, Meg, I am so sorry for deceiving you. My only excuse is that I wanted a new life. Once I had that new life, it didn't seem like a lie anymore. I know I was greedy and selfish."

"Greedy to work in a bookshop in Last Word? No," Meg said gently.

"Why here?" I asked. This abrupt question earned me a frown from Meg, but a nod from Ms. Ridge.

"Prescott and I bought the vacation house here. I fell in love with the town and especially the Book Chalet. After we divorced, I left everything behind, but I kept yearning for this beautiful place. I dreamed of it. The quiet. The books. People who love books."

I had to ask. "Why change your name?"

"You won't understand," Ms. Ridge said, eyes on the puzzle. "You're such a supportive family. But mine . . . I knew that if I used my real name, I'd be hounded. By my relatives. By Prescott's troubles."

She smiled, ruefully. "Maybe I've read too many mysteries— I thought that no one would expect me to return here."

Ghosting. The chief had been right. If we hadn't found Ms. Ridge, would she have moved on? She'd said she was only waiting for Prescott to leave.

And now he was gone for good . . .

Meg said gently, "Did you tell anyone? Our mother . . . ?"

Ms. Ridge flushed. "I felt guilty, asking for a job, so I did tell her. I said I didn't want a paycheck—I still had my own money— but she wouldn't hear of it."

She methodically clicked together puzzle pieces as she talked of her old life. How people pressed her to be someone she didn't want to be, to work for her family's businesses and boards. "And Prescott. At first, I thought he loved me. Then I saw that he loved my family's money more. I've wondered, though. If I'd stayed and given him more funding, maybe he wouldn't have stolen from his investors."

Meg murmured that Ms. Ridge wasn't to blame. I was prepared to issue more strident denials, but Ms. Ridge was speaking again.

"I never asked Prescott about his business either." She smiled sadly. "Head in the sand. That's what I did Saturday morning, running off to L'Auberge. The following afternoon, a maid told me. A man murdered on the gondola. Prescott! I was shocked. Horrified. Poor Prescott, he served his time and never deserved such cruelty. I couldn't face any of it. I just stayed where I was."

"The inn is a quiet place to reflect," Meg said kindly.

Ms. Ridge nodded. "Lena is a very nice hostess."

A very secretive hostess. I replayed some of Lena's words. *There is no Katherine Ridge checked in at my inn.* Maybe she hadn't lied.

"You checked in under another name?" I guessed.

Ms. Ridge's reddening cheeks confirmed my guess.

I made another guess. "Cecelia St. James?"

"Cecelia Carling-Thorne," Ms. Ridge whispered.

Like Agatha Christie during her missing days, checked into a spa under a name she dreaded. The sounds of clanging pans filtered from the kitchen. Rosie and Gram, laughing.

Ms. Ridge said quietly, "I didn't think of the troubles I'd bring to your family."

"No troubles," said my kind sister.

"Except the break-in," I murmured.

Ms. Ridge rushed to say she'd cover the costs of repairs.

I felt bad. "No, no, I was just thinking about our involvement. Us seeing Prescott the night he died, that was unlucky chance. But someone broke into the Chalet on purpose. The only thing they stole was Prescott's satchel with a book inside."

Ms. Ridge laid down her puzzle piece. "The chief hinted at a book, but wouldn't explain. All she'd show me were those emails to Prescott. They did sound like me. I can understand why the chief thought I wrote them. Why Prescott might have believed that too. But I didn't send them. I didn't want Prescott to find me."

She sounded baffled, anxious, and, to my ears, sincere.

"What was the book?" she asked. "I told Chief Sunnie it might help explain things. Books often do."

Meg and I had a conversation in micro-gestures. Meg gave the tiniest of negative head-shakes. I shrugged. Meg shrugged. Yes, we'd promised the chief we'd keep the book a secret. But what if the book could provide an explanation?

Meg nodded. I felt like we'd reached agreement.

We'd helped blow Ms. Ridge's cover. We'd gotten her name splashed around the community forum. If she was innocent, we had to help clear her name.

And if she wasn't innocent? If she'd killed her ex-husband and broken into the Chalet? Well, then she'd already know about the book, wouldn't she?

I took a breath. "*Absent in the Spring* by Mary—"

Ms. Ridge gasped and leaped up. The coffee table tipped, sending puzzle pieces skittering.

"I'm sorry," she said, tears brimming. "I'm sorry, but I have to go."

Meg and I converged with Gram and Rosie in the hallway, facing the front door that had just slammed.

Gram removed an oven mitt and pulled aside the filmy curtain covering the door's upper window. Against the golden glow of the streetlamp, a figure hustled away in the direction of the little red cottage.

"Should we go after her?" Meg asked.

Someone already was. A vehicle followed. The headlamps were off, but I recognized the police SUV. I shivered. Ms. Ridge might not be under arrest, but she wasn't free of suspicion.

Gram dropped the curtain. "Goodness, what happened?"

"We told her the title of the stolen book," I said. "The Mary Westmacott."

Rosie said, "That Christie but not a Christie? Why would that freak her out? What's it about?"

"Middle-aged regrets," I said.

"Which are terrifying," Meg added.

"Secrets," said Gram. "Ms. Ridge has those. Unfulfilled dreams. Massive misperceptions and misunderstandings, both personal and cultural."

"People who don't express what they want," Meg said. She added, "And then blame others. It wasn't *all* the protagonist's fault in that story!"

Rosie uttered a lengthy groan. "Okay, fine, but what *happens?*"

I said, "A woman is on a train from Baghdad to Istanbul. The train gets stuck at a remote desert station. She's alone and has run out of books and has nothing to do but think. She comes to unhappy realizations."

Rosie's extreme eye roll nearly toppled her. "Oh my gosh, that sounds like a horror novel without any fun monsters. No wonder Ms. Ridge ran off." She added with teenage overconfidence, "People should stick to nice, solvable mysteries."

✳

CHAPTER 28

Nice Solvable Mysteries

"Where was Simon Trent immediately before he crashed his convertible?" I spoke this as I wrote it in my notebook the next morning. Agatha and I sat in the Reading Lounge. A mug of coffee steamed on the side table. A sunrise in pinks and peach painted the peaks.

My notebook was filling up with far more questions than answers. I underlined the latest question twice, added an exclamation point, pondered, came up with nothing, and penciled in a star.

I might have added a constellation of doodles, but Agatha intervened and attacked my pencil.

I closed the notebook, petted my favorite feline sleuth, and remembered to admire the fleeting solar light show. I'd returned home to my loft and Agatha last night. Gram's guest room was undeniably the best in town, but my digs had their own comforts. Agatha, for one, even if she decided to knead my scalp as I was falling asleep. My tantalizing to-be-read stack and my engrossing current read, so close to the final few chapters. And this, the joy of waking up to a readers' paradise.

I'd angled my seat for the best of both views: the vast, awe-inspiring mountains and the equally awesome wall of books rising to the rafters. Alone with Agatha, I could fantasize that this was our private library, larger and grander than even Morgan Marin's.

Like a library fairy godmother waved her wand, Morgan had said of hers. It hadn't been a magic wand. That library was Cece's biblio-magic.

I still had a hard time merging Ms. Ridge with the mysterious, wealthy Cece. Ms. Ridge had explained her love for Last Word and the Book Chalet. I completely understood that.

I also understood the urge to erase Prescott and his associated problems (such as Simon Trent) from her life. But to cut herself off from her family? Her books? She'd said that Meg and I wouldn't understand, but I wanted to try.

Risking Agatha's annoyance, I got out my phone and typed "Cecelia Carling-Thorne" into the search bar. I'd done this yesterday under the giddy notion that Morgan Marin and I had pinpointed a killer. I hadn't found much then. Now I cringed to find a full page of screaming headlines. "Murderess." "Incognito Killer." "Bookshop Black Widow." "Gone Gondola!"

"Gone gondola, does that even make sense?" I asked Agatha. She frowned at the phone. I tapped a headline from a respected national publication, "She Disappeared in Books." That sounded reasonable.

"No recent photos of Ms. Ridge. That's good," I informed Agatha. The sole photo resembled the one I'd shown Meg yesterday, dated and pixelated. A caption gave the "presumed location" as the Carling-Thorne "family compound."

I glanced around. Could a multigenerational chalet of books on a prime piece of alpine meadowland count as a family compound? To me, a compound implied walls, gates, and more entry checks than our policy of all-bibliophiles-welcome. If that was so, I didn't crave a compound.

As I read, I became certain that I didn't want to be a Carling-Thorne, gobs of old money or not.

"Family disputes, inheritance disputes . . ." I summarized

for Agatha. "Properties, pedigree dogs, racehorses, trusts, all in dispute."

I learned of estranged siblings, chilly patriarchs, and conflicts within the family business, which seemed to involve squashing little companies for fun and profit. Yeesh! Even reading about them made me anxious. There was a little mystery, solved. I understood why Ms. Ridge—Cecelia—would yearn for a quiet life. I got why she changed her name to avoid them too.

I went back to the search results and found a recent article that had dug up details of Cecelia's marriage to Prescott St. James. A whirlwind romance. A private ceremony. A low-key honeymoon. No photos of her, but lots of him. Florid-faced with thick, swooped-back dark hair, he posed with a social set that favored slick suits, sparkly little dresses, and raised flutes of bubbly.

I scanned for a reticent blond but didn't see Cecelia. Where had she been? Home, reading in her library? That's what I would have preferred.

Agatha head-bumped my phone. She took the cat-vs-Internet competition very seriously.

"Yes, yes, I know," I said, rubbing her ears. "But this is important."

It was, I assured myself, shoving aside an icky feeling that I was prying.

Ms. Ridge *said* she was innocent. Meg, Gram, and I had agreed last night. We believed her. Or, to be totally honest, we *wanted* to believe her. We knew one thing for sure: If she was innocent, we needed to help her.

"To do that, we need to understand her," I told Agatha, who was now purring and rubbing her whiskers on my phone case. "Prescott too. Then we might figure out who lured him here and who killed him." I felt that the lurer and killer were the same person, although not necessarily. I forced myself to ponder unpleasant possibilities.

What if Ms. Ridge had written to Prescott and agreed to meet him? That didn't mean she'd killed him. She could have gotten cold feet. Then, after the murder, fear would have kept her hiding at the inn. Fear of the police and the killer.

A new article popped up. A tabloid promising a "rare, newly unearthed photo of the reclusive heiress, Cecelia St. James."

I felt tawdry, but the photographer had been way worse. The shot looked like it had been sneaked through a hedge. Cece sat in a flower garden, partially turned away from the camera. Blond hair floated down her back, so different from her present blunt salt-and-pepper bob. She wore a long, summery dress. Legs leisurely crossed. Face turned down toward an open book.

I thought back to Prescott, slowly pacing our shop. He'd beelined for the blond customer in the cherry-red outfit, hoping she was Cece. Someone special. He'd been eager to see her, yet then he'd hurried off, leaving behind a book that made the real Cece tear up and run off.

I put down my phone and, seeing that Agatha was snoozing, carefully reopened my notebook and added two questions the chief had surely already asked and a third that she probably hadn't.

Where did Prescott go?
Where was Ms. Ridge the night of the murder?
What's up with the Mary Westmacott?

I doodled around the second question. If Ms. Ridge had an alibi for the time of the murder, wouldn't she have said so? Lena might know, but I doubted the innkeeper would tell me. However, the woman in question might. I just wouldn't mention Mary Westmacott books, for now at least.

Agatha grouched when I, her human pillow, rose. I wanted to phone from the shop's landline, thinking I'd have a better chance of Ms. Ridge answering. Who could resist a call from the Book Chalet?

I counted rings. One, two . . . five . . .

Then I remembered the time. Barely seven-thirty. Ms. Ridge was an early riser, but I was still risking rudeness. At nine rings, I was about to hang up when a breathless "Hello?" reached my ears.

"Sorry!" I said by way of greeting. "Good morning, sorry. It's me, Ellie. I know it's early but . . ."

Ms. Ridge assured me that she'd been up for hours. "I was out sweeping the walks."

I smiled, picturing Glynis, grumpily waking to pristine walkways.

Ms. Ridge said, "Then I took some coffee to the deputy sitting outside in his car, but he declined. Poor man. It's too cold to sit out there."

"Deputy Garza?" I asked, warming up my questioning muscles.

A younger junior deputy, Ms. Ridge reported. "Practically a child. I assured him I didn't plan to go anywhere, so he could go get a warm breakfast." She hesitated. "Were you calling about work, Ellie? I want to come up and help, I do, but . . ."

"Probably best you lie low," I assured her. I dove in. "I have some questions I thought only you could answer."

"Oh," Ms. Ridge said. "Is the shop okay?"

Worry sparked. *Was it?* Would I know? Meg had shipped out books and gone by the bank, and I *thought* the utilities were all paid. I blustered that all was great. "I wanted to ask you about Saturday, some details."

Weariness seeped through the phone line. "I told you, I was so shocked to see Prescott that I abandoned Mountains of Mystery."

"And then?" I prompted. "Were you in your cabin the entire time? Did you go out? Maybe thinking you could go back home?"

Ms. Ridge said that she hadn't dared. She'd feared that

Prescott would be there. "Somehow, he knew where I worked. I assumed if he knew that, then he knew *everything*, my new name, my address. So, no, I couldn't go home. I did peek out in the early afternoon, as I told Chief Sunnie. I wanted to stretch my legs and as long as Prescott wasn't around, I thought no one would notice me. Then I noticed *him*."

"Prescott?"

An intake of breath, then, quietly. "No, Simon Trent. The man who recognized me at the inn. He was coming toward the inn, stomping angry. I rushed back to my cabin before he noticed me."

With some prompting, Ms. Ridge estimated the time of Simon's ill-tempered return. She also confirmed what I already knew. That Prescott had hooked Simon Trent into his sketchy financial scheme.

Then she told me something I didn't know.

"Before everything fell apart, Prescott invited Mr. Trent to stay with us at our house here. There's a little—well, not so little—guesthouse on the property. Simon had money to invest, his sister Morgan's money. Prescott promised him pie-in-the-sky returns."

"So, you knew he was related to Morgan Marin?"

A sad sigh came across the line. "Yes. Morgan was thinking about retiring from acting at the time. Simon had the idea she should get into directing movies. I got the impression that she wasn't as enthusiastic. The one nice thing that came out of it was that Morgan visited too and fell in love with Last Word."

By the time Meg arrived a few hours later, I was abuzz with coffee and news.

"Ms. Ridge saw Simon Trent on Saturday," I announced as Meg tugged off a boot. "A little after half past one, she thought. He was returning to L'Auberge, looking angry."

Meg froze, boot in hand. "Interesting. Around the time Prescott got into the fight? A coincidence?"

Or not. Miss Marple would say that coincidences were worth noting. Trying to temper my excitement, I said, "I did some more digging on Simon. He has a record. Disorderly conduct. He got belligerent with a police officer who pulled him over for drunk driving. He pulled a *do you know who my sister is*."

Meg padded toward the storeroom to change into work-wear.

I followed, laying out more incriminating information. "After Prescott was arrested and his investment pyramid crumbled, Simon hounded Cece. Called her. Showed up at her house. Harassed her with legal threats, fake and real. He's one of the reasons she changed her name. She didn't anticipate Morgan moving here too."

I waited until Meg had a fresh mug of coffee in hand to tell her my zinger.

"Simon came to stay in Prescott and Cece's guest cottage. Morgan flew in for a few days as well. Ms. Ridge doesn't recall meeting her. Things were strained between her and Prescott, so she stayed holed up in her library."

Meg cupped her mug in both hands. Steam and the delicious scent of dark roast wafted. She frowned. "But wait . . . You were there when Morgan talked to the chief. Didn't you say that Morgan told Chief Sunnie she hadn't met Prescott?"

I'd been replaying Morgan's words. "Morgan talked about her angry decorator and twenty shades of beige paint. She said her lawyers handled the sale. I don't think she said either way. She didn't exactly lie . . ."

She didn't exactly tell the truth either.

Inconsistencies, Chief Sunnie had told Deputy Garza. Look for the inconsistencies and little lies. I just hoped that the chief was still looking and hadn't settled on her own version of the perfect suspect: Ms. Ridge.

✳

CHAPTER 29

The Old Gang

Fourteen minutes past closing, I held the door for Piper Tuttle. She had her hands full with a stuffed picnic basket, her prize for finding Ms. Ridge. Technically, Agatha had done the finding, but Agatha prized tuna treats more than books.

Meg and I had filled the basket with mysteries old and new, a hefty book of magic, and the mysterious vintage book in Greek. Piper adored the Greek tome, feeling it had a powerful aura. Gram added a tin filled with her famous gingersnaps, and Rosie contributed a coupon for a free homemade birthday cake.

Piper delighted in the books, the cookies, the promise of cake, and the overall developments.

"I feel safer already," she declared in a stage whisper capable of reaching half the hamlet. "Ms. Ridge has to be the frontrunner among murder suspects, which is good news for us. I don't think she'd kill any fellow book club members, do you?"

"No!" Before I could clarify that my "no" encompassed Ms. Ridge as the prime suspect, Piper said, "Let's face facts. It's always—usually—the spouse. That's another reason my divorce was so well timed. I got out before I did something murderous I *might* regret."

She laughed.

I pointed out that Cece had also arranged a well-timed divorce. "She got out before Prescott was arrested and his assets seized."

Piper was undeterred. "What was that funny little sticky note we found in his book? *Love is terrifying?* She might have still loved him enough to kill him. Something to speculate about . . ."

She trilled a goodbye and staggered off with her basket.

I shut the door and turned the sign from OPEN to CLOSED. Then I went to the storeroom and tapped gently.

"Coast is clear," I announced, hoping Ms. Ridge hadn't heard Piper's theories.

Ms. Ridge looked up. She sat in my great-grandmother's rocker with Agatha and a book. Glynis had dropped her off earlier, gleefully reporting that they'd "foiled" police surveillance by leaving out their back doors and driving away.

Ms. Ridge had wanted to stop and let the deputy know, but he'd been napping.

"Thank you, Ellie," she said. "I do appreciate this. I so wanted time with the books and Agatha."

"Thank *you*," I said with a smile. "You've already made Agatha's night."

"I hope you'll have a nice evening," Ms. Ridge said. "You're meeting Sydney? A date?"

I downplayed the date part. "A bunch of us are getting together at Lifties. The old gang."

Ms. Ridge smiled at "old" and said she should let me get ready.

A good idea. Syd had said "around six-thirty," which it would soon be. I needed to change into something nicer that didn't look like I was trying.

"I'll lock up when I leave," Ms. Ridge said.

She had a key, I thought again. Ms. Ridge had no reason to break in. At the top of the stairs, I looked down at the most convincing evidence of Ms. Ridge's innocence: Agatha adored her.

Over an hour later, I twirled a pint glass half-filled with tepid beer, wishing I was home. I'd arrived on the early side of fashionably late. Syd was just plain late. So late that most of the friends I remembered—and some friendly new folks I'd just met—had already left.

I figured that I'd waited so long, I couldn't give up now. Besides, Lifties was one of the few places I'd found that was comfortingly the same.

Ski paraphernalia covered the plank-wood walls. Bartenders with goggle tans jostled and blustered. Noise bounced all around. Chatter, laughter, the bluegrass strumming of a one-man banjo band, and Venessa Upshaw yelling in my ear.

Ven, a year ahead of me in school, was determined to catch me up on everything I'd missed since graduation. *Everything!* By which she meant every marriage, baby, divorce, personal tragedy, and triumph.

I tried to follow along, inserting an occasional *oh, hmmm,* and *uh-huh.*

"Wow," I said, learning of a former classmate's kid who'd made the high-school football team. A child in high school! Here I was, single again and living in my family's loft. A loft I felt an increasing urge to dash home to. Visions of a dreamy evening wafted through my mind. A bubbly soak in the magnificent clawfoot. Flannel PJs. Curling up under the covers with Agatha and my book.

Nope! I'd vowed to get out and reconnect.

The trouble was, I'd never connected with Ven in school. She'd moved in a different crowd, the kind that supplies storylines for popular-clique cheerleading movies. Currently, Ven sold real estate. When she learned I was living in a loft, she gripped my arm and offered to show me places.

I had to disappoint her. I was happy where I was. "For now," I added.

She added me to her email list. "You never know when you'll see something that grabs you. Maybe you'll find that special someone and need a nursery or two, *mmmm*?" She nudged me with a really sharp elbow.

"How about you?" I asked as Ven paused to order another beer from a dimple-chinned bartender. "Are you, ah . . ."

I generally dreaded interrogations about my relationship status. Ven was delighted to report that she was one-year single. Finally, we had something in common.

"So great," she said, gulping down a third of her pint.

"Liberating," I said.

"I can go out all night whenever I please."

I can read in bed all night with my cat . . . "Cheers to that," I said.

Another acquaintance, Isa Goldberry née Duran, joined us, to an automatic glass of Pinot and flirtations from the bartender. With some prompting from Ven, Isa recalled that we'd been in the same class.

"Oh, yes, of course. You were that quiet girl who was always reading at football games?"

I nodded, as quiet girls do, even if it wasn't quite true. The "always reading"? Okay, exaggerated but valid. But always reading at *football*? I could count the number of football matches (or was it games?) I'd attended on a single hand. I'd had better things to do. Like staying home to read.

"Ellie works at the *book*store," Ven said. "That pretty chalet at the end of the hamlet? Location, location, location, that place is a *gem*! She and her sister witnessed the murder. She just moved back. She's single. Syd invited her." Ven and Isa shared a look I couldn't interpret. I'd never been good at reading cool-girl.

"Not here, is he?" Isa observed dryly.

"Typical," Ven said. "Not my problem. Not anymore."

Oh. Okay, I got the look. "Syd and I have just been catching up," I said. "We happened to bump into each other at . . . er, something."

"At the crime scene," Ven clarified. "Isn't this murder just awful? I had an out-of-state homebuyer pull out of a deal. He said the town was tarnished. Terrible about Syd's dad being suspected again too. Has to have Syd down."

Isa sipped her wine and shrugged. "Syd used to be such *fun*."

Ven snorted. "You mean *rich*? That's why *you* chased after him."

They drifted back to high school glory days before moving on to Isa's husband, a man who worked too much, but that was okay with Isa. She wanted to merge two bedrooms to create her own "closet retreat." Ven was "soooo into that."

I thought of Syd's game again, gathering points for extreme fun. He might not be rich, but he had his passion and his business dreams. Better than working overtime for an extreme closet.

Said the woman with no closets, I acknowledged, although my loft did have a massive magic-portal-worthy armoire. Plus, I got to sleep above a bookshop. *Location, location, location!* I decided that Syd and I had it pretty good. Just as I thought this, Ven squealed.

"Sydney Z, there you are! You're keeping Ellie here up past her bedtime."

I remembered why Ven and I hadn't been great pals.

Isa looked away, twinkling at the bartender.

"Hey!" Syd was rosy-cheeked, beaming, and accompanied by a pal with a self-assured strut. The other guy looked familiar.

"Sorry we're late," Syd said, swiping two chairs from a nearby table. "Demetrious and I had to crush Bookman's Peak."

Ah, Demetrious. The waiter from the pizza restaurant. He was nearly unrecognizable in his ski gear. I waved across the table and turned my nodding and appreciative sounds to Demetrious's rendition of their accomplishments. They'd ripped. They'd shredded. They'd totally destroyed, etc., etc.

"You boys!" Ven said.

"Living the life," Syd said. He inched his seat over to mine, turning more serious. "Hey, sorry I'm late, El. You doing okay? Cecelia—I mean, Ms. Ridge—hasn't bothered you, has she? If you ever feel worried or threatened, you can call me." He grinned. "I'll ski down any slope to get there."

"No," I said, and wanted to say more, to thank him, to stand up for Ms. Ridge's character and—I hoped—her innocence. To ask about his dad too. I hadn't seen Rusty since we'd found Ms. Ridge and her link to Prescott St. James.

Demetrious clanged a spoon to a glass.

"Next round's on . . ." Demetrious drew out the pause and suspense. "Syd, the man!" Laughter and whoops rose.

Syd grinned, stood, and bowed. "On me!" he said, raising his glass.

"What are we celebrating?" Ven asked. "Oh, Sydney, if you're selling that land of yours, you need a realtor. I can get you *millions.*" She batted mascara-heavy eyes.

At the mention of millions, Isa tuned back in.

Hadn't they just been bad-mouthing Syd as no fun anymore? Oh, right, they'd been bashing his lack of money.

Syd snorted. "Selling? In your dreams, Ven. Demetrious and I have our first big investor."

More whoops. We all clinked glasses.

A while later, when the din lowered to a loud hum, I asked Syd. "Who's your investor? Or is it a secret?"

He combed back strawberry-blond locks. Blue eyes gleamed. Leaning in, he said, "Simon Trent. Didn't I tell you? Perfect candidate! The guy can be annoying, but he's smart enough to invest in a solid concept."

"Oh," I said weakly and then tried again with enthusiasm. "That's great. Fabulous!"

Great unless Simon was a killer.

"What?" Syd said, eyeing me.

I wasn't about to burst his excitement with my wishful Simon-is-a-murderer thinking. "Sorry," I said. "I guess Ven was right. I'm tired, not used to late nights. Tell me about your run. You and Demetrious went down Bookman's Peak? That's a sheer drop-off!"

"Sure is. It was dusk by the time we climbed to the top. Figured we'd take the fastest way down. Wanna see?" He got out his phone and opened a video he said came from his helmet cam. I leaned in close. The video had an eerie night-vision quality. A headlamp beam zigzagged and bounded. Boulders loomed all around like crouching giants. At some points, the light sailed out over nothing. In another, it flipped. He'd been airborne and upside down.

He turned it off. "Awesome, right?"

I sat back, woozy. "That gave me vertigo just looking at it."

This delighted Syd. "Best run I've ever done."

Other friends came in. Talk drifted to people I didn't know and events I'd missed. I had a lot of catching up to do. Stifling another yawn, I assured myself that I couldn't do it all in one night.

I touched Syd's elbow. "This has been great, but I'm beat. I think I'm going to head back."

Syd had just ordered a basket of wings. He flagged the bartender and asked for the order to be put on hold. "I'll walk with you."

"No, thanks, I'm fine," I insisted. "Enjoy your wings." It was a short walk, a nice night with gentle snow and streetlamps to light the way.

"Yeah? What about the killer that's still out there?"

Put that way, I accepted.

*

CHAPTER 30

Under the Weather

The night was beautifully silent, tucked under clouds resting so low they brushed the rooftops. Snowflakes floated as if waltzing. Syd bubbled on about his good fortune with Simon Trent, how they'd skied to his favorite "secret" rock-climbing spot, far from the crowds.

"His own private adventure, the real deal," Syd said. "He loved it, but he can't handle the climbs or the altitude. So, I pitched the helicopter concept again. With a 'copter, he could access the best of the backcountry and prime powder all day long."

"Yeah," I said, thinking of peaceful fluffy white snow fleeing under thumping rotors. We were strolling past L'Auberge when I heard something. Not loud or thumping, but out of place.

I stopped. As soon as I did, the sound vanished.

"Did you hear that?" I asked. "Like a moan?"

"Probably wildlife. A raccoon? Deer will be hungry with all this snow." Syd put his arm through mine and said, jokingly, "Or that murderer I'm heroically protecting you from."

I stalled. The noise came again, a low grunt. A growl? "I think it's coming from L'Auberge, the back garden."

"I don't think you're welcome there. You or your cat."

Syd was right, but if I was already banned, I couldn't get

more banned, could I? "I'm just going to peek. You can go back to Lifties. Honestly, I'm fine. Go get those wings." I slipped my arm from his and opened the gate, grateful for its well-oiled silence.

"Eat wings? While you get mauled by a mad moose or a murderer? No way. If you're going in, so am I."

"Thanks," I said, not trying to hide my relief. We walked in silence, my eyes scanning, ears grasping. Another moan. Did moose moan? I didn't think so.

When we reached the boulder blocking the view of the cabin, Syd touched my elbow.

"Uh, El, what if we're busting up someone's romantic evening? Maybe we make a tactful retreat."

The sound came again. It didn't sound like sweet romance.

Telling myself I'd only die of embarrassment if we crashed a honeymoon, I stepped around the boulder. Steam circled the hot-spring pool, but the sight was all too clear. A person lay on the slick rocks. His head hung dangerously close to the water.

Syd rushed by and fell to his knees in front of the body. "El, call 911!" A blurt of cursing and then an anguished cry. "It's Simon!"

I jabbed out 911 with shaky fingers, three times before I believed the phone's comeback: no reception.

The inn. I'd call from inside.

Moments later, I ran along the dark, coiled path, absurdly thinking of Agatha Christie. Her characters couldn't summon help with a handy cellphone either. They had to dash next door, to the next manor, the next village. They sent servants running over moors or cranked up Model Ts and chugged off in slow motion, which was how I felt.

It would be okay, I prayed. Syd knew first aid. He was a volunteer for mountain rescue. He'd yelled out Simon's symptoms earlier so I could relay them. Disoriented, possible head contusion. I repeated them like a chant so I wouldn't forget.

Bursting out from under snow-heavy pines, I skidded to a stop and checked the phone again. A single bar wavered. I pressed the three numbers. To my joy, rings wobbled. I jogged on until I reached the inn's imposing front door.

The icy metal knob slipped in my palm. A lock held it firm. I was banging a silver knocker when both the door and the phone line opened simultaneously.

"Last Word emergency services. What is your emergency?" asked a disembodied phone voice.

"Ellie Christie, what on earth is your urgency?" Lena demanded. "Tell me it is not about your cat."

I answered them both in urgent staccato. "Medical emergency! Back garden of L'Auberge, the upper hamlet. Hurry!" Even as the words came out, I questioned them. Medical emergency sounded like a heart attack or stroke. Meg and I had hoped the same for Prescott St. James. We'd been dead wrong.

Lena gasped and whipped around, leaving me with the sound of her footsteps thudding down the hall.

Shivering, I answered the operator's questions. Name. Address. Phone number. Details I didn't know about Simon Trent.

"Is the subject still breathing?" the operator asked.

I hoped so. I told the operator I'd call back. By the time I returned to the serene pool, Lena was wrapping a still body in blankets. Syd sat back on his heels, head in his hands.

"Hey," I said gently, reaching out and touching his shoulder. "I got through. Help is coming."

Help would be a while, winding up the mountain in the snow.

I said, "I need to go back and give the 911 operator more information. What should I tell him?"

Syd listed symptoms in a stunned monotone.

Simon Trent was breathing, but unconscious.

"Could be an overdose?" Syd speculated. "Or hypother-mia? Heartbeat's low. Skin's kinda bluish. There's a gash on his head too. Maybe he fell?"

Or maybe someone struck him.

CHAPTER 31

✳

Room at the Inn

Sirens converged, the wail of an ambulance and the *whoop-whoop* of the police.

Chief Sunnie stomped in after the EMTs. She wore her earflap cap, enough outerwear for an Arctic expedition, and a frown. She wanted Syd, Lena, and me out of the way yet waiting nearby.

I'd already guessed that. I was becoming a pro non-witnessing witness.

Syd slumped off down the path. Poor Syd. I was grateful he'd been with me. I couldn't have called 911 and tried to help Simon at the same time. On the other hand, if he hadn't been so gallant about walking me home, he'd still be at Lifties, spinning ski stories as big as fish tales, dreaming of helicopters and his key investor.

I prayed that Simon would recover, for his sake, of course, but also for Syd's. For mine too. I felt awful. I'd pretty much hoped the man was a murderer.

He still could be, hissed my mystery-reader mind. Killers faced medical emergencies just like the rest of us.

At the risk of sounding rude, I asked the chief why *she* was here. "Do you think it wasn't a health problem or an accident?"

Chief Sunnie drew a breath. I waited for a variant of "I cannot discuss an ongoing inquiry."

She puffed a frosty sigh. "You tell me. You and your friend called this in. What were *you* thinking?"

I shuffled my boots, scraping a messy sunburst pattern in the snow.

"Yeah, I thought so," the chief said.

"I read a lot of mysteries," I said in my defense. "I have a suspicious mind. There is still a murderer walking around."

The chief said, "I have a suspicious mind too."

We stood in mutual suspicion, watching as the EMTs bundled Simon Trent onto a stretcher. Running in, they'd barked questions.

Did Simon have any known health conditions? Did he take medications? Use drugs?

Syd didn't know. Lena said he had lactose intolerance but ate many croissants.

There were other conditions, though. Invisible ones. A murderer might try to escape soul-squeezing guilt. I didn't know Simon, but I couldn't see him as the overly contrite type.

"So, why'd you come back here?" the chief asked as stretcher legs clacked into place.

I told her about Syd walking me home. "I heard something, like a moan. Syd thought it might be a romantic evening. Or wildlife. A deer or moose—"

Chief Sunnie muttered that she *still* hadn't seen a moose.

I scuffed at more snow. "Maybe you don't want to. They're dangerous. Tourists think they're cute, but moose attacks are more common than bear or mountain lion attacks."

The chief frowned.

Now I felt bad for being a downer—a downer at a possible crime scene, no less. I offered, "They're amazing from a distance!"

The chief sighed. "Go find your friend and wait inside. Tell the innkeeper I said so if she gives you any trouble. I'm not going to be responsible for frozen witnesses."

The EMTs hurried past, pushing a stretcher that skidded in the snow. The chief strode after them.

I held back. I couldn't tromp around a potential crime scene, but I could look from where I stood.

Steam rose languidly. Smoke whispered from the chimney. Someone was staying in the cabin. Simon?

After we'd found Ms. Ridge, I'd peeked at the L'Auberge website and been stunned by the cabin's nightly rate, the highest among the exorbitant others. Our customer Daphne had said that Simon had been pestering Lena for upgrades. Maybe he'd gotten one.

I took a step. I could just peek inside . . .

A tapping sound stopped me cold. Harsh, like a woodpecker attacking glass. I looked around. Trees, boulders, darkness, steam, snowflakes . . . Then I looked up.

A face peered down from a second-story window, shrouded in white. For a second, my heart skipped. I quickly realized that I wasn't seeing my first apparition. Rather, I'd been spotted by a gossip columnist, wrapped up for a spa.

Piper stopped tapping and started gesturing. A white towel towered above her head. A fluffy robe rose to her chin. Her desire was clear. She wanted me inside, where the chief wanted me too.

More than ever, I yearned to run home to Agatha, cozy quilts, and quiet books.

Yet I also needed to know. Why was Piper here? What had she seen? What was going on?

Before my boots crossed the threshold, Piper rattled off similar questions.

"Ohhh . . . Ellie, what'd you see? Were you following the killer? Who did it?"

Piper had removed the towel, leaving her hair in damp spikes. She still wore the robe and matching woolly slippers. "Is he dead? Was it another murder? Oh. My. Goodness! Mountains of Mystery predicted *two* dead men. Poor, poor Morgan. She'll feel awful that she never reunited with Simon. We could summon his spirit and let her say her good-byes."

"He's not dead," I interjected. *Not yet.*

Piper patted her hair demurely. "Well, he *looked* dead when I saw all the commotion," she said, and switched the subject back to me. "So? What drew *you* here? Were you looking into him too?"

I caught the "too," but answered her questions first. "I was walking home from Lifties. I heard something odd." I stood on a doormat that seemed too precious for boots and took in the space. I hadn't been inside the inn since Lena's posh redo. The air smelled of pine and vanilla. Rough-hewn timbers criss-crossed pale plaster walls and a fire crackled in a fireplace sized for giants.

"Walking home with a certain *friend*?" Piper twinkled. "Aw, a second date?"

"We met up with a bunch of friends," I said, thus avoiding any labeling or numbering. "Have you seen Syd?"

Piper tightened her robe sash. "He's in the drawing room. Poor dear is rattled, understandably. You look like you need a boost too. Follow me. Lena stocks a fabulous bar."

The drawing room. I imagined finding Poirot there, ready to lay out the workings of his little gray cells. My little gray cells felt shaken and muddled.

We found no Poirot preening his mustache, a pity since the drawing room was a perfect setting for a big reveal. I took in moody oil paintings, dark timbers, and tall French doors, overlooking spotlighted aspens and a small burbling pool. Syd stood facing the windows. His reflection looked back at me, grim-faced.

"Drinks," Piper proclaimed, beelining toward a well-stocked bar cart.

Piper poured a glass of something clear and handed it to Syd. She was about to do the same for me.

"Is there sherry?" I asked quickly. It sounded like something Miss Marple would choose, sweet and restorative.

Piper was still searching bottles when Lena breezed in with a cut-glass decanter.

"Port?" the innkeeper inquired.

"Close enough," said Piper.

Lena poured some for herself and then me. All of us except Syd took seats in the leather armchairs. It would have been cozy, except for the circumstances. I sipped and sipped some more. Then I asked. "Piper, what are *you* doing here?"

"Same as you, I suspect," Piper said, winking. "Snooping around Simon Trent. I decided to get myself an up-close view."

Lena huffed. "You said you were here for the restorative waters and spa services. I knew you were fibbing."

"Not a fib," Piper said. "Your spa is lovely, Lena, and I do feel restored. I feel the glow of a big-time scoop." She patted her cheeks, which did have a rosy dewiness.

I leaned forward eagerly. "What did you see?"

Syd turned expectantly. Even Lena looked like she wanted to hear.

Unexpectedly, Piper clammed up.

"What?" Lena asked in clear exasperation. "Oh, come, Piper, you spill everything. Tell us. I cannot have my inn associated with crime and criminal business. This *must* be solved."

Syd came over to refill my glass and his. "She didn't see anything," he whispered, leaning close to my ear. "If she did, why didn't *she* call the police?"

Piper did have excellent hearing. She sat up straighter. "Fine. I was trying to spare Ellie's feelings."

My feelings?

"Ellie's?" Syd said. "What's Ellie have to do with this?"

Piper downed the rest of her glass. "Ellie, I know you want a certain someone to be innocent, but I'm afraid they're not." She held her glass out for Syd to top up. "I looked outside from my very lovely room a little bit before seven. I had my facial and spa session at seven, so I know the time exactly." She diverged into spa treatments. She'd enjoyed a soak, a massage, and she recommended that Lena look into mud minerals.

My pulse quickened. *Just say it!*

Someone said it for me, with authority. "Who'd you see?" Chief Sunnie stood in the doorway. She'd either moved silently or I'd been deafened by the blood thumping between my ears.

Piper drew out her moment of witnessing glory. "Who'd I see, visiting Simon Trent's luxury cabin? Mr. Trent, who had recognized said person when no one else did . . . or would admit to?"

My stomach dropped. Rosie's *dun, dun, dun* drummed in my head as the name came out. All the names.

"Katherine Ridge. Or, I should say, Cecelia 'Cece' Carling-Thorne St. James?" Piper shook her head. "For once, I am sorry to be so right."

Lena gasped. Syd cursed.

The chief was unmoved. "Can't be," she said firmly. "Ridge is down at her house. I have a deputy watching."

I couldn't keep in my groan. All eyes turned to me. The chief raised an eyebrow.

I took a bolstering sip of port, which suddenly tasted sour. "Ms. Ridge came up to spend some time in the Book Chalet this evening. She got a ride with her neighbor, Glynis, and was there when I left. She's probably still there now."

But I knew what the chief was thinking. I was thinking it too. Ms. Ridge might indeed be there now, but she could have easily dropped by the inn for an unfriendly visit.

✳

An Arresting Development

Ms. Ridge dozed in the Reading Lounge to the glow of a table lamp. Agatha snoozed on her lap. A book rested on her chest, closed to protect its spine.

"See?" I whispered to Chief Sunnie, who'd insisted on both tiptoeing and excluding Piper Tuttle and all others. "Our cat trusts her. She's tender with books."

The chief cleared her throat.

Ms. Ridge blinked awake with fluttery apologies. "Ellie, you're back. Sorry, I should get out of your hair. Oh, Chief Sundstrom. Is everything all right?"

I opened my mouth.

The chief raised a silencing hand. "Did you go out this evening, ma'am?"

"Yes," Ms. Ridge said calmly. "I went—"

The chief had told me to be silent, but I couldn't stop myself. A warning came tumbling out. "Ms. Ridge, don't say anything. Piper Tuttle knows a lawyer. She says he's good but expensive, but you could probably afford him and—"

Ms. Ridge smiled gently and rubbed Agatha's ears. "Ellie, thank you, but I'm fine telling the chief what I did this evening. I did step out. I went over to the inn. Why? What's happening?"

The chief looked delighted. I was not.

"Let's talk about your visit first," the chief said. "Why did you go?"

Ms. Ridge scratched Agatha's chin. They both frowned. "It was very odd," Ms. Ridge said. "A man called from the inn, saying I'd left some personal items at the cabin and was to come retrieve them immediately. I didn't recall leaving anything."

"Okay," the chief said. "What happened next?"

I felt like we were at a very dangerous story hour.

Ms. Ridge said, "Next? That was even odder. I went back to the cabin, but it looked occupied. I didn't want to intrude, so I peeked in the window and, well . . ."

She hesitated, looking like she might just heed my remain-silent advice. Then she took a deep breath and said, "I saw a blue snowsuit draped over the sofa. Like something I'd seen Mr. Trent wear. I . . . Oh, honestly, I thought I'd been tricked. He's been after me for money he thinks I owe him. He's been very rude and insistent."

"I see," the chief said. She was about to say more when I butted in.

"And then you came right back here?" I said, raising my eyebrows, willing her to agree.

The chief sighed, seemingly resigned to my defense of Ms. Ridge.

Ms. Ridge said she had returned. "I was upset, but Agatha came to sit with me. We've been reading." Ms. Ridge gently lifted her reading companion in preparation for getting up herself.

Agatha scowled hard at me. *It's not my fault,* I wanted to tell her. *I'm trying!*

"I've overstayed," Ms. Ridge said. "I'll take the gondola down and say hello to Rusty if he's there."

"How about I give you a ride?" the chief said. "I'd like to hear more about your interactions with Simon Trent."

Ms. Ridge brushed kitty fluff from her dark slacks. "Do I have to? What's going on? I'm not under arrest, am I?"

The chief's smile was frighteningly pleasant. "No, ma'am, no one's under arrest. For now."

Agatha and I watched them go. Piper Tuttle, her spa robe poking out from a puffer jacket, jogged behind them.

"For now," I repeated to Agatha. Ms. Ridge wasn't under arrest, but not for long, I feared. I called Meg with the grim news and put up no protest when she insisted that I come down and stay with them.

"Do you want me to come up and ride back down with you?" Meg asked.

I laughed off the idea. "I can get to the gondola station on my own. I'm not worried." But on my way, I didn't casually stroll and let my mind wander. Glynis would have been proud. I armed myself with a pointy-tipped hiking stick and strode briskly, scanning my surroundings until I was safe in my glass bubble, floating down to Gram's.

* * *

The next morning, Gram was as bright as I was bleary.

"Good or bad news first?" Gram asked as I entered the kitchen, again lured from my bed by tempting scents of coffee and baked goods.

Meg poured me an extra-large mug of coffee and refilled her own.

"Good?" I needed coffee before a jolt of bad news.

"Good choice," Gram said. "Mr. Trent is alive, although he's still unconscious." Gram then launched into the trail of contacts through which she'd learned this. I took the opportunity to gulp coffee. Alive was very good. Unconscious? Not so great.

"Was that the bad news?" I asked. "That he hasn't regained consciousness?"

Meg ducked the question by checking the oven. I glimpsed two full trays of muffins. She and Gram were on a comfort-baking binge. Which could mean really bad news.

Gram fussed with her apron ties. "Yes, that is bad news, you're right. There's more, though. I probably should have said immediately. Ms. Ridge was arrested late last night."

I processed this as Gram acknowledged another long list of informants. A bird-watcher with a police scanner who'd called a woman in Gram's knitting circle, who'd group-texted half the town. Gram had called Lottie Nez over at the jail, who'd confirmed it.

Gram wrapped up with, "And then Glynis Goodman texted Meg this morning."

"Which is why we made muffins," Meg said. She brought out two trays of plump golden muffins. "For Ms. Ridge, if she gets out of jail, and as a thank-you for Glynis. She texted me, insisting she has vital information."

Meg left the muffins to cool and handed me her phone, the screen open to a text.

Glynis texted like she spoke. Direly.

First message: **Arrest all wrong. Come see me. Vital clue!**

Second message: **Hahahaha. Vital clue! In a book, I'd be dead when you get here. Better hurry!!**

She'd added a smiley face emoji, the kind that's disturbingly laughing and weeping simultaneously.

"Oh my gosh, should we go right now?" I asked.

Gram dipped muffins in melted butter, followed by a dunk in cinnamon sugar. "Glynis will be okay while we finish our breakfast," she said. "She's protected herself by acknowledging the threat. When fictional characters announce a vital clue, they never seem to realize they're tempting a murderer. That's where they go wrong."

That made sense, kind of. More than that, Glynis seemed like she could hold her own against any predator.

"Donut muffins," Gram said, plunking down a platter. "The recipe says they're French, but I have doubts."

I took a bite and had no doubt they were delicious.

Later, Meg and I set out with a bag of muffins big enough to serve as a defensive weapon. As we approached Ms. Ridge's house, the front door swung open at the cottage next door. Mint green with eggplant-purple trim and pristinely shoveled sidewalks.

"Not murdered and chopped up to pieces yet!" Glynis crowed triumphantly. She practically skipped down her front steps in her big purple parka.

Meg and I expressed relief.

"Let 'em try," Glynis declared, scowling around defiantly.

Meg handed over the bag of muffins. Glynis dove right in, to the breakfast treat and her vital information.

"Come with me," she said, in between bites. "You Christies will appreciate this, even if our big-city chief failed to leap on the significance. I took photos, but I want you to back up my deductions."

Glynis led us around to the back of the little red cottage, where she stopped abruptly at the stoop.

"Observe," she said. "About three inches of snow on that railing, am I right?"

Meg and I agreed.

"Now look at those porch boards. What do you see?"

"Snow?" I ventured.

"Less snow?" Meg added quickly when Glynis glared.

"Exactly! As you know, I drove Katherine Ridge up to your bookshop so she could hang out with your cat and books last night."

We nodded. Glynis described how she'd then spent the evening at the pizza place with her friend Barb. We learned what they'd ordered. How it had gotten late without Glynis realizing. They had been having such a good time talking.

A date? I hoped so and couldn't be impatient with Glynis for veering from relevant information. She was happy and not thinking about dead bodies for once.

"Then I get home," Glynis said. "It had been snowing, so I think I'll come over and shovel out Katherine's place before she gets back. What do I find?" She pointed to the porch. "Already shoveled and *swept*! The snow you see is from overnight, but when I got back, it looked like this." She extracted a phone from her purple pockets and displayed a photo of bare porch boards.

She said, excitedly, "They swept to the back alley and left the broom out by the garage. Katherine would never leave the broom out there. What's that tell you?"

I asked, "Could it have been another neighbor?"

Glynis thought little of her neighbors' snow-clearing abilities and ambitions. "No, this was nefarious brooming. I think they broke in. See? Can you see over to the lock? Scratches! Then they brushed away all their footprints, thinking they'd cover up their presence. 'Cept it didn't work. The absence of snow tipped me off."

But what would a thief want from Ms. Ridge? Now, we knew that she had money, but her home had seemed humble. I thought about our burglary. Half to myself, I murmured, "Did they steal a book?"

Glynis clapped her hands. "You're good, even though you're totally wrong. They *left* a book, from what I gather. Katherine let the police search her place, see? She came back with the chief and that deputy a while after I got home. She likely thought she had nothing to hide. Well . . . the deputy got looking on her shelves, pulled out a book, and it was downhill to arrest-ville from there. Katherine looked thunderstruck."

Glynis then mused about the word "thunderstruck" and

whether lightning-struck would be more accurate. "Zapped, that's how she looked."

In my shock, I forgot that I was supposed to keep mum about the Westmacott. "A book was stolen from our shop! Did the book have a light green cover?"

Glynis confirmed that it did.

Wise Meg asked the key question. "How do you know all this, Glynis?"

Glynis burst into a grin. "Lace curtains, like I said before. Anyone can look right in those things. They're an invitation and I accepted."

✳

CHAPTER 33

Chance of Sunny

M eg and I rode to the hamlet in silence. My sister gazed out the window. I opened my notebook, filling a page with yet more questions adorned in underlines, stars, and no answers.

Who swept the back walk at Ms. Ridge's?
Who left and/or planted the book?
Where are the satchel and notes?
What happened to Simon?

I should have simply soaked in the serenity, because Meg and I didn't receive a sunny welcome at the upper station.

Rusty Zeller stomped out of his hut. His hair was mussed, his eyes tired but flaming. "I knew it, didn't I? I said that Katherine Ridge was a quiet woman who wanted to be left to her own business. Now look at her—exposed, maligned, accused."

"Rusty," Meg said, stepping away from slowly circling gondolas. "We only wanted to make sure she was okay."

The track rumbled overhead. Rusty grumbled louder. "She's not okay, is she? That poor woman, the whole town whipping up wild, unfounded falsities."

What could we say? Sorry? I was sorry, but that didn't help prove Ms. Ridge's innocence. Neither would pat assurances that the truth would prevail. If Glynis was right, then Ms. Ridge had been cleverly framed.

I thought of the questions filling my notebook.

One fit the moment: Who knew that Ms. Ridge was Cece?

Simon Trent had recognized Cece. Now he was in the hospital.

I'd penciled in another name too. That person was standing right here, casting recriminations on us.

"You knew, didn't you?" I asked.

Rusty looked away, resolutely waving to a party of six piling out of a gondola. When an empty gondola followed, he muttered, "I just said, didn't I? Everyone knows that poor woman's troubles."

I restated so there was no way he could feign miscomprehension. "Rusty, you knew that Ms. Ridge was Cecelia St. James, the wife of your former business partner. Why didn't you tell us when we were looking for her?"

It occurred to me that I could be treading dangerously. Rusty had been the first suspect and for good reason. Lying didn't bolster his claim to innocence in my mind.

Rusty's chest puffed. I steeled myself for an outburst. Then his broad shoulders slumped. He nodded toward his glass hut and trudged back, sagging heavily into his swivel chair. Meg and I stood just outside.

My eyes swept around the little space. His whiteboard and notes, filled with quotes and inspirations from books. A stack of books. Nero Wolfe, Tony Hillerman, and a guide to orchid propagation.

Crazy for mysteries, Syd had said of his dad. A man who knew mysteries could plot a devious crime. He might even try to throw us off track by feigning concern for the new prime suspect.

"Okay," he said grudgingly. "Yeah, I knew she was Cece. But what if I'd told you gals? Would you have kept her secret? Hindered a murder investigation? I couldn't put that burden on you." He smiled sadly. "Can't have my favorite bookshop shut down because you go to jail."

Rusty's gravelly voice dipped low. "Truth is, I was glad you were looking. I was worried that she might have been hurt too. Or worse . . ."

Meg murmured soothing understandings.

I asked, "Do the police know?" If not, Meg and I would still be burdened with doing the right thing. How would I explain it to Syd?

His head dropped. "Yeah, I told 'em after you found her. The chief seemed pretty ticked, especially after I'd half fibbed about recognizing Prescott."

"*Half* fibbed?" Meg asked.

"I couldn't recognize him in that photo they showed me the night of the murder. My mind refused to comprehend. He shouldn't have been here, for one. He didn't look like himself either. He'd *aged*. Plus, he was, you know, dead."

Rusty straightened to a height looming above us. "I didn't lie to the police about Katherine Ridge, though. They never asked about her."

"*We* asked about Ms. Ridge," Meg said.

Rusty rumbled again. "And I told you straight—I didn't know where she was."

"I get it," I said quickly. "No one asked the right questions."

Rather, no one asked the exact words. So, yes, Rusty may not have technically lied about Ms. Ridge, but he'd hidden something big.

"That's right!" he said. "It wasn't my place to tell Cece's secret."

Meg made more comforting sounds. I wished we'd brought an extra bag of the French donut muffins.

With gentle prompting from Meg, Rusty recalled the mo-ment he'd realized that Ms. Ridge was Cece. "It's a wonder I didn't startle right out of my boots. She'd been working at your shop for almost a year. Driving up to the hamlet and back, not taking the gondola. Her hair tricked me—gone natural gray and that plain cut. Different clothes too. But mostly, I wasn't expecting to see her, not back here and not working at your shop."

I empathized. Seeing people out of place always challenged my memory.

Rusty was saying he'd been so shocked he walked off. "Then one day, I was at the Chalet. No one else was around but us. I said, 'Cece,' and she shook her head no. 'Okay' was all I said. Eventually, she started riding the gondola. We'd say 'hello' and 'nice weather' and whatnot. I thought, if that's how it's gotta be, I'll take it. Made me sad, though. I'd like to think we were friends, back before. We used to talk books."

Now that Rusty was talking, all Meg and I had to do was nod. He continued on, fondly recalling how they'd shared books. "If she read a book she thought I'd like, she'd lend it to me. I'd find notes inside. When I was done reading, I'd send it back with my own notes."

"Notes?" Meg and I said as one. I thought of the notes we'd found in Prescott's satchel, and uncertainty gnawed up my middle. Had we uncovered more evidence pointing to Ms. Ridge, the woman we were trying to help?

Rusty blustered again. "Now, don't go twisting nice things. She'd mention the plot or a character or a turn of phrase. Bookish stuff. We never cheated on our spouses, even if hers ended up in the federal pen and mine ran off with a stockbroker."

Syd hadn't mentioned his mother. I should have asked, or asked Gram for the backstory. Rusty was saying Syd had blamed him for that. "I blamed myself too."

The phone rang in the hut. Rusty pivoted in his chair, turning his back pointedly to us.

Meg and I went on our way, me kicking at snowdrifts. "For a morning that started with donut muffins, this day's not going great."

"That means it has to get better," Meg said. She listed positives. The sun was shining. Birds were singing. We'd ask Sadie to put Italian hot cocoa on the specials menu again, and Gram and Rosie planned to come up after Rosie's school let out.

"We have Glynis on Ms. Ridge's side now too," Meg said. "If Glynis can come around to believe in Ms. Ridge's innocence, so can the chief."

Meg was great at selling the sunny side. I let myself believe until we neared the Book Chalet.

A stout figure in a flap-eared cap waited outside. Chief Sunnie flashed a smile so cheery it scared me.

"I have something I want you to see," she said, waving her phone. "I know you won't like it, but being smart, logical women, I think you'll agree, it's a case changer."

Meg let us in. Agatha issued a loud meow, then turned tail for her breakfast room.

The chief stepped to the nearest display table and placed her phone on a stack of true crime, apologizing for the small screen. "We can have you visit the station and see the item in person, if you'd like."

I could guess what we'd see. A book with a pale green cover.

The chief scrolled slowly through images of just that.

I let Meg answer. "That *looks* like one of the stolen items."

I appreciated Meg's emphasis on "looks."

The chief had more photos. "Thought you'd appreciate the copyright and publishing details, and didn't you say there was a water stain? Like this? Oh, and that special signature too."

We nodded glumly. All matched the stolen book.

"We already heard that you found a book in Ms. Ridge's home," I said. "Someone else could have planted it there."

Chief Sunnie's smile turned indulgent. "Yes, yes, I heard about the reverse burglar who leaves books and helpfully sweeps sidewalks. I'm assuming you talked to her neighbor? I'm keeping an open mind."

While piling up evidence.

"What about the other items? The satchel and notes?" I asked.

"Glad you asked," the chief said. She swiped to another photo. "The only sticky note we found was this one. Garza discovered it under a chair, like it might've fallen. Made his day, let me tell you." She asked if the note looked familiar.

"Love is indeed terrifying," Meg read weakly.

"Yep," the chief said. She reported they hadn't found the black satchel or the rest of the notes. "I have this theory. Our suspect—your friend—ditched the bag and notes. Being a big-time book lover, she couldn't part with that special, signed book."

The chief watched our reactions. I hoped, for once, my thoughts weren't as clear as large print.

What she said made awful sense. The Ms. Ridge I knew (or thought I knew) would never hurt a book.

She wouldn't hurt a person either.

"What does Ms. Ridge say?" Meg asked.

The chief shrugged. "She's taken your advice and gotten that lawyer. He's good, I hear, but so are my experts. Once I get their reports, I can move on with additional charges."

The chief was sharing way more than usual. She was trying to convince us. Was she also trying to convince herself?

Something else occurred to me. "Additional charges? What is she charged with now?"

"Burglary. The break-in at your bookshop. That's all for the time being. I don't like to rush a murder charge."

When Meg stammered protests, the chief held up a palm.

"You reported a crime. You don't get to pick your culprit. When I get the tox report and analysis of Mr. Trent's contusions, I expect I'll be adding murder and attempted murder."

Meg repeated the words. "Attempted murder? Tox report? Contusions?"

I'd been at the scene of another crime? I didn't want to believe it. "There's no chance that he accidentally hurt himself? An overdose or trip and fall or . . ." My list wasn't filled with happy options, but they were better than attempted murder.

The chief acknowledged the possibility. "His symptoms suggested some kind of drug overdose, possibly a tranquilizer. Not opiate-based, since his symptoms didn't respond to Narcan treatment."

I opened my mouth for a rebuttal. I'd recently read that tranquilizer abuse was on the rise, even in little Last Word.

The chief read my mind. "I know, folks hide and lie about addictions. However, Mr. Trent's acquaintances swear up, down, and sideways that his only substance vice is being a top-tier wine snob. Won't touch anything that wasn't plucked from an old French vine. Then there's the physical evidence, enough to make Deputy Garza's heart go pitter-patter."

She described more than I wanted to know about signs that Simon Trent had been dragged out to the pool.

"Good you and your friend found him when you did," she said, heading for the door. "Let's hope he wakes up. Then it's only attempted murder."

"I was wrong," Meg said when the chief was gone. "Today is not getting better."

I felt the need to step up as the positive sibling. "There's still lots of time for it to improve. And, hey, Ms. Ridge isn't arrested for murder. That's good news."

By noon, however, I still wasn't seeing much chance of good news.

Rosie and Gram arrived a little after the cuckoos had tucked back into their clocks. Gram had been on the phone half the morning.

"Folks I hadn't heard from in ages were calling out of the blue," Gram said, tsking at their ill manners. "Not fair-weather friends but gossip-weather friends. Some reporters tried to trick me into talking too. I had to take the phone off the hook."

Rosie's school had let out early, but she wasn't having a great day either. A mean-girl type had teased her about being friends with a murderess.

"You *have* to clear Ms. Ridge," Rosie said. "People are saying awful things about her!"

Meg assured her, we would if we could.

Then an unlikely bearer of joy arrived. Renée-Claude swept inside and cut off a customer heading for me and the cash register.

"Morgan wishes to see you at three," she announced. "She wants you to take charge of the . . ." She waved a bothered hand. "The murderess's books, in the library. She needs them sorted, gone. You can be there?"

Our invitation to Morgan Marin's library.

Meg appeared at my side. "We'll be there," she said.

✳

CHAPTER 34

Like a Box of Chocolates

"Tactical error." I glanced anxiously at the cuckoo clock in the storeroom. We were due at Morgan's in half an hour. The error? None of us had a car. I'd been borrowing Gram's old Subaru for out-of-town errand runs. The Subaru sat serenely in Gram's garage. Gram, Meg, and barista Sadie had all arrived by gondola. An influx of customers—and a new rush of gossipers—had delayed our exit.

"No worries," Meg said, reaching for snowshoes I'd considered antique decoration. As a kid, I'd played with them, their paddles so wide, you walked like a drunk duck.

Not that I wouldn't benefit from a brisk waddle, but . . . "Doesn't Morgan live way up the road?"

Meg slung a pair over her shoulder. "Far away by car because of the switchbacks, but practically next door if we take the trail. There's a new spur trail that goes up that way. Rattlers Cove Connector."

The name didn't exactly inspire eagerness, but rattlesnakes would be hibernating, I reminded myself. We changed into boots and layers, anticipating a sweaty effort.

Before we left, Gram took us aside. "Don't worry, I'll watch out for Rosie. You be careful too. I don't think Ms. Ridge did this, especially the burglary. She'd be much stealthier."

Rosie met us at the front door, where she beckoned us close and whispered, "I've got an eye on Gram." She thrust fists to her hips. "Watch your backs! Don't accept rides or drinks from strangers!"

Meg kissed her. "We're just going to see a library."

"I want text check-ins on the half hours," Rosie demanded. She gave me a cool-aunt fist bump.

They both waved from the bay window as we set off, carrying the snowshoes over our shoulders, frames clacking like wooden teeth.

"Role reversal," Meg said. "My teenager is demanding check-ins."

I laughed, and we chatted about Rosie until we reached the chocolate shop.

Meg stopped.

I breathed in divine scents of sugar and chocolate. My mind turned to a fight. "This is where Prescott got into that scuffle."

"It's also where the connector trail starts," Meg said. "Through the passage and up the hill."

We stood and pondered, and then Meg had two good ideas. "We could get a box of chocolates for Morgan," she said. "And chat with Keiko, the chocolatier?"

On cue, Keiko stepped out. "Sold out," she announced cheerily, folding up her sidewalk signboard.

Meg made introductions. "Keiko, this is my sister, Ellie, back in the book roost. El, this is Keiko Mori, chocolate wizard." Meg added that we were on our way to see Morgan's library.

"Lucky you!" Keiko mimed heart-thudding swooning. "I've only seen it on Shelf Indulgence. Beyond beautiful! I'd climb any mountain to see it."

I would too. I told my legs that they better not fail me.

Meg forged ahead with our non-chocolate-related mission. "We heard you witnessed an incident the other day."

Keiko shuddered. "Thank goodness, nothing like the incidents you've been witnessing."

Or failing to witness. "Did you remember anything about the other person involved?" I asked.

Keiko hadn't. "My assistant won't go back there to take out the trash anymore, but I heard the police made an arrest, so we don't have to worry."

Keiko, I guessed, kept her mind to sweeter topics. She was telling Meg how it had been salted-caramel truffle day. Now I really felt bad that we'd missed out. Morgan surely would have shared with us.

Meg expressed similar regrets. "We hoped to take a box to Morgan."

Keiko was backing in her door, signboard in arms.

"She gets lots of chocolate," Keiko said with a wink. "Always with a card too, 'Sweets for the sweet, with a ponderosity of affection.'"

"A ponderosity?" I mused.

Meg was more concerned with the time. "Ready for a cardio workout?"

No.

I looked down the street and recognized a familiar face. "What about hitching a ride?" Before Meg could answer, I took off at an awkward jog, snowshoes clacking over my shoulder.

An older, beat-up SUV was stopped at the intersection, waiting for pedestrians to cross.

As I panted my way up—clearly in need of cardio training—Syd rolled down the window. He smiled but looked drained. "Hey, El, I was going to call you. I can't believe any of this. You must be even more freaked. Do you think she did it?"

I was making a case for Ms. Ridge's innocence when Meg jogged up.

"Hi, Syd," Meg said, sounding not at all out of breath. She touched my arm. "El, we're going to be late. It's all uphill."

I didn't even have to ask.

Syd said, "Uphill? I'm going that way. Need a lift?"

We gratefully accepted. At Meg's urging, I climbed in the front. Syd apologized for the mess in the back. He was off to meet Demetrious for backwoods boarding that involved climbing and plunging. Gear was mounded in the back. Helmet, cleats, hooks, ropes, picks, clips, headlamps, and a veritable wardrobe of jackets, socks, boots, and hats. Meg squeezed in next to a snowboard.

"Where to?" Syd asked. "Unless you want to come along? I've got extra gear, but I warn you, we're gonna push ourselves. Outdoor therapy, that's what I need."

No, thanks! I recalled my wooziness just looking at Syd's video last night. I buckled up and announced that we were off to extreme-library therapy.

Meg gave directions. "Morgan Marin's. She's just around the second big hairpin."

Syd made unsure sounds.

"Prescott St. James's old place," I said.

That, Syd knew. We accelerated upward with me gripping the chicken bar.

"You've probably seen the library?" I asked to distract myself from the drop-off just below my window. "Cecelia St. James designed it."

We skidded around a bend, Syd driving with a casual single hand.

"I went to the house a few times, sure," Syd said. "Man, seems like ages ago. Must have been in high school, the last time I was there. After that, it was college and a gap year. Man, that year was the best. Demetrious and I, we hit all the big slopes. Vancouver, the Alps . . . Then . . ."

Then Prescott went to jail, and Rusty almost did too, along with losing the family fortune.

Syd frowned. "I can't remember seeing a library there. I didn't come up much. Prescott mostly came over to our place."

No one could forget a library like that, I assured myself, not even a ski-obsessed high-schooler.

"We upset your dad this morning about Ms. Ridge," I confessed.

Syd frowned. "Yeah, well, *I'm* upset if Ms. Ridge, or Cece, did what everyone's saying. Why's Dad upset with *you*?"

"He's upset *for* Ms. Ridge," I said. "He thinks she's innocent and we stirred up trouble for her."

"What? You were trying to help her. She was the one lying." Syd surged around a hairpin. I decided it wasn't a good moment to tell him that his father had been keeping Ms. Ridge's secret too.

The road leveled out to a new-to-me view. Mansions had sprouted in former forestland, enclosed by grand gates and rustic log fences.

Thinking I'd introduce a happier topic, I mentioned the fences. Syd's hands left the wheel in exasperation.

"Old-timers made fences like that because split rails were all they had. Do you know how much a log fence costs now? More than we make, I bet. All so the wealthy can pretend to be 'rustic' and 'western.'"

We wheeled around another bend and slid to a stop in front of an elaborately scrolled metal gate framed in tall timbers.

Syd huffed. "Don't get me started on gates."

He'd started himself. "Ranch gates were built tall like that to guide visitors to remote properties. Now . . ." He glared out at the artistic landscaping. Boulders. Blue spruce. A gate that could block three lanes of traffic and admit giraffes. "Now they're fancy keep-out signs."

He leaned back and sighed. "Sorry. Guess I'm on edge

today. After what happened to Prescott and then not being able to help Simon . . ."

"Simon will be okay," I assured him, with no basis other than hope.

Syd seemed unconvinced. "But thanks for thinking the best. I'll try to do the same. I know you like Ms. Ridge and don't want her to be guilty."

We climbed out, shouldering our unused snowshoes and thanking Syd.

He leaned out the window. "I'm also still hoping for that ski date, El." The SUV rattled off, his arm waving out the window.

"Ohhh . . ." Meg said, nudging me.

I ignored her and concentrated on keeping my grin tamped down.

We approached the gate. Down a long, winding lane, I could just make out the snowy peak of a roofline and smoke curling above.

Meg stepped up to a panel with a flashing red light. She was lowering her mouth to the intercom when the screen flashed on with Morgan's face. Meg jumped back. We both waved.

"Christie sisters, my daring book detectives! You're here! Come rescue my library!"

The gate buzzed. The screen went blank, but not before Morgan's voice said in a rush, "Stay where you are. Renée-Claude will collect you. Renée, don't leave my favorite book-sellers out in the cold. Hurry, hurry!"

Favorite booksellers. There was a bit of sunshine. I couldn't help smiling, and when I glanced at Meg, she was too.

✳

CHAPTER 35

A Clue in the Library

"My dears, prepare yourselves. The library is a mess. A horrible, awful, frightful mess." Morgan led us across a great room that lived up to its name. She too had a wall of windows, hers facing the sunsets. A flagstone fireplace rose to meet log-beamed ceilings. The furniture was creamy suede and the rugs seemed too fluffy and pristine to tread on, even in the brand-new "house slippers" Morgan provided us.

Along the way, I glimpsed a chef's kitchen in marble and metal. We passed by a den, a media room, and museum-lit art before arriving at a solid wood door.

"The library," Morgan announced. "Look away from the clutter."

Meg and I gasped, not from a mess.

"Gorgeous," I breathed. Floor-to-ceiling shelves with wooden roller ladders. A cushioned window seat overlooking a mountain view. Plump chairs in leather and velvety fabrics, artfully draped with throw blankets.

Gram sure could get a lot of reading and dozing work done here.

Morgan swooped past. "That nice Officer Garza offered to put everything back, but I said, 'I cannot have the murderess's aura lingering.'"

That broke my spell. I stopped gaping at the library's beauty, and the gaps glared back. Empty sores on the shelves. Books piled unceremoniously in a corner.

"There's been no arrest for the murder." I would have said more, but Renée-Claude returned from parking the SUV in which she'd driven us and our snowshoes a few hundred yards.

"It is true," Renée-Claude said grimly. "The killer could still be close among us." She flicked the end of a thundercloud-gray linen scarf and announced she must respond to fan mail. "So much mail. Always too much."

"Remember to be *me* this time," Morgan called after her. She tsked. "Renée replied to lovely Quebecois fans recently and told them—in French I'd never know to use—that I was preparing to 'endure' a long winter of 'frigid isolation.' A tabloid got hold of that letter and declared me depressed, loveless, and tipping toward cabin-fever insanity. One must be very careful dealing with fans."

"Yes, I imagine," said Meg, who'd warned me to tread carefully among the famous.

Morgan led us to the stacked books. "These have Cece signatures or inscriptions to her. I know, I know, they're books, and books are innocent, but they give me a *bad* feeling."

I couldn't argue with feelings, especially since Morgan didn't want to trash the books. "You can have them all, free of course. Sell them, donate them, whatever you like as long as I'm not involved."

Morgan turned on her glowing smile. "Then we'll have *fun* filling up all this shelf space. I warned Renée-Claude, we'll have to take a wagon to the Book Chalet."

I liked the sound of that.

Morgan waved at an entire north wall. "These books came with the house. Deputy Garza looked about but he couldn't take the time to inspect every book."

"What was he looking for?" I asked.

Morgan was vague on that. "Notes? A writing sample from Cece? I set out a few, but he wanted to look for more."

I guessed he'd wanted to linger.

Meg asked for details about the notes. "Anything you can remember might help."

Morgan described them as "this and that." "Some were lists of characters, keeping track while she read. I do that sometimes, if the book doesn't provide a list. Others seemed to be comments or quotes or things like 'you'll like this' and 'don't you love so-and-so' or 'doesn't she seem guilty?' Like she was talking to someone else while reading. Rather off-putting."

Meg said, "She shared her books with a friend, like a private reading club."

"That's a relief," Morgan exclaimed. "Deputy Garza suggested she might have multiple personalities, including a murderous one." Her mood dipped quickly. "Someone's hiding their murderous self, though, and Ms. Ridge was in hiding. I'm just thankful that Simon is hanging on. We have our differences, but I don't want to see him hurt."

Meg and I said how sorry we were about Simon.

I added, "Ms. Ridge says she didn't see Simon at the inn, let alone hurt him. Hopefully, he'll regain consciousness soon and can tell the police what happened."

Morgan sighed. "Not to sound too harsh, darlings, but I wouldn't count on my half brother being helpful." She turned to go. "I must check on Renée-Claude and make sure she's being *nice*. I'll have her bring tea by in an hour or so. She has no stamina for letter-writing. She becomes increasingly ill-tempered."

I wasn't sure I wanted ill-tempered tea. However, I was eager to get started.

"What's our strategy?" I asked Meg.

"Let's double-check each book for anything personal or handwritten. Maybe we'll find more notes."

Some forty-five minutes later, we'd found several Cece bookplates, a few character lists and quotes from books, as well as a shopping list suggesting holiday baking. Cinnamon, cloves, brown sugar, and molasses. We'd also found books with signatures by famous authors, some quite valuable. Meg set them aside to show Morgan.

The library was more than good looks. It had an impressive collection too. I couldn't understand how Ms. Ridge had left it behind.

"We should wait to remove these books," I said, eyeing the growing stacks. "When Ms. Ridge is cleared, Morgan might feel differently. Maybe she'll even return them to Ms. Ridge?"

Meg looked up. "I wonder if Ms. Ridge would want them? She left them before. Perhaps they gave *her* a bad feeling."

I frowned.

"Not the books, of course. Morgan's right, the books are blameless, but you know how you remember where and when you've read certain books? Especially if it was somewhere special or during an exceptional time?"

I did. Scents or music swept some people time-traveling into memories. Books did that to me. I could recall what I'd read on my first international flight, the book I'd wept over beside Gramps's hospital bed, happy books binged on beaches and long-distance rail trips.

I could see how Ms. Ridge might not want them. In that case, we'd find the books good homes.

We worked on, me climbing the ladder to reach the upper shelves. I didn't look down, fearful of another vertigo swirl. I was about to descend empty-handed when I noticed a paperback shoved behind hardbacks. The cover was well worn and the pages yellowed. Inside was a folded note. I leaned on the ladder and held my breath as I unfolded the paper.

In novels, this would be the moment. The final book, revealing the case-solving clue.

"Anything interesting?" Meg called up.

"Butter, oats, raisins, brown sugar."

Ever supportive, Meg said, "Ms. Ridge makes wonderful oatmeal raisin cookies. Maybe she and Cece aren't that different."

Hardly the clue to prove her innocence. I climbed down and browsed the other shelves. Morgan's acting trophies rested among decorative items. Pretty glass paperweights. Porcelain teapots. Framed photos of Morgan at parties and ceremonies. There were unusual objects too. A glass slipper and long lace gloves. Antique hats that would usually be hidden away in attics. I liked that Morgan kept hers out.

There was a familiar one as well. The feathered hat Morgan had worn to "inhabit" Emily Trefusis. A hat is transformative, she'd said. I looked around. A gilt-framed mirror hung by the door. Carefully—guiltily—I lifted the hat, took it to the mirror, and hovered it just over my head. I angled and turned and failed to transform into an Agatha Christie super-sleuth.

Something seemed off, and not just my hair, floaty with static in the warm indoor air. I thought back to Saturday morning, to Prescott barging into book club, and Morgan disdainfully bored, fussing with the hat.

"Feathers," I murmured.

"Is that a curse? Like Gram says 'sugar'?" Meg sat cross-legged on the floor, reading rather than searching inside a book.

I replaced the hat in its spot. Blocking it from Meg's view with my body, I asked, "When Morgan arrived at Mountains of Mystery on Saturday, where were the feathers on her hat?"

"Feathers?" Meg frowned. "I'm not sure."

I urged her to try to recall. "It's important."

Meg's face squinched so dramatically her glasses tilted. "Maybe here, on the side?" She gestured above her left ear. "I remember thinking it would make a great kitty toy." Meg closed her book. "Why?"

I needed Rosie to sing her big-reveal song. Instead, I stepped aside and pointed urgently. "Feathers on *both* sides. Remember? Morgan repositioned them when Prescott was interrupting the book club."

"Okay." Meg raised eyebrows at the hat with its two tufts of feathers.

"Right," I said. "Exactly, but remember when Piper showed us the photo from Morgan's Shelf Indulgence chat? The hat had a single tuft. I'm sure of it because I was thinking of Agatha and feathery toys too." I grabbed my phone and scrolled back through Morgan's posts. The photos took agonizingly long to load. Finally, I found the one I wanted.

Meg looked, agreed, and said, "Yes, but El, it's nothing nefarious. She probably used an older photo. I find that unsettling about social media. You never know what's real, what people are actually doing, or where they are."

I lowered my voice to a hissy whisper. "Shelf Indulgence is her *alibi*."

I stared at the photo. It didn't change. I reread the caption. *Well, such is life in the wilderness! Heroic, darling Renée-Claude is working to fix . . .*

Morgan gushed praise on everyone. Everyone except her long-suffering assistant. I read aloud to Meg. "Does this sound like Morgan or is it—"

"It sounds like you will leave, immediately."

Those words—like the caption—came straight from Renée-Claude.

✳

CHAPTER 36

Dishonored Guests

Renée-Claude herded us to the door. I felt like a misbehaving child, padding away in slippers and shame, banished from my dream library.

Morgan stood in the foyer, greeting a guest who'd brought smiles and chocolates rather than suspicions.

"Christies!" Emmet Jackson exclaimed, brushing snow from a caped oilskin coat reminiscent of a wild-west Sherlock Holmes. "I hear you're adding invaluable shelf space to the library. I was just, ah, delivering a poem."

He placed a box of chocolates on the sideboard and twirled the ends of his handlebar mustache. Several days of stubble fluffed around his chin.

Morgan peeked under the chocolate-box lid. "A mixed selection, how sweet. I love a surprise."

Sweets for the sweet, Keiko had said. And something about "ponderosity." I kicked myself for not recognizing Emmet's voice in that.

So, he'd been bringing Morgan chocolate? For a moment, I worried about his tender feelings. Poor sweet man, hauling chocolate up the mountain for a woman far beyond his reach. Then I remembered how strenuously Morgan had defended Emmet.

Glynis's words came back too. She'd blatantly hinted that Emmet wasn't the lonely cowpoke his poems portrayed. And what else had she said? The last to know about a secret were those thinking they were keeping it?

"You brought a new poem too?" Morgan said. "Cowboy poetry, my favorite! Emmet, darling, come in and join us for tea. Would Miss Calamity like anything? Renée-Claude, did you stock us up on more organic carrots?"

Renée-Claude jerked her head toward the door, indicating that she wanted Morgan to follow. I expected Morgan to balk, but something passed between her and her assistant. The two stepped out to the wide porch, Morgan trilling hello to "dear, sweet Calamity."

Before the door shut, I glimpsed the little dappled pony. She was hitched to a railing and chewing industriously on her lead.

Emmet, Meg, and I made stiff small talk about the weather until Meg cleverly brought up an easy topic.

"How's Calamity?" Meg asked.

Emmet reported that the pony had been clamoring for a hike. "Nothing the old girl likes better than a walk in the woods on a snowy day. I think she's part Icelandic pony."

Emmet then regaled us with a tale of trying to put Janet into a sweater. "That garment came all the way from the Faroe Islands. Handmade. Did she care? Took off every button and spit 'em out, then started unraveling the yarn."

I had to smile, even if my coat did sport a pony-bite repair patch, expertly sewn on by Gram. I saw an opening for a question too. "Do you two hike up this way a lot?"

"We amble all over, like troubadours of the forest," Emmet said. He'd again dodged a direct answer, but I guessed they visited enough to deplete Morgan's carrot supply.

Morgan returned, rubbing her arms to warm them, followed by a chilly Renée-Claude.

Meg quickly switched the subject to books. "We found some amazing items on your shelves, Morgan. We set aside author-signed copies that would make a fine collection, and you have a wonderful variety of mysteries and—"

"Renée-Claude said you were questioning a photograph I posed for, for Shelf Indulgence," Morgan said. She sounded wounded.

I'd been prepared for a chiding, even anger. Wounded hurt so much more.

"No, no," I protested. "I was just trying to work out when it was taken because, ah . . . your hair. Your bob looked so convincing at Mountains of Mystery. I could have sworn you'd gotten it cut. Did you do the styling yourself?"

Morgan patted her curls, bouncing at her shoulders as they had in the photo. "I did, with Renée's help with the pins and gel. The photo you saw for my club was a day old, I'll admit." She laughed. "A younger me, innocent, before I knew of the hair-pulling frustration of video-upload troubles. You caught me, Ellie. Lock me up and throw away my social-media keys."

We laughed way too heartily, all of us except Renée-Claude.

"I had to show the Shelf Indulgers something," Renée-Claude said tersely. "That horrid weather and the video system, unmanageable. So I posted the photo. It is no crime."

"Right, of course," I said, thinking they were both quite focused on crime. Kettle calling the pot black, I chided myself. We Christies had been pretty fixated on murder and clues too. So far, it had only brought more trouble, to us and especially Ms. Ridge.

"And a gorgeous photo it was," Emmet said heartily.

Morgan called him a doll. "Of course I was here for my own book club," she added. "I'd never, ever miss it, right, Renée?"

"Yes, *oui*, I can affirm she was here. Very much always here," Renée-Claude said firmly.

"I can too," Emmet said, stepping defensively to Morgan's side. "I dropped by beforehand to wish her a beautiful and book-filled evening. That's why I was delayed getting down to my poetry event. That and the accident, of course."

Morgan's smile faltered a second. Then she looped her arm around Emmet's waist and kissed him on the cheek. He blushed furiously.

"Emmet, you're such a sweet," Morgan declared. "Speaking of sweet, let's have some chocolates, shall we? Ellie, Meg, will you stay or do you have to run back to my favorite bookshop? I must get photos at the shop sometime. Renée-Claude, we'll have to set it up."

Renée-Claude remained stone-faced.

"When all this is over, of course," Morgan added briskly. "I can't think of making any appointments until then. It's all been so emotionally disruptive. You understand."

I thought I understood all too clearly. She'd be by for that promotional photo op if and when we backed off.

Meg and I stayed long enough to explain our sorting method.

"You'll have lots of empty spaces for new books," Meg said, in bookseller mode. "We'll be happy to help remove the others whenever you like. We could also put them back, arranged by author. There may be new developments in the case that will change your feelings."

Morgan walked us out to the porch. Calamity perked her ears.

"My dears," Morgan said, as we hefted our snowshoes. "Speaking of my feelings . . . I hope you'll respect the sensitivity of my relationship with Emmet. That darling man thinks he's protecting *me* by keeping our fledgling romance private. I'm protecting him. He has no idea how cruel and intrusive the world can be."

Meg and I nodded.

"I can't have Emmet hurt," Morgan said in a steely tone. "I won't."

Meg and I kept nodding. We didn't want to see Emmet hurt either, although both he and Morgan had only raised my suspicions.

"Then we do understand each other," Morgan said, smiling again. "I knew we would. Thank you for all your hard work in the library. You've done a brilliant job, simply marvelous." She beamed and blew air kisses before the door shut behind her.

Calamity Janet gave a mocking raspberry as we passed.

"Were we just threatened or bribed?" I asked when we reached the trail.

"Threatened with compliments?" Meg shuddered. "I didn't like the feeling back there."

I didn't either.

We hurried, carrying our snowshoes to make better time. Boots, snowshoes, skis, and pony hooves had tamped down the trail before us. Along the way, we met a group of hikers, a friendly gray jay, and an Abert's squirrel with tall tufted ears. Those tufts and the squirrel's scolding chittering reminded me of the feathered hat and how I should have kept quiet, at least until we were out of Morgan's home.

"Sorry," I said, as we neared the hamlet.

"Why are you sorry?" Meg asked, grasping on to a spindly sapling to navigate a steep, icy patch.

I inched along behind. "You warned me to be careful around famous people, and you were right."

"Rosie and Gram warned us to be careful around possible suspects," Meg said. "Do you think that includes Emmet and Morgan? I can see why Morgan would gloss over her alibi. Everyone was saying she had one. She just didn't correct them."

Giving up on inching, I let go and jogged down the steep patch. Meg braced herself and caught me, a nice feeling.

I thanked my big sis and said, "Did you notice how Morgan looked surprised when Emmet said he'd been with her?"

Meg had. "Her assistant isn't a rock-solid alibi either."

Not the alibi of thousands that we'd assumed. If Morgan hadn't been home, where had she been?

Meg and I reached the passage between the chocolate shop and the oxygen bar. Now we knew that Emmet came this way often, buying sweets and trekking up the trail. He could have encountered Prescott here and confronted him.

When we came out on the other side of the narrow passage, I spotted Daphne, our visiting customer who yearned to spot Morgan Marin.

Maybe she already had . . .

Meg was eager to get back to the shop and help Gram and Rosie close up. I promised her I'd catch up and waited to chat with Daphne.

Daphne merrily recounted what a lovely time she'd been having. Hikes, sledding, gondola rides just for fun, and loads of reading.

"The perfect extended vacation. Well, except for the murder and the almost murder at our inn . . ." She reported that Lena had comped their extra days of stay and given them free spa services too. "It's definitely a vacation to remember, just not all of it good."

I stressed the good parts. "Plus, didn't you say you might have seen Morgan Marin too? The night of the big blizzard?"

"The night of the *murder*?" Daphne specified. "I really thought it was her. Then I realized that she would have been at her book club."

"They say everyone has a twin somewhere," I said. "Where did you see this person?"

"My husband and I were at the fondue place over there," Daphne said, pointing down the street. "The Morgan *twin* was on this side of the street, going toward L'Auberge. That's when my heart skipped—Morgan Marin, at my inn! I was already plotting how I'd casually bump into her, me having an arm-load of Shelf Indulgence books she might like to sign."

Daphne rolled her eyes at herself. "Silly. Of course it wasn't her. She doesn't need an inn, unless she knows someone stay-ing there." Daphne brightened. "Maybe I still have a chance of bumping into her. I should always carry a book!"

"Good policy." I forced a smile. Morgan did know someone staying there. Her estranged brother. Her brother who'd sped down the mountain around the time of the murder and who now lay in the hospital unconscious.

Morgan supposedly had no contact with Simon, yet they shared more than a blood bond. They'd both been swindled by Prescott St. James. That gave them a motive for murder, and now it seemed that they'd both been nearby when that murder occurred.

✳

CHAPTER 37

Clues and Confession

Rosie greeted me when I returned to the Chalet. My niece held Agatha in her arms, the cat's paws draped over her left shoulder. She turned so I could see them both frown.

"Hi!" I said with extra cheer.

Rosie said, "Agatha got stalked by selfie-takers trying to get her in their photos. I've been protecting her by carrying her around."

I reached to scratch behind Agatha's ear. "Poor baby." Agatha purred. Now to soothe my favorite niece. "And? Why are you frowning?"

"Mom's lying," Rosie said. "She said nothing happened at Morgan Marin's library, but Mom's a terrible liar. Worse than Gram."

"What about me?" I asked, curious where I fell on the family fibbing scale.

Rosie eyed me. "That depends. What'd you guys find at Morgan Marin's?"

Ah, a test. Meg must have been evasive, and I knew why. We had nothing firm, and what mother wants her fourteen-year-old dwelling on murder? I went with a partial truth.

"We didn't get anything to go *dun, dun, dun* about."

Rosie said, "You're cheating by kind of telling me the truth, aren't you? You guys are so easy to read. Gram'll tell me. We're going home to make dinner."

Chili was on the menu, I was happy to hear. Rosie was making cornbread. "With real corn. Later!"

Gram and Rosie left a few minutes later, rustling in their winter jackets. Gram, like Rosie, issued a trendy fist bump and another "later."

"I'm in favor of grandmotherly hugs," I said to Meg after they'd gone.

"I'm in favor of a daughter who isn't quite so clever," Meg said.

Uh-huh, sure. Rosie was right, her mother was a very bad liar.

Unlike Morgan Marin.

I told Meg what I'd learned from Daphne as we closed up, tidied up, and spoiled Agatha with cuddles and a fishy dinner. We were getting into our jackets when we interrupted each other in another burst of sisterly sync.

"I've been thinking—" I started.

"I don't know if this is a good idea—" Meg began.

I deferred to her seniority and because my idea, although the right thing to do, could possibly go terribly wrong for us.

Meg took a deep breath. "We have to call Chief Sunnie and tell her about Morgan and Emmet."

Exactly what I'd been thinking.

Meg said, "The risk is that Morgan finds out and we become her least favorite local bookstore."

Yep, but then I knew that Meg and I were in accord about something more important too. No matter the repercussions, we *had* to spill everything we knew. We couldn't risk an innocent person taking the blame.

* * *

I called Chief Sunnie on her personal cellphone number.

"Good timing," the chief said after I blurted out that we

had information. "I'm up at the gondola station. Meet me there?"

"It's Ellie," I remembered to say. "Ellie Christie, and Meg too. From the Book Chalet?"

"I know," she said patiently. "Who else would be offering up clues?"

We kissed Agatha's frowny face for good luck. "If this all goes wrong and the shop suffers, you'll have to become a full-time feline influencer," I told her.

Agatha turned tail and stalked off toward the lounge.

Meg laughed. "She probably has the case all figured out. If only we could ask her."

She had seen the burglar. Someone who scared her. She'd given us that clue.

Meg and I walked swiftly before we could change our minds. We found Chief Sunnie inside, leaning on the doorframe to Rusty's glass hut. He spun in his chair in agitated quarter circles, creating such a stir, the sticky notes fringing his whiteboard fluttered.

Meg and I slowed our pace to hesitant.

Rusty's voice rumbled out, scratchy and gruff. "That's crazy. Illogical." He spotted us and bolted upright, filling the small station hut. If I'd been Chief Sunnie, I would have backed away.

If anything, Chief Sunnie looked more casual. She turned almost languidly in her bulky winter gear. For once, her earflapped hat was perfectly level. She nodded to us.

Rusty blustered. "Ellie and Meg'll tell you. You gals know Ms. Ridge. She's a good person by any name. She wouldn't harm a soul."

I murmured agreement. Meg nodded enthusiastically.

The chief eased from the doorway. "Okay, then. Meg, Ellie, how about you two ride down with me and tell me about Katherine Ridge? I know, we've already talked, but sometimes new details emerge."

I realized what she was doing. And thank goodness! If we'd flagged her down in a public place, gossip would get around. Everyone would know we'd spilled something, including Morgan.

"Either that or we schedule an interview at the station," Chief Sunnie said sternly, either well acted or gruffly heartfelt, I couldn't tell.

"The gondola," Meg said. "We'll tell you all about how kind and generous Ms. Ridge is."

"Come on, then," Chief Sunnie said. "Let's go."

The chief, Meg, and I made our way toward the gondolas, with Rusty trailing behind us, rumbling affirmations of Ms. Ridge's good nature.

The chief stutter-stepped alongside a moving gondola before plunging in. Meg and I slid into the seat opposite, for a view of Rusty stomping back toward his hut.

Our glass capsule chugged to the edge and dipped in a merry plummet.

The chief exhaled. "I'm no fan of that roller-coaster bit. Garza tells me I'll get used to it."

"Let's hope," I said, thinking of my own pesky vertigo swirl.

"So?" Chief Sunnie prompted. "What do you know?"

Meg and I shared a where-to-start look.

"You found the hat," Meg whispered.

Like the gondola, I plunged right in. I told the chief about our visit to Morgan's library. Meg described our book searches.

I took over to explain the hat. "Morgan's vintage beret, which she'd worn to Mountains of Mystery the day of the murder. I tried it on—held it over my head—and I realized the feathers were different and—"

Chief Sunnie half rose from her seat. If we hadn't been swinging in the sky, I'd have thought she was bolting from my rambling story.

Meg stiffened beside me, and I realized what was happening.

We'd stopped. The gondola hung in midair, slightly swaying.

"What's going on?" The chief frowned up, back, forward, and suspiciously down.

"Ah, routine?" I suggested. Except the last time we'd gotten stuck in a gondola, the reason had been anything but routine.

Meg offered other innocent explanations. "Sometimes people ask the gondolier to stop the line so they can load on a baby stroller, a wheelchair, a reluctant dog . . ."

The chief sat back down with on-alert stiffness. "Okay, so you're in a library with a hat. Tell me the rest. We appear to have time."

Time or not, I hurried. I wanted the words out. I told her about Emmet and the box of chocolates. About Morgan, possibly absent from her online book chat, and Renée-Claude, who impersonated her boss in fan mail. I ended with Daphne, seeing someone who looked like Morgan Marin entering Simon Trent's inn around the time of the murder.

I returned to Morgan's Shelf Indulgence chat. "She gets thousands of participants. It's a big deal. If she'd been home, I can't see why she'd let Renée-Claude write the posts. Renée-Claude was supposed to be fixing the video problem—if there actually was one."

I took a breath. There, I'd said it.

The chief said, "Renée-Claude gave her boss an alibi before. That's not new. But now you say Emmet Jackson did as well? First I'm hearing of it. He told me he went from his house, straight down to the base village, delayed by that accident."

Meg said hesitantly, "Please keep this quiet, if you can, especially about where you heard it. Emmet and Morgan are, uh, dating? He might have just said that to be gallant."

The chief mulled this in silence. Meg got out her phone to text Rosie that we might be late. I looked out the window. From where we hung, I could see the cliffs where I'd gotten stuck as a kid, goaded down by my supposed friend. In the dusk, the boulders loomed like crouching giants, the spaces between as dark as infinite drop-offs. I scanned the ledges, trying to find "ours."

Maybe it was looking back in time that got me. The airy vertigo swirl struck. I gripped the edge of my seat, closed my eyes, and waited for it to pass.

When I opened my eyes, Chief Sunnie was keenly assessing me. "You okay?"

"Ellie?" Meg looked up, concerned.

I put on what I hoped was a firm smile. "Vertigo. Hopefully, Deputy Garza is right and it goes away."

The chief groaned. The gondola stuttered and then began to glide. I felt like cheering. We were moving on. Meg and I could move on too. We'd told the chief what we knew.

I swiveled in my seat and gazed toward our destination. That's when I saw it, emerging from a grove of aspens, dark against the snow and the bone-white bark.

"A moose!" I jabbed at the glass. "Chief, look!"

She scrambled up. Meg did too. The gondola swung.

The bull moose took off at a gangly lope. Before the chief could spot it, we passed directly overhead. "He's underneath," I said. "Wait, maybe we'll see him on the other side."

A grove of pines blocked the view. The moose was gone. Or running below us. I pictured him laughing like a wily cartoon character.

"Shoot!" Chief Sunnie slumped back. "I'll never see one."

The chief's pocket rang. She dug out her phone and barked, "Sundstrom."

I looked out into the dusky landscape, pretending I wasn't

listening. It was impossible not to hear. The gloomy mumble on the other end sounded like Deputy Garza.

"What?" the chief demanded incredulously. "Rusty Zeller? I just talked to the man. I was standing right in front of him."

More muffled glum.

Then the chief: "To the murder? What about to the assault on Simon Trent?"

I gave up on manners and stared. Meg did the same.

The chief had turned in her seat, staring up toward the hamlet. "All right, hold him there. I'm on the gondola. I'll loop back up. Wait for me."

Garza was still talking when she hung up.

She turned back, her expression a mix of disbelief and elation. "I suppose you got the gist of that?"

"Rusty Zeller confessed?" Meg said, incredulous.

"No," I protested. "That makes no sense. Why?" I sounded like Rusty had, just minutes ago, stammering about the illogic of it all.

Meg and I staggered out at the base station.

"I don't believe it," I said as we stood, stunned, watching the chief and her gondola head back up the mountain. "Do you think he did it? He was so upset about Ms. Ridge. Could he be trying to help her?"

Meg shivered. "It's no help to anyone if he lets a killer go free."

CHAPTER 38

That Feeling

Gram fluffed her headphone-flattened curls. "Is it like that feeling when you're far from home, and suddenly fear you've left a burner on? Or the iron? Back in the day, I'd get that feeling all the time. Your gramps would get grumbly as a bear if I made him turn back. The solution was to learn to love wrinkles." Her smile lines crinkled.

I sensed a deeper moral in Gram's iron story, but I was too distracted trying to pinpoint my feeling. Something had been bugging me for days. A feeling that I was missing something, that it was right in front of me.

It was Wednesday, almost closing time, nearly a week since Rusty Zeller confessed to the murder of his former business partner, Prescott St. James. That I did have firm feelings about. Namely, I *still* couldn't believe it. Gram and Meg had their doubts too, but how could we argue with a man's firm confession? Gram had gotten the scoop straight from Lottie Nez at the jail.

Rusty had adamantly confessed, to everything.

I knew what I *should* feel. Relief. Relief that the killer was caught. Relief for Ms. Ridge. Sorrow for Syd and for his father too.

"It's something like that," I said to Gram.

Out in the lobby, I could hear Meg wishing a customer goodnight. I'd already dimmed the lights and checked the aisles. On my rounds, I'd come to the lounge, where I'd found Rosie, Gram, Agatha, and Glynis in a neat row of armchairs facing the windows.

Gram had urged me to sit and talk. I'd relocated Agatha to my lap and tried to explain my feeling.

Unease, I'd said. Scary but formless. Dreadful with nothing in particular to dread.

"Sounds like a riddle," said Gram.

To my left, Glynis cradled a stack of freshly purchased thrillers. She stretched long legs, groaned about her back, and offered her version of that feeling.

"Like you forgot to lock a door? And then it's midnight, you're all alone, and there's footsteps up the stairs?" She glanced meaningfully up in the direction of my loft.

To Gram's right, Rosie removed her headphones. "What about, like, wildlife watching you? Aunt El, I read that if you've walked in the forest here fourteen times, chances are a mountain lion has watched you and you didn't know it. If you do see one, back away and look large."

"Wise advice," said Glynis. "Same goes for stalkers, except for the slow part. Do you think it's that, Ellie? A stalker? You meet anyone with a strange, intense fixation on crime lately?"

Yes! Someone with a bad back and a stack of Nordic-noir thrillers.

I smiled with false bravado. "Great. Thanks bunches. No more vague unease for me. Now I can go around checking for hot stoves, psycho killers, stalkers, and mountain lions."

"Mountain lions can leap forty feet," Rosie informed us.

"Bear spray can reach thirty feet and deter predators of all sorts," added Glynis.

Gram, as always, had the best suggestion. "I don't like this unease. It means something. You won't be staying here tonight, Ellie. You're coming down for dinner and a sleepover with us. I insist."

She invited Glynis to dinner too, but Glynis had plans. She was meeting Barb.

"That's why I'm here, waiting until our fondue reservation," Glynis said. "I got Barb the first book in my Ice Carver series too." She patted her book stack and then said, with rare uncertainty, "I hope she likes it."

Gram, refreshed from her nap, was a font of wise grandmotherly advice. "Even if she doesn't, just remember, you don't have to like the same books. What's important is that she likes to read."

Another deep message, I thought vaguely.

Glynis rose and said she'd check in later. "Regarding our mutual friend. When I left, those drapes were still closed behind the lace, but I could tell she was in there."

Ms. Ridge had reverted to recluse mode, hiding away in her little red cottage. Gram had taken over muffins and a casserole and gotten as far as the front porch. Ms. Ridge had been gracious but eager to shut the door.

She needed time, Gram said. We understood—as much as we could—but we still worried about her.

"The next snow'll get her out," Glynis predicted. "She'll feel compelled to beat me to the shoveling. Sixty percent chance of accumulation starting on Friday. I'll even give her a head start."

I hoped that Glynis and the forecasters were right. Fresh powder might boost Syd's spirits too.

He also needed time, although I worried that his father's actions had carved deep and painful wounds. I'd run into him on the street the other night, after my texts and a call went unanswered. I'd offered a friendly listening ear, a shoulder to cry on.

"I can't believe Dad," he'd said, sounding more angry than sad. "What was he thinking?"

He'd turned down my offer of a beer and/or s'mores. Boarding, climbing, pushing away the pain, that's all he wanted to do, he'd said, and trudged off with his snowboard.

I'd gone on to Lifties, hoping for a lift myself. Ven and Isa were there, flirty with the bartender and chilly about Syd.

"He'll ski it off," Ven said.

"Ski, ski, ski," Isa agreed. "That's all Syd's ever cared about. He'll be fine. He has what he wants."

But he didn't. Far from it. His father had been ripped away. So had the dream of his business. Heli-skiing wouldn't take off anytime soon. Simon Trent, would-be investor, had regained consciousness and would hopefully leave the hospital soon. That was the great news.

The bad? Simon Trent reportedly had a case of amnesia to rival Agatha Christie's missing days.

From her hospital sources, Gram had learned that certain readily available veterinary tranquilizers could cause such amnesia. So could knocks on the noggin and almost drowning in a luxury hot spring.

I lapsed back into the awful memory of discovering Simon. Syd, urging me to hurry. The phone, faltering. The ambulance, delayed by the icy road. Ms. Ridge, admitting she'd gone to the inn earlier, lured by what she said was a trick call. I couldn't see Rusty making such a call. He cared about Ms. Ridge.

Gram bundled up her knitting, preparing to go home. Rosie insisted on going along to "bodyguard" her.

"I'm bodyguarding *you*," Gram countered. "I have the knitting needles."

"I have a big book in my backpack," Rosie said.

Meg balanced the cash register for the day's purchases, while I treated Agatha to her favorite dinner and told her (unnecessarily) to feel free to sleep on my pillow. Before we left, I peered out the bay window, checking for more than the weather.

Rusty's arrest had coincided with the reopening of the road into town. Tourists and snow-aficionados had arrived in droves, as expected. So had reporters, a handful of true-crime podcasters, and the Colorado Bureau of Investigation in a big blue bus with CBI emblazoned across the sides.

Tabloid-leaning newshounds had tried to get us to talk about Morgan Marin, her estranged half sibling, and her role in the dead-man prediction. No way! We'd referred them to Renée-Claude, a more effective barrier than Morgan's gates. Morgan had been keeping a low profile, but hadn't been lonely. I'd seen Emmet and Calamity Janet headed her way every day.

Some national reporters had dropped by the Chalet too, clearly seeing us as a comic aside for their serious stories. The little bookshop of mystery lovers who thought they could predict murder. Pretty much everyone—from snow tourist to CBI detective—had wanted a photo with Agatha, who'd scowled her way to even greater online feline fame.

Through it all, Meg kept repeating the calming mantra of *any publicity is good publicity.* She also kept assuring me (and herself) that everyone would soon lose interest. They already had, to some extent. With no fresh news, most of the reporters and the big blue CBI bus had departed. Somehow, however, that only added to my unease.

"All clear," said Meg, who'd taken to checking the windows too.

We set out, pressing through a bracing wind to the gondola station, where everything was back to normal, yet unsettlingly different. Trevor, the young gondolier who'd tried to revive Prescott St. James, had taken over Rusty's glass hut. The whiteboard still hung on the wall, but the colorful quotes and sticky notes were gone. We received no friendly wave. No book chats.

Meg and I stepped into the nearest gondola. The doors were within an inch of sealing when two hands pried them open.

"Christies!" Piper Tuttle burst in, landing with a *whoosh* on the opposite seat. "Oh my goodness, I have been meaning to find you and here you are!"

"Here we are," Meg agreed.

Piper chattered at high-speed-train speed. "Have you ladies felt there's something off with all this?"

I jerked upright. "Yes!"

Piper knew what was bugging her. "Why didn't Rusty enjoy more last moments of freedom? If he'd kept quiet, he might not have been caught. You know what else I wonder? Why he went after Simon Trent. There's hardly a reason for that, unless, of course, Trent saw him knock off Prescott. That Trent was watchful. I know the type."

Said the woman who'd checked into Trent's inn to watch him. But Piper had a point. Simon had watched me at the pizza restaurant and then later from his original second-floor room at the inn.

"Simon wanted his money back from the failed investment scheme," Meg said. "Maybe he tried to get it from Rusty, the other business partner?"

Piper and Meg discussed other victims of Prescott's scheme.

I turned my gaze to the serene aspens. When we neared the cliffs, I looked away, only to now find Piper watching me.

"Are you ill?" Piper asked. "You look . . ." She made a swirly motion with her hand.

"You're not getting vertigo again, are you?" Meg said. "I was hoping you just needed to adjust to the altitude."

I decided to tell them. Maybe laughing at myself would

cure me. I started with a "Did you know" to Meg, who hadn't known about my childhood misadventure.

"You tried to climb down those cliffs?" Meg said. "El, you could have fallen to your death!"

"I know," I said. "It was a stupid dare. I think it's the memory that's giving me vertigo when I look down at that spot."

Piper brightened. "You're in luck. I have the cure, for vertigo and bad memories."

Before I could react, the gossip columnist reached over and grabbed my head. "Relax."

I tensed, as I always did when someone told me to relax.

Piper firmed her grip. "Move with my words. Up, down, to the left, right, and twist and—relax! Okay, now, upside-down. That's the trick, hold the upside-down."

I found myself peering out at cliff and sky, spinning like I was falling.

"Now, sit up and repeat as necessary," Piper said. "Oh, and I think there's some breathing I missed, but you can catch up with that. Feel better?"

If by better, she meant that now I knew *why* my head was spinning, yeah, I was cured.

Piper said, "It works for hiccups too. Sometimes for anxiety attacks."

I could see it causing anxiety.

She returned to dissecting Rusty Zeller, concluding he must have blamed Prescott for the loss of his home, wife, and fortune. "Vengeance, that had to be the motivation."

"He's so friendly," Meg said.

"Hiding his festering anger?" Piper suggested, but she couldn't convince herself. "I know, it still feels wrong, doesn't it?"

We'd reached the base.

Piper was first out the doors. "If you figure out your unease, Ellie, call me! Remember, I called first dibs on your tell-all!"

Meg had gathered her bags and mittens. The gondola kept moving. I remained seated, pinned by my unease.

"Meg," I said. "This is going to sound strange, but I'm going to ride up and back again. You go on. Let Gram know I'll be a little late?"

"Did you forget something?" Meg was standing. Our gondola had rounded the tight oval and would soon be leaving the station.

Just the opposite. I felt like something was right there on the edge of my memory. The precipice. I told Meg that I needed to think.

Meg sat back down. "You can think all you want, but I'm coming with you."

We rode up the mountain and back down. Sitting by my sister in a sailing glass bubble, I looked at the world—and the murder—from all sides and upside-down.

That was the key, Piper had said. The upside-down. Back on solid ground, walking to Gram's, I dared tell Meg a theory that might turn everything on its head. When we reached Gram's, she bustled us in with grandmotherly fuss.

"There you are." She drew us in for a hug and said, "Ellie, did you figure out your feeling? Oh dear, girls, what's wrong? The looks on your faces . . ."

I told Gram a plan that, said out loud, sounded as far-fetched as my theory.

"We want to hold another séance," I said.

To her credit, Gram didn't check my forehead for fever-driven delusions. "If you like. That could be fun."

Meg shook her head. "Not for fun."

No fun at all, we explained. We feared that Rusty Zeller might be lying. If that was so, maybe we could summon the real killer to speak.

✴

CHAPTER 39

Summoning a Killer

"What a perfect morning for a séance!" Morgan Marin nearly bowled me over with air kisses and déjà vu. Two weeks ago, she'd arrived at book club announcing a perfect day for murder. Since then, there'd been a murder, a burglary, an attempted murder, and blizzards of fibs, lies, and little incongruities.

"*Alors.*" Renée-Claude trudged in, lugging the oversized bag. "Again, on a Saturday. Too early, too much snow."

It was just before nine, later than last time, but still early. I thanked them effusively and reminded Renée-Claude that we hoped she'd stay.

"If I must."

"You must," said her boss. "Ellie says we're essential. It'll be grand fun!"

Morgan was an excellent actor. She didn't want to be here, I was sure. When I'd finally gotten in touch with her—by begging via her gate intercom—she'd fended off my séance invitation with busy, busy excuses. Curiosity had finally lured her. I'd promised that truths would be revealed.

Now I added tasty enticements. "There's fresh coffee in the Reading Lounge. Donut muffins too. Ms. Ridge is in there setting up with Gram and Meg. Piper Tuttle is already there as well."

Piper Tuttle had been thrilled to get our séance invite.

"The dead man will finally speak!" she'd exclaimed.

I sure hoped that someone would.

Renée-Claude sighed and headed toward the lounge.

Morgan fluttered about the lobby, picking up books and putting them back.

"I'm so glad you convinced dear, dear Ms. Ridge to attend," she said. "I feel awful that I almost evicted her books. I must apologize and make it up to her. I brought you a little something too, Ellie. I fear Renée-Claude may have been rude on your previous library visit."

She opened a purse resembling a designer version of a bowling-ball bag. Inside was a hat. *The* hat. The 1920s beret with its feathers returned to a single fluffy side tuft.

"There's nothing like a fancy hat for extra courage." Morgan deftly bobby-pinned the beret to my too-casual-for-feathers ponytail. "There!" She stepped back to admire. "Transformed." She reached back into the bag and found a compact.

"You are Emily Trefusis," she intoned, holding the little mirror to my face. "Believe. Inhabit. Be . . ."

I stared at myself, tired-eyed from a night of fitful sleep, feathers sprouting above my ear. The hat looked like what it was—a costume. Was there any hint of Emily Trefusis, determined, brave, and wise? I decided I'd have to settle for Ellie Christie in a hat.

Cowbells clanged and Emmet strode in, dapper in a black Stetson with silver ornaments. His mustache was extravagantly curled and coiffed, his chin clean-shaven and showing barely a trace of his previous injury.

He blushed at a beaming Morgan, issued us a "howdy, la-

dies," and asked if he could park his pony outside. "Miss Calamity is all set up with carrots and her puffer jacket."

Morgan looked out and cooed. "The sunset pink in that
jacket brings out her dapples. It fits her just perfectly too. My
tailor swore it would."

A tailor? Grinning, I assured Emmet that anything that
was okay with Calamity was fine with me. Emmet offered
Morgan his elbow and escorted her to the lounge, telling a tale
of great drama and danger: dressing a pony in a puffer coat.

Glynis arrived next, also full of tall tales. "What'd I tell you?
Nothing like fresh snow to lure you-know-who from her se-
clusion. Just so we're clear, I *let* her beat me to the shoveling
this morning."

Uh-huh. I took that as a warm-up for my fib-detection muscles and offered to hang up Glynis's purple parka.

"Nah, I'll hold on to it in case we go chasing after a killer.
That's why we're here, I assume? Pursuit?" Her eyes glittered
eagerly.

"We're summoning the deceased's spirit so it may rest," I
said stiffly. I'd practiced this line numerous times. In the bath.
In front of a mirror and a dubious Agatha. It hadn't sounded
convincing then either.

"Right," said Glynis knowingly. "I better go claim a prime
spot. I want to see everyone's eyes."

After she'd left, a figure stepped out from a Mystery aisle.
"Is everyone here?" Syd asked.

"Just about. We're only waiting on Simon and his nurse." I
checked out the window again. I needed Simon here for this to
work.

Syd joined me, scraping a hand through rumpled locks.
"El, I know I asked for your help, but now? I appreciate the
effort, but there's not much hope."

I'd tracked Syd down at Lifties and requested his assistance.

I needed backup and an extra set of eyes, I'd told him. Someone was hiding something.

He hadn't hidden his skepticism. "It's not a game, El. My dad's in jail."

"For murder and only because he confessed," I'd countered. The chief still hadn't brought charges for the assault on Simon Trent or for our robbery. I told Syd how I'd been to see the chief.

"Chief Sunnie said she's still lining up evidence, but I think she has doubts, especially about what happened to Simon. That could account for the CBI coming to town too."

Syd hadn't been convinced. "Those bigwig detectives came because of his connection to Morgan Marin."

I told him a theory I suspected he wouldn't like. "Right before your dad confessed, he was upset about Ms. Ridge being blamed. Maybe he thinks he's helping her?"

I'd been right. Syd wasn't happy.

"Simon Trent has agreed to attend too," I'd told him. "Morgan helped me convince him."

Syd shook his head. "You think Simon truly can't remember what happened? You know what I think? He took a bunch of meds, fell into the hot spring, and is too embarrassed to fess up."

I wondered about that too. "The doctors believe in the amnesia, though. If we can jog his memory, it might help your dad. Maybe he'll remember to fund your helicopter business too."

Syd finally agreed to attend.

"Go back and get coffee and a muffin," I said. "Find a seat." He'd been restlessly pacing since he got here, making me nervous.

He balked. "If you think someone here murdered Prescott, I need to stick by you." He said, all seriousness, "In those mysteries Dad loves, this would totally be when someone tries to knock you off."

I tamped back a shiver, remembering Gram's theory that realizing such a threat would dispel it. "All the more reason to go back and watch everyone. Seriously, listen in on what people are saying. They won't suspect you of eavesdropping. I'll be there soon. I think Simon is arriving."

I watched a tank-sized SUV lumber across the nearest two no-parking spots.

Agatha, who'd been bathing in the bay window, swished her tail.

"I know," I said.

A woman in pastel-peach nurse's scrubs got out and fussed over Simon Trent. He wore a bandage on his head and a petulant expression.

"There's a hostile horse outside," he said by way of greeting. "It tried to attack us."

"Maybe we shouldn't have insulted the nice little horse," the nurse said. She was a round-faced woman who looked unused to frowning.

"*We?* You were no help. *I* told it the truth. It looks ridiculous in that puffy coat." He wore a velour baby-blue tracksuit that Calamity Janet probably also deemed silly. He frowned at my hat. "I don't know why I agreed to this."

I cranked up a bright smile and led the way to the Reading Lounge.

"We can get started now," I announced briskly, as the nurse settled Simon in. "We're here to settle a restless spirit."

Agatha hopped to a high shelf to watch. Gram took up her knitting.

I sat between her and Meg, the Ouija board in front of me, the wall of windows and gently falling snow to my back. I touched the hat. Morgan was right. I did feel a touch more powerful.

"Spirit," I said, "spirit of Prescott St. James, are you here? Speak . . ."

Simon scoffed. Piper drew a hopeful breath. Ms. Ridge inched her chair back under the suspicious eye of Syd.

The tremor in my hand helped add authenticity, I told myself. The planchette looked spirit-guided as it jiggled toward *Y*.

"Yes," I pronounced. "He's here." I paused for effect, drew the planchette back, and posed another question.

"Spirit, did someone in this room hurt you? Point, show us . . ."

I rattled the planchette across the board, toward Piper.

"Me?" Piper squawked. "That spirit has no gripe with me. I had no ill will toward Prescott St. James. My divorce lawyer and I made out like bandits."

I jerked the planchette abruptly toward Glynis, who chuckled ominously.

"Oh, you just try," Glynis said.

Simon faked a yawn.

Gram whispered, "You're doing very well, dear."

I took that as a prompt to get moving. Closing my eyes, I veered the planchette toward Morgan and Emmet.

When I opened my eyes, Morgan had that look. Disdainful queen. I nudged the pointer in Emmet's direction.

His mustache twitched, his expression wry but without a smile. "I see where this is going. An airing of fibs, facts, and fables, is it? I might as well tell one of those. Let's say, I hurt that man by my chin getting in the way of his knuckles." He touched the faded bruise. "I came across him on that fateful Saturday afternoon and encouraged him to mosey on out of Last Word. He told me to mind my own business. When I helpfully turned him in the direction of the station, he hauled off and belted me."

Morgan leaned over and kissed his blushing cheek. "He did it for me, silly, stubborn man."

Piper Tuttle slapped both hands to her mouth, but couldn't contain a whoop of glee. "What? You two! You're a . . . ah . . ."

Glynis said, "A hot item. Catch up, Tuttle. I've known for ages." She waggled a finger at Emmet. "All that snowshoeing on public lands, you thought that was private? Silly to think you could keep a secret in Last Word. Sillier to make yourself a murder suspect by refusing to explain yourself to the police."

"He still could be the murderer," Syd muttered. "He just admitted that he fought with Prescott."

"Emmet wouldn't hurt anyone," Morgan said. "I will vouch for his sweet nature. Besides, we were together at the time of the murder."

Simon snorted. "Don't lie. It's unbecoming, Morgan. You were with *me*. I remember that much."

He touched his bandaged head and frowned as if gripped by an unpleasant memory. "You dropped by to accuse me of bringing Prescott St. James back to town. Then, when *I* was brainstorming how to recoup *our* money, you realized you were late for your little online book chat and ditched me."

Morgan huffed. "*You* ditched me. You were supposed to go get your absurd convertible and drive me home. I waited and waited until I gave up and called Emmet to come rescue me."

She turned to Meg and me. "I apologize. You were correct. I wasn't home for much of my own book club, but I had no reason to hurt Prescott."

"He stole your money," Syd pointed out. "*You* just admitted you lied."

Morgan waved a hand as if she couldn't be bothered. "My own *brother* stole my money." To Simon, she said, "Later, I heard you'd gone charging down the mountain in yet another bad decision. Why? What were you doing?"

Simon frowned. "I saw Prescott going into the gondola station. I was going to catch him . . ."

"There, there, let's not talk too much," the nurse said, probably good advice for Simon, although not as helpful for revealing clues.

"Let's hear him out," Glynis said. "You saw Prescott, eh? Did *you* stab him? Chase after him to finish him off?"

Simon's face went a lurid shade of red.

The nurse threatened to remove her patient. "I thought this was a *bookshop*," she added peevishly. "Bookshops should be calm."

"Ha!" Glynis laughed. "You ever read a book? Lady, you're surrounded by murder, conflict, and mayhem."

"Secrets," Gram said, knitting serenely. "Devious twists. Nemeses."

"Dark motivations," Glynis added. *"Lies."*

At least they were enjoying themselves. Ms. Ridge looked terrified. Morgan was channeling her disdainful queen. Syd glared at Simon, who fussed at his shushing nurse. Meg nodded to me.

Right. Time to summon my inner Emily Trefusis. "Spirit," I intoned, raising my voice above the chattering. "With whom do you wish to speak?"

The room fell silent.

I felt awful about my next move. Meg squirmed in her seat, and I knew she felt the same. Taking a deep breath, I nudged the planchette toward the person I dreaded exposing. The person we'd been trying to help.

Ms. Ridge, aka Cecelia St. James.

CHAPTER 40

Ellie Tells a Story

"Prescott St. James came to town with little but a book," I said, abandoning the fiction of speaking through a spirit.

All eyes clung to me.

Gram paused her knitting.

Meg held up our copy of *Absent in the Spring*.

Piper, in a scandalized whisper, said, "That's the Agatha Christie with no murders."

I smiled at Piper. Unwittingly, she'd given me a nudge with her upside-down "cure." I'd thank her later.

For now, I continued with my story. "The book features a character who realizes she's hurt people she loves. Ms. Ridge— Cecelia—you know this book, don't you?"

All the eyes turned to Ms. Ridge.

She swiped at a tear. "If I'd known that Prescott had brought *that* book, I wouldn't have run off like a coward."

"Run off after you killed him?" Syd demanded, taking my advice to seriously suspect everybody.

Glynis leaned back in her armchair. "Well, well, well. Always the person you first suspect, isn't it? That's what throws you off." She nodded approvingly at Ms. Ridge. "Well done."

Ms. Ridge had the look of a baby bunny in a den of foxes.

"You were upset to learn about the book," I said, in what I hoped was a soothing tone. "Why?"

Ms. Ridge studied her clasped hands, saying nothing. I forced myself to wait.

Agatha broke the impasse by hopping from her high shelf and nuzzling her way onto Ms. Ridge's lap.

Over Agatha's comforting purrs, Ms. Ridge said, "When I left Prescott, I gave him that book and ordered him to read it. He'd been obsessed with his business for some time and uncaring about our marriage and my feelings. Oh, and I did lie—"

"I knew it!" Syd interjected.

Ms. Ridge stammered on. "I suspected that his business wasn't quite . . . legitimate? That book is about hurting others and self-reflection. It's about being alone with your thoughts, too, which is how I'd decided to leave Prescott. Ellie and Meg, when you told me the title, I felt awful. I never thought he'd actually *read* the book, let alone bring it back to me. I should have spoken with Prescott. He came all this way to discuss a book and I ran away."

Glynis handed Ms. Ridge a packet of tissues.

Emmet said, "That book sounds like harsh truth. Being alone with yourself? Most people are terrified of that. Scared of what they may see." He preened his mustache. "Others of us, well . . . lonely meditation leads to poetry." He reached over and took Morgan's hand. "And love."

Piper Tuttle declared that she loathed being alone.

Glynis said, "You can't run forever. You always end up finding yourself."

I took the book from Meg and slid it across the table toward Ms. Ridge. "Do you think Prescott came to apologize?"

Louder sniffles affirmed my guess.

"Eh, sure," Glynis said dismissively. "He'd have said what you wanted to hear and then reverted right back to his true nature. Can't run from that either."

Ms. Ridge bit her lip, suggesting she might agree.

I said, "Prescott came to the Book Chalet to meet Cece. He'd received emails and letters, presumably from her. When we looked in his satchel, there were also notes. Like you used to write when you were reading and sharing books, Ms. Ridge?"

Ms. Ridge looked up from her crumpled tissue. "Those emails, I didn't send them, I swear. The chief showed me the note they found in my house. That was my handwriting, but I didn't summon Prescott here. Why would I and then avoid him?"

"Cold feet?" Morgan suggested.

"Very cold," Renée-Claude agreed with something close to admiration.

"Vengeance?" Piper supplied.

"Sneak up on him? Element of surprise?" Glynis offered.

"Kill him?" Syd muttered.

Gram gave me a nod.

I took a deep breath and touched my feathered hat. "There's a stronger emotion than hate," I said, looking around.

When no one else answered, Gram said, "Love." She knitted on, cool-blue fluffy wool in neat loops. "Love can be most dangerous."

Piper gasped. "Love is terrifying! That was on one of those notes in Prescott's bag. I was there to discover it."

I nodded. "Ms. Ridge, do you recognize those words?"

She did. "Agatha Christie wrote that. I forget the exact words but something like 'love can be a terrifying thing . . . Most love stories are tragedies.' She certainly cut to the truth, didn't she?"

Gram, Meg, Piper, Glynis, Emmet, Morgan, Simon's nurse,

and even Renée-Claude agreed. Simon continued his bored surly act. Syd stared hard at Ms. Ridge.

I knew I had to keep her talking. "You used to have a two-person book club, didn't you? Back when you were Cece? You and Rusty Zeller would write notes in books."

Her cheeks reddened. "I discovered that Rusty was a book lover. We exchanged books and thoughts, that's all. I didn't know anyone else in town at the time. We had the same reading taste."

Meg said, "You made quite an impression on him. He still keeps notes."

Syd muttered, "Lotta good it did him."

"He recognized you as Cecelia St. James," I said. "He kept your secret."

"Ohh . . ." Glynis cooed ominously. "So, what are you Christies suspecting? Rusty actually did it, but his motive wasn't vengeance? It was for love?"

Syd made an exasperated sound.

I said, "Someone who loved Prescott killed him."

Piper hastily qualified that she'd loved her divorce settlement, not the man who sparked it. The group eyed one another suspiciously, all except Syd. He'd let his hair lop over his forehead. Squinting to a blur, I could picture him as that ski-obsessed guy who'd "pull a Zeller," ditching school—and friends and prom dates—for fresh snow.

I said, "Syd, you liked Prescott."

He smoothed his hair back, blue eyes fixed firmly to mine. "You know I did, El. I told you, he was like an uncle to me. What are you saying?"

What *was* I saying? Fear skittered up my middle. If I was right, I'd invited friends and loved ones to a parlor game with a killer. If I was wrong, well, that would be awful too. I wouldn't just lose a friend. I'd be the person no one would ever trust to befriend again.

I could still laugh it off, return to the Ouija board, have the "spirit" accuse everyone in turn, even Agatha.

I wanted to, desperately. I couldn't.

"You didn't plan to kill him," I said quietly, watching Syd. "You wanted to get Prescott to Last Word, but he wouldn't risk his parole for just anyone. So, you impersonated Cece. He couldn't resist her."

Syd was shaking his head in apparent disbelief.

I hurried on. "Did you think he couldn't resist your business idea once he heard it? That he owed you? For finding Cece for him? For losing your family's fortune? When we were in school, you had money for the easy ski-bum life."

Syd rubbed his forehead. "A *wealthy* ski bum? El, you're embarrassing yourself. You don't know what you're talking about. And you're still thinking about high school?"

I was thinking about Syd, first on the scene at the gondola station, claiming he was there to catch a ride up to visit his father. Yet Rusty and Syd hadn't seemed that close. In my time home, Rusty hadn't mentioned his son. Syd knew that Meg and I had the dead man's satchel at the shop. We'd told him. We'd even discussed Christie-worthy methods of murder, including tranquilizers.

Easy to get, Syd had said . . .

Syd, who'd been alone with stricken Simon Trent while I rushed off to call 911.

Most of all, I was thinking of that video.

"Your most awesome snowboarding run," I said. "The night we met at Lifties. You were late and showed me a video to prove why and—"

"I wasn't late," Syd snapped. "We weren't on a *date*, El. I was trying to help you get out and meet people. What're you doing otherwise? Reading with your cat?"

Agatha's tail swished.

My cheeks burned, but he'd just reinforced my theory. He hadn't been interested in me except to keep an eye on the case.

"That video," I repeated. "It didn't click at the time, but later I realized. I recognized that slope, the cliffs. That's why it made me feel so woozy when I saw it. It wasn't right, not Bookman's Peak like you claimed. Those were the cliffs under the gondola line."

My heart raced as if I was careening over the rocks, flipping, falling, weaving through a deadly maze of trees and boulders. I tried to make my next guess sound confident. "Did Prescott rebuff you? You lashed out. He made it onto the gondola, and you snowboarded down after him." I added, with hope I didn't believe, "To try to help him?"

Syd's look was one I now recalled from our school days. Superior and mocking, the cool guy who didn't have time for the likes of me. "Those cliffs are murder. No one boards down them, especially at night. Anyway, there's no way *you've* seen those cliffs, El, except from the gondola."

He made to rise. "I agreed to this *game* to help Dad, not to be insulted."

Ms. Ridge spoke up. "Your father confessed. He did that for love, Sydney. For you."

Syd snarled. "If that's true, then he did it for *you*. He loved your book swaps and those notes you'd pass each other. He kept 'em all. Pathetic."

Meg reached over and took my hand. I squeezed back hard, processing the implication. Syd knew about the notes, meaning he could have used them to impersonate Ms. Ridge and lure Prescott here.

He shoved his chair back, no longer the laid-back fun guy.

Simon gripped his bandaged head. Was he remembering? Maybe he'd never forgotten.

"Someone saw you," I said quickly before Syd could leave.

"Mr. Trent, you saw Prescott the night of the murder. Did you see Syd strike him, hurt him? Is that why you sped down the mountain too, to reach Prescott first? To watch how it played out?"

Simon tightened his lips like a drawstring purse.

I went out on a brittle limb. "You've been trying to buy property here. You wanted Syd's place. It's a prime location. He didn't want to sell. If you saw him attack Prescott St. James, you'd have leverage."

"Blackmail," breathed Piper. "I should've guessed."

Simon put on an act—a very bad act—of offense. "Blackmail? Insulting! Yeah, sure, I made my struggling ski guide a reasonable offer on his land. Minus detriments like that old shack." He paused, his eyes widening at Syd. "The other night, you came to the inn. We were going to sign the contract."

"The night you said you and Demetrius were skiing?" I asked Syd. "When you came to Lifties late and claimed that Simon was going to fund your heli-ski business?"

Simon scoffed, then suddenly seemed to realize the implications. He reached back for the nurse, who put protective hands on his shoulders.

Syd said, "Ah, Simon? Of course, you saw me at the inn, remember? I saved you from your overdose?"

The overdose that Syd had administered, I bet. Syd hadn't wanted me to check on the disturbing sounds coming from the inn's back garden. When I'd gone anyway, he'd insisted on accompanying me.

"You were alone with him." I shuddered at the thought. "I went to call for help. When I returned, he was unconscious."

Syd threw up his hands. "You people are crazy. This isn't one of your mystery novels. Simon took too much horse tranq and doesn't want to admit it."

"How'd you know it was horse stuff?" Glynis asked. "Let's

see that video Ellie was talking about. I'll clear this up. I know those cliffs, day or night."

Syd grabbed his backpack and rose. Glynis did too, looping her purple parka over his head. Chairs pushed back, their legs scraping the floor. Meg and I jumped in front of Gram. Emmet and Morgan vied to shield each other. Piper stared, as if in popcorn-munching agog at the movies. Ms. Ridge covered her eyes, while Agatha and Renée-Claude frowned from safe distances. The disapproving nurse hustled Simon from the fray.

Syd slipped from Glynis's parka and ran. His footsteps pounded through the shop. The cowbells clanged.

We all froze, stunned.

Then Piper yelled, "He's getting away!"

Emmet charged after him. I caught up in the lobby. We reached the door as a bellow erupted from outside, accompanied by curses, a whinny, and a merry chuckle.

I stepped out to find Syd facedown in the snow. Chief Sunnie was clicking on handcuffs. A single ski lay at her feet. Calamity Janet watched, idly munching a sleeve of her puffer jacket.

"Best use I've found for a ski yet," the chief said, winded, her earflap lopsided. "Tripping people up. That and a bucking bronco." She smiled up at Calamity. "Janet, we make a good team."

My head spun with a mix of relief, horror, and sorrow. Yet, I still noticed. "You called her Janet."

Janet bared hay-stained teeth. I didn't care. We'd just summoned a killer and survived. I seized my moment of bravery and kissed the pony's velvety muzzle.

CHAPTER 41

✳

A Good Day for Reading

Monday, our day off, Chief Sunnie came by. Most of the séance group had gathered in the lounge again, with the addition of my favorite niece. Rosie had *almost* forgiven her mom, aunt, and great-gram for excluding her from Saturday's big (and potentially dangerous) reveal. Absent were Piper, who was busy giving interviews, and Simon Trent, who'd flown out of town.

We were also missing Syd, who was down in the jail.

I felt awful about Syd but worse about what he'd done.

The chief settled into a pine-green wingback and accepted a cup of hot tea from Gram.

Gram, Rosie, and Glynis nudged their armchairs protectively around Ms. Ridge, as if to buffer her from any further upset. Morgan and Emmet shared a loveseat. Renée-Claude was ensconced in the Sci-fi aisle. Meg added a log to the fire. Agatha surveyed us from a high shelf, and I helped myself to more tea, peppermint for clarity. I hoped the chief had brought answers too.

"Nice," the chief said, appreciatively sipping and nodding toward the windows. "Glad to see that snow melting away."

She, Emmet, and Glynis chatted about weather, the return of autumn, and a good season for spotting moose.

Eventually, Morgan tapped her fingers with impatience. "So, Chief, did he do it? You're certain? Sydney Zeller was going to let his own father go to prison?"

The chief set down her teacup and reeled off evidence. The video was the clincher, time and location deleted but recoverable. Then there was the murder weapon, a mountaineering pickax, slender and sharp, still with microscopic traces of blood.

Morgan's hand fluttered at her heart. "Simply awful, and he first tried to pin the blame on you, Ms. Ridge? Horrible!"

Ms. Ridge stared at her lap. "I spoke with Rusty. He admitted he'd hoped to clear my name by confessing. Silly man! He wouldn't talk about Sydney, but he must have suspected what his son had done. As a young man, Sydney idolized Prescott, his money, his cunning. Rusty blamed himself for bringing Prescott into their lives. For Sydney's unhappiness too. That boy, he tried so hard to have fun, but he never could grasp it. He was always too bitter, wanting more."

That tragedy panged from my heart to my fingertips.

Agatha hopped to Ms. Ridge's lap. "We'll keep checking in with Rusty, won't we?" Ms. Ridge said to the purring cat. "We could start sharing books again."

The chief said, "If it's any comfort, Syd claims the attack was an accident. He said he tried to 'reach out' and stop Prescott from leaving. Just happened to have that pickax in his hand when he did." Her shrug expressed disbelief. "He said he then boarded down the mountain, 'risking his life' to try to help the wounded man."

"Whoa . . ." Rosie breathed.

Meg shuddered. "We probably passed over him in our gondola. It was dark. I didn't look down."

"Can't see what's directly underneath you," the chief said. "Ellie and a moose taught me that." She turned to me. "I'll admit, I doubted your séance scheme. I'm glad you and Meg invited me, and that Garza set me up with the live video feed."

I was beyond grateful that she'd shown up. The chief had waited outside with Calamity Janet, watching the séance as recorded by a tiny video camera Deputy Garza had installed on a shelf the night before.

Morgan beamed. "I had a sixth sense about throwing the first séance." More modestly, she added, "Of course, I was only following the great Agatha Christie. Ms. Ridge, we never got to discuss those wonderful red herrings in *The Sittaford Mystery*. Why, our case was just like—"

"Shhh!" Glynis ordered. "I'm reading that book right now. No spoilers."

I returned to our mystery. "Chief, did you find out if Syd tried to contact Prescott in his own name?"

She had. "Yep, pretty sad, all around. Prescott saved letters he got in prison. Lotta hate mail, weird marriage proposals, and then Syd, talking up his big business ideas and talking down his dad."

The chief moved on to the notes we'd found in Prescott's bag. "Syd found those notes you and Rusty wrote to each other, Ms. Ridge. His father kept a stash of them in a little room he calls his library. Had a photo of you both too, that must have helped Syd recognize you. Syd 'borrowed' some of the notes to send along in letters. He copied your writing style for the emails too." She shook her head. "He thought that you were the only way to lure Prescott back. He was probably right about that. Syd guided Prescott to the Book Chalet, but then you spotted your ex and ran off."

Ms. Ridge hung her head.

"No one's blaming you for that," the chief said, adding that Demetrius had filled in some of the gaps. "Demetrius said that Syd called Prescott later on Saturday, saying he knew where to find Cece. Syd wanted to get Prescott alone. But then, on the way to meet Syd, Prescott ran into you, Emmet."

"His fist ran into my chin," Emmet grumbled but then

flushed. "I had no idea that man was seeking love and forgiveness."

Glynis was less romantic. "Either that or he was seeking his ex-wife's money."

"Did Sydney know I was at the inn?" Ms. Ridge said, sounding as anxious as if she was still hiding.

The chief didn't think so. "They drove around for a while looking. I take it Syd came clean about sending those Cece notes and emails. He was under the misimpression that Prescott would be grateful he'd 'discovered' where you were."

Ms. Ridge looked grim. "Prescott didn't like deception."

"Always the case with deceivers," Glynis said.

The chief agreed. "They went back to Syd's. Syd pitched him the business idea, still hoping they'd bond. Prescott refused and insisted Syd take him to the gondola station. That's where things went deadly wrong."

"Reconnecting is not easy," Morgan said, almost sympathetically. "Even under honest circumstances."

"Tell me about it," I murmured.

Morgan said, "What about Simon? Before my half sibling left town, was he at all helpful?"

The chief shrugged. "I think he does have some memory loss from the tranquilizer and concussion. He did admit that he'd offered a low price on the Zeller property and speculated that *perhaps* that's what caused Syd to attack him. *Twice.* Syd likely thought he'd given Simon enough drugs to kill him the first time. When you two found him alive later, Syd tried to finish the job."

I shivered.

Gram was knitting a long throw blanket. She stretched an end over me.

"I can't believe his audacity," I said. "I was only gone for a few minutes calling 911. What if I'd had better reception and stayed there?"

"Let's not think about that, dear," Gram said, tucking over more of the blanket.

"A few minutes is all it takes," the chief said. "Syd had already arranged for a handy scapegoat in you, Ms. Ridge. He called you from the inn, saying he worked there. You obligingly went and left footprints all over. A bonus was you getting spotted by Piper Tuttle. After you were gone, he dragged Trent outside and left him head down in the pool. In a way, he was looking out for his father by framing you."

"Cold way," Glynis said.

"Super-cold," breathed Rosie, who'd been listening, wide-eyed and rapt.

"Did Demetrious know about the murder and attempted murder?" I asked. "He seemed so honestly happy that night at Lifties."

The chief didn't think he knew about either crime. "Demetrious admitted that he lied to you about why they were late to Lifties, Ellie. He pretended he and Syd had been snowboarding, when really they'd just met up. Syd told him he'd been out with another woman and didn't want you to know. Syd lied to his pal too. He told Demetrious that Simon was going to fund their enterprise. Demetrious was pretty crushed about the business. Even more so by his friend's betrayal."

Meg shuddered. "I wonder if it was a thrill to Syd, like a risky sport? To think, he robbed our shop and then came by to repair the door he'd broken. He must have worried that Prescott had left something incriminating here."

I thought of Syd, gliding in from the Rim Trail to "help" fix our door. Taking that route, he wouldn't have been detected by the security cam that caught Emmet snowshoeing home from Morgan's.

"Yep, I warned ya," Glynis said, stretching legs and back. "I said, look out for anyone hovering around too close."

I groaned. I wasn't off to a great start to reconnecting with old friends. But then, Syd hadn't been a real friend when we were in school. He'd always been out for himself, like Ven and Isa had said.

Glynis turned to the chief. "Did you ask him if he swept the sidewalk at Katherine's place? That was a key clue."

"So it was," the chief acknowledged. "We found forensic evidence—boot and tire tracks—that put him at her house. It would have been a pretty good frame-up, except then his father confessed."

"I knew it," Glynis said, pleased. "The suspicious absence of snow."

The chief smiled. "You'll note, I didn't charge Rusty Zeller with the bookshop robbery or the assault. Your sweeping story put a doubt in my mind."

"The little incongruities," I said. "They added up."

Meg made another pot of tea. Emmet announced he had to go feed his herd. Morgan insisted that she and Renée-Claude would drive him home.

"It's blustery out," Morgan said. "And I want to visit Calamity. I promised my tailor I'd measure her for that cape."

Glynis left too, saying she needed a brisk walk to clear away the grim.

The chief stood. "Gotta get going myself. Mountains of paperwork to file." She paused in the doorway. "Thanks for your help. I am grateful, but I still have to say it: no more sleuthing. It's probably best to keep away from séances too."

We locked the door and settled back in, Meg, Gram, Rosie, Ms. Ridge, Agatha, and me.

Gram broached the question Meg and I had been too afraid to ask. "Ms. Ridge, you'll stay on, won't you?"

Ms. Ridge protested that she'd brought us trouble.

"Do you still *want* to work here?" I asked.

"I do. More than anything."

"Then you have to stay," Rosie declared. "It's your birthday next week and I'm making your cake."

Gram smiled. "Well, good. That's settled. You can start by picking the next book for Mountains of Mystery, Ms. Ridge, and your favorite cake flavor."

Ms. Ridge swished away a tear. "Thank you all. I'll choose a book this afternoon. My favorite cake is the baker's choice."

"Chocolate," Rosie said firmly. "With Gram's marshmallow frosting and graham cracker sprinkles. S'mores cake!"

We toasted these good things with clinks of our teacups.

"One more," Gram said, topping up our cups with the last drops from the pot. "A toast to no more sleuthing?"

We laughed, clinked again, and downed our tea.

Gram's eyes twinkled. "Whatever will we do instead?"

The fire crackled, Agatha softly snored, and a blustery autumn afternoon stretched before us.

"It's a perfect day to read," I said.

We toasted that by opening books. Mysteries, of course, and happily fictional.

ACKNOWLEDGMENTS

I've just written a lot of words, yet now I find myself at a loss for them. How can I thank everyone enough? I owe more than I can express to my family. If they've questioned my desire to make up mysteries (which *surely* they have), they've never told me outright. Any writer knows that this is a treasure beyond measure. Heartfelt thanks and love to my parents, in-laws, aunts, nieces, and especially my husband. Eric, thank you for our time together and for enduring way too much talk of murder.

Many thanks to my amazing agent, Christina Hogrebe, for believing in my writing and connecting me with Jenny Chen, my brilliant editor. Jenny, thank you for your insights and keen edits, which strengthened the story and reminded me and the Christie sisters that no one is above suspicion. Thanks, too, to Mae Donicia Martinez for your assistance and for keeping the many moving parts—and me—on schedule.

As I write this, a book is becoming real, from cover art to carefully considered design and typesetting. I'm humbled to be working with the fabulous team at Bantam Books and Random House and am afraid I might miss acknowledging all who've helped out. If I do, please know you have my gratitude.

Sincere thanks to Kara Cesare, Kim Hovey, Jennifer Hershey, and Kara Welsh at Bantam editorial and to Luke Epplin, production editor, and Katie Zilberman, production manager. For helping the book reach the eyes of readers, I'm grateful to publicist Courtney Mocklow and marketers Allison Schuster and Corina Diez. Many thanks to designers Ella Laytham and Virginia Norey, and art director Carlos Beltran. I absolutely adore the cover, cats, and snowflakes.

Since I began writing mysteries, I've been buoyed and inspired by the writers of Sisters in Crime, especially the Colorado chapter. Cynthia Kuhn, thank you for being the best of writing partners and friends.

Most of all, thank you to readers, librarians, booksellers, and fellow bibliophiles. Believe me, I know—reading time is precious and my own to-be-read stack grows taller by the hour. I'm humbled and honored that you've chosen to spend time in Last Word.

ABOUT THE AUTHOR

ANN CLAIRE earned degrees in geography, which took her across the world. Now Claire lives with her geographer husband in Colorado, where the mountains beckon from their kitchen windows. When she's not writing, you can find Claire hiking, gardening, herding house-cats, and enjoying a good mystery, especially one by Agatha Christie.

Facebook: facebook.com/AnnClaireMysteries
Instagram: @annclaireauthor

ABOUT THE TYPE

This book was set in Legacy, a typeface family designed by Ronald Arnholm (b. 1939) and issued in digital form by ITC in 1992. Both its serifed and unserifed versions are based on an original type created by the French punchcutter Nicholas Jenson in the late fifteenth century. While Legacy tends to differ from Jenson's original in its proportions, it maintains much of the latter's characteristic modulations in stroke.